TALES OF MYSTERY & THE SUPERNATURAL

General Editor: David Stuart Davies

TALES OF MYSTERY
AND THE MACABRE

Tales of Mystery and the Macabre

by Elizabeth Gaskell

with an introduction by
David Stuart Davies

WORDSWORTH EDITIONS

For my husband
ANTHONY JOHN RANSON
with love from your wife, the publisher
Eternally grateful for your
unconditional love

Readers who are interested in other titles from
Wordsworth Editions are invited to visit our
website at www.wordsworth-editions.com

First published 2008 by Wordsworth Editions Limited
8B East Street, Ware, Hertfordshire SG12 9HJ

ISBN 978 1 84022 095 7

Wordsworth Editions is
the company founded in 1987 by
MICHAEL TRAYLER

Typeset in Great Britain by Roperford Editorial
Printed and bound in Italy by Elcograf S.p.A.

CONTENTS

INTRODUCTION

In the nineteenth century, women writers emerged as major con-
tributors to the world of supernatural and macabre literature. It was
perhaps the young Mary Shelley with her daring and ground-breaking
narrative concerning the revolutionary scientist Victor Frankenstein
and his experimentations which led to the creation of a man-made
creature who lived and breathed and indeed killed that provided the
guiding light for other female writers to follow on this mysterious and
sinister path. The novel *Frankenstein* (1818) is a wonderful blend of
the gothic, the dark fairy tale and scientific fantasy – elements which,
particularly the first two, were taken by such writers as Emily Brontë,
Catherine Crowe, Edith Nesbit, Mrs Riddell and Amelia B. Edwards
to weave into their own unsettling fiction.

There was also one other woman, a renowned author of her day,
who contributed a pleasing body of work to the genre with some
splendid ghost stories, gothic tales and uncanny narratives. This was
Elizabeth Gaskell – better known to her readers as simply Mrs
Gaskell. However, today she tends to be overlooked as a contributor
to this particular form of fiction because her fame is based on her
pioneering novels, major works which aimed to illuminate the foibles,
failings and injustices of society. There were novels such as *Mary
Barton* (1848), which presents a vivid and harsh vision of the poverty
of the working classes; *Cranford* (1853), which exposes the effects
change and industry were to bring to the quaint English country
towns; and *North and South* (1855), which included such themes as
religious doubt and female servitude and, as the title suggests, exam-
ines the contrast between the way of life in the industrial north of
England and the wealthier south. Nevertheless, despite attaching
great importance to these books, hoping that they would alert
the public to the plight of the less well off, Gaskell also enjoyed flirt-
ing with the world of the supernatural, in which she was a strong
believer. Indeed, she claimed to have actually seen a ghost in 1849.
While it would be wrong to claim that she was an innovator or a

major contributor to the world of supernatural fiction, it would be fair to state that she created a very effective corner for herself in this shadowy realm. She contributed to the genre of the gothic and ghost story with some fine tales, which are collected here together for the first time.

The real charm of this volume is its variety. Unlike so many writers of this kind of material, she allows the story to fit the style rather than the other way around and as result there is a charming freshness to each tale. Gaskell uses different voices, tones and topics to engage her readers and as you turn from one story to the next you cannot be quite sure what to expect.

Elizabeth Cleghorn Gaskell was born Elizabeth Stevenson in 1810 in London. However, much of her childhood was spent in Knutsford in Cheshire where she lived with an aunt, Mrs Hannah Lumb. In 1832 Elizabeth married William Gaskell, the minister at Cross Street Unitarian Chapel in Manchester, and they had a happy and fruitful marriage. Elizabeth had always had a desire to write, and her husband encouraged her. The Gaskells settled in Manchester, where the industrial surroundings would offer inspiration for her first novel, *Mary Barton*. Gaskell won instant recognition with the book, attracting the attention of Charles Dickens who was most impressed with her powerful writing.

In 1850 Dickens had been soliciting Mrs Gaskell to contribute to his weekly publication *Household Words*, but surprisingly for a relative newcomer to the realms of fiction, she appeared reluctant. She was a strong woman with a fierce independent streak and was not all at impressed or flattered by the famous author's overtures. But Dickens persevered and she succumbed to his entreaties. We have a lot to thank Dickens for in this respect, for it was his encouragement, enthusiasm and support that prompted Gaskell to create most of the stories in this collection. In fact all but two these – 'The Doom of the Griffiths' and 'Curious If True' – first appeared in a Dickens periodical.

At first Mrs Gaskell presented Dickens with a series of tales which were eventually collected together in the novel *Cranford*. They were originally published in *Household Words* between December 1851 and May 1853. But for the special Christmas issue in 1852, Dickens requested a ghost story and Gaskell came up with 'The Old Nurse's Story', a powerful and atmospheric piece which is perhaps the most famous and certainly the most anthologised of her spooky narratives. It appeared as one of 'A Round of Stories by the Christmas Fire'. Initially Dickens was unhappy with the ending and set about rewriting it to his own taste. He then sent it to Mrs Gaskell for her approval. He did not get it. She replied, insisting that her version remained unaltered. Dickens relented, telling her that ' . . . there is no doubt of the story being admirable as it stands.'

Like so much of her novel-length fiction, 'The Old Nurse's Story' has its basis in fact. In Gaskell's biographical study of her fellow-novelist, *The Life of Charlotte Brontë* (1857), she recounts a story which had 'made a deep impression on Charlotte's mind'. It is a tale of Haworth in Yorkshire, where the Brontë sisters lived and wrote their novels, and concerns a local woman seduced by her brother-in-law, who then became pregnant. Her father, beside himself with anger at the girl's fall from grace, locked her in her room while 'her sisters flouted at and scorned her'. Charlotte Brontë related the events of this unnerving incident to her biographer, and Gaskell replicated them in 'The Old Nurse's Story'.

However, the Brontë connection with this tale does not end there. The scenes in which the ghost of the little girl stands at the window in the darkness, beseeching Rosamund to join her out in the cold and the snow, are strongly reminiscent of the scene in Emily Brontë's *Wuthering Heights* (1847) where the ghost of Catherine appears at the window begging the visitor Mr Lockwood to let her in to the house, as the fingers of 'her ice cold hand' hold on to his.

'The Old Nurse's Tale' is typical of many of the stories in this collection in that it begins realistically enough, lulling the reader with this false sense of normality, and then Gaskell slowly introduces elements of the sinister or macabre in such a way that they also seem real.

'The Squire's Story' unfolds in a similar simple fashion and through a series of subtle revelations we are led to realise that Mr Higgins, the rich and personable young man who has arrived in the little town of Barford, is not all that he would have us believe. When, in the closing moments of the story, we learn the terrible truth of his true nature, we are perhaps reminded of how, at the beginning of the tale, Higgins treated the children in the town.

There are also moments of *Cranford*-like social satire in 'The Squire's Story'. Mr Dudgeon represents the aspiring middle-class man who attempts to mimic the aristocracy by building a house that is a smaller version of the grander homes he serves.

In 'The Poor Clare' we move nearer to what the modern critic would class as horror fiction with the central character Lucy who is afflicted by means of a curse with a dual image, her evil self. Gaskell experiments here with the form of storytelling, for while the unnamed lawyer is the general narrator, parts of the tale are recounted by other individuals involved in the events. As a result we have a diverse and fully detailed account. What is particularly effective in this story is when Lucy herself speaks to the reader and describes seeing her other self reflected in the mirror. The marked contrast between the innocent Lucy staring at her evil alter ego within the mirror is doubly chilling because it is recounted by the victim herself.

> In the great mirror opposite I saw myself, and right behind, another wicked fearful self, so like me my soul seemed to quiver within me, as though not knowing to which similitude of body it belonged . . . I suddenly swooned away . . . even while I lay [unconscious in my sickbed] my double was seen by all flitting about the house and garden, always about some mischievous or detestable work.

Gaskell takes the idea of multiple personalities a stage further in 'The Grey Woman' when the central character Anna looking in the mirror is confronted by a series sinister multiple reflections of herself: 'I caught my own face and figure reflected in all the mirrors which showed only a mysterious background . . . I trembled in silence at the fantastic figures and shapes which my imagination called up.'

We can see that this is a recurring theme in some of Gaskell's work, the notion that we harbour another self within us, one that is not entirely wholesome. Our outer shell is therefore a mask concealing the unpleasantness beneath, rather like the Squire in the earlier story.

'Lois the Witch' was something a departure in content for Gaskell. It is in essence a short novel set in the times of the notorious witch trials in Salem, Massachusetts in 1692. (It was aimed at the American market but was first published in Dickens's new magazine *All the Year Round* in 1858.) There is a strong factual element to the story: Gaskell's central character Rebecca Nurse, who was persecuted as a witch, was a real person, and much of Gaskell's historical material was gleaned from *Lectures on Witchcraft* by Charles Upham, a volume published in the 1830s. Gaskell has been criticised for inserting into her narrative verbatim the statement of the Salem jurors who admitted their guilt and remorse for their complicity in persecuting over seventy-five people. But this is in keeping with Gaskell's belief that if we are to accept the unusual happenings presented in these stories, reality and truth must be felt; they are the great persuaders.

Another story which claims to take a view on an historical event is 'The Doom of the Griffiths'. Here we are given an exciting and dramatic account of the legend of Owen Glendower and the curse that he places on the descendants of Rhys ap Gryfydd, the man who was reputed to have slain Glendower. The curse involves a son murdering his father, thus executing a revenge for Glendower. The fact that there are resonances in this scenario with the situation as presented in Sophocles' tragedy *Oedipus Tyranns*, that of a son killing his father, is emphasised by Gaskell herself by having the son, whose fate it is to commit patricide, idly opening a copy of the very same play. This is an example of Gaskell's dark sense of humour: a surreal wink to the reader.

'The Ghost in the Garden Room' is more commonly known as 'The Crooked Branch'. Originally the tale under the latter title was submitted by Mrs Gaskell to Dickens for the 1859 Christmas issue of *All the Year Round*. The basic premise of this edition was a story cycle created by Dickens himself called 'The Haunted House' where each room in an old house harboured a particular ghost whose tale is told. Each entry was preceded by a brief introductory prologue. To fit in with the format of the edition, where all the narratives had to have the word 'room' in the title, Dickens himself renames the piece 'The Ghost in The Garden Room'. Subsequent reprintings of the story have reverted to the original title and left out the prologue, thus obscuring some of the references within the tale. This volume reprints the whole narrative, including the prologue, and therefore Dickens's title is used.

I referred to the variety of Gaskell's work in an earlier section of this introduction, and there is there is no greater evidence of this trait than the cunning and comic tale 'Curious if True', which has a modern satirical edge to it. It purports to be an 'Extract from a letter from Richard Whitingham'. We encounter well-known characters from fairy tales who have moved on and to some extent entered the real world, such as Cinderella who has now grown lame and overweight. There are veiled references to Puss in Boots and Red Riding Hood, Beauty and her Beast as well as some others. It is presented as a dream sequence, a party in a ghostly château filled with these fantastic characters and rich in whimsy. The real strength of this piece is Gaskell's ability to conjure up this fantasy while at the same time making it seem real.

Perhaps the oddest story in this collection is 'Disappearances', partly because it is not a story at all. It is a collection of anecdotes, legends and gossip about individuals who have mysteriously disappeared without trace. While some of these tales are fanciful, others are based on supposed fact, thus giving the whole the stamp of authenticity. It is likely that Gaskell's interest in this subject – one which still has pertinent and powerful resonances today – was stimulated by her own distress at the disappearance of her brother at sea on his way to India. She may well have considered such an exercise a cathartic experience. The piece remains a fascinating document.

This is a unique collection because of the range and differing tones of the tales – a stark contrast to the social realism of Gaskell's novels. This darker and more unusual style of writing can for the collector of ghost stories and supernatural fiction be a little surprising at times, but the volume provides something that is rather unusual, and extremely entertaining.

DAVID STUART DAVIES

TALES OF MYSTERY
AND THE MACABRE

The Old Nurse's Story

You know, my dears, that your mother was an orphan, and an only child; and I dare say you have heard that your grandfather was a clergyman up in Westmoreland, where I come from. I was just a girl in the village school, when, one day, your grandmother came in to ask the mistress if there was any scholar there who would do for a nurse-maid; and mighty proud I was, I can tell ye, when the mistress called me up, and spoke of me being a good girl at my needle, and a steady, honest girl, and one whose parents were very respectable, though they might be poor. I thought I should like nothing better than to serve the pretty young lady, who was blushing as deep as I was, as she spoke of the coming baby, and what I should have to do with it. However, I see you don't care so much for this part of my story, as for what you think is to come, so I'll tell you at once. I was engaged and settled at the parsonage before Miss Rosamond (that was the baby, who is now your mother) was born. To be sure, I had little enough to do with her when she came, for she was never out of her mother's arms, and slept by her all night long; and proud enough was I sometimes when missis trusted her to me. There never was such a baby before or since, though you've all of you been fine enough in your turns; but for sweet, winning ways, you've none of you come up to your mother. She took after her mother, who was a real lady born; a Miss Furnivall, a grand-daughter of Lord Furnivall's, in Northumberland. I believe she had neither brother nor sister, and had been brought up in my lord's family till she had married your grandfather, who was just a curate, son to a shopkeeper in Carlisle – but a clever, fine gentleman as ever was – and one who was a right-down hard worker in his parish, which was very wide, and scattered all abroad over the Westmoreland Fells. When your mother, little Miss Rosamond, was about four or five years old, both her parents died in a fortnight – one after the other. Ah! that was a sad time. My pretty young mistress and me was looking for another baby, when my master came home from one of his long rides, wet and tired, and took the fever he died of; and then she never held up her head again, but just lived to see her dead baby, and have it laid on her breast, before she sighed away her life. My mistress had asked me, on her death-bed, never to leave Miss Rosamond; but if she had never spoken a word, I would have gone with the little child to the end of the world.

The next thing, and before we had well stilled our sobs, the executors and guardians came to settle the affairs. They were my poor young mistress's own cousin, Lord Furnivall, and Mr Esthwaite, my master's brother, a shopkeeper in Manchester; not so well to do then as he was afterwards, and with a large family rising about him. Well! I don't know if it were their settling, or because of a letter my mistress wrote on her death-bed to her cousin, my lord; but somehow it was settled that Miss Rosamond and me were to go to Furnivall Manor House, in Northumberland, and my lord spoke as if it had been her mother's wish that she should live with his family, and as if he had no objections, for that one or two more or less could make no difference in so grand a household. So, though that was not the way in which I should have wished the coming of my bright and pretty pet to have been looked at – who was like a sunbeam in any family, be it never so grand – I was well pleased that all the folks in the Dale should stare and admire, when they heard I was going to be young lady's maid at my Lord Furnivall's at Furnivall Manor.

But I made a mistake in thinking we were to go and live where my lord did. It turned out that the family had left Furnivall Manor House fifty years or more. I could not hear that my poor young mistress had ever been there, though she had been brought up in the family; and I was sorry for that, for I should have liked Miss Rosamond's youth to have passed where her mother's had been.

My lord's gentleman, from whom I asked as many questions as I durst, said that the Manor House was at the foot of the Cumberland Fells, and a very grand place; that an old Miss Furnivall, a great-aunt of my lord's, lived there, with only a few servants; but that it was a very healthy place, and my lord had thought that it would suit Miss Rosamond very well for a few years, and that her being there might perhaps amuse his old aunt.

I was bidden by my lord to have Miss Rosamond's things ready by a certain day. He was a stern, proud man, as they say all the Lords Furnivall were; and he never spoke a word more than was necessary. Folk did say he had loved my young mistress; but that, because she knew that his father would object, she would never listen to him, and married Mr Esthwaite; but I don't know. He never married, at any rate. But he never took much notice of Miss Rosamond; which I thought he might have done if he had cared for her dead mother. He sent his gentleman with us to the Manor House, telling him to join him at Newcastle that same evening; so there was no great length of time for him to make us known to all the strangers before he, too, shook us off; and we were left, two lonely young things (I was not eighteen) in the great old Manor House. It seems like yesterday that we drove there. We had left our own dear parsonage very early, and we had both cried as if our hearts would break, though we were travelling in my lord's carriage, which I thought so much of once. And now it was long past noon on a September day, and we stopped to change horses for the last time at a little smoky town, all full of colliers and miners. Miss Rosamond had fallen asleep, but Mr Henry told me to waken her, that she might see the park and the Manor House as we drove up. I thought it rather a pity; but I did what he bade me, for fear he should complain of me to my lord. We had left all signs of a town, or even a village, and were then inside the gates of a large wild park – not like the parks here in the south, but with rocks, and the noise of running water, and gnarled thorn-trees, and old oaks, all white and peeled with age.

The road went up about two miles, and then we saw a great and stately house, with many trees close around it, so close that in some places their branches dragged against the walls when the wind blew; and some hung broken down; for no-one seemed to take much charge of the place – to lop the wood, or to keep the moss-covered carriage-way in order. Only in front of the house all was clear. The great oval drive was without a weed; and neither tree nor creeper was allowed to grow over the long, many-windowed front; at both sides of which a wing projected, which were each the ends of other side fronts; for the house, although it was so desolate, was even grander than I expected. Behind it rose the Fells, which seemed unenclosed and bare enough; and on the left hand of the house, as you stood facing it, was a little, old-fashioned flower-garden, as I found out afterwards. A door opened out upon it from the west front; it had been scooped out of the thick, dark wood for some old Lady Furnivall; but the branches of the great forest-trees had grown and overshadowed it again, and there were very few flowers that would live there at that time.

When we drove up to the great front entrance, and went into the hall, I thought we would be lost – it was so large, and vast and grand.

There was a chandelier all of bronze, hung down from the middle of the ceiling; and I had never seen one before, and looked at it all in amaze. Then, at one end of the hall, was a great fire-place, as large as the sides of the houses in my country, with massy andirons and dogs to hold the wood; and by it were heavy, old-fashioned sofas. At the opposite end of the hall, to the left as you went in – on the western side – was an organ built into the wall, and so large that it filled up the best part of that end. Beyond it, on the same side, was a door; and opposite, on each side of the fire-place, were also doors leading to the east front; but those I never went through as long as I stayed in the house, so I can't tell you what lay beyond.

The afternoon was closing in, and the hall, which had no fire lighted in it, looked dark and gloomy, but we did not stay there a moment. The old servant, who had opened the door for us, bowed to Mr Henry, and took us in through the door at the further side of the great organ, and led us through several smaller halls and passages into the west drawing-room, where he said that Miss Furnivall was sitting. Poor little Miss Rosamond held very tight to me, as if she were scared and lost in that great place; and as for myself, I was not much better. The west drawing-room was very cheerful-looking, with a warm fire in it, and plenty of good, comfortable furniture about. Miss Furnivall was an old lady not far from eighty, I should think, but I do not know. She was thin and tall, and had a face as full of fine wrinkles as if they had been drawn all over it with a needle's point. Her eyes were very watchful, to make up, I suppose, for her being so deaf as to be obliged to use a trumpet. Sitting with her, working at the same great piece of tapestry, was Mrs Stark, her maid and companion, and almost as old as she was. She had lived with Miss Furnivall ever since they both were young, and now she seemed more like a friend than a servant; she looked so cold, and grey, and stony, as if she had never loved or cared for anyone; and I don't suppose she did care for anyone, except her mistress; and, owing to the great deafness of the latter, Mrs Stark treated her very much as if she were a child. Mr Henry gave some message from my lord, and then he bowed goodbye to us all – taking no notice of my sweet little Miss Rosamond's outstretched hand – and left us standing there, being looked at by the two old ladies through their spectacles.

I was right glad when they rung for the old footman who had shown us in at first, and told him to take us to our rooms. So we went out of that great drawing-room and into another sitting-room, and out of that, and then up a great flight of stairs, and along a broad gallery – which was something like a library, having books all down one side, and windows and writing-tables all down the other – till we came to our rooms, which I was not sorry to hear were just over the kitchens; for I began to think I should be lost in that wilderness of a house. There was an old nursery, that had been used for all the little lords and ladies long ago, with a pleasant fire burning in the grate, and the kettle boiling on the hob, and tea-things spread out on the table; and out of that room was the night-nursery, with a little crib for Miss Rosamond close to my bed. And old James called up Dorothy, his wife, to bid us welcome; and both he and she were so hospitable and kind, that by-and-by Miss Rosamond and me felt quite at home; and by the time tea was over, she was sitting on Dorothy's knee, and chattering away as fast as her little tongue could go. I soon found out that Dorothy was from Westmoreland, and that bound her and me together, as it were; and I would never wish to meet with kinder people than were old James and his wife. James had lived pretty nearly all his life in my lord's family, and thought there was no-one so grand as they. He even looked down a little on his wife; because, till he had married her, she had never lived in any but a farmer's household. But he was very fond of her, as well he might be. They had one servant under them, to do all the rough work. Agnes they called her; and she and me, and James and Dorothy, with Miss Furnivall and Mrs Stark, made up the family; always remembering my sweet little Miss Rosamond! I used to wonder what they had done before she came, they thought so much of her now. Kitchen and drawing-room, it was all the same. The hard, sad Miss Furnivall, and the cold Mrs Stark, looked pleased when she came fluttering in like a bird, playing and pranking hither and thither, with a continual murmur, and pretty prattle of gladness. I am sure, they were sorry many a time when she flitted away into the kitchen, though they were too proud to ask her to stay with them, and were a little surprised at her taste; though to be sure, as Mrs Stark said, it was not to be wondered at, remembering what stock her father had come of. The great, old rambling house was a famous place for little Miss Rosamond. She made expeditions all over it, with me at her heels; all, except the east wing, which was never opened, and whither we never thought of going. But in the western and northern part was many a pleasant room; full of things that were curiosities to us, though they might not have been to people who had seen more. The windows were darkened by the sweeping boughs of the trees, and the ivy which had overgrown them; but, in the green gloom, we could manage to see old china jars and carved ivory boxes, and great heavy books, and, above all, the old pictures!

Once, I remember, my darling would have Dorothy go with us to tell us who they all were; for they were all portraits of some of my lord's family, though Dorothy could not tell us the names of every-one. We had gone through most of the rooms, when we came to the old state drawing-room over the hall, and there was a picture of Miss Furnivall; or, as she was called in those days, Miss Grace, for she was the younger sister. Such a beauty she must have been! but with such a set, proud look, and such scorn looking out of her handsome eyes, with her eyebrows just a little raised, as if she wondered how any-one could have the impertinence to look at her, and her lip curled at us, as we stood there gazing. She had a dress on, the like of which I had never seen before, but it was all the fashion when she was young; a hat of some soft white stuff like beaver, pulled a little over her brows, and a beautiful plume of feathers sweeping round it on one side; and her gown of blue satin was open in front to a quilted white stomacher.

'Well, to be sure!' said I, when I had gazed my fill. 'Flesh is grass, they do say; but who would have thought that Miss Furnivall had been such an out-and-out beauty, to see her now.'

'Yes,' said Dorothy. 'Folks change sadly. But if what my master's father used to say was true, Miss Furnivall, the elder sister, was handsomer than Miss Grace. Her picture is here somewhere; but, if I show it you, you must never let on, even to James, that you have seen it. Can the little lady hold her tongue, think you?' asked she.

I was not so sure, for she was such a little sweet, bold, open-spoken child, so I set her to hide herself; and then I helped Dorothy to turn a great picture, that leaned with its face towards the wall, and was not hung up as the others were. To be sure, it beat Miss Grace for beauty; and, I think, for scornful pride, too, though in that matter it might be hard to choose. I could have looked at it an hour, but Dorothy seemed half frightened at having shown it to me, and hurried it back again, and bade me run and find Miss Rosamond, for that there were some ugly places about the house, where she should like ill for the child to go. I was a brave, high-spirited girl, and thought little of what the old woman said, for I liked hide-and-seek as well as any child in the parish; so off I ran to find my little one.

As winter drew on, and the days grew shorter, I was sometimes almost certain that I heard a noise as if someone was playing on the great organ in the hall. I did not hear it every evening; but, certainly,

I did very often, usually when I was sitting with Miss Rosamond, after I had put her to bed, and keeping quite still and silent in the bedroom. Then I used to hear it booming and swelling away in the distance. The first night, when I went down to my supper, I asked Dorothy who had been playing music, and James said very shortly that I was a gowk to take the wind soughing among the trees for music; but I saw Dorothy look at him very fearfully, and Bessy, the kitchen-maid, said something beneath her breath, and went quite white. I saw they did not like my question, so I held my peace till I was with Dorothy alone, when I knew I could get a good deal out of her. So, the next day, I watched my time, and I coaxed and asked her who it was that played the organ; for I knew that it was the organ and not the wind well enough, for all I had kept silence before James. But Dorothy had had her lesson, I'll warrant, and never a word could I get from her. So then I tried Bessy, though I had always held my head rather above her, as I was evened to James and Dorothy, and she was little better than their servant. So she said I must never, never tell; and if ever I told, I was never to say *she* had told me; but it was a very strange noise, and she had heard it many a time, but most of all on winter nights, and before storms; and folks did say it was the old lord playing on the great organ in the hall, just as he used to do when he was alive; but who the old lord was, or why he played, and why he played on stormy winter evenings in particular, she either could not or would not tell me. Well! I told you I had a brave heart; and I thought it was rather pleasant to have that grand music rolling about the house, let who would be the player; for now it rose above the great gusts of wind, and wailed and triumphed just like a living creature, and then it fell to a softness most complete, only it was always music, and tunes, so it was nonsense to call it the wind. I thought at first, that it might be Miss Furnivall who played, un-known to Bessy; but one day, when I was in the hall by myself, I opened the organ and peeped all about it and around it, as I had done to the organ in Crosthwaite church once before, and I saw it was all broken and destroyed inside, though it looked so brave and fine; and then, though it was noonday, my flesh began to creep a little, and I shut it up, and run away pretty quickly to my own bright nursery; and I did not like hearing the music for some time after that, any more than James and Dorothy did. All this time Miss Rosamond was making herself more and more beloved. The old ladies liked her to dine with them at their early dinner. James stood behind Miss Furnivall's chair, and I behind Miss Rosamond's all in state; and after dinner, she would play about in a corner of the great drawing-room as still as any mouse, while Miss Furnivall slept, and I had my dinner in the kitchen. But she was glad enough to come to me in the nursery afterwards; for, as she said, Miss Furnivall was so sad, and Mrs Stark so dull; but she and I were merry enough; and by-and-by, I got not to care for that weird rolling music, which did one no harm, if we did not know where it came from.

That winter was very cold. In the middle of October the frosts began, and lasted many, many weeks. I remember one day, at dinner, Miss Furnivall lifted up her sad, heavy eyes, and said to Mrs Stark, 'I am afraid we shall have a terrible winter,' in a strange kind of meaning way. But Mrs Stark pretended not to hear, and talked very loud of something else. My little lady and I did not care for the frost; not we! As long as it was dry, we climbed up the steep brows behind the house, and went up on the Fells, which were bleak and bare enough, and there we ran races in the fresh, sharp air; and once we came down by a new path, that took us past the two old gnarled holly-trees, which grew about half-way down by the east side of the house. But the days grew shorter and shorter, and the old lord, if it was he, played away, more and more stormily and sadly, on the great organ. One Sunday afternoon – it must have been towards the end of November – I asked Dorothy to take charge of little missy when she came out of the drawing-room, after Miss Furnivall had had her nap; for it was too cold to take her with me to church, and yet I wanted to go. And Dorothy was glad enough to promise, and was so fond of the child, that all seemed well; and Bessy and I set off very briskly, though the sky hung heavy and black over the white earth, as if the night had never fully gone away, and the air, though still, was very biting and keen.

'We shall have a fall of snow,' said Bessy to me. And sure enough, even while we were in church, it came down thick, in great large flakes – so thick, it almost darkened the windows. It had stopped snowing before we came out, but it lay soft, thick and deep beneath our feet, as we tramped home. Before we got to the hall, the moon rose, and I think it was lighter then – what with the moon, and what with the white dazzling snow – than it had been when we went to church, between two and three o'clock. I have not told you that Miss Furnivall and Mrs Stark never went to church; they used to read the prayers together, in their quiet, gloomy way; they seemed to feel the Sunday very long without their tapestry-work to be busy at. So when I went to Dorothy in the kitchen, to fetch Miss Rosamond and take her upstairs with me, I did not much wonder when the old woman told me that the ladies had kept the child with them, and that she had never come to the kitchen, as I had bidden her, when she was tired of behaving pretty in the drawing-room. So I took off my things and went to find her, and bring her to her supper in the nursery. But when I went into the best drawing-room, there sat the two old ladies, very still and quiet, dropping out a word now and then, but looking as if nothing so bright and merry as Miss Rosamond had ever been near them. Still I thought she might be hiding from me; it was one of her pretty ways – and that she had persuaded them to look as if they knew nothing about her; so I went softly peeping under this sofa, and behind that chair, making believe I was sadly frightened at not finding her.

'What's the matter, Hester?' said Mrs Stark, sharply. I don't know if Miss Furnivall had seen me, for, as I told you, she was very deaf, and she sat quite still, idly staring into the fire, with her hopeless face. 'I'm only looking for my little Rosy Posy,' replied I, still thinking that the child was there, and near me, though I could not see her.

'Miss Rosamond is not here,' said Mrs Stark. 'She went away, more than an hour ago, to find Dorothy.' And she, too, turned and went on looking into the fire.

My heart sank at this, and I began to wish I had never left my darling. I went back to Dorothy and told her. James was gone out for the day, but she, and me, and Bessy took lights, and went up into the nursery first; and then we roamed over the great, large house, calling and entreating Miss Rosamond to come out of her hiding-place, and not frighten us to death in that way. But there was no answer; no sound.

'Oh!' said I, at last, 'can she have got into the east wing and hidden there?'

But Dorothy said it was not possible, for that she herself had never been in there; that the doors were always locked, and my lord's steward had the keys, she believed; at any rate, neither she nor James had ever seen them: so I said I would go back, and see if, after all, she was not hidden in the drawing-room, unknown to the old ladies; and if I found her there, I said, I would whip her well for the fright she had given me; but I never meant to do it. Well, I went back to the west drawing-room, and I told Mrs Stark we could not find her anywhere, and asked for leave to look all about the furniture there, for I thought now that she might have fallen asleep in some warm, hidden corner; but no! we looked – Miss Furnivall got up and looked, trembling all over – and she was nowhere there; then we set off again, everyone in the house, and looked in all the places we had searched before, but we could not find her. Miss Furnivall shivered and shook so much, that Mrs Stark took her back into the warm drawing-room; but not before they had made me promise to bring her to them when she was found. Well-a-day! I began to think she never would be found, when I bethought me to look into the great front court, all covered with snow. I was upstairs when I looked out; but, it was such clear moonlight, I could see, quite plain, two little footprints, which might be traced from the hall-door and round the corner of the east wing. I don't know how I got down, but I tugged open the great stiff hall-door, and, throwing the skirt of my gown over my head for a cloak, I ran out. I turned the east corner, and there a black shadow fell on the snow; but when I came again into the moonlight, there were the little foot-marks going up – up to the Fells. It was bitter cold; so cold, that the air almost took the skin off my face as I ran; but I ran on, crying to think how my poor little darling must be perished and frightened. I was within sight of the holly-trees, when I saw a shepherd coming down the hill, bearing something in his arms wrapped in his maud. He shouted to me, and asked me if I had lost a bairn; and, when I could not speak for crying, he bore towards me, and I saw my wee bairnie, lying still, and white, and stiff in his arms, as if she had been dead. He told me he had been up the Fells to gather in his sheep, before the deep cold of night came on, and that under the holly-trees (black marks on the hill-side, where no other bush was for miles around) he had found my little lady – my lamb – my queen – my darling – stiff and cold in the terrible sleep which is frost-begotten. Oh! the joy and the tears of having her in my arms once again! for I would not let him carry her; but took her, maud and all, into my own arms, and held her near my own warm neck and heart, and felt the life stealing slowly back again into her little gentle limbs. But she was still insensible when we reached the hall, and I had no breath for speech. We went in by the kitchen-door.

'Bring me the warming-pan,' said I; and I carried her upstairs and began undressing her by the nursery fire, which Bessy had kept up. I called my little lammie all the sweet and playful names I could think of – even while my eyes were blinded by my tears; and at last, oh! at length she opened her large blue eyes. Then I put her into her warm bed, and sent Dorothy down to tell Miss Furnivall that all was well; and I made up my mind to sit by my darling's bedside the live-long night. She fell away into a soft sleep as soon as her pretty head had touched the pillow, and I watched by her till morning light; when she wakened up bright and clear – or so I thought at first – and, my dears, so I think now.

She said, that she had fancied that she should like to go to Dorothy, for that both the old ladies were asleep, and it was very dull in the drawing-room; and that, as she was going through the west lobby, she saw the snow through the high window falling – falling – soft and steady; but she wanted to see it lying pretty and white on the ground; so she made her way into the great hall; and then, going to the window, she saw it bright and soft upon the drive; but while she stood there, she saw a little girl, not so old as she was, 'but so pretty,' said my darling, 'and this little girl beckoned to me to come out; and oh, she was so pretty and so sweet, I could not choose but go.' And then this other little girl had taken her by the hand, and side by side the two had gone round the east corner.

'Now you are a naughty little girl, and telling stories,' said I. 'What would your good mamma, that is in heaven, and never told a story in her life, say to her little Rosamond, if she heard her – and I dare say she does – telling stories!'

'Indeed, Hester,' sobbed out my child, 'I'm telling you true. Indeed I am.'

'Don't tell me!' said I, very stern. 'I tracked you by your foot-marks through the snow; there were only yours to be seen: and if you had had a little girl to go hand-in-hand with you up the hill, don't you think the footprints would have gone along with yours?'

'I can't help it, dear, dear Hester,' said she, crying, 'if they did not; I never looked at her feet, but she held my hand fast and tight in her little one, and it was very, very cold. She took me up the Fell-path, up to the holly-trees; and there I saw a lady weeping and crying; but when she saw me, she hushed her weeping, and smiled very proud and grand, and took me on her knee, and began to lull me to sleep; and that's all, Hester – but that is true; and my dear mamma knows it is,' said she, crying. So I thought the child was in a fever, and pretended to believe her, as she went over her story – over and over again, and always the same. At last Dorothy knocked at the door with Miss Rosamond's breakfast; and she told me the old ladies were down in the eating parlour, and that they wanted to speak to me. They had both been into the night-nursery the evening before, but it was after Miss Rosamond was asleep; so they had only looked at her – not asked me any questions.

'I shall catch it,' thought I to myself, as I went along the north gallery. 'And yet,' I thought, taking courage, 'it was in their charge I left her; and it's they that's to blame for letting her steal away unknown and unwatched.' So I went in boldly, and told my story. I told it all to Miss Furnivall, shouting it close to her ear; but when I came to the mention of the other little girl out in the snow, coaxing and tempting her out, and willing her up to the grand and beautiful lady by the holly-tree, she threw her arms up – her old and withered arms – and cried aloud, 'Oh! Heaven forgive! Have mercy!'

Mrs Stark took hold of her; roughly enough, I thought; but she was past Mrs Stark's management, and spoke to me, in a kind of wild warning and authority.

'Hester! keep her from that child! It will lure her to her death! That evil child! Tell her it is a wicked, naughty child.' Then, Mrs Stark hurried me out of the room; where, indeed, I was glad enough to go; but Miss Furnivall kept shrieking out, 'Oh, have mercy! Wilt Thou never forgive! It is many a long year ago – '

I was very uneasy in my mind after that. I durst never leave Miss Rosamond, night or day, for fear lest she might slip off again, after some fancy or other; and all the more, because I thought I could make out that Miss Furnivall was crazy, from their odd ways about her; and I was afraid lest something of the same kind (which might be in the family, you know) hung over my darling. And the great frost never ceased all this time; and, whenever it was a more stormy night than usual, between the gusts, and through the wind, we heard the old lord playing on the great organ. But, old lord, or not, wherever Miss Rosamond went, there I followed; for my love for her, pretty, helpless orphan, was stronger than my fear for the grand and terrible sound. Besides, it rested with me to keep her cheerful and merry, as beseemed her age. So we played together, and wandered together, here and there, and everywhere; for I never dared to lose sight of her again in that large and rambling house. And so it happened, that one afternoon, not long before Christmas-day, we were playing together on the billiard-table in the great hall (not that we knew the right way of playing, but she liked to roll the smooth ivory balls with her pretty hands, and I liked to do whatever she did); and, by-and-by, without our noticing it, it grew dusk indoors, though it was still light in the open air, and I was thinking of taking her back into the nursery, when, all of a sudden, she cried out, 'Look, Hester! look! there is my poor little girl out in the snow!'

I turned towards the long narrow windows, and there, sure enough, I saw a little girl, less than my Miss Rosamond – dressed all unfit to be out-of-doors such a bitter night – crying, and beating against the window-panes, as if she wanted to be let in. She seemed to sob and wail, till Miss Rosamond could bear it no longer, and was flying to the door to open it, when, all of a sudden, and close upon us, the great organ pealed out so loud and thundering, it fairly made me tremble; and all the more, when I remembered me that, even in the stillness of that dead-cold weather, I had heard no sound of little battering hands upon the windowglass, although the phantom child had seemed to put forth all its force; and, although I had seen it wail and cry, no faintest touch of sound had fallen upon my ears. Whether I remembered all this at the very moment, I do not know; the great organ sound had so stunned me into terror; but this I know, I caught up Miss Rosamond before she got the hall-door opened, and clutched her, and carried her away, kicking and screaming, into the large, bright kitchen, where Dorothy and Agnes were busy with their mince-pies.

'What is the matter with my sweet one?' cried Dorothy, as I bore in Miss Rosamond, who was sobbing as if her heart would break.

'She won't let me open the door for my little girl to come in; and she'll die if she is out on the Fells all night. Cruel, naughty Hester,' she said, slapping me; but she might have struck harder, for I had seen a look of ghastly terror on Dorothy's face, which made my very blood run cold.

'Shut the back-kitchen door fast, and bolt it well,' said she to Agnes. She said no more; she gave me raisins and almonds to quiet Miss Rosamond; but she sobbed about the little girl in the snow, and would not touch any of the good things. I was thankful when she cried herself to sleep in bed. Then I stole down to the kitchen, and told Dorothy I had made up my mind. I would carry my darling back to my father's house in Applethwaite; where, if we lived humbly, we lived at peace. I said I had been frightened enough with the old lord's organ-playing; but now that I had seen for myself this little moaning child, all decked out as no child in the neighbourhood could be, beating and battering to get in, yet always without any sound or noise – with the dark wound on its right shoulder; and that Miss Rosamond had known it again for the phantom that had nearly lured her to her death (which Dorothy knew was true); I would stand it no longer.

I saw Dorothy change colour once or twice. When I had done, she told me she did not think I could take Miss Rosamond with me, for that she was my lord's ward, and I had no right over her; and she asked me would I leave the child that I was so fond of just for sounds and sights that could do me no harm; and that they had all had to get used to in their turns? I was all in a hot, trembling passion; and I said it was very well for her to talk; that knew what these sights and noises betokened, and that had, perhaps, had something to do with the spectre child while it was alive. And I taunted her so, that she told me all she knew at last; and then I wished I had never been told, for it only made me more afraid than ever.

She said she had heard the tale from old neighbours that were alive when she was first married; when folks used to come to the hall sometimes, before it had got such a bad name in the countryside: it might not be true, or it might, what she had been told.

The old lord was Miss Furnivall's father – Miss Grace, as Dorothy called her, for Miss Maude was the elder, and Miss Furnivall by rights. The old lord was eaten up with pride. Such a proud man was never seen or heard of; and his daughters were like him. No-one was good enough to wed them, although they had choice enough; for they were the great beauties of their day, as I had seen by their portraits, where they hung in the state drawing-room. But, as the old saying is, 'Pride will have a fall'; and these two haughty beauties fell in love with the same man, and he no better than a foreign musician, whom their father had down from London to play music with him at the Manor House. For, above all things, next to his pride, the old lord loved music. He could play on nearly every instrument that ever was heard of, and it was a strange thing it did not soften him; but he was a fierce dour old man, and had broken his poor wife's heart with his cruelty, they said. He was mad after music, and would pay any money for it. So he got this foreigner to come; who made such beautiful music, that they said the very birds on the trees stopped their singing to listen. And, by degrees, this foreign gentleman got such a hold over the old lord, that nothing would serve him but that he must come every year; and it was he that had the great organ brought from Holland, and built up in the hall, where it stood now. He taught the old lord to play on it; but many and many a time, when Lord Furnivall was thinking of nothing but his fine organ, and his finer music, the dark foreigner was walking abroad in the woods with one of the young ladies; now Miss Maude, and then Miss Grace.

Miss Maude won the day and carried off the prize, such as it was; and he and she were married, all unknown to anyone; and before he made his next yearly visit, she had been confined of a little girl at a farm-house on the Moors, while her father and Miss Grace thought she was away at Doncaster Races. But though she was a wife and a mother, she was not a bit softened, but as haughty and as passionate as ever; and perhaps more so, for she was jealous of Miss Grace, to whom her foreign husband paid a deal of court – by way of blinding her – as he told his wife. But Miss Grace triumphed over Miss Maude, and Miss Maude grew fiercer and fiercer, both with her husband and with her sister; and the former – who could easily shake off what was disagreeable, and hide himself in foreign countries – went away a month before his usual time that summer, and half-threatened that he would never come back again. Meanwhile, the little girl was left at the farm-house, and her mother used to have her horse saddled and gallop wildly over the hills to see her once every week, at the very least; for where she loved she loved, and where she hated she hated. And the old lord went on playing – playing on his organ; and the servants thought the sweet music he made had soothed down his awful temper, of which (Dorothy said) some terrible tales could be told. He grew infirm too, and had to walk with a crutch; and his son – that was the present Lord Furnivall's father – was with the army in America, and the other son at sea; so Miss Maude had it pretty much her own way, and she and Miss Grace grew colder and bitterer to each other every day; till at last they hardly ever spoke, except when the old lord was by. The foreign musician came again the next summer, but it was for the last time; for they led him such a life with their jealousy and their passions, that he grew weary, and went away, and never was heard of again. And Miss Maude, who had always meant to have her marriage acknowledged when her father should be dead, was left now a deserted wife, whom nobody knew to have been married, with a child that she dared not own, although she loved it to distraction; living with a father whom she feared, and a sister whom she hated. When the next summer passed over, and the dark foreigner never came, both Miss Maude and Miss Grace grew gloomy and sad; they had a haggard look about them, though they looked handsome as ever. But, by-and-by, Maude brightened; for her father grew more and more infirm, and more than ever carried away by his music; and she and Miss Grace lived almost entirely apart, having separate rooms, the one on the west side, Miss Maude on the east – those very rooms which were now shut up. So she thought she might have her little girl with her, and no-one need ever know except those who dared not speak about it, and were bound to believe that it was, as she said, a cottager's child she had taken a fancy to. All this, Dorothy said, was pretty well known; but what came afterwards no-one knew, except Miss Grace and Mrs Stark, who was even then her maid, and much more of a friend to her than ever her sister had been. But the servants supposed, from words that were dropped, that Miss Maude had triumphed over Miss Grace, and told her that all the time the dark foreigner had been mocking her with pretended love – he was her own husband. The colour left Miss Grace's cheek and lips that very day for ever, and she was heard to say many a time that sooner or later she would have her revenge; and Mrs Stark was for ever spying about the east rooms.

One fearful night, just after the New Year had come in, when the snow was lying thick and deep; and the flakes were still falling – fast enough to blind anyone who might be out and abroad – there was a great and violent noise heard, and the old lord's voice above all, cursing and swearing awfully, and the cries of a little child, and the proud defiance of a fierce woman, and the sound of a blow, and a dead stillness, and moans and wailings dying away on the hill-side! Then the old lord summoned all his servants, and told them, with terrible oaths, and words more terrible, that his daughter had disgraced herself, and that he had turned her out of doors – her, and her child – and that if ever they gave her help, or food, or shelter, he prayed that they might never enter heaven. And, all the while, Miss Grace stood by him, white and still as any stone; and, when he had ended, she heaved a great sigh, as much as to say her work was done, and her end was accomplished. But the old lord never touched his organ again, and died within the year; and no wonder! for, on the morrow of that wild and fearful night, the shepherds, coming down the Fell side, found Miss Maude sitting, all crazy and smiling, under the holly-trees, nursing a dead child, with a terrible mark on its right shoulder. 'But that was not what killed it,' said Dorothy: 'it was the frost and the cold. Every wild creature was in its hole, and every beast in its fold, while the child and its mother were turned out to wander on the Fells! And now you know all! and I wonder if you are less frightened now?'

I was more frightened than ever; but I said I was not. I wished Miss Rosamond and myself well out of that dreadful house for ever; but I would not leave her, and I dared not take her away. But oh, how I watched her, and guarded her! We bolted the doors, and shut the window-shutters fast, an hour or more before dark, rather than leave them open five minutes too late. But my little lady still heard the weird child crying and mourning; and not all we could do or say could keep her from wanting to go to her, and let her in from the cruel wind and the snow. All this time I kept away from Miss Furnivall and Mrs Stark, as much as ever I could; for I feared them – I knew no good could be about them, with their grey, hard faces, and their dreamy eyes, looking back into the ghastly years that were gone. But, even in my fear, I had a kind of pity for Miss Furnivall, at least. Those gone down to the pit can hardly have a more hopeless look than that which was ever on her face. At last I even got so sorry for her – who never said a word but what was quite forced from her – that I prayed for her; and I taught Miss Rosamond to pray for one who had done a deadly sin; but often when she came to those words, she would listen, and start up from her knees, and say, 'I hear my little girl plaining and crying very sad – oh, let her in, or she will die!'

One night – just after New Year's Day had come at last, and the long winter had taken a turn, as I hoped – I heard the west drawing-room bell ring three times, which was the signal for me. I would not leave Miss Rosamond alone, for all she was asleep – for the old lord had been playing wilder than ever – and I feared lest my darling should waken to hear the spectre child; see her, I knew she could not. I had fastened the windows too well for that. So I took her out of her bed, and wrapped her up in such outer clothes as were most handy, and carried her down to the drawing-room, where the old ladies sat at their tapestry-work as usual. They looked up when I came in, and Mrs Stark asked, quite astounded, 'Why did I bring Miss Rosamond there, out of her warm bed?' I had begun to whisper, 'Because I was afraid of her being tempted out while I was away, by the wild child in the snow,' when she stopped me short (with a glance at Miss Furnivall), and said Miss Furnivall wanted me to undo some work she had done wrong, and which neither of them could see to unpick. So I laid my pretty dear on the sofa, and sat down on a stool by them, and hardened my heart against them, as I heard the wind rising and howling.

Miss Rosamond slept on sound, for all the wind blew so; and Miss Furnivall said never a word, nor looked round when the gusts shook the windows. All at once she started up to her full height, and put up one hand, as if to bid us to listen.

'I hear voices!' said she. 'I hear terrible screams – I hear my father's voice!'

Just at that moment my darling wakened with a sudden start: 'My little girl is crying, oh, how she is crying!' and she tried to get up and go to her, but she got her feet entangled in the blanket, and I caught her up; for my flesh had begun to creep at these noises, which they heard while we could catch no sound. In a minute or two the noises came, and gathered fast, and filled our ears; we, too, heard voices and screams, and no longer heard the winter's wind that raged abroad. Mrs Stark looked at me, and I at her, but we dared not speak. Suddenly Miss Furnivall went towards the door, out into the ante-room, through the west lobby, and opened the door into the great hall. Mrs Stark followed, and I durst not be left, though my heart almost stopped beating for fear. I wrapped my darling tight in my arms, and went out with them. In the hall the screams were louder than ever; they seemed to come from the east wing – nearer and nearer – close on the other side of the locked-up doors – close behind them. Then I noticed that the great bronze chandelier seemed all alight, though the hall was dim, and that a fire was blazing in the vast hearth-place, though it gave no heat; and I shuddered up with terror, and folded my darling closer to me. But as I did so the east door shook, and she, suddenly struggling to get free from me, cried, 'Hester! I must go. My little girl is there! I hear her; she is coming! Hester, I must go!'

I held her tight with all my strength; with a set will, I held her. If I had died, my hands would have grasped her still, I was so resolved in my mind. Miss Furnivall stood listening, and paid no regard to my darling, who had got down to the ground, and whom I, upon my knees now, was holding with both my arms clasped round her neck; she still striving and crying to get free.

All at once, the east door gave way with a thundering crash, as if torn open in a violent passion, and there came into that broad and mysterious light, the figure of a tall old man, with grey hair and gleaming eyes. He drove before him, with many a relentless gesture of abhorrence, a stern and beautiful woman, with a little child cling-ing to her dress.

'Oh, Hester! Hester!' cried Miss Rosamond; 'it's the lady! the lady below the holly-trees; and my little girl is with her. Hester! Hester! let me go to her; they are drawing me to them. I feel them – I feel them. I must go!'

Again she was almost convulsed by her efforts to get away; but I held her tighter and tighter, till I feared I should do her a hurt; but rather that than let her go towards those terrible phantoms. They passed along towards the great hall-door, where the winds howled and ravened for their prey; but before they reached that, the lady turned; and I could see that she defied the old man with a fierce and proud defiance; but then she quailed – and then she threw up her arms wildly and piteously to save her child – her little child – from a blow from his uplifted crutch.

And Miss Rosamond was torn as by a power stronger than mine and writhed in my arms, and sobbed (for by this time the poor darling was growing faint).

'They want me to go with them on to the Fells – they are drawing me to them. Oh, my little girl! I would come, but cruel, wicked Hester holds me very tight.' But when she saw the uplifted crutch, she swooned away, and I thanked God for it. Just at this moment – when the tall old man, his hair streaming as in the blast of a furnace, was going to strike the little shrinking child – Miss Furnivall, the old woman by my side, cried out, 'Oh father! father! spare the little innocent child!' But just then I saw – we all saw – another phantom shape itself, and grow clear out of the blue and misty light that filled the hall; we had not seen her till now, for it was another lady who stood by the old man, with a look of relentless hate and triumphant scorn. That figure was very beautiful to look upon, with a soft, white hat drawn down over the proud brows, and a red and curling lip. It was dressed in an open robe of blue satin. I had seen that figure before. It was the likeness of Miss Furnivall in her youth; and the terrible phantoms moved on, regardless of old Miss Furnivall's wild entreaty – and the uplifted crutch fell on the right shoulder of the little child, and the younger sister looked on, stony, and deadly serene. But at that moment, the dim lights, and the fire that gave no heat, went out of themselves, and Miss Furnivall lay at our feet stricken down by the palsy – death-stricken.

Yes! she was carried to her bed that night never to rise again. She lay with her face to the wall, muttering low, but muttering always: 'Alas! alas! what is done in youth can never be undone in age! What is done in youth can never be undone in age!'

The Squire's Story

In the year 1769 the little town of Barford was thrown into a state of great excitement by the intelligence that a gentleman (and 'quite the gentleman', said the landlord of the George Inn) had been looking at Mr Clavering's old house. This house was neither in the town nor in the country. It stood on the outskirts of Barford, on the roadside leading to Derby. The last occupant had been a Mr Clavering – a Northumberland gentleman of good family who had come to live in Barford while he was but a younger son; but when some elder branches of the family died, he had returned to take possession of the family estate. The house of which I speak was called the White House, from its being covered with a greyish kind of stucco. It had a good garden to the back, and Mr Clavering had built capital stables, with what were then considered the latest improvement. The point of good stabling was expected to let the house, as it was in a hunting county; otherwise it had few recommendations. There were many bedrooms; some entered through others, even to the number of five, leading one beyond the other; several sitting-rooms of the small and poky kind, wainscoted round with wood, and then painted a heavy slate colour; one good dining-room, and a drawing-room over it, both looking into the garden, with pleasant bow-windows.

Such was the accommodation offered by the White House. It did not seem to be very tempting to strangers, though the good people of Barford rather piqued themselves on it, as the largest house in the town; and as a house in which 'townspeople' and 'county people' had often met at Mr Clavering's friendly dinners. To appreciate this circumstance of pleasant recollection, you should have lived some years in a little country town, surrounded by gentlemen's seats. You would then understand how a bow or a courtesy from a member of a county family elevates the individuals who receive it almost as much, in their own eyes, as the pair of blue garters fringed with silver did Mr Bickerstaff's ward. They trip lightly on air for a whole day afterwards. Now Mr Clavering was gone, where could town and county mingle?

I mention these things that you may have an idea of the desirability of the letting of the White House in the Barfordites' imagination; and to make the mixture thick and slab, you must add for yourselves the bustle, the mystery, and the importance which every little event either causes or assumes in a small town; and then, perhaps, it will be no wonder to you that twenty ragged little urchins accompanied the 'gentleman' aforesaid to the door of the White House; and that, although he was above an hour inspecting it, under the auspices of Mr Jones, the agent's clerk, thirty more had joined themselves on to the wondering crowd before his exit, and awaited such crumbs of intelligence as they could gather before they were threatened or whipped out of hearing distance. Presently, out came the 'gentleman' and the lawyer's clerk. The latter was speaking as he followed the former over the threshold. The gentleman was tall, well-dressed, handsome; but there was a sinister cold look in his quick-glancing, light blue eye, which a keen observer might not have liked. There were no keen observers among the boys, and ill-conditioned gaping girls. But they stood too near; inconveniently close; and the gentleman, lifting up his right hand, in which he carried a short riding-whip, dealt one or two sharp blows to the nearest, with a look of savage enjoyment on his face as they moved away whimpering and crying. An instant after, his expression of countenance had changed.

'Here!' said he, drawing out a handful of money, partly silver, partly copper, and throwing it into the midst of them. 'Scramble for it! fight it out, my lads! Come this afternoon, at three, to the George, and I'll throw you out some more.' So the boys hurrahed for him as he walked off with the agent's clerk. He chuckled to himself, as over a pleasant thought. 'I'll have some fun with those lads,' he said; 'I'll teach 'em to come prowling and prying about me. I'll tell you what I'll do. I'll make the money so hot in the fire-shovel that it shall burn their fingers. You come and see the faces and the howling. I shall be very glad if you will dine with me at two; and by that time I may have made up my mind respecting the house.'

Mr Jones, the agent's clerk, agreed to come to the George at two, but, somehow, he had a distaste for his entertainer. Mr Jones would not like to have said, even to himself, that a man with a purse full of money, who kept many horses, and spoke familiarly of noblemen – above all, who thought of taking the White House – could be anything but a gentleman; but still the uneasy wonder as to who this Mr Robinson Higgins could be, filled the clerk's mind long after Mr

Higgins, Mr Higgins's servants, and Mr Higgins's stud had taken possession of the White House.

The White House was re-stuccoed (this time of a pale yellow colour), and put into thorough repair by the accommodating and delighted landlord; while his tenant seemed inclined to spend any amount of money on internal decorations, which were showy and effective in their character, enough to make the White House a nine days' wonder to the good people of Barford. The slate-coloured paints became pink, and were picked out with gold; the old-fashioned banisters were replaced by newly gilt ones; but, above all, the stables were a sight to be seen. Since the days of the Roman Emperor never was there such provision made for the care, the comfort, and the health of horses. But everyone said it was no wonder, when they were led through Barford, covered up to their eyes, but curving their arched and delicate necks, and prancing with short high steps, in repressed eagerness. Only one groom came with them; yet they required the care of three men. Mr Higgins, however, preferred engaging two lads out of Barford; and Barford highly approved of his preference. Not only was it kind and thoughtful to give employment to the lounging lads themselves, but they were receiving such a training in Mr Higgins's stables as might fit them for Doncaster or Newmarket. The district of Derbyshire in which Barford was situated, was too close to Leicestershire not to support a hunt and a pack of hounds. The master of the hounds was a certain Sir Harry Manley, who was *aut* a huntsman *aut nullus*. He measured a man by the 'length of his fork', not by the expression of his countenance, or the shape of his head. But as Sir Harry was wont to observe, there was such a thing as too long a fork, so his approbation was withheld until he had seen a man on horseback; and if his seat there was square and easy, his hand light, and his courage good, Sir Harry hailed him as a brother.

Mr Higgins attended the first meet of the season, not as a subscriber but as an amateur. The Barford huntsmen piqued themselves on their bold riding; and their knowledge of the country came by nature; yet this new strange man, whom nobody knew, was in at the death, sitting on his horse, both well breathed and calm, without a hair turned on the sleek skin of the latter, supremely addressing the old huntsman as he hacked off the tail of the fox; and he, the old man, who was testy even under Sir Harry's slightest rebuke, and flew out on any other member of the hunt that dared to utter a word against his sixty years' experience as stable-boy, groom, poacher, and what not – he, old Isaac Wormeley, was meekly listening to the wisdom of this stranger, only now and then giving one of his quick, up-turning, cunning glances, not unlike the sharp o'er-canny looks of the poor deceased Reynard, round whom the hounds were howling, unadmonished by the short whip, which was now tucked into Wormeley's well-worn pocket. When Sir Harry rode into the copse – full of dead brushwood and wet tangled grass – and was followed by the members of the hunt, as one by one they cantered past, Mr Higgins took off his cap and bowed – half deferentially, half insolently – with a lurking smile in the corner of his eye at the discomfited looks of one or two of the laggards.

'A famous run, sir,' said Sir Harry. 'The first time you have hunted in our country; but I hope we shall see you often.'

'I hope to become a member of the hunt, sir,' said Mr Higgins.

'Most happy – proud, I am sure, to receive so daring a rider among us. You took the Copper-gate, I fancy; while some of our friends here' – scowling at one or two cowards by way of finishing his speech. 'Allow me to introduce myself – master of the hounds.' He fumbled in his waistcoat pocket for the card on which his name was formally inscribed. 'Some of our friends here are kind enough to come home with me to dinner; might I ask for the honour?'

'My name is Higgins,' replied the stranger, bowing low. 'I am only lately come to occupy the White House at Barford, and I have not as yet presented my letters of introduction.'

'Hang it!' replied Sir Harry; 'a man with a seat like yours, and that good brush in your hand, might ride up to any door in the county (I'm a Leicestershire man!), and be a welcome guest. Mr Higgins, I shall be proud to become better acquainted with you over my dinner table.'

Mr Higgins knew pretty well how to improve the acquaintance thus begun. He could sing a good song, tell a good story, and was well up in practical jokes; with plenty of that keen worldly sense, which seems like an instinct in some men, and which in this case taught him on whom he might play off such jokes, with impunity from their resentment, and with a security of applause from the more boisterous, vehement, or prosperous. At the end of twelve months Mr Robinson Higgins was, out-and-out, the most popular member of the Barford hunt; had beaten all the others by a couple of lengths, as his first patron, Sir Harry, observed one evening, when they were just leaving the dinner-table of an old hunting squire in the neighbourhood.

'Because, you know,' said Squire Hearn, holding Sir Harry by the button – 'I mean, you see, this young spark is looking sweet upon Catherine; and she's a good girl, and will have ten thousand pounds down, the day she's married, by her mother's will; and – excuse me, Sir Harry – but I should not like my girl to throw herself away.'

Though Sir Harry had a long ride before him, and but the early and short light of a new moon to take it in, his kind heart was so much touched by Squire Hearn's trembling, tearful anxiety, that he stopped and turned back into the dining-room to say, with more asseverations than I care to give: 'My good Squire, I may say, I know that man pretty well by this time; and a better fellow never existed. If I had twenty daughters he should have the pick of them.'

Squire Hearn never thought of asking the grounds for his old friend's opinion of Mr Higgins; it had been given with too much earnestness for any doubts to cross the old man's mind as to the possibility of its not being well founded. Mr Hearn was not a doubter, or a thinker, or suspicious by nature; it was simply his love for Catherine, his only daughter, that prompted his anxiety in this case; and, after what Sir Harry had said, the old man could totter with an easy mind, though not with very steady legs, into the drawing-room, where his bonny, blushing daughter Catherine and Mr Higgins stood close together on the hearth-rug – he whispering, she listening with downcast eyes. She looked so happy, so like her dead mother had looked when the Squire was a young man, that all his thought was how to please her most. His son and heir was about to be married, and bring his wife to live with the Squire; Barford and the White House were not distant an hour's ride; and, even as these thoughts passed through his mind, he asked Mr Higgins if he could not stay all night – the young moon was already set – the roads would be dark – and Catherine looked up with a pretty anxiety, which, however, had not much doubt in it, for the answer.

With every encouragement of this kind from the old Squire, it took everybody rather by surprise when, one morning, it was discovered that Miss Catherine Hearn was missing; and when, according to the usual fashion in such cases, a note was found, saying that she had eloped with 'the man of her heart', and gone to Gretna Green, no-one could imagine why she could not quietly have stopped at home and been married in the parish church. She had always been a romantic, sentimental girl; very pretty and very affectionate, and very much spoiled, and very much wanting in common sense. Her indulgent father was deeply hurt at this want of confidence in his never-varying affection; but when his son came, hot with indignation from the Baronet's (his future father-in-law's house, where every form of law and of ceremony was to accompany his own impending marriage), Squire Hearn pleaded the cause of the young couple with imploring cogency, and protested that it was a piece of spirit in his daughter, which he admired and was proud of. However, it ended with Mr Nathaniel Hearn's declaring that he and his wife would have nothing to do with his sister and her husband. 'Wait till you've seen him, Nat!' said the old Squire, trembling with his distressful anticip-ations of family discord. 'He's an excuse for any girl. Only ask Sir Harry's opinion of him.'

'Confound Sir Harry! So that a man sits his horse well, Sir Harry cares nothing about anything else. Who is this man – this fellow? Where does he come from? What are his means? Who are his family?'

'He comes from the south – Surrey or Somersetshire, I forget which; and he pays his way well and liberally. There's not a trades-man in Barford but says he cares no more for money than for water; he spends like a prince, Nat, I don't know who his family are, but he seals with a coat of arms, which may tell you if you want to know – and he goes regularly to collect his rents from his estates in the south. Oh, Nat! if you would but be friendly, I should be as well pleased with Kitty's marriage as any father in the county.'

Mr Nathaniel Hearn gloomed, and muttered an oath or two to himself. The poor old father was reaping the consequences of his weak indulgence to his two children. Mr and Mrs Nathaniel Hearn kept apart from Catherine and her husband; and Squire Hearn durst never ask them to Levison Hall, though it was his own house. Indeed, he stole away as if he were a culprit whenever he went to visit the White House; and if he passed a night there, he was fain to equivocate when he returned home the next day; an equivocation which was well interpreted by the surly, proud Nath-aniel. But the younger Mr and Mrs Hearn were the only people who did not visit at the White House. Mr and Mrs Higgins were decidedly more popular than their brother and sister-in-law. She made a very pretty, sweet-tempered hostess, and her education had not been such as to make her intolerant of any want of refinement in the associates who gathered round her husband. She had gentle smiles for townspeople as well as county people; and unconsciously played an admirable second in her husband's project of making himself universally popular.

But there is someone to make ill-natured remarks, and draw ill-natured conclusions from very simple premises, in every place; and in Barford this bird of ill-omen was a Miss Pratt. She did not hunt – so Mr Higgins's admirable riding did not call out her admiration. She did not drink – so the well-selected wines, so lavishly dispensed among his guests, could never mollify Miss Pratt. She could not bear comic songs, or buffo stories – so, in that way, her approbation was impregnable. And these three secrets of popularity constituted Mr Higgins's great charm. Miss Pratt sat and watched. Her face looked immovably grave at the end of any of Mr Higgins's best stories; but there was a keen, needle-like glance of her unwinking little eyes, which Mr Higgins felt rather than saw, and which made him shiver, even on a hot day, when it fell upon him. Miss Pratt was a dissenter, and, to propitiate this female Mordecai, Mr Higgins asked the dissenting minister whose services she attended, to dinner; kept himself and his company in good order; gave a handsome donation to the poor of the chapel. All in vain – Miss Pratt stirred not a muscle more of her face towards graciousness; and Mr Higgins was conscious that, in spite of all his open efforts to captivate Mr Davis, there was a secret influence on the other side, throwing in doubts and suspicions, and evil interpretations of all he said or did. Miss Pratt, the little, plain old maid, living on eighty pounds a year, was the thorn in the popular Mr Higgins's side, although she had never spoken one uncivil word to him; indeed, on the contrary, had treated him with a stiff and elaborate civility.

The thorn – the grief to Mrs Higgins was this. They had no children! Oh! how she would stand and envy the careless, busy motion of half a dozen children; and then, when observed, move on with a deep, deep sigh of yearning regret. But it was as well.

It was noticed that Mr Higgins was remarkably careful of his health. He ate, drank, took exercise, rested, by some secret rules of his own; occasionally bursting into an excess, it is true, but only on rare occasions – such as when he returned from visiting his estates in the south, and collecting his rents. That unusual exertion and fatigue – for there were no stage-coaches within forty miles of Barford, and he, like most country gentlemen of that day, would have preferred riding if there had been – seemed to require some strange excess to compensate for it; and rumours went through the town that he shut himself up, and drank enormously for some days after his return. But no-one was admitted to these orgies.

One day – they remembered it well afterwards – the hounds met not far from the town; and the fox was found in a part of the wild heath, which was beginning to be enclosed by a few of the more wealthy townspeople, who were desirous of building themselves houses rather more in the country than those they had hitherto lived in. Among these, the principal was a Mr Dudgeon, the attorney of Barford, and the agent for all the county families about. The firm of Dudgeon had managed the leases, the marriage-settlements, and the wills, of the neighbourhood for generations. Mr Dudgeon's father had the responsibility of collecting the landowners' rents just as the present Mr Dudgeon had at the time of which I speak: and as his son and his son's son have done since. Their business was an hereditary estate to them; and with something of the old feudal feeling was mixed a kind of proud humility at their position towards the squires whose family secrets they had mastered, and the mysteries of whose fortunes and estates were better known to the Messrs Dudgeon than to themselves.

Mr John Dudgeon had built himself a house on Wildbury Heath; a mere cottage as he called it: but though only two storeys high, it spread out far and wide, and work-people from Derby had been sent for on purpose to make the inside as complete as possible. The gardens too were exquisite in arrangement, if not very extensive; and not a flower was grown in them but of the rarest species. It must have been somewhat of a mortification to the owner of this dainty place when, on the day of which I speak, the fox, after a long race, during which he had described a circle of many miles, took refuge in the garden; but Mr Dudgeon put a good face on the matter when a gentleman hunter, with the careless insolence of the squires of those days and that place, rode across the velvet lawn, and tapping at the window of the dining-room with his whip-handle, asked permission – no! that is not it, rather informed Mr Dudgeon of their intention to enter his garden in a body, and have the fox unearthed. Mr Dudgeon compelled himself to smile assent, with the grace of a masculine Griselda; and then he hastily gave orders to have all that the house afforded of provision set out for luncheon, guessing rightly enough that a six-hours' run would give even homely fare an acceptable welcome. He bore without wincing the entrance of the dirty boots into his exquisitely clean rooms; he only felt grateful for the care with which Mr Higgins strode about, laboriously and noiselessly moving on the tip of his toes, as he reconnoitred the rooms with a curious eye.

'I'm going to build a house myself, Dudgeon; and, upon my word, I don't think I could take a better model than yours.'

'Oh! my poor cottage would be too small to afford any hints for such a house as you would wish to build, Mr Higgins,' replied Mr Dudgeon, gently rubbing his hands nevertheless at the compliment.

'Not at all! Not at all! Let me see. You have dining-room, drawing-room,' he hesitated, and Mr Dudgeon filled up the blank as he expected.

'Four sitting-rooms and the bedrooms. But allow me to show you over the house. I confess I took some pains in arranging it, and, though far smaller than what you would require, it may, nevertheless, afford you some hints.'

So they left the eating gentlemen with their mouths and their plates quite full, and the scent of the fox overpowering that of the hasty rashers of ham; and they carefully inspected all the ground-floor rooms.

Then Mr Dudgeon said: 'If you are not tired, Mr Higgins, it is rather my hobby, so you must pull me up if you are, we will go upstairs, and I will show you my sanctum.'

Mr Dudgeon's sanctum was the centre room, over the porch, which formed a balcony, and which was carefully filled with choice flowers in pots. Inside, there were all kinds of elegant contrivances for hiding the real strength of all the boxes and chests required by the particular nature of Mr Dudgeon's business: for although his office was in Barford, he kept (as he informed Mr Higgins) what was the most valuable here, as being safer than an office which was locked up and left every night. But, as Mr Higgins reminded him with a sly poke in the side, when next they met, his own house was not over-secure. A fortnight after the gentlemen of the Barford hunt lunched there, Mr Dudgeon's strong-box – in his sanctum upstairs, with the mysterious spring-bolt to the window invented by himself, and the secret of which was only known to the inventor and a few of his most intimate friends, to whom he had proudly shown it – this strong-box, containing the collected Christmas rents of half-a-dozen landlords (there was then no bank nearer than Derby), was rifled; and the secretly rich Mr Dudgeon had to stop his agent in his purchases of paintings by Flemish artists, because the money was required to make good the missing rents.

The Dogberries and Verges of those days were quite incapable of obtaining any clue to the robber or robbers; and though one or two vagrants were taken up and brought before Mr Dunover and Mr Higgins, the magistrates who usually attended in the court-room at Barford, there was no evidence brought against them, and after a couple of nights' durance in the lock-ups they were set at liberty. But it became a standing joke with Mr Higgins to ask Mr Dudgeon, from time to time, whether he could recommend him a place of safety for his valuables; or, if he had made any more inventions lately for securing houses from robbers.

About two years after this time – about seven years after Mr Higgins had been married – one Tuesday evening Mr Davis was sitting reading the news in the coffee-room of the George Inn. He belonged to a club of gentlemen who met there occasionally to play at whist, to read what few newspapers and magazines were published in those days, to chat about the market at Derby, and prices all over the country. This Tuesday night it was a black frost; and few people were in the room. Mr Davis was anxious to finish an article in the *Gentleman's Magazine*; indeed, he was making extracts from it, intending to answer it, and yet unable with his small income to purchase a copy. So he stayed late; it was past nine, and at ten o'clock the room was closed. But while he wrote, Mr Higgins came in. He was pale and haggard with cold. Mr Davis, who had had for some time sole possession of the fire, moved politely on one side, and handed to the newcomer the sole London newspaper which the room afforded. Mr Higgins accepted it, and made some remark on the intense coldness of the weather; but Mr Davis was too full of his article, and intended reply, to fall into conversation readily. Mr Higgins hitched his chair nearer to the fire, and put his feet on the fender, giving an audible shudder. He put the newspaper on one end of the table near him, and sat gazing into the red embers of the fire, crouching down over them as if his very marrow were chilled.

At length he said: 'There is no account of the murder at Bath in that paper?'

Mr Davis, who had finished taking his notes, and was preparing to go, stopped short, and asked: 'Has there been a murder at Bath? No! I have not seen anything of it – who was murdered ?'

'Oh! it was a shocking, terrible murder!' said Mr Higgins, not raising his look from the fire, but gazing on with his eyes dilated till the whites were seen all round them. 'A terrible, terrible murder! I wonder what will become of the murderer? I can fancy the red glowing centre of that fire – look and see how infinitely distant it seems, and how the distance magnifies it into something awful and unquenchable.'

'My dear sir, you are feverish; how you shake and shiver !' said Mr Davis, thinking privately that his companion had symptoms of fever, and that he was wandering in his mind.

'Oh, no!' said Mr Higgins. 'I am not feverish. It is the night which is so cold.' And for a time he talked with Mr Davis about the article in the *Gentleman's Magazine*, for he was rather a reader himself, and could take more interest in Mr Davis's pursuits than most of the people at Barford. At length it drew near to ten, and Mr Davis rose up to go home to his lodgings.

'No, Davis, don't go. I want you here. We will have a bottle of port together, and that will put Saunders into good humour. I want to tell you about this murder,' he continued, dropping his voice, and speaking hoarse and low. 'She was an old woman, and he killed her, sitting reading her Bible by her own fireside!' He looked at Mr Davis with a strange searching gaze, as if trying to find some sympathy in the horror which the idea presented to him.

'Who do you mean, my dear sir? What is this murder you are so full of? No-one has been murdered here.'

'No, you fool! I tell you it was in Bath!' said Mr Higgins, with sudden passion; and then calming himself to most velvet-smoothness of manner, he laid his hand on Mr Davis's knee, there, as they sat by the fire, and gently detaining him, began the narration of the crime he was so full of; but his voice and manner were constrained to a stony quietude: he never looked in Mr Davis's face; once or twice, as Mr Davis remembered afterwards, his grip tightened like a compressing vice.

'She lived in a small house in a quiet old-fashioned street, she and her maid. People said she was a good old woman; but for all that, she hoarded and hoarded, and never gave to the poor. Mr Davis, it is wicked not to give to the poor – wicked – wicked, is it not? I always give to the poor, for once I read in the Bible that "Charity covereth a multitude of sins". The wicked old woman never gave, but hoarded her money, and saved, and saved. Someone heard of it; I say she threw temptation in his way, and God will punish her for it. And this man – or it might be a woman, who knows? – and this person – heard also that she went to church in the mornings, and her maid in the afternoons; and so – while the maid was at church, and the street and the house quite still, and the darkness of a winter afternoon coming on – she was nodding over the Bible – and that, mark you! is a sin, and one that God will avenge sooner or later; and a step came in the dusk up the stair, and that person I told you of stood in the room. At first he – no! at first, it is supposed – for, you understand, all this is mere guesswork – it is supposed that he asked her civilly enough to give him her money, or to tell him where it was; but the old miser defied him, and would not ask for mercy and give up her keys, even when he threatened her, but looked him in the face as if he had been a baby – Oh, God! Mr Davis, I once dreamt when I was a little innocent boy that I should commit a crime like this, and I wakened up crying; and my mother comforted me – that is the reason I tremble so now – that and the cold, for it is very very cold!'

'But did he murder the old lady?' asked Mr Davis. 'I beg your pardon, sir, but I am interested by your story.'

'Yes! he cut her throat; and there she lies yet in her quiet little parlour, with her face upturned and all ghastly white, in the middle of a pool of blood. Mr Davis, this wine is no better than water; I must have some brandy!'

Mr Davis was horror-struck by the story, which seemed to have fascinated him as much as it had done his companion.

'Have they got any clue to the murderer?' said he.

Mr Higgins drank down half a tumbler of raw brandy before he answered. 'No! No clue whatever. They will never be able to discover him; and I should not wonder, Mr Davis – should not wonder if he repented after all, and did bitter penance for his crime; and if so – will there be mercy for him at the last day?'

'God knows!' said Mr Davis, with solemnity. 'It is an awful story,' continued he, rousing himself; 'I hardly like to leave this warm light room and go out into the darkness after hearing it. But it must be done,' – buttoning on his greatcoat – 'I can only say I hope and trust they will find out the murderer and hang him. If you'll take my advice, Mr Higgins, you'll have your bed warmed, and drink a treacle-posset just the last thing; and, if you'll allow me, I'll send you my answer to Philologus before it goes up to old Urban.'

The next morning, Mr Davis went to call on Miss Pratt, who was not very well; and, by way of being agreeable and entertaining, he related to her all he had heard the night before about the murder at Bath; and really he made a very pretty connected story out of it, and interested Miss Pratt very much in the fate of the old lady – partly because of a similarity in their situations; for she also privately hoarded money, and had but one servant, and stopped at home alone on Sunday afternoons to allow her servant to go to church.

'And when did all this happen?' she asked.

'I don't know if Mr Higgins named the day; and yet I think it must have been on this very last Sunday.'

'And today is Wednesday. Ill news travels fast.'

'Yes, Mr Higgins thought it might have been in the London newspaper.'

'That it could never be. Where did Mr Higgins learn all about it?'

'I don't know; I did not ask. I think he only came home yesterday: he had been south to collect his rents, somebody said.'

Miss Pratt grunted. She used to vent her dislike and suspicions of Mr Higgins in a grunt whenever his name was mentioned.

'Well, I shan't see you for some days. Godfred Merton has asked me to go and stay with him and his sister; and I think it will do me good. Besides,' added she, 'these winter evenings – and these murderers at large in the country – I don't quite like living with only Peggy to call to in case of need.'

Miss Pratt went to stay with her cousin, Mr Merton. He was an active magistrate, and enjoyed his reputation as such. One day he came in, having just received his letters.

'Bad account of the morals of your little town here, Jessy!' said he, touching one of his letters. 'You've either a murderer among you, or some friend of a murderer. Here's a poor old lady at Bath had her throat cut last Sunday week; and I've a letter from the Home Office, asking to lend them "my very efficient aid", as they are pleased to call it, towards finding out the culprit. It seems he must have been thirsty, and of a comfortable jolly turn; for before going to his horrid work he tapped a barrel of ginger wine the old lady had set by to work; and he wrapped the spigot round with a piece of a letter taken out of his pocket, as may be supposed; and this piece of a letter was found afterwards; there are only these letters on the outside, "*ns, Esq., -arford, -egworth*," which someone has ingeniously made out to mean Barford, near Kegworth. On the other side there is some allusion to a race-horse, I conjecture, though the name is singular enough: "Church-and-King-and-down-with-the-Rump".'

Miss Pratt caught at this name immediately; it had hurt her feelings as a dissenter only a few months ago, and she remembered it well.

'Mr Nat Hearn has – or had (as I am speaking in the witness-box, as it were, I must take care of my tenses), a horse with that ridiculous name.'

'Mr Nat Hearn,' repeated Mr Merton, making a note of the intell-igence; then he recurred to his letter from the Home Office again.

'There is also a piece of a small key, broken in the futile attempt to open a desk – well, well. Nothing more of consequence. The letter is what we must rely upon.'

'Mr Davis said that Mr Higgins told him – ' Miss Pratt began.

'Higgins!' exclaimed Mr Merton, '*ns*. Is it Higgins, the blustering fellow that ran away with Nat Hearn's sister?'

'Yes!' said Miss Pratt. 'But though he has never been a favourite of mine – '

'*ns*,' repeated Mr Merton. 'It is too horrible to think of; a member of the hunt – kind old Squire Hearn's son-in-law! Who else have you in Barford with names that end in *ns*?'

'There's Jackson, and Higginson, and Blenkinsop, and Davis, and Jones. Cousin! One thing strikes me – how did Mr Higgins know all about it to tell Mr Davis on Tuesday what had happened on Sunday afternoon?'

There is no need to add much more. Those curious in lives of the highwaymen may find the name of Higgins as conspicuous among those annals as that of Claude Duval. Kate Hearn's husband collec-ted his rents on the highway, like many another 'gentleman' of the day; but, having been unlucky in one or two of his adventures, and hearing exaggerated accounts of the hoarded wealth of the old lady at Bath, he was led on from robbery to murder, and was hung for his crime at Derby, in 1775.

He had not been an unkind husband; and his poor wife took lodgings in Derby to be near him in his last moments – his awful last moments. Her old father went with her everywhere but into her husband's cell; and wrung her heart by constantly accusing himself of having promoted her marriage with a man of whom he knew so little. He abdicated his squireship in favour of his son Nathaniel. Nat was prosperous, and the helpless silly father could be of no use to him; but to his widowed daughter the foolish fond old man was all in all; her knight, her protector, her companion – her most faithful loving companion. Only, he ever declined assuming the office of her counsellor – shaking his head sadly, and saying – 'Ah! Kate, Kate! if I had had more wisdom to have advised thee better, thou need'st not have been an exile here in Brussels, shrinking from the sight of every English person as if they knew thy story.'

I saw the White House not a month ago; it was to let, perhaps for the twentieth time since Mr Higgins occupied it; but still the tradition goes in Barford that once upon a time a highwayman lived there, and amassed untold treasures; and that the ill-gotten wealth yet remains walled up in some unknown concealed chamber; but in what part of the house no-one knows.

Will any of you become tenants, and try to find out this mysterious closet? I can furnish the exact address to any applicant who wishes for it.

The Poor Clare

Chapter 1

December 12th, 1747. – My life has been strangely bound up with extraordinary incidents, some of which occurred before I had any connection with the principal actors in them, or, indeed, before I even knew of their existence. I suppose, most old men are, like me, more given to looking back upon their own career with a kind of fond interest and affectionate remembrance, than to watching the events – though these may have far more interest for the multitude – immediately passing before their eyes. If this should be the case with the generality of old people, how much more so with me! . . . If I am to enter upon that strange story connected with poor Lucy, I must begin a long way back. I myself only came to the knowledge of her family history after I knew her; but, to make the tale clear to anyone else, I must arrange events in the order in which they occurred – not that in which I became acquainted with them.

There is a great old hall in the north-east of Lancashire, in a part they call the Trough of Bolland, adjoining that other district named Craven. Starkey Manor-house is rather like a number of rooms clustered round a grey, massive, old keep than a regularly-built hall. Indeed, I suppose that the house only consisted of the great tower in the centre, in the days when the Scots made their raids terrible as far south as this; and that after the Stuarts came in, and there was a little more security of property in those parts, the Starkeys of that time added the lower building, which runs, two storeys high, all round the base of the keep. There has been a grand garden laid out in my days, on the southern slope near the house; but when I first knew the place, the kitchen-garden at the farm was the only piece of cultivated ground belonging to it. The deer used to come within sight of the drawing-room windows, and might have browsed quite close up to the house if they had not been too wild and shy. Starkey Manor-house itself stood on a projection or peninsula of high land, jutting out from the abrupt hills that form the sides of the Trough of Bolland. These hills were rocky and bleak enough towards their summit; lower down they were clothed with tangled copsewood and green depths of fern, out of which a grey giant of an ancient forest-tree would tower here and there, throwing up its ghastly white branches, as if in imprecation, to the sky. These trees, they told me, were the remnants of that forest which existed in the days of the Heptarchy, and were even then noted as landmarks. No wonder that their upper and more exposed branches were leafless, and that the dead bark had peeled away, from sapless old age.

Not far from the house there were a few cottages, apparently of the same date as the keep, probably built for some retainers of the family, who sought shelter – they and their families and their small flocks and herds – at the hands of their feudal lord. Some of them had pretty much fallen to decay. They were built in a strange fashion. Strong beams had been sunk firm in the ground at the requisite distance, and their other ends had been fastened together, two and two, so as to form the shape of one of those rounded waggon-headed gipsy-tents, only very much larger. The spaces between were filled with mud, stones, osiers, rubbish, mortar – anything to keep out the weather. The fires were made in the centre of these rude dwellings, a hole in the roof forming the only chimney. No Highland hut or Irish cabin could be of rougher construction.

The owner of this property, at the beginning of the present century, was a Mr Patrick Byrne Starkey. His family had kept to the old faith, and were staunch Roman Catholics, esteeming it even a sin to marry anyone of Protestant descent, however willing he or she might have been to embrace the Romish religion. Mr Patrick Starkey's father had been a follower of James the Second; and, during the disastrous Irish campaign of that monarch, he had fallen in love with an Irish beauty, a Miss Byrne, as zealous for her religion and for the Stuarts as himself. He had returned to Ireland after his escape to France, and married her, bearing her back to the court at St Germains. But some licence on the part of the disorderly gentlemen who surrounded King James in his exile, had insulted his beautiful wife, and disgusted him; so he removed from St Germains to Antwerp, whence, in a few years' time, he quietly returned to Starkey Manor-house – some of his Lancashire neighbours having lent their good offices to reconcile him to the powers that were. He was as firm a Roman Catholic as ever, and as staunch an advocate for the Stuarts and the divine right of kings; but his religion almost amounted to

asceticism, and the conduct of those with whom he had been brought
in such close contact at St Germains would little bear the inspection of a stern moralist. So he gave his allegiance where he could not
give his esteem, and learned to respect sincerely the upright and
moral character of one whom he yet regarded as an usurper. King
William's government had little need to fear such a one. So he
returned, as I have said, with a sobered heart and impoverished
fortunes, to his ancestral house, which had fallen sadly to ruin while
the owner had been a courtier, a soldier, and an exile. The roads into
the Trough of Bolland were little more than cart-ruts; indeed, the
way up to the house lay along a ploughed field before you came to
the deer-park. Madam, as the country-folk used to call Mrs Starkey,
rode on a pillion behind her husband, holding on to him with a light
hand by his leather riding-belt. Little master (he that was afterwards
Squire Patrick Byrne Starkey) was held on to his pony by a serving-
man. A woman past middle age walked, with a firm and strong step,
by the cart that held much of the baggage; and, high up on the mails
and boxes, sat a girl of dazzling beauty, perched lightly on the
topmost trunk, and swaying herself fearlessly to and fro, as the
cart rocked and shook in the heavy roads of late autumn. The girl
wore the Antwerp *faille*, or black Spanish mantle, over her head,
and altogether her appearance was such that the old cottager, who
described the procession to me many years after, said that all the
country-folk took her for a foreigner. Some dogs, and the boy who
held them in charge, made up the company. They rode silently
along, looking with grave, serious eyes at the people, who came out
of the scattered cottages to bow or curtsy to the real Squire, 'come
back at last', and gazed after the little procession with gaping wonder, not deadened by the sound of the foreign language in which the
few necessary words that passed among them were spoken. One lad,
called from his staring by the Squire to come and help about the cart,
accompanied them to the Manor-house. He said that when the lady
had descended from her pillion, the middle-aged woman whom I
have described as walking while the others rode, stepped quickly
forward, and taking Madam Starkey (who was of a slight and delicate
figure) in her arms, she lifted her over the threshold, and set her
down in her husband's house, at the same time uttering a passionate
and outlandish blessing. The Squire stood by, smiling gravely at
first; but when the words of blessing were pronounced, he took off
his fine feathered hat, and bent his head. The girl with the black
mantle stepped onward into the shadow of the dark hall, and kissed

the lady's hand; and that was all the lad could tell to the group that gathered round him on his return, eager to hear everything, and to know how much the Squire had given him for his services.

From all I could gather, the Manor-house, at the time of the Squire's return, was in the most dilapidated state. The stout grey walls remained firm and entire; but the inner chambers had been used for all kinds of purposes. The great withdrawing-room had been a barn; the state tapestry-chamber had held wool, and so on. But, by-and-by, they were cleared out; and if the Squire had no money to spend on new furniture, he and his wife had the knack of making the best of the old. He was no despicable joiner; she had a kind of grace in whatever she did, and imparted an air of elegant picturesqueness to whatever she touched. Besides, they had brought many rare things from the Continent; perhaps I should rather say, things that were rare in that part of England – carvings, and crosses, and beautiful pictures. And then, again, wood was plentiful in the Trough of Bolland, and great log-fires danced and glittered in all the dark, old rooms, and gave a look of home and comfort to everything.

Why do I tell you all this? I have little to do with the Squire and Madam Starkey; and yet I dwell upon them, as if I were unwilling to come to the real people with whom my life was so strangely mixed up. Madam had been nursed in Ireland by the very woman who lifted her in her arms, and welcomed her to her husband's home in Lancashire. Excepting for the short period of her own married life, Bridget Fitzgerald had never left her nursling. Her marriage – to one above her in rank – had been unhappy. Her husband had died, and left her in even greater poverty than that in which she was when he had first met with her. She had one child, the beautiful daughter who came riding on the waggon-load of furniture that was brought to the Manor-house. Madam Starkey had taken her again into her service when she became a widow. She and her daughter had followed 'the mistress' in all her fortunes; they had lived at St Germains and at Antwerp, and were now come to her home in Lancashire. As soon as Bridget had arrived there, the Squire gave her a cottage of her own, and took more pains in furnishing it for her than he did in anything else out of his own house. It was only nominally her residence. She was constantly up at the great house; indeed, it was but a short cut across the woods from her own home to the home of her nursling. Her daughter Mary, in like manner, moved from one house to the other at her own will. Madam loved both mother and child dearly. They had great influence over her, and, through her, over her husband. Whatever Bridget or Mary willed was sure to come to pass. They were not disliked; for, though wild and passionate, they were also generous by nature. But the other servants were afraid of them, as being in secret the ruling spirits of the household. The Squire had lost his interest in all secular things; Madam was gentle, affectionate, and yielding. Both husband and wife were tenderly attached to each other and to their boy; but they grew more and more to shun the trouble of decision on any point; and hence it was that Bridget could exert such despotic power. But if everyone else yielded to her 'magic of a superior mind', her daughter not unfrequently rebelled. She and her mother were too much alike to agree. There were wild quarrels between them, and wilder reconciliations. There were times when, in the heat of passion, they could have stabbed each other. At all other times they both – Bridget especially – would have willingly laid down their lives for one another. Bridget's love for her child lay very deep – deeper than that daughter ever knew; or I should think she would never have wearied of home as she did, and prayed her mistress to obtain for her some situation – as waiting-maid – beyond the seas, in that more cheerful continental life, among the scenes of which so many of her happiest years had been spent. She thought, as youth thinks, that life would last for ever, and that two or three years were but a small portion of it to pass away from her mother, whose only child she was. Bridget thought differently, but was too proud ever to show what she felt. If her child wished to leave her, why – she should go. But people said Bridget became ten years older in the course of two months at this time. She took it that Mary wanted to leave her. The truth was, that Mary wanted for a time to leave the place, and to seek some change, and would thankfully have taken her mother with her. Indeed, when Madam Starkey had gotten her a situation with some grand lady abroad, and the time drew near for her to go, it was Mary who clung to her mother with passionate embrace, and, with floods of tears, declared that she would never leave her; and it was Bridget, who at last loosened her arms, and, grave and tearless herself, bade her keep her word, and go forth into the wide world. Sobbing aloud, and looking back continually, Mary went away. Bridget was still as death, scarcely drawing her breath, or closing her stony eyes; till at last she turned back into her cottage, and heaved a ponderous old settle against the door. There she sat, motionless, over the grey ashes of her extinguished fire, deaf to Madam's sweet voice, as she begged leave to enter and comfort her nurse. Deaf, stony, and motionless, she sat for more than twenty hours; till, for the third time, Madam came across the snowy path from the great house, carrying with her a young spaniel, which had been Mary's pet up at the hall, and which had not ceased all night long to seek for its absent mistress, and to whine and moan after her. With tears Madam told this story, through the closed door – tears excited by the terrible look of anguish, so steady, so immovable – so the same today as it was yesterday – on her nurse's face. The little creature in her arms began to utter its piteous cry, as it shivered with the cold. Bridget stirred; she moved – she listened. Again that long whine; she thought it was for her daughter; and what she had denied to her nursling and mistress she granted to the dumb creature that Mary had cherished. She opened the door, and took the dog from Madam's arms. Then Madam came in, and kissed and comforted the old woman, who took but little notice of her or anything. And sending up Master Patrick to the hall for fire and food, the sweet young lady never left her nurse all that night. Next day, the Squire himself came down, carrying a beautiful foreign picture: Our Lady of the Holy Heart, the Papists call it. It is a picture of the Virgin, her heart pierced with arrows, each arrow representing one of her great woes. That picture hung in Bridget's cottage when I first saw her; I have that picture now.

Years went on. Mary was still abroad. Bridget was still and stern, instead of active and passionate. The little dog, Mignon, was indeed her darling. I have heard that she talked to it continually; although, to most people, she was so silent. The Squire and Madam treated her with the greatest consideration, and well they might; for to them she was as devoted and faithful as ever. Mary wrote pretty often, and seemed satisfied with her life. But at length the letters ceased – I hardly know whether before or after a great and terrible sorrow came upon the house of the Starkeys. The Squire sickened of a putrid fever; and Madam caught it in nursing him, and died. You may be sure, Bridget let no other woman tend her but herself; and in the very arms that had received her at her birth, that sweet young woman laid her head down, and gave up her breath. The Squire recovered, in a fashion. He was never strong – he had never the heart to smile again. He fasted and prayed more than ever; and people did say that he tried to cut off the entail, and leave all the property away to found a monastery abroad, of which he prayed that some day little Squire Patrick might be the reverend father. But he could not do this, for the strictness of the entail and the laws against the Papists. So he could only appoint gentlemen of his own faith as guardians to his son, with many charges about the lad's soul, and a few about the land, and the way it was to be held while he was a minor. Of course, Bridget was not forgotten. He sent for her as he lay on his death-bed, and asked her if she would rather have a sum down, or have a small annuity settled upon her. She said at once she would have a sum down; for she thought of her daughter, and how she could bequeath the money to her, whereas an annuity would have died with her. So the Squire left her her cottage for life, and a fair sum of money. And then he died, with as ready and willing a heart as, I suppose, ever any gentleman took out of this world with him. The young Squire was carried off by his guardians, and Bridget was left alone.

I have said that she had not heard from Mary for some time. In her last letter, she had told of travelling about with her mistress, who was the English wife of some great foreign officer, and had spoken of her chances of making a good marriage, without naming the gentleman's name, keeping it rather back as a pleasant surprise to her mother; his station and fortune being, as I had afterwards reason to know, far superior to anything she had a right to expect. Then came a long silence; and Madam was dead, and the Squire was dead; and Bridget's heart was gnawed by anxiety, and she knew not whom to ask for news of her child. She could not write, and the Squire had managed her communication with her daughter. She walked off to Hurst; and got a good priest there – one whom she had known at Antwerp – to write for her. But no answer came. It was like crying into the awful stillness of night.

One day, Bridget was missed by those neighbours who had been accustomed to mark her goings-out and comings-in. She had never been sociable with any of them; but the sight of her had become a part of their daily lives, and slow wonder arose in their minds, as morning after morning came, and her house-door remained closed, her window dead from any glitter, or light of fire within. At length, someone tried the door; it was locked. Two or three laid their heads together, before daring to look in through the blank, unshuttered window. But, at last, they summoned up courage; and then saw that Bridget's absence from their little world was not the result of accident or death, but of premeditation. Such small articles of furniture as could be secured from the effects of time and damp by being packed up, were stowed away in boxes. The picture of the Madonna was taken down, and gone. In a word, Bridget had stolen away from her home, and left no trace whither she was departed. I knew afterwards, that she and her little dog had wandered off on the long search for her lost daughter. She was too illiterate to have faith in letters, even had she had the means of writing and sending many. But she had faith in her own strong love, and believed that her passionate instinct would guide her to her child. Besides, foreign travel was no new thing to her, and she could speak enough of French to explain the object of her journey, and had, moreover, the advantage of being, from her faith, a welcome object of charitable hospitality at many a distant convent. But the country people round Starkey Manor-house knew nothing of all this. They wondered what had become of her, in a torpid, lazy fashion, and then left off thinking of her altogether. Several years passed. Both Manor-house and cottage were deserted. The young Squire lived far away under the direction of his guardians. There were inroads of wool and corn into the sitting-rooms of the Hall; and there was some low talk, from time to time, among the hinds and country people, whether it would not be as well to break into old Bridget's cottage, and save such of her goods as were left from the moth and rust which must be making sad havoc. But this idea was always quenched by the recollection of her strong character and passionate anger; and tales of her masterful spirit, and vehement force of will, were whispered about, till the very thought of offending her, by touching any article of hers, became invested with a kind of horror: it was believed that, dead or alive, she would not fail to avenge it.

Suddenly she came home; with as little noise or note of preparation as she had departed. One day, someone noticed a thin, blue curl of smoke, ascending from her chimney. Her door stood open to the noonday sun; and, ere many hours had elapsed, someone had seen an old travel-and-sorrow-stained woman dipping her pitcher in the well; and said, that the dark, solemn eyes that looked up at him were more like Bridget Fitzgerald's than anyone else's in this world; and yet, if it were she, she looked as if she had been scorched in the flames of hell, so brown, and scared, and fierce a creature did she seem. By-and-by many saw her; and those who met her eye once cared not to be caught looking at her again. She had got into the habit of perpetually talking to herself; nay, more, answering herself, and varying her tones according to the side she took at the moment. It was no wonder that those who dared to listen outside her door at night, believed that she held converse with some spirit; in short, she was unconsciously earning for herself the dreadful reputation of a witch.

Her little dog, which had wandered half over the Continent with her, was her only companion; a dumb remembrancer of happier days. Once he was ill; and she carried him more than three miles, to ask about his management from one who had been groom to the last Squire, and had then been noted for his skill in all diseases of animals. Whatever this man did, the dog recovered; and they who heard her thanks, intermingled with blessings (that were rather promises of good fortune than prayers), looked grave at his good luck when, next year, his ewes twinned, and his meadow-grass was heavy and thick.

Now it so happened that, about the year seventeen hundred and eleven, one of the guardians of the young Squire, a certain Sir Philip Tempest, bethought him of the good shooting there must be on his ward's property; and, in consequence, he brought down four or five gentlemen, of his friends, to stay for a week or two at the Hall. From all accounts, they roystered and spent pretty freely. I never heard any of their names but one, and that was Squire Gisborne's. He was hardly a middle-aged man then; he had been much abroad, and there, I believe, he had known Sir Philip Tempest, and done him some service. He was a daring and dissolute fellow in those days: careless and fearless, and one who would rather be in a quarrel than out of it. He had his fits of ill-temper beside, when he would spare neither man nor beast. Otherwise, those who knew him well, used to say he had a good heart, when he was neither drunk, nor angry, nor in any way vexed. He had altered much when I came to know him.

One day, the gentlemen had all been out shooting, and with but little success, I believe; anyhow, Mr Gisborne had had none, and was in a black humour accordingly. He was coming home, having his gun loaded, sportsman-like, when little Mignon crossed his path, just as he turned out of the wood by Bridget's cottage. Partly for wantonness, partly to vent his spleen upon some living creature, Mr Gisborne took his gun, and fired – he had better have never fired gun again, than aimed that unlucky shot. He hit Mignon; and at the creature's sudden cry, Bridget came out, and saw at a glance what had been done. She took Mignon up in her arms, and looked hard at the wound; the poor dog looked at her with his glazing eyes, and tried to wag his tail and lick her hand, all covered with blood. Mr Gisborne spoke in a kind of sullen penitence: 'You should have kept the dog out of my way – a little poaching varmint.'

At this very moment, Mignon stretched out his legs, and stiffened in her arms – her lost Mary's dog, who had wandered and sorrowed with her for years. She walked right into Mr Gisborne's path, and fixed his unwilling, sullen look with her dark and terrible eye.

'Those never throve that did me harm,' said she. 'I'm alone in the world, and helpless; the more do the Saints in Heaven hear my prayers. Hear me, ye blessed ones! Hear me while I ask for sorrow on this bad, cruel man. He has killed the only creature that loved me – the dumb beast that I loved. Bring down heavy sorrow on his head for it, O ye Saints! He thought that I was helpless, because he saw me lonely and poor; but are not the armies of Heaven for the like of me?'

'Come, come,' said he, half-remorseful, but not one whit afraid. 'Here's a crown to buy thee another dog. Take it, and leave off cursing! I care none for thy threats.'

'Don't you?' said she, coming a step closer, and changing her imprecatory cry for a whisper which made the gamekeeper's lad, following Mr Gisborne, creep all over. 'You shall live to see the creature you love best, and who alone loves you – ay, a human creature, but as innocent and fond as my poor, dead darling – you shall see this creature, for whom death would be too happy, become a terror and a loathing to all, for this blood's sake. Hear me, O holy Saints, who never fail them that have no other help!'

She threw up her right hand, filled with poor Mignon's life-drops; they spurted, one or two of them, on his shooting-dress – an ominous sight to the follower. But the master only laughed a little, forced, scornful laugh, and went on to the Hall. Before he got there, how-ever, he took out a gold piece, and bade the boy carry it to the old woman on his return to the village. The lad was 'afeard', as he told me in after years; he came to the cottage, and hovered about, not daring to enter. He peeped through the window at last; and by the flickering wood-flame, he saw Bridget kneeling before the picture of our Lady of the Holy Heart, with dead Mignon lying between her and the Madonna. She was praying wildly, as her outstretched arms betokened. The lad shrank away in redoubled terror; and contented himself with slipping the gold piece under the ill-fitting door. The next day it was thrown out upon the midden; and there it lay, no-one daring to touch it.

Meanwhile Mr Gisborne, half curious, half uneasy, thought to lessen his uncomfortable feelings by asking Sir Philip who Bridget was? He could only describe her – he did not know her name. Sir Philip was equally at a loss. But an old servant of the Starkeys, who had resumed his livery at the Hall on this occasion – a scoundrel whom Bridget had saved from dismissal more than once during her palmy days – said: 'It will be the old witch, that his worship means. She needs a ducking, if ever woman did, does that Bridget Fitzgerald.'

'Fitzgerald!' said both the gentlemen at once. But Sir Philip was the first to continue.

'I must have no talk of ducking her, Dickon. Why, she must be the very woman poor Starkey bade me have a care of; but when I came here last she was gone, no-one knew where. I'll go and see her tomorrow. But mind you, sirrah, if any harm comes to her, or any more talk of her being a witch – I've a pack of hounds at home, who can follow the scent of a lying knave as well as ever they followed a dog-fox; so take care how you talk about ducking a faithful old servant of your dead master's.'

'Had she ever a daughter?' asked Mr Gisborne, after a while.

'I don't know – yes! I've a notion she had; a kind of waiting-woman to Madam Starkey.'

'Please your worship,' said humbled Dickon, 'Mistress Bridget had a daughter – one Mistress Mary – who went abroad, and has never been heard on since; and folk do say that has crazed her mother.'

Mr Gisborne shaded his eyes with his hand.

'I could wish she had not cursed me,' he muttered. 'She may have power – no-one else could.' After a while, he said aloud, no-one understanding rightly what he meant, 'Tush! it's impossible!' – and called for claret; and he and the other gentlemen set to to a drinking-bout.

Chapter 2

I now come to the time in which I myself was mixed up with the people that I have been writing about. And to make you understand how I became connected with them, I must give you some little account of myself. My father was the younger son of a Devonshire gentleman of moderate property; my eldest uncle succeeded to the estate of his forefathers, my second became an eminent attorney in London, and my father took orders. Like most poor clergymen, he had a large family; and I have no doubt was glad enough when my London uncle, who was a bachelor, offered to take charge of me, and bring me up to be his successor in business.

In this way I came to live in London, in my uncle's house, not far from Gray's Inn, and to be treated and esteemed as his son, and to labour with him in his office. I was very fond of the old gentleman. He was the confidential agent of many country squires, and had attained to his present position as much by knowledge of human nature as by knowledge of law; though he was learned enough in the latter. He used to say his business was law, his pleasure heraldry. From his intimate acquaintance with family history, and all the tragic courses of life therein involved, to hear him talk, at leisure times, about any coat of arms that came across his path was as good as a play or a romance. Many cases of disputed property, dependent on a love of genealogy, were brought to him, as to a great authority on such points. If the lawyer who came to consult him was young, he would take no fee, only give him a long lecture on the importance of attending to heraldry; if the lawyer was of mature age and good standing, he would mulct him pretty well, and abuse him to me afterwards as negligent of one great branch of the profession. His house was in a stately new street called Ormond Street, and in it he had a handsome library; but all the books treated of things that were past; none of them planned or looked forward into the future. I worked away – partly for the sake of my family at home, partly because my uncle had really taught me to enjoy the kind of practice in which he himself took such delight. I suspect I worked too hard; at any rate, in seventeen hundred and eighteen I was far from well, and my good uncle was disturbed by my ill looks.

One day, he rang the bell twice into the clerk's room at the dingy office in Gray's Inn Lane. It was the summons for me, and I went into his private room just as a gentleman – whom I knew well enough by sight as an Irish lawyer of more reputation than he deserved – was leaving.

My uncle was slowly rubbing his hands together and considering. I was there two or three minutes before he spoke. Then he told me that I must pack up my portmanteau that very afternoon, and start that night by post-horse for West Chester. I should get there, if all went well, at the end of five days' time, and must then wait for a packet to cross over to Dublin; from thence I must proceed to a certain town named Kildoon, and in that neighbourhood I was to remain, making certain inquiries as to the existence of any descendants of the younger branch of a family to whom some valuable estates had descended in the female line. The Irish lawyer whom I had seen was weary of the case, and would willingly have given up the property, without further ado, to a man who appeared to claim them; but on laying his tables and trees before my uncle, the latter had foreseen so many possible prior claimants, that the lawyer had begged him to undertake the management of the whole business. In his youth, my uncle would have liked nothing better than going over to Ireland himself, and ferreting out every scrap of paper or parchment, and every word of tradition respecting the family. As it was, old and gouty, he deputed me.

Accordingly, I went to Kildoon. I suspect I had something of my uncle's delight in following up a genealogical scent, for I very soon found out, when on the spot, that Mr Rooney, the Irish lawyer, would have got both himself and the first claimant into a terrible scrape, if he had pronounced his opinion that the estates ought to be given up to him. There were three poor Irish fellows, each nearer of kin to the last possessor; but, a generation before, there was a still nearer relation, who had never been accounted for, nor his existence ever discovered by the lawyers, I venture to think, till I routed him out from the memory of some of the old dependants of the family. What had become of him? I travelled backwards and forwards; I crossed over to France, and came back again with a slight clue, which ended in my discovering that, wild and dissipated himself, he had left one child, a son, of yet worse character than his father; that this same Hugh Fitzgerald had married a very beautiful serving-woman of the Byrnes – a person below him in hereditary rank, but above him in character; that he had died soon after his marriage, leaving one child, whether a boy or a girl I could not learn, and that the mother had returned to live in the family of the Byrnes. Now, the chief of this latter family was serving in the Duke of Berwick's regiment, and it was long before I could hear from him; it was more than a year before I got a short, haughty letter – I fancy he had a soldier's contempt for a civilian, an Irishman's hatred for an Englishman, an exiled Jacobite's jealousy of one who prospered and lived tranquilly under the government he looked upon as an usurpation. 'Bridget Fitzgerald,' he said, 'had been faithful to the fortunes of his sister – had followed her abroad, and to England when Mrs Starkey had thought fit to return. Both his sister and her husband were dead; he knew nothing of Bridget Fitzgerald at the present time: probably Sir Philip Tempest, his nephew's guardian, might be able to give me some information.' I have not given the little contemptuous terms; the way in which faithful service was meant to imply more than it said – all that has nothing to do with my story. Sir Philip, when applied to, told me that he paid an annuity regularly to an old woman named Fitzgerald, living at Coldholme (the village near Starkey Manor-house). Whether she had any descendants he could not say.

One bleak March evening, I came in sight of the places described at the beginning of my story. I could hardly understand the rude dialect in which the direction to old Bridget's house was given.

'Yo' see yon furleets,' all run together, gave me no idea that I was to guide myself by the distant lights that shone in the windows of the Hall, occupied for the time by a farmer who held the post of steward, while the Squire, now four or five and twenty, was making the grand tour. However, at last, I reached Bridget's cottage – a low, moss-grown place; the palings that had once surrounded it were broken and gone; and the underwood of the forest came up to the walls, and must have darkened the windows. It was about seven o'clock – not late to my London notions – but, after knocking for some time at the door and receiving no reply, I was driven to conjecture that the occupant of the house was gone to bed. So I betook myself to the nearest church I had seen, three miles back on the road I had come, sure that close to that I should find an inn of some kind; and early the next morning I set off back to Coldholme, by a field-path which my host assured me I should find a shorter cut than the road I had taken the night before. It was a cold, sharp morning; my feet left prints in the sprinkling of hoar-frost that covered the ground; nevertheless, I saw an old woman, whom I instinctively suspected to be the object of my search, in a sheltered covert on one side of my path. I lingered and watched her. She must have been considerably above the middle size in her prime, for when she raised herself from the stooping position in which I first saw her, there was something fine and commanding in the erectness of her figure. She drooped again in a minute or two, and seemed looking for something on the ground, as, with bent head, she turned off from the spot where I gazed upon her, and was lost to my sight. I fancy I missed my way, and made a round in spite of the landlord's directions; for by the time I had reached Bridget's cottage she was there, with no semblance of hurried walk or discomposure of any kind. The door was slightly ajar. I knocked, and the majestic figure stood before me, silently awaiting the explanation of my errand. Her teeth were all gone, so the nose and chin were brought near together; the grey eyebrows were straight, and almost hung over her deep, cavernous eyes, and the thick white hair lay in silvery masses over the low, wide, wrinkled forehead. For a moment, I stood uncertain how to shape my answer to the solemn questioning of her silence.

'Your name is Bridget Fitzgerald, I believe?' She bowed her head in assent.

'I have something to say to you. May I come in? I am unwilling to keep you standing.'

'You cannot tire me,' she said, and at first she seemed inclined to deny me the shelter of her roof. But the next moment – she had searched the very soul in me with her eyes during that instant – she led me in, and dropped the shadowing hood of her grey, draping cloak, which had previously hid part of the character of her countenance. The cottage was rude and bare enough. But before that picture of the Virgin, of which I have made mention, there stood a little cup filled with fresh primroses. While she paid her reverence to the Madonna, I understood why she had been out seeking through the clumps of green in the sheltered copse. Then she turned round, and bade me be seated. The expression of her face, which all this time I was studying, was not bad, as the stories of my last night's landlord had led me to expect; it was a wild, stern, fierce, indomitable countenance, seamed and scarred by agonies of solitary weeping; but it was neither cunning nor malignant.

'My name is Bridget Fitzgerald,' said she, by way of opening our conversation.

'And your husband was Hugh Fitzgerald, of Knock-Mahon, near Kildoon, in Ireland?'

A faint light came into the dark gloom of her eyes.

'He was.'

'May I ask if you had any children by him?'

The light in her eyes grew quick and red. She tried to speak, I could see; but something rose in her throat, and choked her, and until she could speak calmly, she would fain not speak at all before a stranger. In a minute or so she said: 'I had a daughter – one Mary Fitzgerald,' – then her strong nature mastered her strong will, and she cried out, with a trembling, wailing cry: 'Oh, man! what of her? – What of her?'

She rose from her seat, and came and clutched at my arm, and looked in my eyes. There she read, as I suppose, my utter ignorance of what had become of her child; for she went blindly back to her chair, and sat rocking herself and softly moaning, as if I were not there; I not daring to speak to the lone and awful woman. After a little pause, she knelt down before the picture of our Lady of the Holy Heart, and spoke to her by all the fanciful and poetic names of the Litany.

'O Rose of Sharon! O Tower of David! O Star of the Sea! Have you no comfort for my sore heart? Am I for ever to hope? Grant me at least despair!' – And so on she went, heedless of my presence. Her prayers grew wilder and wilder, till they seemed to me to touch on the borders of madness and blasphemy. Almost involuntarily, I spoke as if to stop her.

'Have you any reason to think that your daughter is dead?'

She rose from her knees, and came and stood before me.

'Mary Fitzgerald is dead,' said she. 'I shall never see her again in the flesh. No tongue ever told me. But I know she is dead. I have yearned so to see her, and my heart's will is fearful and strong: it would have drawn her to me before now, if she had been a wanderer on the other side of the world. I wonder often it has not drawn her out of the grave to come and stand before me, and hear me tell her how I loved her. For, sir, we parted unfriends.'

I knew nothing but the dry particulars needed for my lawyer's quest, but I could not help feeling for the desolate woman; and she must have read the unusual sympathy with her wistful eyes.

'Yes, sir, we did. She never knew how I loved her; and we parted unfriends; and I fear me that I wished her voyage might not turn out well, only meaning – O, blessed Virgin! you know I only meant that she should come home to her mother's arms as to the happiest place on earth; but my wishes are terrible – their power goes beyond my thought – and there is no hope for me, if my words brought Mary harm.'

'But,' I said, 'you do not know that she is dead. Even now, you hoped she might be alive. Listen to me,' and I told her the tale I have already told you, giving it all in the driest manner, for I wanted to recall the clear sense that I felt almost sure she had possessed in her younger days, and by keeping up her attention to details, restrain the vague wildness of her grief.

She listened with deep attention, putting from time to time such questions as convinced me I had to do with no common intelligence, however dimmed and shorn by solitude and mysterious sorrow. Then she took up her tale; and in few brief words, told me of her wanderings abroad in vain search after her daughter; sometimes in the wake of armies, sometimes in camp, sometimes in city. The lady, whose waiting-woman Mary had gone to be, had died soon after the date of her last letter home; her husband, the foreign officer, had been serving in Hungary, whither Bridget had followed him, but too late to find him. Vague rumours reached her that Mary had made a great marriage; and this sting of doubt was added – whether the mother might not be close to her child under her new name, and even hearing of her every day, and yet never recognising the lost one under the appellation she then bore. At length the thought took possession of her, that it was possible that all this time Mary might be at home at Coldholme, in the Trough of Bolland, in Lancashire, in

England; and home came Bridget, in that vain hope, to her desolate hearth, and empty cottage. Here she had thought it safest to remain; if Mary was in life, it was here she would seek for her mother.

I noted down one or two particulars out of Bridget's narrative that I thought might be of use to me; for I was stimulated to further search in a strange and extraordinary manner. It seemed as if it were impressed upon me, that I must take up the quest where Bridget had laid it down; and this for no reason that had previously influenced me (such as my uncle's anxiety on the subject, my own reputation as a lawyer, and so on), but from some strange power which had taken possession of my will only that very morning, and which forced it in the direction it chose.

'I will go,' said I. 'I will spare nothing in the search. Trust to me. I will learn all that can be learnt. You shall know all that money, or pains, or wit can discover. It is true she may be long dead: but she may have left a child.'

'A child!' she cried, as if for the first time this idea had struck her mind. 'Hear him, Blessed Virgin! he says she may have left a child. And you have never told me, though I have prayed so for a sign, waking or sleeping!'

'Nay,' said I, 'I know nothing but what you tell me. You say you heard of her marriage.'

But she caught nothing of what I said. She was praying to the Virgin in a kind of ecstacy, which seemed to render her unconscious of my very presence.

From Coldholme I went to Sir Philip Tempest's. The wife of the foreign officer had been a cousin of his father's, and from him I thought I might gain some particulars as to the existence of the Count de la Tour d'Auvergne, and where I could find him; for I knew questions *de vive voix* aid the flagging recollection, and I was determined to lose no chance for want of trouble. But Sir Philip had gone abroad, and it would be some time before I could receive an answer. So I followed my uncle's advice, to whom I had mentioned how wearied I felt, both in body and mind, by my will-o'-the-wisp search. He immediately told me to go to Harrogate, there to await Sir Philip's reply. I should be near to one of the places connected with my search, Coldholme; not far from Sir Philip Tempest, in case he returned, and I wished to ask him any further questions; and, in conclusion, my uncle bade me try to forget all about my business for a time.

This was far easier said than done. I have seen a child on a common blown along by a high wind, without power of standing still and

resisting the tempestuous force. I was somewhat in the same predica-
ment as regarded my mental state. Something resistless seemed to
urge my thoughts on, through every possible course by which there
was a chance of attaining to my object. I did not see the sweeping
moors when I walked out: when I held a book in my hand, and read
the words, their sense did not penetrate to my brain. If I slept, I went
on with the same ideas, always flowing in the same direction. This
could not last long without having a bad effect on the body. I had an
illness, which, although I was racked with pain, was a positive relief
to me, as it compelled me to live in the present suffering, and not in
the visionary researches I had been continually making before. My
kind uncle came to nurse me; and after the immediate danger was
over, my life seemed to slip away in delicious languor for two or
three months. I did not ask – so much did I dread falling into the old
channel of thought – whether any reply had been received to my
letter to Sir Philip. I turned my whole imagination right away from
all that subject. My uncle remained with me until nigh midsummer,
and then returned to his business in London; leaving me perfectly
well, although not completely strong. I was to follow him in a fortnight; when, as he said, 'we would look over letters, and talk about
several things.' I knew what this little speech alluded to, and shrank
from the train of thought it suggested, which was so intimately
connected with my first feelings of illness. However, I had a fortnight more to roam on those invigorating Yorkshire moors.

In those days, there was one large, rambling inn at Harrogate, close
to the Medicinal Spring; but it was already becoming too small for the
accommodation of the influx of visitors, and many lodged round
about, in the farm-houses of the district. It was so early in the season,
that I had the inn pretty much to myself; and, indeed, felt rather like a
visitor in a private house, so intimate had the landlord and landlady
become with me during my long illness. She would chide me for being
out so late on the moors, or for having been too long without food,
quite in a motherly way; while he consulted me about vintages and
wines, and taught me many a Yorkshire wrinkle about horses. In my
walks I met other strangers from time to time. Even before my uncle
had left me, I had noticed, with half-torpid curiosity, a young lady of
very striking appearance, who went about always accompanied by an
elderly companion, hardly a gentlewoman, but with something in her
look that prepossessed me in her favour. The younger lady always put
her veil down when anyone approached; so it had been only once or
twice, when I had come upon her at a sudden turn in the path, that I

had even had a glimpse of her face. I am not sure if it was beautiful, though in after-life I grew to think it so. But it was at this time over-shadowed by a sadness that never varied: a pale, quiet, resigned look of intense suffering, that irresistibly attracted me, not with love, but with a sense of infinite compassion for one so young yet so hopelessly unhappy. The companion wore something of the same look: quiet, melancholy, hopeless, yet resigned. I asked my landlord who they were. He said they were called Clarke, and wished to be considered as mother and daughter; but that, for his part, he did not believe that to be their right name, or that there was any such relationship between them. They had been in the neighbourhood of Harrogate for some time, lodging in a remote farm-house. The people there would tell nothing about them; saying that they paid handsomely, and never did any harm; so why should they be speaking of any strange things that might happen? That, as the landlord shrewdly observed, showed there was something out of the common way: he had heard that the elderly woman was a cousin of the farmer's where they lodged, and so the regard existing between relations might help to keep them quiet.

'What did he think, then, was the reason for their extreme seclusion?' asked I.

'Nay, he could not tell, not he. He had heard that the young lady, for all as quiet as she seemed, played strange pranks at times.' He shook his head when I asked him for more particulars, and refused to give them, which made me doubt if he knew any, for he was in general a talkative and communicative man. In default of other interests, after my uncle left, I set myself to watch these two people. I hovered about their walks, drawn towards them with a strange fascination, which was not diminished by their evident annoyance at so frequently meeting me. One day, I had the sudden good fortune to be at hand when they were alarmed by the attack of a bull, which, in those unenclosed grazing districts, was a particularly dangerous occurrence. I have other and more important things to relate, than to tell of the accident which gave me an opportunity of rescuing them; it is enough to say, that this event was the beginning of an acquaintance, reluctantly acquiesced in by them, but eagerly prosecuted by me. I can hardly tell when intense curiosity became merged in love, but in less than ten days after my uncle's departure I was passionately enamoured of Mrs Lucy, as her attendant called her; carefully – for this I noted well – avoiding any address which appeared as if there was an equality of station between them. I noticed also that Mrs Clarke, the elderly woman, after her first reluctance to allow me to pay them any attentions had been overcome, was cheered by my evident attachment to the young girl; it seemed to lighten her heavy burden of care, and she evidently favoured my visits to the farm-house where they lodged. It was not so with Lucy. A more attractive person I never saw, in spite of her depression of manner, and shrink-ing avoidance of me. I felt sure at once, that whatever was the source of her grief, it rose from no fault of her own. It was difficult to draw her into conversation; but when at times, for a moment or two, I beguiled her into talk, I could see a rare intelligence in her face, and a grave, trusting look in the soft, grey eyes that were raised for a minute to mine. I made every excuse I possibly could for going there. I sought wild flowers for Lucy's sake; I planned walks for Lucy's sake; I watched the heavens by night, in hopes that some unusual beauty of sky would justify me in tempting Mrs Clarke and Lucy forth upon the moors, to gaze at the great purple dome above.

It seemed to me that Lucy was aware of my love; but that, for some motive which I could not guess, she would fain have repelled me; but then again I saw, or fancied I saw, that her heart spoke in my favour, and that there was a struggle going on in her mind, which at times (I loved so dearly) I could have begged her to spare herself, even though the happiness of my whole life should have been the sacrifice; for her complexion grew paler, her aspect of sorrow more hopeless, her delicate frame yet slighter. During this period I had written, I should say, to my uncle, to beg to be allowed to prolong my stay at Harrogate, not giving any reason; but such was his tenderness to-wards me, that in a few days I heard from him, giving me a willing permission, and only charging me to take care of myself, and not use too much exertion during the hot weather.

One sultry evening I drew near the farm. The windows of their parlour were open, and I heard voices when I turned the corner of the house, as I passed the first window (there were two windows in their little ground-floor room). I saw Lucy distinctly; but when I had knocked at their door – the house-door stood always ajar – she was gone, and I saw only Mrs Clarke, turning over the work-things lying on the table, in a nervous and purposeless manner. I felt by instinct that a conversation of some importance was coming on, in which I should be expected to say what was my object in paying these frequent visits. I was glad of the opportunity. My uncle had several times alluded to the pleasant possibility of my bringing home a young wife, to cheer and adorn the old house in Ormond Street. He was rich, and I was to succeed him, and had, as I knew, a fair reputation for so young a lawyer. So on my side I saw no obstacle. It was true that Lucy was shrouded in mystery; her name (I was convinced it was not Clarke), birth, parentage, and previous life were unknown to me. But I was sure of her goodness and sweet innocence, and although I knew that there must be something painful to be told, to account for her mournful sadness, yet I was willing to bear my share in her grief, whatever it might be.

Mrs Clarke began, as if it was a relief to her to plunge into the subject.

'We have thought, sir – at least I have thought – that you know very little of us, nor we of you, indeed; not enough to warrant the intimate acquaintance we have fallen into. I beg your pardon, sir,' she went on, nervously; 'I am but a plain kind of woman, and I mean to use no rudeness; but I must say straight out that I – we – think it would be better for you not to come so often to see us. She is very unprotected, and – '

'Why should I not come to see you, dear madam?' asked I, eagerly, glad of the opportunity of explaining myself. 'I come, I own, because I have learnt to love Mistress Lucy, and wish to teach her to love me.'

Mistress Clarke shook her head, and sighed.

'Don't, sir – neither love her, nor, for the sake of all you hold sacred, teach her to love you! If I am too late, and you love her already, forget her – forget these last few weeks. O! I should never have allowed you to come!' she went on, passionately; 'but what am I to do? We are forsaken by all, except the great God, and even He permits a strange and evil power to afflict us – what am I to do? Where is it to end?' She wrung her hands in her distress; then she turned to me: 'Go away, sir; go away, before you learn to care any more for her. I ask it for your own sake – I implore. You have been good and kind to us, and we shall always recollect you with gratitude; but go away now, and never come back to cross our fatal path!'

'Indeed, madam,' said I, 'I shall do no such thing. You urge it for my own sake. I have no fear, so urged – nor wish, except to hear more – all. I cannot have seen Mistress Lucy in all the intimacy of this last fortnight, without acknowledging her goodness and innocence; and without seeing – pardon me, madam – that for some reason you are two very lonely women, in some mysterious sorrow and distress. Now, though I am not powerful myself, yet I have friends who are so wise and kind, that they may be said to possess power. Tell me some particulars. Why are you in grief – what is your secret – why are you here? I declare solemnly that nothing you have said has daunted me in

my wish to become Lucy's husband; nor will I shrink from any difficulty that, as such an aspirant, I may have to encounter. You say you are
friendless – why cast away an honest friend? I will tell you of people to
whom you may write, and who will answer any questions as to my
character and prospects. I do not shun inquiry.'

She shook her head again. 'You had better go away, sir. You know
nothing about us.'

'I know your names,' said I, 'and I have heard you allude to the part
of the country from which you came, which I happen to know as a
wild and lonely place. There are so few people living in it that, if I
chose to go there, I could easily ascertain all about you; but I would
rather hear it from yourself.' You see I wanted to pique her into
telling me something definite.

'You do not know our true names, sir,' said she, hastily.

'Well, I may have conjectured as much. But tell me, then, I conjure
you. Give me your reasons for distrusting my willingness to stand by
what I have said with regard to Mistress Lucy.'

'Oh, what can I do?' exclaimed she. 'If I am turning away a true
friend as he says? – Stay!' coming to a sudden decision – 'I will tell
you something – I cannot tell you all – you would not believe it. But,
perhaps, I can tell you enough to prevent your going on in your
hopeless attachment. I am not Lucy's mother.'

'So I conjectured,' I said. 'Go on.'

'I do not even know whether she is the legitimate or illegitimate
child of her father. But he is cruelly turned against her; and her
mother is long dead; and, for a terrible reason, she has no other
creature to keep constant to her but me. She – only two years ago –
such a darling and such a pride in her father's house! Why, sir, there
is a mystery that might happen in connection with her any moment;
and then you would go away like all the rest; and, when you next
heard her name, you would loathe her. Others, who have loved her
longer, have done so before now. My poor child, whom neither God
nor man has mercy upon – or, surely, she would die!'

The good woman was stopped by her crying. I confess, I was a
little stunned by her last words; but only for a moment. At any rate,
till I knew definitely what was this mysterious stain upon one so
simple and pure, as Lucy seemed, I would not desert her, and so I
said; and she made answer.

'If you are daring in your heart to think harm of my child, sir, after
knowing her as you have done, you are no good man yourself; but I
am so foolish and helpless in my great sorrow, that I would fain hope

to find a friend in you. I cannot help trusting that, although you may no longer feel towards her as a lover, you will have pity upon us; and perhaps, by your learning, you can tell us where to go for aid.'

'I implore you to tell me what this mystery is,' I cried, almost maddened by this suspense.

'I cannot,' said she, solemnly. 'I am under a deep vow of secrecy. If you are to be told, it must be by her.' She left the room, and I remained to ponder over this strange interview. I mechanically turned over the few books, and with eyes that saw nothing at the time, examined the tokens of Lucy's frequent presence in that room.

When I got home at night, I remembered how all these trifles spoke of a pure and tender heart and innocent life. Mistress Clarke returned; she had been crying sadly.

'Yes,' said she, 'it is as I feared: she loves you so much that she is willing to run the fearful risk of telling you all herself – she acknowledges it is but a poor chance; but your sympathy will be a balm, if you give it. Tomorrow, come here at ten in the morning; and as you hope for pity in your hour of agony, repress all show of fear or repugnance you may feel towards one so grievously afflicted.'

I half smiled. 'Have no fear,' I said. It seemed too absurd to imagine my feeling dislike to Lucy.

'Her father loved her well,' said she, gravely, 'yet he drove her out like some monstrous thing.'

Just at this moment came a peal of ringing laughter from the garden. It was Lucy's voice; it sounded as if she were standing just on one side of the open casement – and as though she were suddenly stirred to merriment – merriment verging on boisterousness, by the doings or sayings of some other person. I can scarcely say why, but the sound jarred on me inexpressibly. She knew the subject of our conversation, and must have been at least aware of the state of agitation her friend was in: she herself usually so gentle and quiet. I half rose to go to the window, and satisfy my instinctive curiosity as to what had provoked this burst of ill-timed laughter; but Mrs Clarke threw her whole weight and power upon the hand with which she pressed and kept me down.

'For God's sake!' she said, white and trembling all over, 'sit still; be quiet. Oh! be patient. Tomorrow you will know all. Leave us, for we are all sorely afflicted. Do not seek to know more about us.'

Again that laugh – so musical in sound, yet so discordant to my heart. She held me tight – tighter; without positive violence I could not have risen. I was sitting with my back to the window, but I felt a shadow pass between the sun's warmth and me, and a strange shudder ran through my frame. In a minute or two she released me.

'Go,' repeated she. 'Be warned, I ask you once more. I do not think you can stand this knowledge that you seek. If I had had my own way, Lucy should never have yielded, and promised to tell you all. Who knows what may come of it?'

'I am firm in my wish to know all. I return at ten tomorrow morning, and then expect to see Mistress Lucy herself.'

I turned away; having my own suspicions, I confess, as to Mistress Clarke's sanity.

Conjectures as to the meaning of her hints, and uncomfortable thoughts connected with that strange laughter, filled my mind. I could hardly sleep. I rose early; and long before the hour I had appointed, I was on the path over the common that led to the old farm-house where they lodged. I suppose that Lucy had passed no better a night than I; for there she was also, slowly pacing with her even step, her eyes bent down, her whole look most saintly and pure. She started when I came close to her, and grew paler as I reminded her of my appointment, and spoke with something of the impatience of obstacles that, seeing her once more, had called up afresh in my mind. All strange and terrible hints, and giddy merriment were forgotten. My heart gave forth words of fire, and my tongue uttered them. Her colour went and came, as she listened; but, when I had ended my passionate speeches, she lifted her soft eyes to me, and said: 'But you know that you have something to learn about me yet. I only want to say this: I shall not think less of you – less well of you, I mean – if you, too, fall away from me when you know all. Stop!' said she, as if fearing another burst of mad words. 'Listen to me. My father is a man of great wealth. I never knew my mother; she must have died when I was very young. When first I remember anything, I was living in a great, lonely house, with my dear and faithful Mistress Clarke. My father, even, was not there; he was – he is – a soldier, and his duties lie abroad. But he came, from time to time, and every time I think he loved me more and more. He brought me rarities from foreign lands, which prove to me now how much he must have thought of me during his absences. I can sit down and measure the depth of his lost love now, by such standards as these. I never thought whether he loved me or not, then; it was so natural, that it was like the air I breathed. Yet he was an angry man at times, even then; but never with me. He was very reckless, too; and, once or twice, I heard a whisper among the servants that a doom was over him, and that he knew it, and tried to drown his knowledge in wild activity, and even sometimes, sir, in wine. So I grew up in this grand mansion, in that lonely place. Everything around me seemed at my disposal, and I think everyone loved me; I am sure I loved them. Till about two years ago – I remember it well – my father had come to England, to us; and he seemed so proud and so pleased with me and all I had done. And one day his tongue seemed loosened with wine, and he told me much that I had not known till then – how dearly he had loved my mother, yet how his wilful usage had caused her death; and then he went on to say how he loved me better than any creature on earth, and how, some day, he hoped to take me to foreign places, for that he could hardly bear these long absences from his only child. Then he seemed to change suddenly, and said, in a strange, wild way, that I was not to believe what he said; that there was many a thing he loved better – his horse – his dog – I know not what.

'And 'twas only the next morning that, when I came into his room to ask his blessing as was my wont, he received me with fierce and angry words. "Why had I," so he asked, "been delighting myself in such wanton mischief – dancing over the tender plants in the flower-beds, all set with the famous Dutch bulbs he had brought from Holland?" I had never been out of doors that morning, sir, and I could not conceive what he meant, and so I said; and then he swore at me for a liar, and said I was of no true blood, for he had seen me doing all that mischief himself – with his own eyes. What could I say? He would not listen to me, and even my tears seemed only to irritate him. That day was the beginning of my great sorrows. Not long after, he reproached me for my undue familiarity – all unbecoming a gentlewoman – with his grooms. I had been in the stable-yard, laughing and talking, he said. Now, sir, I am something of a coward by nature, and I had always dreaded horses; besides that, my father's servants – those whom he brought with him from foreign parts – were wild fellows, whom I had always avoided, and to whom I had never spoken, except as a lady must needs from time to time speak to her father's people. Yet my father called me by names of which I hardly know the meaning, but my heart told me they were such as shame any modest woman; and from that day he turned quite against me; – nay, sir, not many weeks after that, he came in with a riding-whip in his hand; and, accusing me harshly of evil doings, of which I knew no more than you, sir, he was about to strike me, and I, all in bewildering tears, was ready to take his stripes as great kindness compared to his harder words, when suddenly he stopped his arm mid-way, gasped and staggered, crying out, "The curse – the curse!" I looked up in terror. In the great mirror opposite I saw myself, and, right behind, another wicked, fearful self, so like me that my soul seemed to quiver within me, as though not knowing to which similitude of body it belonged. My father saw my double at the same moment, either in its dreadful reality, whatever that might be, or in the scarcely less terrible reflection in the mirror; but what came of it at that moment I cannot say, for I suddenly swooned away; and when I came to myself I was lying in my bed, and my faithful Clarke sitting by me. I was in my bed for days; and even while I lay there my double was seen by all, flitting about the house and gardens, always about some mischievous or detestable work. What wonder that everyone shrank from me in dread – that my father drove me forth at length, when the disgrace of which I was the cause was past his patience to bear. Mistress Clarke came with me; and here we try to live such a life of piety and prayer as may in time set me free from the curse.'

All the time she had been speaking, I had been weighing her story in my mind. I had hitherto put cases of witchcraft on one side, as mere superstitions; and my uncle and I had had many an argument, he supporting himself by the opinion of his good friend Sir Matthew Hale. Yet this sounded like the tale of one bewitched; or was it merely the effect of a life of extreme seclusion telling on the nerves of a sensitive girl? My scepticism inclined me to the latter belief, and when she paused I said: 'I fancy that some physician could have disabused your father of his belief in visions – '

Just at that instant, standing as I was opposite to her in the full and perfect morning light, I saw behind her another figure – a ghastly resemblance, complete in likeness, so far as form and feature and minutest touch of dress could go, but with a loathsome demon soul looking out of the grey eyes, that were in turns mocking and voluptuous. My heart stood still within me; every hair rose up erect; my flesh crept with horror. I could not see the grave and tender Lucy – my eyes were fascinated by the creature beyond. I know not why, but I put out my hand to clutch it; I grasped nothing but empty air, and my whole blood curdled to ice. For a moment I could not see; then my sight came back, and I saw Lucy standing before me, alone, deathly pale, and, I could have fancied, almost, shrunk in size.

'It has been near me?' she said, as if asking a question.

The sound seemed taken out of her voice; it was husky as the notes on an old harpsichord when the strings have ceased to vibrate. She read her answer in my face, I suppose, for I could not speak. Her look was one of intense fear, but that died away into an aspect of most humble patience. At length she seemed to force herself to face behind and around her: she saw the purple moors, the blue distant hills, quivering in the sunlight, but nothing else.

'Will you take me home?' she said, meekly.

I took her by the hand, and led her silently through the budding heather – we dared not speak; for we could not tell but that the dread creature was listening, although unseen – but that IT might appear and push us asunder. I never loved her more fondly than now when – and that was the unspeakable misery – the idea of her was becoming so inextricably blended with the shuddering thought of IT. She seemed to understand what I must be feeling. She let go my hand, which she had kept clasped until then, when we reached the garden gate, and went forwards to meet her anxious friend, who was standing by the window looking for her. I could not enter the house: I needed silence, society, leisure, change – I knew not what – to shake off the sensation of that creature's presence. Yet I lingered about the garden – I hardly know why; I partly suppose, because I feared to encounter the resemblance again on the solitary common, where it had vanished, and partly from a feeling of inexpressible compassion for Lucy. In a few minutes Mistress Clarke came forth and joined me. We walked some paces in silence.

'You know all now,' said she, solemnly.

'I saw IT,' said I, below my breath.

'And you shrink from us, now,' she said, with a hopelessness which stirred up all that was brave or good in me.

'Not a whit,' said I. 'Human flesh shrinks from encounter with the powers of darkness: and, for some reason unknown to me, the pure and holy Lucy is their victim.'

'The sins of the fathers shall be visited upon the children,' she said.

'Who is her father?' asked I. 'Knowing as much as I do, I may surely know more – know all. Tell me, I entreat you, madam, all that you can conjecture respecting this demoniac persecution of one so good.'

'I will; but not now. I must go to Lucy now. Come this afternoon, I will see you alone; and oh, sir! I will trust that you may yet find some way to help us in our sore trouble!'

I was miserably exhausted by the swooning affright which had taken possession of me. When I reached the inn, I staggered in like one overcome by wine. I went to my own private room. It was some time before I saw that the weekly post had come in, and brought me my letters. There was one from my uncle, one from my home in

Devonshire, and one, re-directed over the first address, sealed with a great coat of arms. It was from Sir Philip Tempest: my letter of inquiry respecting Mary Fitzgerald had reached him at Liège, where it so happened that the Count de la Tour d'Auvergne was quartered at the very time. He remembered his wife's beautiful attendant; she had had high words with the deceased countess, respecting her intercourse with an English gentleman of good standing, who was also in the foreign service. The countess augured evil of his intentions; while Mary, proud and vehement, asserted that he would soon marry her, and resented her mistress's warnings as an insult. The consequence was, that she had left Madame de la Tour d'Auvergne's service, and, as the Count believed, had gone to live with the Englishman; whether he had married her, or not, he could not say. 'But,' added Sir Philip Tempest, 'you may easily hear what particulars you wish to know respecting Mary Fitzgerald from the Englishman himself, if, as I suspect, he is no other than my neighbour and former acquaintance, Mr Gisborne, of Skipford Hall, in the West Riding. I am led to the belief that he is no other by several small particulars, none of which are in themselves conclusive, but which, taken together, make a mass of presumptive evidence. As far as I could make out from the Count's foreign pronunciation, Gisborne was the name of the Englishman: I know that Gisborne of Skipford was abroad and in the foreign service at that time – he was a likely fellow enough for such an exploit, and, above all, certain expressions recur to my mind which he used in reference to old Bridget Fitzgerald, of Coldholme, whom he once en-countered while staying with me at Starkey Manor-house. I remem-ber that the meeting seemed to have produced some extraordinary effect upon his mind, as though he had suddenly discovered some connection which she might have had with his previous life. I beg you to let me know if I can be of any further service to you. Your uncle once rendered me a good turn, and I will gladly repay it, so far as in me lies, to his nephew.'

I was now apparently close on the discovery which I had striven so many months to attain. But success had lost its zest. I put my letters down, and seemed to forget them all in thinking of the morning I had passed that very day. Nothing was real but the unreal presence, which had come like an evil blast across my bodily eyes, and burnt itself down upon my brain. Dinner came, and went away untouched. Early in the afternoon I walked to the farm-house. I found Mistress Clarke alone, and I was glad and relieved. She was evidently prepared to tell me all I might wish to hear.

'You asked me for Mistress Lucy's true name; it is Gisborne,' she began.

'Not Gisborne of Skipford?' I exclaimed, breathless with anticipation.

'The same,' said she, quietly, not regarding my manner. 'Her father is a man of note; although, being a Roman Catholic, he cannot take that rank in this country to which his station entitles him. The consequence is that he lives much abroad – has been a soldier, I am told.'

'And Lucy's mother?' I asked.

She shook her head. 'I never knew her,' said she. 'Lucy was about three years old when I was engaged to take charge of her. Her mother was dead.'

'But you know her name? – you can tell if it was Mary Fitzgerald?'

She looked astonished. 'That was her name. But, sir, how came you to be so well acquainted with it? It was a mystery to the whole household at Skipford Court. She was some beautiful young woman whom he lured away from her protectors while he was abroad. I have heard said he practised some terrible deceit upon her, and when she came to know it, she was neither to have nor to hold, but rushed off from his very arms, and threw herself into a rapid stream and was drowned. It stung him deep with remorse, but I used to think the remembrance of the mother's cruel death made him love the child yet dearer.'

I told her, as briefly as might be, of my researches after the descendant and heir of the Fitzgeralds of Kildoon, and added – something of my old lawyer spirit returning into me for the moment – that I had no doubt but that we should prove Lucy to be by right possessed of large estates in Ireland.

No flush came over her grey face; no light into her eyes. 'And what is all the wealth in the whole world to that poor girl?' she said. 'It will not free her from the ghastly bewitchment which persecutes her. As for money, what a pitiful thing it is; it cannot touch her.'

'No more can the Evil Creature harm her,' I said. 'Her holy nature dwells apart, and cannot be defiled or stained by all the devilish arts in the whole world.'

'True! but it is a cruel fate to know that all shrink from her, sooner or later, as from one possessed – accursed.'

'How came it to pass?' I asked.

'Nay, I know not. Old rumours there are, that were bruited through the household at Skipford.'

'Tell me,' I demanded.

'They came from servants, who would fain account for everything. They say that, many years ago, Mr Gisborne killed a dog belonging to an old witch at Coldholme; that she cursed, with a dreadful and mysterious curse, the creature, whatever it might be, that he should love best; and that it struck so deeply into his heart that for years he kept himself aloof from any temptation to love aught. But who could help loving Lucy?'

'You never heard the witch's name?' I gasped.

'Yes – they called her Bridget; they said he would never go near the spot again for terror of her. Yet he was a brave man!'

'Listen,' said I, taking hold of her arm, the better to arrest her full attention; 'if what I suspect holds true, that man stole Bridget's only child – the very Mary Fitzgerald who was Lucy's mother; if so, Bridget cursed him in ignorance of the deeper wrong he had done her. To this hour she yearns after her lost child, and questions the saints whether she be living or not. The roots of that curse lie deeper than she knows: she unwittingly banned him for a deeper guilt than that of killing a dumb beast. The sins of the fathers are indeed visited upon the children.'

'But,' said Mistress Clarke, eagerly, 'she would never let evil rest on her own grandchild? Surely, sir, if what you say be true, there are hopes for Lucy. Let us go – go at once, and tell this fearful woman all that you suspect, and beseech her to take off the spell she has put upon her innocent grandchild.'

It seemed to me, indeed, that something like this was the best course we could pursue. But first it was necessary to ascertain more than what mere rumour or careless hearsay could tell. My thoughts turned to my uncle – he could advise me wisely – he ought to know all. I resolved to go to him without delay; but I did not choose to tell Mistress Clarke of all the visionary plans that flitted through my mind. I simply declared my intention of proceeding straight to London on Lucy's affairs. I bade her believe that my interest on the young lady's behalf was greater than ever, and that my whole time should be given up to her cause. I saw that Mistress Clarke distrusted me, because my mind was too full of thoughts for my words to flow freely. She sighed and shook her head, and said, 'Well, it is all right!' in such a tone that it was an implied reproach. But I was firm and constant in my heart, and I took confidence from that.

I rode to London. I rode long days drawn out into the lovely summer nights: I could not rest. I reached London. I told my uncle all, though in the stir of the great city the horror had faded away, and I could hardly imagine that he would believe the account I gave him of the fearful double of Lucy which I had seen on the lonely moor-side. But my uncle had lived many years, and learnt many things; and, in the deep secrets of family history that had been confided to him, he had heard of cases of innocent people bewitched and taken possession of by evil spirits yet more fearful than Lucy's. For, as he said, to judge from all I told him, that resemblance had no power over her – she was too pure and good to be tainted by its evil, haunting presence. It had, in all probability, so my uncle conceived, tried to suggest wicked thoughts and to tempt to wicked actions; but she, in her saintly maidenhood, had passed on undefiled by evil thought or deed. It could not touch her soul: but true, it set her apart from all sweet love or common human intercourse. My uncle threw himself with an energy more like six-and-twenty than sixty into the consideration of the whole case. He undertook the proving Lucy's descent, and volunteered to go and find out Mr Gisborne, and ob-tain, firstly, the legal proofs of her descent from the Fitzgeralds of Kildoon, and, secondly, to try and hear all that he could respecting the working of the curse, and whether any and what means had been taken to exorcise that terrible appearance. For he told me of instances where, by prayers and long fasting, the evil possessor had been driven forth with howling and many cries from the body which it had come to inhabit; he spoke of those strange New England cases which had happened not so long before; of Mr Defoe, who had written a book, wherein he had named many modes of subduing apparitions, and sending them back whence they came; and, lastly, he spoke low of dreadful ways of compelling witches to undo their witchcraft. But I could not endure to hear of those tortures and burnings. I said that Bridget was rather a wild and savage woman than a malignant witch; and, above all, that Lucy was of her kith and kin; and that, in putting her to the trial, by water or by fire, we should be torturing – it might be to the death – the ancestress of her we sought to redeem.

My uncle thought awhile, and then said, that in this last matter I was right – at any rate, it should not be tried, with his consent, till all other modes of remedy had failed; and he assented to my proposal that I should go myself and see Bridget, and tell her all.

In accordance with this, I went down once more to the wayside inn near Coldholme. It was late at night when I arrived there; and, while I supped, I inquired of the landlord more particulars as to Bridget's ways. Solitary and savage had been her life for many years. Wild and despotic were her words and manner to those few people who came across her path. The country-folk did her imperious bidding, because they feared to disobey. If they pleased her, they prospered; if, on the contrary, they neglected or traversed her behests, misfortune, small or great, fell on them and theirs. It was not detestation so much as an indefinable terror that she excited.

In the morning I went to see her. She was standing on the green outside her cottage, and received me with the sullen grandeur of a throneless queen. I read in her face that she recognised me, and that I was not unwelcome; but she stood silent till I had opened my errand.

'I have news of your daughter,' said I, resolved to speak straight to all that I knew she felt of love, and not to spare her. 'She is dead!'

The stern figure scarcely trembled, but her hand sought the support of the door-post.

'I knew that she was dead,' said she, deep and low, and then was silent for an instant. 'My tears that should have flowed for her were burnt up long years ago. Young man, tell me about her.'

'Not yet,' said I, having a strange power given me of confronting one, whom, nevertheless, in my secret soul I dreaded.

'You had once a little dog,' I continued. The words called out in her more show of emotion than the intelligence of her daughter's death.

She broke in upon my speech: 'I had! It was hers – the last thing I had of hers – and it was shot for wantonness! It died in my arms. The man who killed that dog rues it to this day. For that dumb beast's blood, his best-beloved stands accursed.'

Her eyes distended, as if she were in a trance and saw the working of her curse. Again I spoke: 'O, woman!' I said, 'that best-beloved, standing accursed before men, is your dead daughter's child.'

The life, the energy, the passion came back to the eyes with which she pierced through me, to see if I spoke truth; then, without another question or word, she threw herself on the ground with fearful vehemence, and clutched at the innocent daisies with convulsed hands.

'Bone of my bone! Flesh of my flesh! Have I cursed thee – and art thou accursed?'

So she moaned, as she lay prostrate in her great agony. I stood aghast at my own work. She did not hear my broken sentences; she asked no more, but the dumb confirmation which my sad looks had given that one fact, that her curse rested on her own daughter's child. The fear grew on me lest she should die in her strife of body and soul; and then might not Lucy remain under the spell as long as she lived?

Even at this moment, I saw Lucy coming through the woodland path that led to Bridget's cottage; Mistress Clarke was with her: I felt at my heart that it was she, by the balmy peace which the look of her sent over me, as she slowly advanced, a glad surprise shining out of her soft quiet eyes. That was as her gaze met mine. As her looks fell on the woman lying stiff, convulsed on the earth, they became full of tender pity; and she came forward to try and lift her up. Seating herself on the turf, she took Bridget's head into her lap; and, with gentle touches, she arranged the dishevelled grey hair streaming thick and wild from beneath her mutch.*

'God help her!' murmured Lucy. 'How she suffers!'

At her desire we sought for water; but when we returned, Bridget had recovered her wandering senses, and was kneeling with clasped hands before Lucy, gazing at that sweet sad face as though her troubled nature drank in health and peace from every moment's contemplation. A faint tinge on Lucy's pale cheeks showed me that she was aware of our return; otherwise it appeared as if she was conscious of her influence for good over the passionate and troubled woman kneeling before her, and would not willingly avert her grave and loving eyes from that wrinkled and careworn countenance.

Suddenly – in the twinkling of an eye – the creature appeared, there, behind Lucy; fearfully the same as to outward semblance, but kneeling exactly as Bridget knelt, and clasping her hands in jesting mimicry as Bridget clasped hers in her ecstasy that was deepening into a prayer. Mistress Clarke cried out – Bridget arose slowly, her gaze fixed on the creature beyond: drawing her breath with a hissing sound, never moving her terrible eyes, that were steady as stone, she made a dart at the phantom, and caught, as I had done, a mere handful of empty air. We saw no more of the creature – it vanished as suddenly as it came, but Bridget looked slowly on, as if watching some receding form. Lucy sat still, white, trembling, drooping – I think she would have swooned if I had not been there to uphold her. While I was attending to her, Bridget passed us, without a word to anyone, and, entering her cottage, she barred herself in, and left us without.

All our endeavours were now directed to get Lucy back to the house where she had tarried the night before. Mistress Clarke told

* A cap, or covering for the head.

me that, not hearing from me (some letter must have miscarried), she had grown impatient and despairing, and had urged Lucy to the enterprise of coming to seek her grandmother; not telling her, indeed, of the dread reputation she possessed, or how we suspected her of having so fearfully blighted that innocent girl; but, at the same time, hoping much from the mysterious stirring of blood, which Mistress Clarke trusted in for the removal of the curse. They had come, by a different route from that which I had taken, to a village inn not far from Coldholme, only the night before. This was the first interview between ancestress and descendant.

All through the sultry noon I wandered along the tangled wood-paths of the old neglected forest, thinking where to turn for remedy in a matter so complicated and mysterious. Meeting a countryman, I asked my way to the nearest clergyman, and went, hoping to obtain some counsel from him. But he proved to be a coarse and common-minded man, giving no time or attention to the intricacies of a case, but dashing out a strong opinion involving immediate action. For instance, as soon as I named Bridget Fitzgerald, he exclaimed.

'The Coldholme witch! The Irish papist! I'd have had her ducked long since but for that other papist, Sir Philip Tempest. He has had to threaten honest folk about here over and over again, or they'd have had her up before the justices for her black doings. And it's the law of the land that witches should be burnt! Ay, and of Scripture, too, sir! Yet you see a papist, if he's a rich squire, can overrule both law and Scripture. I'd carry a fagot myself to rid the country of her!'

Such a one could give me no help. I rather drew back what I had already said; and tried to make the parson forget it, by treating him to several pots of beer, in the village inn, to which we had adjourned for our conference at his suggestion. I left him as soon as I could, and returned to Coldholme, shaping my way past deserted Starkey Manor-house, and coming upon it by the back. At that side were the oblong remains of the old moat, the waters of which lay placid and motionless under the crimson rays of the setting sun; with the forest-trees lying straight along each side, and their deep-green foliage mirrored to blackness in the burnished surface of the moat below – and the broken sun-dial at the end nearest the hall – and the heron, standing on one leg at the water's edge, lazily looking down for fish – the lonely and desolate house scarce needed the broken windows, the weeds on the door-sill, the broken shutter softly flapping to and fro in the twilight breeze, to fill up the picture of desertion and decay. I lingered about the place until the growing darkness warned me on.

And then I passed along the path, cut by the orders of the last lady of Starkey Manor-house, that led me to Bridget's cottage. I resolved at once to see her; and, in spite of closed doors – it might be of resolved will – she should see me. So I knocked at her door, gently, loudly, fiercely. I shook it so vehemently that at length the old hinges gave way, and with a crash it fell inwards, leaving me suddenly face to face with Bridget – I, red, heated, agitated with my so long-baffled efforts – she, stiff as any stone, standing right facing me, her eyes dilated with terror, her ashen lips trembling, but her body motionless. In her hands she held her crucifix, as if by that holy symbol she sought to oppose my entrance. At sight of me, her whole frame relaxed, and she sank back upon a chair. Some mighty tension had given way. Still her eyes looked fearfully into the gloom of the outer air, made more opaque by the glimmer of the lamp inside, which she had placed before the picture of the Virgin.

'Is she there?' asked Bridget, hoarsely.

'No! Who? I am alone. You remember me.'

'Yes,' replied she, still terror-stricken. 'But she – that creature – has been looking in upon me through that window all day long. I closed it up with my shawl; and then I saw her feet below the door, as long as it was light, and I knew she heard my very breathing – nay, worse, my very prayers; and I could not pray, for her listening choked the words ere they rose to my lip. Tell me, who is she? – what means that double girl I saw this morning? One had a look of my dead Mary; but the other curdled my blood, and yet it was the same!'

She had taken hold of my arm, as if to secure herself some human companionship. She shook all over with the slight, never-ceasing tremor of intense terror. I told her my tale, as I have told it you, sparing none of the details.

How Mistress Clarke had informed me that the resemblance had driven Lucy forth from her father's house – how I had disbelieved, until, with mine own eyes, I had seen another Lucy standing behind my Lucy, the same in form and feature, but with the demon-soul looking out of the eyes. I told her all, I say, believing that she – whose curse was working so upon the life of her innocent grandchild – was the only person who could find the remedy and the redemption. When I had done, she sat silent for many minutes.

'You love Mary's child?' she asked.

'I do, in spite of the fearful working of the curse – I love her. Yet I shrink from her ever since that day on the moor-side. And men must shrink from one so accompanied; friends and lovers must stand afar off. Oh, Bridget Fitzgerald! loosen the curse! Set her free!'

'Where is she?'

I eagerly caught at the idea that her presence was needed, in order that, by some strange prayer or exorcism, the spell might be reversed.

'I will go and bring her to you,' I exclaimed. But Bridget tightened her hold upon my arm.

'Not so,' said she, in a low, hoarse voice. 'It would kill me to see her again as I saw her this morning. And I must live till I have worked my work. Leave me!' said she, suddenly, and again taking up the cross. 'I defy the demon I have called up. Leave me to wrestle with it!'

She stood up, as if in an ecstasy of inspiration, from which all fear was banished. I lingered – why, I can hardly tell – until once more she bade me begone. As I went along the forest way, I looked back, and saw her planting the cross in the empty threshold, where the door had been.

The next morning Lucy and I went to seek her, to bid her join her prayers with ours. The cottage stood open and wide to our gaze. No human being was there: the cross remained on the threshold, but Bridget was gone.

Chapter 3

What was to be done next? was the question that I asked myself. As for Lucy, she would fain have submitted to the doom that lay upon her. Her gentleness and piety, under the pressure of so horrible a life, seemed over-passive to me. She never complained. Mrs Clarke complained more than ever. As for me, I was more in love with the real Lucy than ever; but I shrunk from the false similitude with an intensity proportioned to my love. I found out by instinct that Mrs Clarke had occasional temptations to leave Lucy. The good lady's nerves were shaken, and, from what she said, I could almost have concluded that the object of the Double was to drive away from Lucy this last and almost earliest friend. At times, I could scarcely bear to own it, but I myself felt inclined to turn recreant; and I would accuse Lucy of being too patient – too resigned. One after another, she won the little children of Coldholme. (Mrs Clarke and she had resolved to stay there, for was it not as good a place as any other to such as they? and did not all our faint hopes rest on Bridget – never seen or heard of now, but still we trusted to come back, or give some token?) So, as I say, one after another, the little children came about my Lucy, won by her soft tones, and her gentle smiles, and kind actions. Alas! one after another they fell away, and shrunk from her path with blanching terror; and we too surely guessed the reason why. It was the last drop. I could bear it no longer. I resolved no more to linger around the spot, but to go back to my uncle, and among the learned divines of the city of London, seek for some power whereby to annul the curse.

My uncle, meanwhile, had obtained all the requisite testimonials relating to Lucy's descent and birth, from the Irish lawyers, and from Mr Gisborne. The latter gentleman had written from abroad (he was again serving in the Austrian army), a letter alternately passionately self-reproachful and stoically repellent. It was evident that when he thought of Mary – her short life – how he had wronged her, and of her violent death, he could hardly find words severe enough for his own conduct; and from this point of view, the curse that Bridget had laid upon him and his was regarded by him as a prophetic doom, to the utterance of which she was moved by a Higher Power, working for the fulfilment of a deeper vengeance than for the death of the poor dog. But then, again, when he came to speak of his daughter, the repugnance which the conduct of the demoniac creature had produced in his mind, was but ill disguised under a show of profound indifference as to Lucy's fate. One almost felt as if he would have been as content to put her out of existence, as he would have been to destroy some disgusting reptile that had invaded his chamber or his couch.

The great Fitzgerald property was Lucy's; and that was all – was nothing.

My uncle and I sat in the gloom of a London November evening, in our house in Ormond Street. *I* was out of health, and felt as if I were in an inextricable coil of misery. Lucy and I wrote to each other, but that was little; and we dared not see each other for dread of the fearful Third, who had more than once taken her place at our meetings. My uncle had, on the day I speak of, bidden prayers to be put up, on the ensuing Sabbath, in many a church and meeting-house in London, for one grievously tormented by an evil spirit. He had faith in prayers – I had none; I was fast losing faith in all things. So we sat – he trying to interest me in the old talk of other days, I oppressed by one thought – when our old servant, Anthony, opened the door, and, without speaking, showed in a very gentle-manly and prepossessing man, who had something remarkable about his dress, betraying his profession to be that of the Roman Catholic priesthood. He glanced at my uncle first, then at me. It was to me he bowed. 'I did not give my name,' said he, 'because you would hardly have recognised it; unless, sir, when in the north, you heard of Father Bernard, the chaplain at Stoney Hurst?'

I remembered afterwards that I had heard of him, but at the time I had utterly forgotten it; so I professed myself a complete stranger to him; while my ever-hospitable uncle, although hating a papist as much as it was in his nature to hate anything, placed a chair for the visitor, and bade Anthony bring glasses and a fresh jug of claret.

Father Bernard received this courtesy with the graceful ease and pleasant acknowledgment which belongs to the man of the world. Then he turned to scan me with his keen glance. After some slight conversation, entered into on his part, I am certain, with an intention of discovering on what terms of confidence I stood with my uncle, he paused, and said gravely: 'I am sent here with a message to you, sir, from a woman to whom you have shown kindness, and who is one of my penitents, in Antwerp – one Bridget Fitzgerald.'

'Bridget Fitzgerald!' exclaimed I. 'In Antwerp? Tell me, sir, all that you can about her.'

'There is much to be said,' he replied. 'But may I inquire if this gentleman – if your uncle is acquainted with the particulars of which you and I stand informed?'

'All that I know, he knows,' said I, eagerly laying my hand on my uncle's arm, as he made a motion as if to quit the room.

'Then I have to speak before two gentlemen who, however they may differ from me in faith, are yet fully impressed with the fact, that there are evil powers going about continually to take cognizance of our evil thoughts; and, if their Master gives them power, to bring them into overt action. Such is my theory of the nature of that sin, of which I dare not disbelieve – as some sceptics would have us do – the sin of witchcraft. Of this deadly sin, you and I are aware Bridget Fitzgerald has been guilty. Since you saw her last, many prayers have been offered in our churches, many masses sung, many penances undergone, in order that, if God and the Holy Saints so willed it, her sin might be blotted out. But it has not been so willed.'

'Explain to me,' said I, 'who you are, and how you come connected with Bridget. Why is she at Antwerp? I pray you, sir, tell me more. If I am impatient, excuse me; I am ill and feverish, and in consequence bewildered.'

There was something to me inexpressibly soothing in the tone of voice with which he began to narrate, as it were from the beginning, his acquaintance with Bridget.

'I had known Mr and Mrs Starkey during their residence abroad, and so it fell out naturally that, when I came as chaplain to the Sherburnes at Stoney Hurst, our acquaintance was renewed; and thus I became the confessor of the whole family, isolated as they were from the offices of the Church, Sherburne being their nearest neighbour who professed the true faith. Of course, you are aware that facts revealed in confession are sealed as in the grave; but I learnt enough of Bridget's character to be convinced that I had to do with no common woman; one powerful for good as for evil. I believe that I was able to give her spiritual assistance from time to time, and that she looked upon me as a servant of that Holy Church, which has such wonderful power of moving men's hearts, and relieving them of the burden of their sins. I have known her cross the moors on the wildest nights of storm, to confess and be absolved; and then she would return, calmed and subdued, to her daily work about her mistress, no-one witting where she had been during the hours that most passed in sleep upon their beds. After her daughter's departure – after Mary's mysterious disappearance – I had to impose many a long penance, in order to wash away the sin of impatient repining that was fast leading her into the deeper guilt of blasphemy. She set out on that long journey of which you have possibly heard – that fruitless journey in search of Mary – and during her absence, my superiors ordered my return to my former duties at Antwerp, and for many years I heard no more of Bridget.

'Not many months ago, as I was passing homewards in the evening, along one of the streets near St Jacques, leading into the Meer Straet, I saw a woman sitting crouched up under the shrine of the Holy Mother of Sorrows. Her hood was drawn over her head, so that the shadow caused by the light of the lamp above fell deep over her face; her hands were clasped round her knees. It was evident that she was someone in hopeless trouble, and as such it was my duty to stop and speak. I naturally addressed her first in Flemish, believing her to be one of the lower class of inhabitants. She shook her head, but did not look up. Then I tried French, and she replied in that language, but speaking it so indifferently, that I was sure she was either English or Irish, and consequently spoke to her in my own native tongue. She recognised my voice; and, starting up, caught at my robes, dragging me before the blessed shrine, and throwing herself down, and forcing me, as much by her evident desire as by her action, to kneel beside her, she exclaimed: "O Holy Virgin! you will never hearken to me again, but hear him; for you know him of old, that he does your bidding, and strives to heal broken hearts. Hear him!"

'She turned to me.

' "She will hear you, if you will only pray. She never hears me: she and all the saints in Heaven cannot hear my prayers, for the Evil One carries them off, as he carried that first away. O, Father Bernard, pray for me!"

'I prayed for one in sore distress, of what nature I could not say; but the Holy Virgin would know. Bridget held me fast, gasping with eagerness at the sound of my words. When I had ended, I rose, and, making the sign of the Cross over her, I was going to bless her in the name of the Holy Church, when she shrank away like some terrified creature, and said.

' "I am guilty of deadly sin, and am not shriven."

' "Arise, my daughter," said I, "and come with me." And I led the way into one of the confessionals of St Jacques.

'She knelt; I listened. No words came. The evil powers had stricken her dumb, as I heard afterwards they had many a time before, when she approached confession.

'She was too poor to pay for the necessary forms of exorcism; and hitherto those priests to whom she had addressed herself were either so ignorant of the meaning of her broken French, or her Irish-English, or else esteemed her to be one crazed – as, indeed, her wild and excited manner might easily have led anyone to think – that they had neglected the sole means of loosening her tongue, so that she might confess her deadly sin, and after due penance, obtain absolution. But I knew Bridget of old, and felt that she was a penitent sent to me. I went through those holy offices appointed by our church for the relief of such a case. I was the more bound to do this, as I found that she had come to Antwerp for the sole purpose of discovering me, and making confession to me. Of the nature of that fearful confession I am forbidden to speak. Much of it you know; possibly all.

'It now remains for her to free herself from mortal guilt, and to set others free from the consequences thereof. No prayer, no masses, will ever do it, although they may strengthen her with that strength by which alone acts of deepest love and purest self-devotion may be performed. Her words of passion, and cries for revenge – her unholy prayers could never reach the ears of the Holy Saints! Other powers intercepted them, and wrought so that the curses thrown up to Heaven have fallen on her own flesh and blood; and so, through her very strength of love, have bruised and crushed her heart. Henceforward her former self must be buried – yea, buried quick, if need be – but never more to make sign, or utter cry on earth! She has become a Poor Clare, in order that, by perpetual penance and constant service of others, she may at length so act as to obtain final absolution and rest for her soul. Until then, the innocent must suffer. It is to plead for the innocent that I come to you; not in the name of the witch, Bridget Fitzgerald, but of the penitent and servant of all men, the Poor Clare, Sister Magdalen.'

'Sir,' said I, 'I listen to your request with respect; only I may tell you it is not needed to urge me to do all that I can on behalf of one, love for whom is part of my very life. If for a time I have absented myself from her, it is to think and work for her redemption. I, a member of the English Church – my uncle, a Puritan – pray morning and night for her by name: the congregations of London, on the next Sabbath, will pray for one unknown, that she may be set free from the Powers of Darkness. Moreover, I must tell you, sir, that those evil ones touch not the great calm of her soul. She lives her own pure and loving life, unharmed and untainted, though all men fall off from her. I would I could have her faith!'

My uncle now spoke.

'Nephew,' said he, 'it seems to me that this gentleman, although professing what I consider an erroneous creed, has touched upon the right point in exhorting Bridget to acts of love and mercy, whereby to wipe out her sin of hate and vengeance. Let us strive after our fashion, by almsgiving and visiting of the needy and fatherless, to make our prayers acceptable. Meanwhile, I myself will go down into the north, and take charge of the maiden. I am too old to be daunted by man or demon. I will bring her to this house as to a home; and let the Double come if it will! A company of godly divines shall give it the meeting, and we will try issue.'

The kindly brave old man! But Father Bernard sat on musing.

'All hate,' said he, 'cannot be quenched in her heart; all Christian forgiveness cannot have entered into her soul, or the demon would have lost its power. You said, I think, that her grandchild was still tormented?'

'Still tormented!' I replied, sadly, thinking of Mistress Clarke's last letter.

He rose to go. We afterwards heard that the occasion of his coming to London was a secret political mission on behalf of the Jacobites. Nevertheless, he was a good and a wise man.

Months and months passed away without any change. Lucy entreated my uncle to leave her where she was – dreading, as I learnt, lest if she came, with her fearful companion, to dwell in the same house with me, that my love could not stand the repeated shocks to which I should be doomed. And this she thought from no distrust of the strength of my affection, but from a kind of pitying sympathy for the terror to the nerves which she observed that the demoniac visitation caused in all.

I was restless and miserable. I devoted myself to good works; but I performed them from no spirit of love, but solely from the hope of reward and payment, and so the reward was never granted. At length, I asked my uncle's leave to travel; and I went forth, a wanderer, with no distincter end than that of many another wanderer – to get away from myself. A strange impulse led me to Antwerp, in spite of the wars and commotions then raging in the Low Countries – or rather, perhaps, the very craving to become interested in something external, led me into the thick of the struggle then going on with the Austrians. The cities of Flanders were all full at that time of civil disturbances and rebellions, only kept down by force, and the presence of an Austrian garrison in every place.

I arrived in Antwerp, and made inquiry for Father Bernard. He was away in the country for a day or two. Then I asked my way to the Convent of Poor Clares; but, being healthy and prosperous, I could only see the dim, pent-up, grey walls, shut closely in by narrow streets, in the lowest part of the town. My landlord told me, that had I been stricken by some loathsome disease, or in desperate case of any kind, the Poor Clares would have taken me, and tended me. He spoke of them as an order of mercy of the strictest kind, dressing scantily in the coarsest materials, going barefoot, living on what the inhabitants of Antwerp chose to bestow, and sharing even those fragments and crumbs with the poor and helpless that swarmed all around; receiving no letters or communication with the outer world; utterly dead to everything but the alleviation of suffering. He smiled at my inquiring whether I could get speech of one of them; and told me that they were even forbidden to speak for the purposes of begging their daily food; while yet they lived, and fed others upon what was given in charity.

'But,' exclaimed I, 'supposing all men forgot them! Would they quietly lie down and die, without making sign of their extremity?'

'If such were their rule, the Poor Clares would willingly do it; but their founder appointed a remedy for such extreme case as you suggest. They have a bell – 'tis but a small one, as I have heard, and has yet never been rung in the memory of man: when the Poor Clares have been without food for twenty-four hours, they may ring this bell, and then trust to our good people of Antwerp for rushing to the rescue of the Poor Clares, who have taken such blessed care of us in all our straits.'

It seemed to me that such rescue would be late in the day; but I did not say what I thought. I rather turned the conversation, by asking my landlord if he knew, or had ever heard, anything of a certain Sister Magdalen.

'Yes,' said he, rather under his breath; 'news will creep out, even from a convent of Poor Clares. Sister Magdalen is either a great sinner or a great saint. She does more, as I have heard, than all the other nuns put together; yet, when last month they would fain have made her mother-superior, she begged rather that they would place her below all the rest, and make her the meanest servant of all.'

'You never saw her?' asked I.

'Never,' he replied.

I was weary of waiting for Father Bernard, and yet I lingered in Antwerp. The political state of things became worse than ever, increased to its height by the scarcity of food consequent on many deficient harvests. I saw groups of fierce, squalid men, at every corner of the street, glaring out with wolfish eyes at my sleek skin and handsome clothes.

At last Father Bernard returned. We had a long conversation, in which he told me that, curiously enough, Mr Gisborne, Lucy's father, was serving in one of the Austrian regiments, then in garrison at Antwerp. I asked Father Bernard if he would make us acquainted; which he consented to do. But, a day or two afterwards, he told me that, on hearing my name, Mr Gisborne had declined responding to any advances on my part, saying he had abjured his country, and hated his countrymen.

Probably he recollected my name in connection with that of his daughter Lucy. Anyhow, it was clear enough that I had no chance of making his acquaintance. Father Bernard confirmed me in my suspicions of the hidden fermentation, for some coming evil, working among the 'blouses' of Antwerp, and he would fain have had me depart from out the city; but I rather craved the excitement of danger, and stubbornly refused to leave.

One day, when I was walking with him in the Place Verte, he bowed to an Austrian officer, who was crossing towards the cathedral.

'That is Mr Gisborne,' said he, as soon as the gentleman was past.

I turned to look at the tall, slight figure of the officer. He carried himself in a stately manner, although he was past middle age, and from his years, might have had some excuse for a slight stoop. As I looked at the man, he turned round, his eyes met mine, and I saw his face. Deeply lined, sallow, and scathed was that countenance; scarred by passion as well as by the fortunes of war. 'Twas but a moment our eyes met. We each turned round, and went on our separate way.

But his whole appearance was not one to be easily forgotten; the thorough appointment of the dress, and evident thought bestowed on it, made but an incongruous whole with the dark, gloomy expression of his countenance. Because he was Lucy's father, I sought instinctively to meet him everywhere. At last he must have become aware of my pertinacity, for he gave me a haughty scowl whenever I passed him. In one of these encounters, however, I chanced to be of some service to him. He was turning the corner of a street, and came suddenly on one of the groups of discontented Flemings of whom I have spoken. Some words were exchanged, when my gentleman out with his sword, and with a slight but skilful cut drew blood from one of those who had insulted him, as he fancied, though I was too far off to hear the words. They would all have fallen upon him had I not rushed forwards and raised the cry, then well known in Antwerp, of rally, to the Austrian soldiers who were perpetually patrolling the streets, and who came in numbers to the rescue. I think that neither Mr Gisborne nor the mutinous group of plebeians owed me much gratitude for my interference. He had planted himself against a wall, in a skilful attitude of fence, ready with his bright glancing rapier to do battle with all the heavy, fierce, unarmed men, some six or seven in number. But when his own soldiers came up, he sheathed his sword; and, giving some careless word of command, sent them away again, and continued his saunter all alone down the street, the workmen snarling in his rear, and more than half-inclined to fall on me for my cry for rescue. I cared not if they did, my life seemed so dreary a burden just then; and, perhaps, it was this daring loitering among them that prevented their attacking me. Instead, they suffered me to fall into conversation with them; and I heard some of their grievances. Sore and heavy to be borne were they, and no wonder the sufferers were savage and desperate.

The man whom Gisborne had wounded across his face would fain have got out of me the name of his aggressor, but I refused to tell it. Another of the group heard his inquiry, and made answer.

'I know the man. He is one Gisborne, aide-de-camp to the General-Commandant. I know him well.'

He began to tell some story in connection with Gisborne in a low and muttering voice; and while he was relating a tale, which I saw excited their evil blood, and which they evidently wished me not to hear, I sauntered away and back to my lodgings.

That night Antwerp was in open revolt. The inhabitants rose in rebellion against their Austrian masters. The Austrians, holding the gates of the city, remained at first pretty quiet in the citadel; only, from time to time, the boom of a great cannon swept sullenly over the town. But, if they expected the disturbance to die away, and spend itself in a few hours' fury, they were mistaken. In a day or two, the rioters held possession of the principal municipal buildings. Then the Austrians poured forth in bright flaming array, calm and smiling, as they marched to the posts assigned, as if the fierce mob were no more to them than the swarms of buzzing summer flies. Their practised manoeuvres, their well-aimed shot, told with terrible effect; but in the place of one slain rioter, three sprang up of his blood to avenge his loss. But a deadly foe, a ghastly ally of the Austrians, was at work. Food, scarce and dear for months, was now hardly to be obtained at any price. Desperate efforts were being made to bring provisions into the city, for the rioters had friends without. Close to the city port nearest to the Scheldt, a great struggle took place. I was there, helping the rioters, whose cause I had adopted. We had a savage encounter with the Austrians. Numbers fell on both sides; I saw them lie bleeding for a moment; then a volley of smoke obscured them; and when it cleared away, they were dead – trampled upon or smothered, pressed down and hidden by the freshly-wounded whom those last guns had brought low. And then a grey-robed and grey-veiled figure came right across the flashing guns, and stooped over someone, whose life-blood was ebbing away; sometimes it was to give him drink from cans which they carried slung at their sides, sometimes I saw the cross held above a dying man, and rapid prayers were being uttered, unheard by men in that hellish din and clangour, but listened to by One above. I saw all this as in a dream: the reality of that stern time was battle and carnage. But I knew that these grey figures, their bare feet all wet with blood, and their faces hidden by their veils, were the Poor Clares – sent forth now because dire agony was abroad and imminent danger at hand. Therefore, they left their cloistered shelter, and came into that thick and evil mêlée.

Close to me – driven past me by the struggle of many fighters – came the Antwerp burgess with the scarce-healed scar upon his face; and in an instant more, he was thrown by the press upon the Austrian officer Gisborne, and ere either had recovered the shock, the burgess had recognised his opponent.

'Ha! the Englishman Gisborne!' he cried, and threw himself upon him with redoubled fury. He had struck him hard – the Englishman was down; when out of the smoke came a dark-grey figure, and threw herself right under the uplifted flashing sword. The burgess's arm stood arrested. Neither Austrians nor Anversois willingly harmed the Poor Clares.

'Leave him to me!' said a low stern voice. 'He is mine enemy – mine for many years.'

Those words were the last I heard. I myself was struck down by a bullet. I remember nothing more for days. When I came to myself, I was at the extremity of weakness, and was craving for food to recruit my strength. My landlord sat watching me. He, too, looked pinched and shrunken; he had heard of my wounded state, and sought me out. Yes! the struggle still continued, but the famine was sore; and some, he had heard, had died for lack of food. The tears stood in his eyes as he spoke. But soon he shook off his weakness, and his natural cheerfulness returned. Father Bernard had been to see me – no-one else. (Who should, indeed?) Father Bernard would come back that afternoon – he had promised. But Father Bernard never came, although I was up and dressed, and looking eagerly for him.

My landlord brought me a meal which he had cooked himself: of what it was composed he would not say, but it was most excellent, and with every mouthful I seemed to gain strength. The good man sat looking at my evident enjoyment with a happy smile of sympathy; but, as my appetite became satisfied, I began to detect a certain wistfulness in his eyes, as if craving for the food I had so nearly devoured – for, indeed, at that time I was hardly aware of the extent of the famine. Suddenly, there was a sound of many rushing feet past our window. My landlord opened one of the sides of it, the better to learn what was going on. Then we heard a faint, cracked, tinkling bell, coming shrill upon the air, clear and distinct from all other sounds. 'Holy Mother!' exclaimed my landlord, 'the Poor Clares!'

He snatched up the fragments of my meal, and crammed them into my hands, bidding me follow. Downstairs he ran, clutching at more food, as the women of his house eagerly held it out to him; and in a moment we were in the street, moving along with the great current, all tending towards the Convent of the Poor Clares. And still, as if piercing our ears with its inarticulate cry, came the shrill tinkle of the bell. In that strange crowd were old men trembling and sobbing, as they carried their little pittance of food; women with the tears running down their cheeks, who had snatched up what provisions they had in the vessels in which they stood, so that the burden of these was in many cases much greater than that which they contained; children, with flushed faces, grasping tight the morsel of bitten cake or bread, in their eagerness to carry it safe to the help of the Poor Clares; strong men – yea, both Anversois and Austrians – pressing onwards with set teeth, and no word spoken; and over all, and through all, came that sharp tinkle – that cry for help in extremity.

We met the first torrent of people returning with blanched and piteous faces: they were issuing out of the convent to make way for the offerings of others. 'Haste, haste!' said they.

'A Poor Clare is dying! A Poor Clare is dead for hunger! God forgive us, and our city!'

We pressed on. The stream bore us along where it would. We were carried through refectories, bare and crumbless; into cells over whose doors the conventual name of the occupant was written. Thus it was that I, with others, was forced into Sister Magdalen's cell. On her couch lay Gisborne, pale unto death, but not dead. By his side was a cup of water, and a small morsel of mouldy bread, which he had pushed out of his reach, and could not move to obtain. Over against his bed were these words, copied in the English version: 'Therefore, if thine enemy hunger, feed him; if he thirst, give him drink.'

Some of us gave him of our food, and left him eating greedily, like some famished wild animal. For now it was no longer the sharp tinkle, but that one solemn toll, which in all Christian countries tells of the passing of the spirit out of earthly life into eternity; and again a murmur gathered and grew, as of many people speaking with awed breath, 'A Poor Clare is dying! a Poor Clare is dead!'

Borne along once more by the motion of the crowd, we were carried into the chapel belonging to the Poor Clares. On a bier before the high altar, lay a woman – lay sister Magdalen – lay Bridget Fitzgerald. By her side stood Father Bernard, in his robes of office, and holding the crucifix on high while he pronounced the solemn absolution of the Church, as to one who had newly confessed herself of deadly sin. I pushed on with passionate force, till I stood close to the dying woman, as she received extreme unction amid the breathless and awed hush of the multitude around. Her eyes were glazing, her limbs were stiffening; but when the rite was over and finished, she raised her gaunt figure slowly up, and her eyes brightened to a strange intensity of joy, as, with the gesture of her finger and the trance-like gleam of her eye, she seemed like one who watched the disappearance of some loathed and fearful creature.

'She is freed from the curse!' said she, as she fell back dead.

Lois the Witch

Chapter 1

In the year 1691, Lois Barclay stood on a little wooden pier, steadying herself on the stable land, in much the same manner as, eight or nine weeks ago, she had tried to steady herself on the deck of the rocking ship which had carried her across from Old to New England. It seemed as strange now to be on solid earth as it had been, not long ago, to be rocked by the sea, both by day and by night; and the aspect of the land was equally strange. The forests which showed in the distance all round, and which, in truth, were not very far from the wooden houses forming the town of Boston, were of different shades of green, and different, too, in shape of outline to those which Lois Barclay knew well in her old home in Warwickshire. Her heart sank a little as she stood alone, waiting for the captain of the good ship *Redemption*, the kind rough old sailor, who was her only known friend in this unknown continent. Captain Holdernesse was busy, however, as she saw, and it would probably be some time before he would be ready to attend to her; so Lois sat down on one of the casks that lay about, and wrapped her grey duffle cloak tight around her, and sheltered herself under her hood, as well as might be, from the piercing wind, which seemed to follow those whom it had tyrannised over at sea with a dogged wish of still tormenting them on land. Very patiently did Lois sit there, although she was weary, and shivering with cold; for the day was severe for May, and the *Redemption*, with store of necessaries and comforts for the Puritan colonists of New England, was the earliest ship that had ventured across the seas.

How could Lois help thinking of the past, and speculating on the future, as she sat on Boston pier, at this breathing-time of her life? In the dim sea-mist which she gazed upon with aching eyes (filled, against her will, with tears, from time to time), there rose the little village church of Barford (not three miles from Warwick – you may see it yet), where her father had preached ever since 1661, long before she was born. He and her mother both lay dead in Barford churchyard; and the old low grey church could hardly come before her vision without her seeing the old parsonage too, the cottage covered with Austrian roses, and yellow jessamine, where she had been born, sole child of parents already long past the prime of youth. She saw the path, not a hundred yards long, from the parsonage to the vestry door: that path which her father trod daily; for the vestry was his study, and the sanctum, where he pored over the ponderous tomes of the Father, and compared their precepts with those of the authorities of the Anglican Church of that day – the day of the later Stuarts; for Barford Parsonage at that time scarcely exceeded in size and dignity the cottages by which it was surrounded: it only contained three rooms on a floor, and was but two storeys high. On the first, or ground floor, were the parlour, kitchen, and back or working kitchen; upstairs, Mr and Mrs Barclay's room, that belonging to Lois, and the maid-servant's room. If a guest came, Lois left her own chamber, and shared old Clemence's bed. But those days were over. Never more should Lois see father or mother on earth; they slept, calm and still, in Barford churchyard, careless of what became of their orphan child, as far as earthly manifestations of care or love went. And Clemence lay there too, bound down in her grassy bed by withies of the briar-rose, which Lois had trained over those three precious graves before leaving England for ever.

There were some who would fain have kept her there; one who swore in his heart a great oath unto the Lord that he would seek her sooner or later, if she was still upon the earth. But he was the rich heir and only son of the Miller Lucy, whose mill stood by the Avonside in the grassy Barford meadows, and his father looked higher for him than the penniless daughter of Parson Barclay (so low were clergymen esteemed in those days!); and the very suspicion of Hugh Lucy's attachment to Lois Barclay made his parents think it more prudent not to offer the orphan a home, although none other of the parishioners had the means, even if they had the will, to do so.

So Lois swallowed her tears down till the time came for crying, and acted upon her mother's words.

'Lois, thy father is dead of this terrible fever, and I am dying. Nay, it is so, though I am easier from pain for these few hours, the Lord be praised! The cruel men of the Commonwealth have left thee very friendless. Thy father's only brother was shot down at Edgehill. I, too, have a brother, though thou hast never heard me speak of him, for he was a schismatic; and thy father and he had words, and he left for that new country beyond the seas, without ever saying farewell to

us. But Ralph was a kind lad until he took up these new-fangled
notions, and for the old days' sake he will take thee in, and love thee
as a child, and place thee among his children. Blood is thicker than
water. Write to him as soon as I am gone – for Lois, I am going – and
I bless the Lord that has letten me join my husband again so soon.'
Such was the selfishness of conjugal love; she thought little of Lois's
desolation in comparison with her rejoicing over her speedy reunion
with her dead husband! 'Write to thine uncle, Ralph Hickson, Salem,
New England (put it down, child, on thy tablets), and say that I,
Henrietta Barclay, charge him, for the sake of all he holds dear in
heaven or on earth – for his salvation's sake, as well as for the sake
of the old home at Lester-bridge – for the sake of the father and
mother that gave us birth, as well as for the sake of the six little
children who lie dead between him and me – that he take thee into
his home as if thou wert his own flesh and blood, as indeed thou art.
He has a wife and children of his own, and no-one need fear having
thee, my Lois, my darling, my baby, among his household. Oh, Lois,
would that thou wert dying with me! The thought of thee makes
death sore!' Lois comforted her mother more than herself, poor
child, by promises to obey her dying wishes to the letter, and by
expressing hopes she dared not feel of her uncle's kindness.

'Promise me' – the dying woman's breath came harder and harder –
'that thou wilt go at once. The money our goods will bring – the letter
thy father wrote to Captain Holdernesse, his old schoolfellow – thou
knowest all I would say – my Lois, God bless thee!'

Solemnly did Lois promise; strictly she kept her word. It was all the
more easy, for Hugh Lucy met her, and told her, in one great burst of
love, of his passionate attachment, his vehement struggles with his
father, his impotence at present, his hope and resolves for the future.
And, intermingled with all this, came such outrageous threats and
expressions of uncontrolled vehemence, that Lois felt that in Barford
she must not linger to be a cause of desperate quarrel between father
and son, while her absence might soften down matters, so that either
the rich old miller might relent, or – and her heart ached to think of
the other possibility – Hugh's love might cool, and the dear playfellow of her childhood learn to forget. If not – if Hugh were to be
trusted in one tithe of what he said – God might permit him to fulfil
his resolve of coming to seek her out before many years were over. It
was all in God's hands, and that was best, thought Lois Barclay.

She was roused out of her trance of recollections by Captain
Holdernesse, who, having done all that was necessary in the way of

orders and directions to his mate, now came up to her, and, praising her for her quiet patience, told her that he would now take her to the Widow Smith's, a decent kind of house, where he and many other sailors of the better order were in the habit of lodging, during their stay on the New England shores. Widow Smith, he said, had a parlour for herself and her daughters, in which Lois might sit, while he went about the business that, as he had told her, would detain him in Boston for a day or two, before he could accompany her to her uncle's at Salem. All this had been to a certain degree arranged on ship-board; but Captain Holdernesse, for want of anything else that he could think of to talk about, recapitulated it as he and Lois walked along. It was his way of showing sympathy with the emotion that made her grey eyes full of tears, as she started up from the pier at the sound of his voice. In his heart he said, 'Poor wench! poor wench! it's a strange land to her, and they are all strange folks, and, I reckon, she will be feeling desolate. I'll try and cheer her up.' So he talked on about hard facts, connected with the life that lay before her, until they reached Widow Smith's; and perhaps Lois was more brightened by this style of conversation, and the new ideas it presented to her, than she would have been by the tenderest woman's sympathy.

'They are a queer set, these New Englanders,' said Captain Holdernesse. 'They are rare chaps for praying; down on their knees at every turn of their life. Folk are none so busy in a new country, else they would have to pray like me, with a "Yo-hoy!" on each side of my prayers, and a rope cutting like fire through my hand. Yon pilot was for calling us all to thanksgiving for a good voyage, and lucky escape from the pirates; but I said I always put up my thanks on dry land, after I had got my ship into harbour. The French colonists, too, are vowing vengeance for the expedition against Canada, and the people here are raging like heathens – at least, as like as godly folk can be – for the loss of their charter. All that is the news the pilot told me; for, for all he wanted us to be thanksgiving instead of casting the lead, he was as down in the mouth as could be about the state of the country. But here we are at Widow Smith's! Now, cheer up, and show the godly a pretty smiling Warwickshire lass!'

Anybody would have smiled at Widow Smith's greeting. She was a comely, motherly woman, dressed in the primmest fashion in vogue twenty years before, in England, among the class to which she belonged. But, somehow, her pleasant face gave the lie to her dress; were it as brown and sober-coloured as could be, folk remembered it bright and cheerful, because it was a part of Widow Smith herself.

She kissed Lois on both cheeks, before she rightly understood who the stranger maiden was, only because she was a stranger, and looked sad and forlorn; and then she kissed her again, because Captain Holdernesse commended her to the widow's good offices. And so she led Lois by the hand into her rough, substantial log-house, over the door of which hung a great bough of a tree, by way of sign of entertainment for man and horse. Yet not all men were received by Widow Smith. To some she could be as cold and reserved as need be, deaf to all inquiries save one – where else they could find accommodation? To this question she would give a ready answer, and speed the unwelcome guest on his way. Widow Smith was guided in these matters by instinct: one glance at a man's face told her whether or not she chose to have him as an inmate of the same house as her daughters; and her promptness of decision in these matters gave her manner a kind of authority which no-one liked to disobey, especially as she had stalwart neighbours within call to back her, if her assumed deafness in the first instance, and her voice and gesture in the second, were not enough to give the would-be guest his dismissal. Widow Smith chose her customers merely by their physical aspect; not one whit with regard to their apparent worldly circumstances. Those who had been staying at her house once, always came again, for she had the knack of making everyone beneath her roof comfortable and at his ease. Her daughters, Prudence and Hester, had somewhat of their mother's gifts, but not in such perfection. They reasoned a little upon a stranger's appearance, instead of knowing at the first moment whether they liked him or no; they noticed the indications of his clothes, the quality and cut thereof, as telling somewhat of his station in society; they were more reserved, they hesitated more than their mother; they had not her prompt authority, her happy power. Their bread was not so light, their cream went sometimes to sleep when it should have been turning into butter, their hams were not always 'just like the hams of the old country', as their mother's were invariably pronounced to be; yet they were good, orderly, kindly girls, and rose and greeted Lois with a friendly shake of the hand, as their mother, with her arm round the stranger's waist, led her into the private room which she called her parlour. The aspect of this room was strange in the English girl's eyes. The logs of which the house was built, showed here and there through the mud plaster, although before both plaster and logs were hung the skins of many curious animals – skins presented to the widow by many a trader of her acquaintance, just as her sailor guests brought her another description of gift – shells, strings of wampum-beads, sea-birds' eggs, and presents from the old country. The room was more like a small museum of natural history of these days than a parlour; and it had a strange, peculiar, but not unpleasant smell about it, neutralised in some degree by the smoke from the enormous trunk of pinewood which smouldered on the hearth.

The instant their mother told them that Captain Holdernesse was in the outer room, the girls began putting away their spinning-wheel and knitting-needles, and preparing for a meal of some kind; what meal, Lois, sitting there and unconsciously watching, could hardly tell. First, dough was set to rise for cakes; then came out of a corner cupboard – a present from England – an enormous square bottle of a cordial called Golden Wasser; next, a mill for grinding chocolate – a rare unusual treat anywhere at that time; then a great Cheshire cheese. Three venison steaks were cut ready for broiling, fat cold pork sliced up and treacle poured over it, a great pie something like a mince-pie, but which the daughters spoke of with honour as the 'punken-pie', fresh and salt fish brandered, oysters cooked in various ways. Lois wondered where would be the end of the provisions for hospitably receiving the strangers from the old country. At length everything was placed on the table, the hot food smoking; but all was cool, not to say cold, before Elder Hawkins (an old neighbour of much repute and standing, who had been invited in by Widow Smith to hear the news) had finished his grace, into which was embodied thanksgivings for the past and prayers for the future lives of every individual present, adapted to their several cases, as far as the elder could guess at them from appearances. This grace might not have ended so soon as it did, had it not been for the somewhat impatient drumming of his knife-handle on the table with which Captain Holdernesse accompanied the latter half of the elder's words.

When they first sat down to their meal, all were too hungry for much talking; but as their appetites diminished their curiosity in-creased, and there was much to be told and heard on both sides. With all the English intelligence Lois was, of course, well acquainted; but she listened with natural attention to all that was said about the new country, and the new people among whom she had come to live. Her father had been a Jacobite, as the adherents of the Stuarts were beginning at this time to be called. His father, again, had been a follower of Archbishop Laud; so Lois had hitherto heard little of the conversation, and seen little of the ways of the Puritans. Elder Hawkins was one of the strictest of the strict, and evidently his presence kept the two daughters of the house considerably in awe. But the widow herself was a privileged person; her known goodness of heart (the effects of which had been experienced by many) gave her the liberty of speech which was tacitly denied to many, under penalty of being esteemed ungodly if they infringed certain conventional limits. And Captain Holdernesse and his mate spoke out their minds, let who would be present. So that on this first landing in New England, Lois was, as it were, gently let down into the midst of the Puritan peculiarities, and yet they were sufficient to make her feel very lonely and strange.

The first subject of conversation was the present state of the colony – Lois soon found out that, although at the beginning she was not a little perplexed by the frequent reference to names of places which she naturally associated with the old country. Widow Smith was speaking: 'In the county of Essex the folk are ordered to keep four scouts, or companies of minute-men, six persons in each company, to be on the look-out for the wild Indians, who are for ever stirring about in the woods, stealthy brutes as they are! I am sure, I got such a fright the first harvest-time after I came over to New England, I go on dreaming, now near twenty years after Lothrop's business, of painted Indians, with their shaven scalps and their war-streaks, lurking behind the trees, and coming nearer and nearer with their noiseless steps.'

'Yes,' broke in one of her daughters; 'and, mother, don't you remember how Hannah Benson told us how her husband had cut down every tree near his house at Deerbrook, in order that no-one might come near him, under cover; and how one evening she was a-sitting in the twilight, when all her family were gone to bed, and her husband gone off to Plymouth on business, and she saw a log of wood, just like a trunk of a felled tree, lying in the shadow, and thought nothing of it, till, on looking again a while after, she fancied it was come a bit nearer to the house, and how her heart turned sick with fright, and how she dared not stir at first, but shut her eyes while she counted a hundred, and looked again, and the shadow was deeper, but she could see that the log was nearer; so she ran in and bolted the door, and went up to where her eldest lad lay. It was Elijah, and he was but sixteen then; but he rose up at his mother's words, and took his father's long duck-gun down, and he tried the loading, and spoke for the first time to put up a prayer that God would give his aim good guidance, and went to a window that gave a view upon the side where the log lay, and fired, and no-one dared to look what came of it, but all the household read the Scriptures, and prayed the whole night long, till morning came and showed a long stream of blood lying on the grass close by the log, which the full sunlight showed to be no log at all, but just a Red Indian covered with bark, and painted most skilfully, with his war-knife by his side.'

All were breathless with listening, though to most the story, or such like it, were familiar. Then another took up the tale of horror.

'And the pirates have been down at Marblehead since you were here, Captain Holdernesse. 'Twas only the last winter they landed – French Papist pirates; and the people kept close within their houses, for they knew not what would come of it; and they dragged folk ashore. There was one woman among those folk – prisoners from some vessel, doubtless – and the pirates took them by force to the inland marsh; and the Marblehead folk kept still and quiet, every gun loaded, and every ear on the watch, for who knew but what the wild sea-robbers might take a turn on land next; and, in the dead of the night, they heard a woman's loud and pitiful outcry from the marsh, 'Lord Jesu! have mercy on me! Save me from the power of man, O Lord Jesu!' And the blood of all who heard the cry ran cold with terror, till old Nance Hickson, who had been stone-deaf and bed-ridden for years, stood up in the midst of the folk all gathered together in her grandson's house, and said, that as they, the dwellers in Marblehead, had not had brave hearts or faith enough to go and succour the helpless, that cry of a dying woman should be in their ears, and in their children's ears, till the end of the world. And Nance dropped down dead as soon as she had made an end of speaking, and the pirates set sail from Marblehead at morning dawn; but the folk there hear the cry still, shrill and pitiful, from the waste marshes, "Lord Jesu! have mercy on me! Save me from the power of man, O Lord Jesu!"'

'And by token,' said Elder Hawkins's deep bass voice, speaking with the strong nasal twang of the Puritans (who, says Butler, 'blasphemed custard through the nose'), 'godly Mr Noyes ordained a fast at Marblehead, and preached a soul-stirring discourse on the words; "Inasmuch as ye did it not unto one of the least of these, my brethren, ye did it not unto me." But it has been borne in upon me at times, whether the whole vision of the pirates and the cry of the woman was not a device of Satan's to sift the Marblehead folk, and see what fruit their doctrine bore, and so to condemn them in the sight of the Lord. If it were so, the enemy had a great triumph, for assuredly it was no part of Christian men to leave a helpless woman unaided in her sore distress.'

'But, Elder,' said Widow Smith, 'it was no vision; they were real living men who went ashore, men who broke down branches and left their footmarks on the ground.'

'As for that matter, Satan hath many powers, and if it be the day when he is permitted to go about like a roaring lion, he will not stick at trifles, but make his work complete. I tell you, many men are spiritual enemies in visible forms, permitted to roam about the waste places of the earth. I myself believe that these Red Indians are indeed the evil creatures of whom we read in Holy Scripture; and there is no doubt that they are in league with those abominable Papists, the French people in Canada. I have heard tell, that the French pay the Indians so much gold for every dozen scalps off Englishmen's heads.'

'Pretty cheerful talk this,' said Captain Holdernesse to Lois, perceiving her blanched cheek and terror-stricken mien. 'Thou art thinking that thou hadst better have stayed at Barford, I'll answer for it, wench. But the devil is not so black as he is painted.'

'Ho! there again!' said Elder Hawkins. 'The devil is painted, it hath been said so from old times; and are not these Indians painted, even like unto their father?'

'But is it all true?' asked Lois, aside, of Captain Holdernesse, letting the elder hold forth unheeded by her, though listened to, however, with the utmost reverence by the two daughters of the house.

'My wench,' said the old sailor, 'thou hast come to a country where there are many perils, both from land and from sea. The Indians hate the white men. Whether other white men' (meaning the French away to the north) 'have hounded on the savages, or whether the English have taken their lands and hunting-grounds without due recompense, and so raised the cruel vengeance of the wild creatures – who knows? But it is true that it is not safe to go far into the woods, for fear of the lurking painted savages; nor has it been safe to build a dwelling far from a settlement; and it takes a brave heart to make a journey from one town to another, and folk do say the Indian creatures rise up out of the very ground to waylay the English; and then others affirm they are all in league with Satan to affright the Christians out of the heathen country over which he has reigned so long. Then, again, the seashore is infested by pirates, the scum of all nations: they land, and plunder, and ravage, and burn, and destroy. Folk get affrighted of the real dangers, and in their fright imagine, perchance, dangers that are not. But who knows? Holy Scripture speaks of witches and wizards, and of the power of the Evil One in desert places; and even in the old country we have heard tell of those who have sold their souls for ever for the little power they get for a few years on earth.'

By this time the whole table was silent, listening to the captain; it was just one of those chance silences that sometimes occur, without any apparent reason, and often without any apparent consequence. But all present had reason, before many months had passed over, to remember the words which Lois spoke in answer, although her voice was low, and she only thought, in the interest of the moment, of being heard by her old friend the captain.

'They are fearful creatures, the witches! and yet I am sorry for the poor old women, whilst I dread them. We had one in Barford, when I was a little child. No-one knew whence she came, but she settled herself down in a mud hut by the common side; and there she lived, she and her cat.' (At the mention of the cat, Elder Hawkins shook his head long and gloomily.) 'No-one knew how she lived, if it were not on nettles and scraps of oatmeal and such-like food given her more for fear than for pity. She went double, always talking and muttering to herself. Folk said she snared birds and rabbits, in the thicket that came down to her hovel. How it came to pass I cannot say, but many a one fell sick in the village, and much cattle died one spring, when I was near four years old. I never heard much about it, for my father said it was ill talking about such things; I only know I got a sick fright one afternoon, when the maid had gone out for milk and had taken me with her, and we were passing a meadow where the Avon, circling, makes a deep round pool, and there was a crowd of folk, all still – and a still, breathless crowd makes the heart beat worse than a shouting, noisy one. They were all gazing towards the water, and the maid held me up in her arms to see the sight above the shoulders of the people; and I saw old Hannah in the water, her grey hair all streaming down her shoulders, and her face bloody and black with the stones and the mud they had been throwing at her, and her cat tied round her neck. I hid my face, I know, as soon as I saw the fearsome sight, for her eyes met mine as they were glaring with fury – poor, helpless, baited creature! – and she caught the sight of me, and cried out, "Parson's wench, parson's wench, yonder, in thy nurse's arms, thy dad hath never tried for to save me, and none shall save thee when thou art brought up for a witch." Oh! the words rang in my ears, when I was dropping asleep, for years after. I used to dream that I was in that pond, all men hating me with their eyes because I was a witch; and, at times, her black cat used to seem living again, and say over those dreadful words.'

Lois stopped: the two daughters looked at her excitement with a kind of shrinking surprise, for the tears were in her eyes. Elder Hawkins shook his head, and muttered texts from Scripture; but cheerful Widow Smith, not liking the gloomy turn of the conversation, tried to give it a lighter cast by saying, 'And I don't doubt but what the parson's bonny lass has bewitched many a one since, with her dimples and her pleasant ways – eh, Captain Holdernesse? It's you must tell us tales of this young lass's doings in England.'

'Ay, ay,' said the captain, 'there's one under her charms in Warwickshire who will never get the better of it, I'm thinking.'

Elder Hawkins rose to speak; he stood leaning on his hands, which were placed on the table: 'Brethren,' said he, 'I must upbraid you if ye speak lightly; charms and witchcraft are evil things. I trust this maiden hath had nothing to do with them, even in thought. But my mind misgives me at her story. The hellish witch might have power from Satan to infect her mind, she being yet a child, with the deadly sin. Instead of vain talking, I call upon you all to join with me in prayer for this stranger in our land, that her heart may be purged from all iniquity. Let us pray.'

'Come, there's no harm in that,' said the captain; 'but, Elder Hawkins, when you are at work, just pray for us all, for I am afeard there be some of us need purging from iniquity a good deal more than Lois Barclay, and a prayer for a man never does mischief.'

Captain Holdernesse had business in Boston which detained him there for a couple of days, and during that time Lois remained with the Widow Smith, seeing what was to be seen of the new land that contained her future home. The letter of her dying mother was sent off to Salem, meanwhile, by a lad going thither, in order to prepare her Uncle Ralph Hickson for his niece's coming, as soon as Captain Holdernesse could find leisure to take her; for he considered her given into his own personal charge, until he could consign her to her uncle's care. When the time came for going to Salem, Lois felt very sad at leaving the kindly woman under whose roof she had been staying, and looked back as long as she could see anything of Widow Smith's dwelling. She was packed into a rough kind of country cart, which just held her and Captain Holdernesse, beside the driver. There was a basket of provisions under their feet, and behind them hung a bag of provender for the horse; for it was a good day's journey to Salem, and the road was reputed so dangerous that it was ill tarrying a minute longer than necessary for refreshment. English roads were bad enough at that period and for long after, but in America the way was simply the cleared ground of the forest; the stumps of the felled trees still remaining in the direct line, forming obstacles, which it required the most careful driving to avoid; and in the hollows, where the ground was swampy, the pulpy nature of it was obviated by logs of wood laid across the boggy part. The deep green forest, tangled into heavy darkness even thus early in the year, came within a few yards of the road all the way, though efforts were regularly made by the inhabitants of the neighbouring settlements to keep a certain space clear on each side, for fear of the lurking Indians, who might otherwise come upon them unawares. The cries of strange birds, the unwonted colour of some of them, all suggested to the imaginative or unaccustomed traveller the idea of war-whoops and painted deadly enemies. But at last they drew near to Salem, which rivalled Boston in size in those days, and boasted the name of one or two streets, although to an English eye they looked rather more like irregularly built houses, clustered round the meeting-house, or rather one of the meeting-houses, for a second was in process of building. The whole place was surrounded with two circles of stockades; between the two were the gardens and grazing ground for those who dreaded their cattle straying into the woods, and the consequent danger of reclaiming them.

The lad who drove them flogged his spent horse into a trot, as they went through Salem to Ralph Hickson's house. It was evening, the leisure time for the inhabitants, and their children were at play before the houses. Lois was struck by the beauty of one wee toddling child, and turned to look after it; it caught its little foot in a stump of wood, and fell with a cry that brought the mother out in affright. As she ran out, her eye caught Lois's anxious gaze, although the noise of the heavy wheels drowned the sound of her words of inquiry as to the nature of the hurt the child had received. Nor had Lois time to think long upon the matter, for the instant after, the horse was pulled up at the door of a good, square, substantial wooden house, plastered over into a creamy white, perhaps as handsome a house as any in Salem; and there she was told by the driver that her uncle, Ralph Hickson, lived. In the flurry of the moment she did not notice, but Captain Holdernesse did, that no-one came out at the unwonted sound of wheels, to receive and welcome her. She was lifted down by the old sailor, and led into a large room, almost like the hall of some English manor-house as to size. A tall, gaunt young man of three or four and twenty, sat on a bench by one of the windows, reading a great folio by the fading light of day. He did not rise when they came in, but looked at them with surprise, no gleam of intelligence coming into his stern, dark face. There was no woman in the house-place. Captain Holdernesse paused a moment, and then said: 'Is this house Ralph Hickson's?'

'It is,' said the young man, in a slow, deep voice. But he added no word further.

'This is his niece, Lois Barclay,' said the captain, taking the girl's arm, and pushing her forwards. The young man looked at her steadily and gravely for a minute; then rose, and carefully marking the page in the folio which hitherto had lain open upon his knee, said, still in the same heavy, indifferent manner, 'I will call my mother, she will know.'

He opened a door which looked into a warm bright kitchen, ruddy with the light of the fire over which three women were apparently engaged in cooking something, while a fourth, an old Indian woman, of a greenish-brown colour, shrivelled up and bent with apparent age, moved backwards and forwards, evidently fetching the others the articles they required.

'Mother,' said the young man; and having arrested her attention, he pointed over his shoulder to the newly-arrived strangers, and returned to the study of his book, from time to time, however, furtively examining Lois from beneath his dark shaggy eyebrows.

A tall, largely made woman, past middle life, came in from the kitchen, and stood reconnoitring the strangers.

Captain Holdernesse spoke.

'This is Lois Barclay, Master Ralph Hickson's niece.'

'I know nothing of her,' said the mistress of the house, in a deep voice, almost as masculine as her son's.

'Master Hickson received his sister's letter, did he not? I sent it off myself by a lad named Elias Wellcome, who left Boston for this place yester morning.'

'Ralph Hickson has received no such letter. He lies bedridden in the chamber beyond. Any letters for him must come through my hands; wherefore I can affirm with certainty that no such letter has been delivered here. His sister Barclay, she that was Henrietta Hickson, and whose husband took the oaths to Charles Stuart, and stuck by his living when all godly men left theirs – '

Lois, who had thought her heart was dead and cold a minute before at the ungracious reception she had met with, felt words come up into her mouth at the implied insult to her father, and spoke out, to her own and the captain's astonishment: 'They might be godly men who left their churches on that day of which you speak, madam; but they alone were not the godly men, and no-one has a right to limit true godliness for mere opinion's sake.'

'Well said, lass,' spoke out the captain, looking round upon her with a kind of admiring wonder, and patting her on the back.

Lois and her aunt gazed into each other's eyes unflinchingly, for a minute or two of silence; but the girl felt her colour coming and going, while the elder woman's never varied; and the eyes of the young maiden were filling fast with tears, while those of Grace Hickson kept on their stare, dry and unwavering.

'Mother!' said the young man, rising up with a quicker motion than anyone had yet used in this house, 'it is ill speaking of such matters when my cousin comes first among us. The Lord may give her grace hereafter, but she has travelled from Boston city today, and she and this seafaring man must need rest and food.'

He did not attend to see the effect of his words, but sat down again, and seemed to be absorbed in his book in an instant. Perhaps he knew that his word was law with his grim mother, for he had hardly ceased speaking before she had pointed to a wooden settle; and smoothing the lines on her countenance, she said, 'What Manasseh says is true. Sit down here, while I bid Faith and Nattee get food ready; and meanwhile I will go tell my husband, that one who calls herself his sister's child is come over to pay him a visit.'

She went to the door leading into the kitchen, and gave some directions to the elder girl, whom Lois now knew to be the daughter of the house. Faith stood impassive, while her mother spoke, scarcely caring to look at the newly-arrived strangers. She was like her brother Manasseh in complexion, but had handsomer features, and large, mysterious-looking eyes, as Lois saw, when once she lifted them up, and took in, as it were, the aspect of the sea-captain and her cousin with one swift searching look. About the stiff, tall, angular mother, and the scarce less pliant figure of the daughter, a girl of twelve years old, or thereabouts, played all manner of impish antics, unheeded by them, as if it were her accustomed habit to peep about, now under their arms, now at this side, now at that, making grimaces all the while at Lois and Captain Holdernesse, who sat facing the door, weary, and somewhat disheartened by their reception. The captain pulled out tobacco, and began to chew it by way of consolation; but in a moment or two, his usual elasticity of spirit came to his rescue, and he said in a low voice to Lois: 'That scoundrel Elias, I will give it him! If the letter had but been delivered, thou wouldst have had a different kind of welcome; but as soon as I have had some victuals, I will go out and find the lad, and bring back the letter, and that will make all right, my wench. Nay, don't be downhearted, for I cannot stand women's tears. Thou'rt just worn out with the shaking and the want of food.'

Lois brushed away her tears, and looking round to try and divert her thoughts by fixing them on present object, she caught her cousin Manasseh's deep-set eyes furtively watching her. It was with no unfriendly gaze, yet it made Lois uncomfortable, particularly as he did not withdraw his looks after he must have seen that she observed him. She was glad when her aunt called her into an inner room to see her uncle, and she escaped from the steady observance of her gloomy, silent cousin.

Ralph Hickson was much older than his wife, and his illness made him look older still. He had never had the force of character that Grace, his spouse, possessed, and age and sickness had now rendered him almost childish at times. But his nature was affectionate, and stretching out his trembling arms from where he lay bedridden, he gave Lois an unhesitating welcome, never waiting for the confirmation of the missing letter before he acknowledged her to be his niece.

'Oh! 'tis kind in thee to come all across the sea to make acquaintance with thine uncle; kind in Sister Barclay to spare thee!'

Lois had to tell him that there was no-one living to miss her at home in England; that in fact she had no home in England, no father nor mother left upon earth; and that she had been bidden by her mother's last words to seek him out, and ask him for a home. Her words came up, half choked from a heavy heart, and his dulled wits could not take their meaning in without several repetitions; and then he cried like a child, rather at his own loss of a sister, whom he had not seen for more than twenty years, than at that of the orphan's standing before him, trying hard not to cry, but to start bravely in this new strange home. What most of all helped Lois in her self-restraint was her aunt's unsympathetic look. Born and bred in New England, Grace Hickson had a kind of jealous dislike to her husband's English relations, which had increased since of late years his weakened mind yearned after them, and he forgot the good reason he had had for his self-exile, and moaned over the decision which had led to it as the great mistake of his life. 'Come,' said she, 'it strikes me that, in all this sorrow for the loss of one who died full of years, ye are forgetting in Whose hands life and death are!'

True words, but ill-spoken at that time. Lois looked up at her with a scarcely disguised indignation; which increased as she heard the contemptuous tone in which her aunt went on talking to Ralph Hickson, even while she was arranging his bed with a regard to his greater comfort.

'One would think thou wert a godless man, by the moan thou art always making over spilt milk; and truth is, thou art but childish in thine old age. When we were wed, thou left all things to the Lord; I would never have married thee else. Nay, lass,' said she, catching the expression on Lois's face, 'thou art never going to browbeat me with thine angry looks. I do my duty as I read it, and there is never a man in Salem that dare speak a word to Grace Hickson about either her works or her faith. Godly Mr Cotton Mather hath said, that even he might learn of me; and I would advise thee rather to humble thyself, and see if the Lord may not convert thee from thy ways, since he has sent thee to dwell, as it were, in Zion, where the precious dew falls daily on Aaron's beard.'

Lois felt ashamed and sorry to find that her aunt had so truly interpreted the momentary expression of her features; she blamed herself a little for the feeling that had caused that expression, trying to think how much her aunt might have been troubled with something before the unexpected irruption of the strangers, and again hoping that the remembrance of this little misunderstanding would soon pass away. So she endeavoured to reassure herself, and not to give way to her uncle's tender trembling pressure of her hand, as, at her aunt's bidding, she wished him good night, and returned into the outer, or 'keeping'-room, where all the family were now assembled, ready for the meal of flour cakes and venison-steaks which Nattee, the Indian servant, was bringing in from the kitchen. No-one seemed to have been speaking to Captain Holdernesse while Lois had been away. Manasseh sat quiet and silent where he did, with the book open upon his knee, his eyes thoughtfully fixed on vacancy, as if he saw a vision, or dreamed dreams. Faith stood by the table, lazily directing Nattee in her preparations; and Prudence lolled against the door-frame, between kitchen and keeping-room, playing tricks on the old Indian woman as she passed backwards and forwards, till Nattee appeared to be in a strong state of expressed irritation, which she tried in vain to repress, as whenever she showed any sign of it, Prudence only seemed excited to greater mischief. When all was ready, Manasseh lifted his right hand, and 'asked a blessing,' as it was termed; but the grace became a long prayer for abstract spiritual blessings, for strength to combat Satan, and to quench his fiery darts, and at length assumed, so Lois thought, a purely personal character, as if the young man had forgotten the occasion, and even the people present, but was searching into the nature of the diseases that beset his own sick soul, and spreading them out before the Lord. He was brought back by a pluck at the coat from Prudence; he opened his shut eyes, cast an angry glance at the child, who made a face at him for sole reply, and then he sat down, and they all fell to. Grace Hickson would have thought her hospitality sadly at fault, if she had allowed Captain Holdernesse to go out in search of a bed. Skins were spread for him on the floor of the keeping-room; a Bible, and a square bottle of spirits were placed on the table, to supply his wants during the night; and in spite of all the cares and troubles, tempt-ations, or sins of the members of that household, they were all asleep before the town clock struck ten.

In the morning, the captain's first care was to go out in search of the boy Elias, and the missing letter. He met him bringing it with an easy conscience, for, thought Elias, a few hours sooner or later will make no difference; tonight or the morrow morning will be all the same. But he was startled into a sense of wrongdoing by a sound box on the ear, from the very man who had charged him to deliver it speedily, and whom he believed to be at that very moment in Boston city.

The letter delivered, all possible proof being given that Lois had a right to claim a home from her nearest relations, Captain Holder-nesse thought it best to take leave.

'Thou'lt take to them, lass, maybe, when there is no-one here to make thee think on the old country. Nay, nay! parting is hard work at all times, and best get hard work done out of hand. Keep up thine heart, my wench, and I'll come back and see thee next spring, if we are all spared till then; and who knows what fine young miller mayn't come with me? Don't go and get wed to a praying Puritan, mean-while. There, there – I'm off! God bless thee!'

And Lois was left alone in New England.

Chapter 2

It was hard uphill work for Lois to win herself a place in this family. Her aunt was a woman of narrow, strong affections. Her love for her husband, if ever she had any, was burnt out and dead long ago. What she did for him she did from duty; but duty was not strong enough to restrain that little member the tongue; and Lois's heart often bled at the continual flow of contemptuous reproof which Grace constantly addressed to her husband, even while she was sparing no pains or trouble to minister to his bodily ease and comfort. It was more as a relief to herself that she spoke in this way, than with any desire that her speeches should affect him; and he was too deadened by illness to feel hurt by them; or, it may be, the constant repetition of her sarcasms had made him indifferent; at any rate, so that he had his food and his state of bodily warmth attended to, he very seldom seemed to care much for anything else. Even his first flow of affection towards Lois was soon exhausted; he cared for her because she arranged his pillows well and skilfully, and because she could prepare new and dainty kinds of food for his sick appetite, but no longer for her as his dead sister's child. Still he did care for her, and Lois was too glad of this little hoard of affection to examine how or why it was given. To him she could give pleasure, but apparently to no-one else in that household. Her aunt looked askance at her for many reasons: the first coming of Lois to Salem was inopportune, the expression of disapprobation on her face on that evening still lingered and rankled in Grace's memory, early prejudices, and feelings, and prepossessions of the English girl were all on the side of what would now be called Church and State, what was then esteemed in that country a superstitious observance of the directions of a Popish rubric, and a servile regard for the family of an oppressing and irreligious king. Nor is it to be supposed that Lois did not feel, and feel acutely, the want of sympathy that all those with whom she was now living manifested towards the old hereditary loyalty (religious as well as political loyalty) in which she had been brought up. With her aunt and Manasseh it was more than want of sympathy; it was positive, active antipathy to all the ideas Lois held most dear. The very allusion, however incidentally made, to the little old grey church at Barford, where her father had preached so long – the occasional reference to the troubles in which her own country had been distracted when she left – and the adherence, in which she had been brought up, to the notion that the king could do no wrong, seemed to irritate Manasseh past endurance. He would get up from his reading, his constant employment when at home, and walk angrily about the room after Lois had said anything of this kind, muttering to himself; and once he had even stopped before her, and in a passionate tone bade her not talk so like a fool. Now this was very different to his mother's sarcastic, contemptuous way of treating all poor Lois's little loyal speeches. Grace would lead her on – at least she did at first, till experience made Lois wiser – to express her thoughts on such subjects, till, just when the girl's heart was opening, her aunt would turn round upon her with some bitter sneer that roused all the evil feelings in Lois's disposition by its sting. Now Manasseh seemed, through all his anger, to be so really grieved by what he considered her error, that he went much nearer to convincing her that there might be two sides to a question. Only this was a view that it appeared like treachery to her dead father's memory to entertain.

Somehow, Lois felt instinctively that Manasseh was really friendly towards her. He was little in the house; there was farming, and some kind of mercantile business to be transacted by him, as real head of the house; and as the season drew on, he went shooting and hunting in the surrounding forests, with a daring which caused his mother to warn and reprove him in private, although to the neighbours she boasted largely of her son's courage and disregard of danger. Lois did not often walk out for the mere sake of walking, there was generally some household errand to be transacted when any of the women of the family went abroad; but once or twice she had caught glimpses of the dreary, dark wood, hemming in the cleared land on all sides – the great wood with its perpetual movement of branch and bough, and its solemn wail, that came into the very streets of Salem when certain winds blew, bearing the sound of the pine-trees clear upon the ears that had leisure to listen. And from all accounts, this old forest, girdling round the settlement, was full of dreaded and mysterious beasts, and still more to be dreaded Indians, stealing in and out among the shadows, intent on bloody schemes against the Christian people; panther-streaked, shaven Indians, in league by their own confession, as well as by the popular belief, with evil powers.

Nattee, the old Indian servant, would occasionally make Lois's blood run cold as she and Faith and Prudence listened to the wild stories she told them of the wizards of her race. It was often in the kitchen, in the darkening evening, while some cooking process was going on, that the old Indian crone, sitting on her haunches by the bright red wood embers which sent up no flame, but a lurid light reversing the shadows of all the faces around, told her weird stories while they were awaiting the rising of the dough, perchance, out of which the household bread had to be made. There ran through these stories always a ghastly, unexpressed suggestion of some human sacrifice being needed to complete the success of any incantation to the Evil One; and the poor old creature, herself believing and shuddering as she narrated her tale in broken English, took a strange, unconscious pleasure in her power over her hearers – young girls of the oppressing race, which had brought her down into a state little differing from slavery, and reduced her people to out-casts on the hunting-grounds which had belonged to her fathers. After such tales, it required no small effort on Lois's part to go out, at her aunt's command, into the common pasture round the town, and bring the cattle home at night. Who knew but what the double-headed snake might start up from each blackberry-bush – that wicked, cunning, accursed creature in the service of the Indian wizards, that had such power over all those white maidens who met the eyes placed at either end of his long, sinuous, creeping body, so that loathe him, loathe the Indian race as they would, off they must go into the forest to seek but some Indian man, and must beg to be taken into his wigwam, abjuring faith and race for ever? Or there were spells – so Nattee said – hidden about the ground by the wizards, which changed that person's nature who found them; so that, gentle and loving as they might have been before, thereafter they took no pleasure but in the cruel torments of others, and had a strange power given to them of causing such torments at their will. Once Nattee, speaking low to Lois, who was alone with her in the kitchen, whispered out her terrified belief that such a spell had Prudence found; and when the Indian showed her arms to Lois, all pinched and black and blue by the impish child, the English girl began to be afraid of her cousin as of one possessed. But it was not Nattee alone, nor young imaginative girls alone, that believed in these stories. We can afford to smile at them now; but our English ancestors enter-tained superstitions of much the same character at the same period, and with less excuse, as the circumstances surrounding them were better known, and consequently more explicable by common sense than the real mysteries of the deep, untrodden forests of New Eng-land. The gravest divines not only believed stories similar to that of the double-headed serpent, and other tales of witchcraft, but they made such narrations the subjects of preaching and prayer; and as cowardice makes us all cruel, men who were blameless in many of the relations of life, and even praiseworthy in some, became, from superstition, cruel persecutors about this time, showing no mercy towards anyone whom they believed to be in league with the Evil One.

Faith was the person with whom the English girl was the most intimately associated in her uncle's house. The two were about the same age, and certain household employments were shared between them. They took it in turns to call in the cows, to make up the butter which had been churned by Hosea, a stiff old out-door servant, in whom Grace Hickson placed great confidence; and each lassie had her great spinning-wheel for wool, and her lesser for flax, before a month had elapsed after Lois's coming. Faith was a grave, silent person, never merry, sometimes very sad, though Lois was a long time in even guessing why. She would try in her sweet, simple fashion to cheer her cousin up, when the latter was depressed, by telling her old stories of English ways and life. Occasionally, Faith seemed to care to listen, occasionally she did not heed one word, but dreamed on. Whether of the past or of the future, who could tell?

Stern old ministers came in to pay their pastoral visits. On such occasions, Grace Hickson would put on clean apron and clean cap, and make them more welcome than she was ever seen to do anyone else, bringing out the best provisions of her store, and setting of all before them. Also, the great Bible was brought forth, and Hosea and Nattee summoned from their work to listen while the minister read a chapter, and, as he read, expounded it at considerable length. After this all knelt, while he, standing, lifted up his right hand, and prayed for all possible combinations of Christian men, for all possible cases of spiritual need; and lastly, taking the individuals before him, he would put up a very personal supplication for each, according to his notion of their wants. At first Lois wondered at the aptitude of one or two prayers of this description to the outward circumstances of each case; but when she perceived that her aunt had usually a pretty long confidential conversation with the minister in the early part of his visit, she became aware that he received both his impressions and his knowledge through the medium of 'that godly woman, Grace Hickson'; and I am afraid she paid less regard to the prayer 'for the maiden from another land, who hath brought the errors of that land as a seed with her, even across the great ocean, and who is letting even now the little seeds shoot up into an evil tree, in which all unclean creatures may find shelter.'

'I like the prayers of our Church better,' said Lois, one day to Faith. 'No clergyman in England can pray his own words, and therefore it is that he cannot judge of others so as to fit his prayers to what he esteems to be their case, as Mr Tappau did this morning.'

'I hate Mr Tappau!' said Faith, shortly, a passionate flash of light coming out of her dark, heavy eyes.

'Why so cousin? It seems to me as if he were a good man, although I like not his prayers.'

Faith only repeated her words, 'I hate him.'

Lois was sorry for this strong bad feeling; instinctively sorry, for she was loving herself, delighted in being loved, and felt a jar run through her at every sign of want of love in others. But she did not know what to say, and was silent at the time. Faith, too, went on turning her wheel with vehemence, but spoke never a word until her thread snapped, and then she pushed the wheel away hastily and left the room.

Then Prudence crept softly up to Lois's side. This strange child seemed to be tossed about by varying moods: today she was caressing and communicative, tomorrow she might be deceitful, mocking, and so indifferent to the pain or sorrows of others that you could call her almost inhuman.

'So thou dost not like Pastor Tappau's prayers?' she whispered.

Lois was sorry to have been overheard, but she neither would nor could take back her words.

'I like them not so well as the prayers I used to hear at home.'

'Mother says thy home was with the ungodly. Nay, don't look at me so – it was not I that said it. I'm none so fond of praying myself, nor of Pastor Tappau for that matter. But Faith cannot abide him, and I know why. Shall I tell thee, cousin Lois?'

'No! Faith did not tell me, and she was the right person to give her own reasons.'

'Ask her where young Mr Nolan is gone to, and thou wilt hear. I have seen Faith cry by the hour together about Mr Nolan.'

'Hush, child, hush!' said Lois, for she heard Faith's approaching step, and feared lest she should overhear what they were saying.

The truth was that, a year or two before, there had been a great struggle in Salem village, a great division in the religious body, and Pastor Tappau had been the leader of the more violent, and, ultimately, the successful party. In consequence of this, the less popular minister, Mr Nolan, had had to leave the place. And him Faith Hickson loved with all the strength of her passionate heart, although he never was aware of the attachment he had excited, and her own family were too regardless of manifestations of mere feeling to ever observe the signs of any emotion on her part. But the old Indian servant Nattee saw and observed them all. She knew, as well as if she had been told the reason, why Faith had lost all care about father or mother, brother and sister, about household work and daily occupation, nay,

about the observances of religion as well. Nattee read the meaning of
the deep smouldering of Faith's dislike to Pastor Tappau aright; the
Indian woman understood why the girl (whom alone of all the white
people she loved) avoided the old minister – would hide in the wood-
stack sooner than be called in to listen to his exhortations and prayers.
With savage, untutored people, it is not 'Love me, love my dog', they
are often jealous of the creature beloved; but it is, 'Whom thou hatest
I will hate'; and Nattee's feeling towards Pastor Tappau was even an
exaggeration of the mute unspoken hatred of Faith.

For a long time, the cause of her cousin's dislike and avoidance of
the minister was a mystery to Lois; but the name of Nolan remained
in her memory whether she would or no, and it was more from
girlish interest in a suspected love affair, than from any indifferent
and heartless curiosity, that she could not help piecing together little
speeches and actions, with Faith's interest in the absent banished
minister, for an explanatory clue, till not a doubt remained in her
mind. And this without any further communication with Prudence,
for Lois declined hearing any more on the subject from her, and so
gave deep offence.

Faith grew sadder and duller as the autumn drew on. She lost
her appetite, her brown complexion became sallow and colourless,
her dark eyes looked hollow and wild. The first of November was
near at hand. Lois, in her instinctive, well-intentioned efforts to
bring some life and cheerfulness into the monotonous household,
had been telling Faith of many English customs, silly enough, no
doubt, and which scarcely lighted up a flicker of interest in the
American girl's mind. The cousins were lying awake in their bed
in the great unplastered room, which was in part store-room, in part
bedroom. Lois was full of sympathy for Faith that night. For long
she had listened to her cousin's heavy, irrepressible sighs, in silence.
Faith sighed because her grief was of too old a date for violent
emotion or crying. Lois listened without speaking in the dark, quiet
night hours, for a long, long time. She kept quite still, because she
thought such vent for sorrow might relieve her cousin's weary heart.
But when at length, instead of lying motionless, Faith seemed to be
growing restless even to convulsive motions of her limbs, Lois began
to speak, to talk about England, and the dear old ways at home,
without exciting much attention on Faith's part, until at length she
fell upon the subject of Hallow-e'en, and told about customs then
and long afterwards practised in England, and that have scarcely yet
died out in Scotland. As she told of tricks she had often played, of the

apple eaten facing a mirror, of the dripping sheet, of the basins of water, of the nuts burning side by side, and many other such innocent ways of divination, by which laughing, trembling English maidens sought to see the form of their future husbands, if husbands they were to have, then Faith listened breathlessly, asking short, eager questions, as if some ray of hope had entered into her gloomy heart. Lois went on speaking, telling her of all the stories that would confirm the truth of the second sight vouchsafed to all seekers in the accustomed methods, half believing, half incredulous herself, but desiring, above all things, to cheer up poor Faith.

Suddenly, Prudence rose up from her truckle-bed in the dim corner of the room. They had not thought that she was awake, but she had been listening long.

'Cousin Lois may go out and meet Satan by the brook-side if she will, but if thou goest, Faith, I will tell mother – ay, and I will tell Pastor Tappau, too. Hold thy stories, Cousin Lois, I am afeard of my very life. I would rather never be wed at all, than feel the touch of the creature that would take the apple out of my hand, as I held it over my left shoulder.' The excited girl gave a loud scream of terror at the image her fancy had conjured up. Faith and Lois sprang out towards her, flying across the moonlit room in their white nightgowns. At the same instant, summoned by the same cry, Grace Hickson came to her child.

'Hush! hush!' said Faith, authoritatively.

'What is it, my wench?' asked Grace. While Lois, feeling as if she had done all the mischief, kept silence.

'Take her away, take her away!' screamed Prudence. 'Look over her shoulder – her left shoulder – the Evil One is there now, I see him stretching over for the half-bitten apple.'

'What is this she says?' said Grace, austerely.

'She is dreaming,' said Faith; 'Prudence, hold thy tongue.' And she pinched the child severely, while Lois more tenderly tried to soothe the alarms she felt that she had conjured up.

'Be quiet, Prudence,' said she, 'and go to sleep. I will stay by thee till thou hast gone off into slumber.'

'No, go! go away,' sobbed Prudence, who was really terrified at first, but was now assuming more alarm than she felt, if from the pleasure she received at perceiving herself the centre of attention. 'Faith shall stay by me, not you, wicked English witch!'

So Faith sat by her sister; and Grace, displeased and perplexed, withdrew to her own bed, purposing to inquire more into the matter in the morning. Lois only hoped it might all be forgotten by that time, and resolved never to talk again of such things. But an event happened in the remaining hours of the night to change the current of affairs. While Grace had been absent from her room, her husband had had another paralytic stroke: whether he, too, had been alarmed by that eldritch scream no-one could ever know. By the faint light of the rush candle burning at the bedside, his wife perceived that a great change had taken place in his aspect on her return: the irregular breathing came almost like snorts – the end was drawing near. The family were roused, and all help given that either the doctor or experience could suggest. But before the late November morning light, all was ended for Ralph Hickson.

The whole of the ensuing day, they sat or moved in darkened rooms, and spoke few words, and those below their breath. Manasseh kept at home, regretting his father, no doubt, but showing little emotion. Faith was the child that bewailed her loss most grievously; she had a warm heart, hidden away somewhere under her moody exterior, and her father had shown her far more passive kindness than ever her mother had done, for Grace made distinct favourites of Manasseh, her only son, and Prudence, her youngest child. Lois was about as unhappy as any of them, for she had felt strongly drawn towards her uncle as her kindest friend, and the sense of his loss renewed the old sorrow she had experienced at her own parents' death. But she had no time and no place to cry in. On her devolved many of the cares, which it would have seemed indecorous in the nearer relatives to interest themselves in enough to take an active part: the change required in their dress, the household preparations for the sad feast of the funeral – Lois had to arrange all under her aunt's stern direction.

But a day or two afterwards – the last day before the funeral – she went into the yard to fetch in some fagots for the oven; it was a solemn, beautiful, starlit evening, and some sudden sense of desolation in the midst of the vast universe thus revealed touched Lois's heart, and she sat down behind the wood-stack, and cried very plentiful tears.

She was startled by Manasseh, who suddenly turned the corner of the stack, and stood before her.

'Lois crying!'

'Only a little,' she said, rising up, and gathering her bundle of fagots, for she dreaded being questioned by her grim, impassive cousin. To her surprise, he laid his hand on her arm, and said: 'Stop one minute. Why art thou crying, cousin?'

'I don't know,' she said, just like a child questioned in like manner; and she was again on the point of weeping.

'My father was very kind to thee, Lois; I do not wonder that thou grievest after him. But the Lord who taketh away can restore tenfold. I will be as kind as my father – yea, kinder. This is not a time to talk of marriage and giving in marriage. But after we have buried our dead, I wish to speak to thee.'

Lois did not cry now, but she shrank with affright. What did her cousin mean? She would far rather that he had been angry with her for unreasonable grieving, for folly.

She avoided him carefully – as carefully as she could, without seeming to dread him – for the next few days. Sometimes she thought it must have been a bad dream; for if there had been no English lover in the case, no other man in the whole world, she could never have thought of Manasseh as her husband; indeed, till now, there had been nothing in his words or actions to suggest such an idea. Now it had been suggested, there was no telling how much she loathed him. He might be good, and pious – he doubtless was – but his dark fixed eyes, moving so slowly and heavily, his lank black hair, his grey coarse skin, all made her dislike him now – all his personal ugliness and ungainliness struck on her senses with a jar, since those few words spoken behind the haystack.

She knew that sooner or later the time must come for further discussion of this subject; but, like a coward, she tried to put it off, by clinging to her aunt's apron-string, for she was sure that Grace Hickson had far different views for her only son. As, indeed, she had, for she was an ambitious, as well as a religious woman; and by an early purchase of land in Salem village, the Hicksons had become wealthy people, without any great exertions of their own; partly, also, by the silent process of accumulation, for they had never cared to change their manner of living from the time when it had been suitable to a far smaller income than that which they at present enjoyed. So much for worldly circumstances. As for their worldly character, it stood as high. No-one could say a word against any of their habits or actions. The righteousness and godliness were patent to everyone's eyes. So Grace Hickson thought herself entitled to pick and choose among the maidens, before she should meet with one fitted to be Manasseh's wife. None in Salem came up to her imaginary standard. She had it in her mind even at this very time – so soon after her husband's death – to go to Boston, and take counsel with the leading ministers there, with worthy Mr Cotton Mather at their head, and see if they could tell her of a well-favoured and godly young maiden in their congregations worthy of being the wife of her son. But, besides good looks and godliness, the wench must have good birth, and good wealth, or Grace Hickson would have put her contemptuously on one side. When once this paragon was found, the ministers had approved, Grace anticipated no difficulty on her son's part. So Lois was right in feeling that her aunt would dislike any speech of marriage between Manasseh and herself.

But the girl was brought to bay one day in this wise. Manasseh had ridden forth on some business, which everyone said would occupy him the whole day; but, meeting the man with whom he had to transact his affairs, he returned earlier than anyone expected. He missed Lois from the keeping-room where his sisters were spinning, almost immediately. His mother sat by at her knitting – he could see Nattee in the kitchen through the open door. He was too reserved to ask where Lois was, but he quietly sought till he found her – in the great loft, already piled with winter stores of fruit and vegetables. Her aunt had sent her there to examine the apples one by one, and pick out such as were unsound, for immediate use. She was stooping down, and intent upon this work, and was hardly aware of his approach, until she lifted up her head and saw him standing close before her. She dropped the apple she was holding, went a little paler than her wont, and faced him in silence.

'Lois,' he said, 'thou rememberest the words that I spoke while we yet mourned over my father. I think that I am called to marriage now, as the head of this household. And I have seen no maiden so pleasant in my sight as thou art, Lois!' He tried to take her hand. But she put it behind her with a childish shake of her head, and, half-crying, said: 'Please, Cousin Manasseh, do not say this to me. I dare say you ought to be married, being the head of the household now; but I don't want to be married. I would rather not.'

'That is well spoken,' replied he, frowning a little, nevertheless. 'I should not like to take to wife an over-forward maiden, ready to jump at wedlock. Besides, the congregation might talk, if we were to be married too soon after my father's death. We have, perchance, said enough, even now. But I wished thee to have thy mind set at ease as to thy future well-doing. Thou wilt have leisure to think of it, and to bring thy mind more fully round to it.' Again he held out his hand. This time she took hold of it with a free, frank gesture.

'I owe you somewhat for your kindness to me ever since I came, Cousin Manasseh; and I have no way of paying you but by telling you truly I can love you as a dear friend, if you will let me, but never as a wife.'

He flung her hand away, but did not take his eyes off her face, though his glance was lowering and gloomy. He muttered something which she did not quite hear, and so she went on bravely although she kept trembling a little, and had much ado to keep from crying.

'Please let me tell you all. There was a young man in Barford – nay, Manasseh, I cannot speak if you are so angry; it is hard work to tell you anyhow – he said that he wanted to marry me; but I was poor, and his father would have none of it, and I do not want to marry anyone; but if I did, it would be – '

Her voice dropped, and her blushes told the rest. Manasseh stood looking at her with sullen, hollow eyes, that had a glittering touch of wilderness in them, and then he said: 'It is borne in upon me – verily I see it as in a vision – that thou must be my spouse, and no other man's. Thou canst not escape what is foredoomed. Months ago, when I set myself to read the old godly books in which my soul used to delight until thy coming, I saw no letters of printers' ink marked on the page, but I saw a gold and ruddy type of some unknown language, the meaning whereof was whispered into my soul; it was, "Marry Lois! marry Lois!" And when my father died, I knew it was the beginning of the end. It is the Lord's will, Lois, and thou canst not escape from it.' And again he would have taken her hand and drawn her towards him. But this time she eluded him with ready movement.

'I do not acknowledge it to be the Lord's will, Manasseh,' said she. 'It is not "borne in upon me", as you Puritans call it, that I am to be your wife. I am none so set upon wedlock as to take you, even though there be no other chance for me. For I do not care for you as I ought to care for my husband. But I could have cared for you very much as a cousin – as a kind cousin.'

She stopped speaking; she could not choose the right words with which to speak to him of her gratitude and friendliness, which yet could never be any feeling nearer and dearer, no more than two parallel lines can ever meet.

But he was so convinced, by what he considered the spirit of prophecy, that Lois was to be his wife, that he felt rather more indignant at what he considered to be her resistance to the preordained decree,

than really anxious as to the result. Again he tried to convince her
that neither he nor she had any choice in the matter, by saying: 'The
voice said unto me "Marry Lois", and I said, "I will, Lord." '

'But,' Lois replied, 'the voice, as you call it, has never spoken such
a word to me.'

'Lois,' he answered, solemnly, 'it will speak. And then wilt thou
obey, even as Samuel did?'

'No, indeed I cannot!' she answered, briskly. 'I may take a dream
to be truth, and hear my own fancies, if I think about them too long.
But I cannot marry anyone from obedience.'

'Lois, Lois, thou art as yet unregenerate; but I have seen thee in a
vision as one of the elect, robed in white. As yet thy faith is too weak
for thee to obey meekly, but it shall not always be so. I will pray that
thou mayest see thy preordained course. Meanwhile, I will smooth
away all worldly obstacles.'

'Cousin Manasseh! Cousin Manasseh!' cried Lois after him, as he
was leaving the room, 'come back. I cannot put it in strong enough
words. Manasseh, there is no power in heaven or earth that can
make me love thee enough to marry thee, or to wed thee without
such love. And this I say solemnly, because it is better that this
should end at once.'

For a moment he was staggered; then he lifted up his hands, and
said, 'God forgive thee thy blasphemy! Remember Hazael, who said,
"Is thy servant a dog, that he should do this great thing?" and went
straight and did it, because his evil courses were fixed and appointed
for him from before the foundation of the world. And shall not thy
paths be laid out among the godly as it hath been foretold to me?'

He went away; and for a minute or two Lois felt as if his words
must come true, and that, struggle as she would, hate her doom as
she would, she must become his wife; and, under the circumstances,
many a girl would have succumbed to her apparent fate. Isolated
from all previous connections, hearing no word from England, living
in the heavy, monotonous routine of a family with one man for head,
and this man esteemed a hero by most of those around him, simply
because he was the only man in the family – these facts alone would
have formed strong presumptions that most girls would have yielded
to the offers of such a one. But, besides this, there was much to
tell upon the imagination in those days, in that place, and time. It
was prevalently believed that there were manifestations of spiritual
influence – of the direct influence both of good and bad spirits –
constantly to be perceived in the course of men's lives. Lots were

drawn, as guidance from the Lord; the Bible was opened, and the leaves allowed to fall apart, and the first text the eye fell upon was supposed to be appointed from above as a direction. Sounds were heard that could not be accounted for; they were made by the evil spirits not yet banished from the desert places of which they had so long held possession. Sights, inexplicable and mysterious, were dimly seen – Satan, in some shape, seeking whom he might devour. And at the beginning of the long winter season, such whispered tales, such old temptations and hauntings, and devilish terrors, were supposed to be peculiarly rife. Salem was, as it were, snowed up, and left to prey upon itself. The long, dark evenings, the dimly-lighted rooms, the creaking passages, where heterogeneous articles were piled away out of reach of the keen-piercing frost, and where occasionally, in the dead of night, a sound was heard, as of some heavy falling body, when, next morning, everything appeared to be in its right place – so accustomed are we to measure noises by comparison with themselves, and not with the absolute stillness of the night-season – the white mist, coming nearer and nearer to the windows every evening in strange shapes, like phantoms – all these, and many other circumstances, such as the distant fall of mighty trees in the mysterious forests girdling them round, the faint whoop and cry of some Indian seeking his camp, and unwittingly nearer to the white men's settlement than either he or they would have liked could they have chosen, the hungry yells of the wild beasts approaching the cattle-pens – these were the things which made that winter life in Salem, in the memorable time of 1691–2, seem strange, and haunted, and terrific to many: peculiarly weird and awful to the English girl in her first year's sojourn in America.

And now imagine Lois worked upon perpetually by Manasseh's conviction that it was decreed that she should be his wife, and you will see that she was not without courage and spirit to resist as she did, steadily, firmly, and yet sweetly. Take one instance out of many, when her nerves were subjected to a shock, slight in relation it is true, but then remember that she had been all day, and for many days, shut up within doors, in a dull light, that at midday was almost dark with a long-continued snow-storm. Evening was coming on, and the wood fire was more cheerful than any of the human beings surrounding it; the monotonous whirr of the smaller spinning-wheels had been going on all day, and the store of flax downstairs was nearly exhausted, when Grace Hickson bade Lois fetch down some more from the store-room, before the light so entirely waned away that it could not be found without a candle, and a candle it would be dangerous to carry into that apartment full of combustible materials, especially at this time of hard frost, when every drop of water was locked up and bound in icy hardness. So Lois went, half-shrinking from the long passage that led to the stairs leading up into the storeroom, for it was in this passage that the strange night sounds were heard, which everyone had begun to notice, and speak about in lowered tones. She sang, however, as she went, 'to keep her courage up' – sang, however, in a subdued voice, the evening hymn she had so often sung in Barford church.

'Glory to Thee, my God, this night – '

and so it was, I suppose, that she never heard the breathing or motion of any creature near her till, just as she was loading herself with flax to carry down, she heard someone – it was Manasseh – say close to her ear.

'Has the voice spoken yet? Speak, Lois! Has the voice spoken yet to thee – that speaketh to me day and night, "Marry Lois?"'

She started and turned a little sick, but spoke almost directly in a brave, clear manner: 'No! Cousin Manasseh. And it never will.'

'Then I must wait yet longer,' he replied, hoarsely, as if to himself. 'But all submission – all submission.'

At last a break came upon the monotony of the long, dark winter. The parishioners once more raised the discussion whether – the parish extending as it did – it was not absolutely necessary for Pastor Tappau to have help. This question had been mooted once before; and then Pastor Tappau had acquiesced in the necessity, and all had gone on smoothly for some months after the appointment of his assistant, until a feeling had sprung up on the part of the elder minister, which might have been called jealousy of the younger, if so godly a man as Pastor Tappau could have been supposed to entertain so evil a passion. However that might be, two parties were speedily formed, the younger and more ardent being in favour of Mr Nolan, the elder and more persistent – and, at the time, the more numerous – clinging to the old grey-headed, dogmatic Mr Tappau, who had married them, baptized their children, and was to them literally as a 'pillar of the church'. So Mr Nolan left Salem, carrying away with him, possibly, more hearts than that of Faith Hickson's; but certainly she had never been the same creature since.

But now – Christmas, 1691 – one or two of the older members of the congregation being dead, and some who were younger men having come to settle in Salem – Mr Tappau being also older, and, some charitably supposed, wiser – a fresh effort had been made, and Mr Nolan was returning to labour in ground apparently smoothed over. Lois had taken a keen interest in all the proceedings for Faith's sake – far more than the latter did for herself, any spectator would have said. Faith's wheel never went faster or slower, her thread never broke, her colour never came, her eyes were never uplifted with sudden interest, all the time these discussions respecting Mr Nolan's return were going on. But Lois, after the hint given by Prudence, had found a clue to many a sigh and look of despairing sorrow, even without the help of Nattee's improvised songs, in which, under strange allegories, the helpless love of her favourite was told to ears heedless of all meaning, except those of the tender-hearted and sympathetic Lois. Occasionally, she heard a strange chant of the old Indian woman's – half in her own language, half in broken English – droned over some simmering pipkin, from which the smell was, to say the least, unearthly. Once, on perceiving this odour in the keeping-room, Grace Hickson suddenly exclaimed: 'Nattee is at her heathen ways again; we shall have some mischief unless she is stayed.'

But Faith, moving quicker than ordinary, said something about putting a stop to it, and so forestalled her mother's evident intention of going into the kitchen. Faith shut the door between the two rooms, and entered upon some remonstrance with Nattee; but no-one could hear the words used. Faith and Nattee seemed more bound together by love and common interest, than any other two among the self-contained individuals comprising this household. Lois sometimes felt as if her presence as a third interrupted some confidential talk between her cousin and the old servant. And yet she was fond of Faith, and could almost think that Faith liked her more than she did either mother, brother, or sister; for the first two were indifferent as to any unspoken feelings, while Prudence delighted in discovering them only to make an amusement to herself out of them.

One day Lois was sitting by herself at her sewing table, while Faith and Nattee were holding one of the secret conclaves from which Lois felt herself to be tacitly excluded, when the outer door opened, and a tall, pale young man, in the strict professional habit of a minister, entered. Lois sprang up with a smile and a look of welcome for Faith's sake, for this must be the Mr Nolan whose name had been on the tongue of everyone for days, and who was, as Lois knew, expected to arrive the day before.

He seemed half surprised at the glad alacrity with which he was received by this stranger: possibly he had not heard of the English girl, who was an inmate in the house where formerly he had seen only grave, solemn, rigid, or heavy faces, and had been received with a stiff form of welcome, very different from the blushing, smiling, dimpled looks that innocently met him with the greeting almost of an old acquaintance. Lois having placed a chair for him, hastened out to call Faith, never doubting but that the feeling which her cousin entertained for the young pastor was mutual, although it might be unrecognised in its full depth by either.

'Faith!' said she, bright and breathless. 'Guess – no,' checking herself to an assumed unconsciousness of any particular importance likely to be affixed to her words, 'Mr Nolan, the new pastor, is in the keeping-room. He has asked for my aunt and Manasseh. My aunt is gone to the prayer meeting at Pastor Tappau's, and Manasseh is away.' Lois went on speaking to give Faith time, for the girl had become deadly white at the intelligence, while, at the same time, her eyes met the keen, cunning eyes of the old Indian with a peculiar look of half-wondering awe, while Nattee's looks expressed triumphant satisfaction.

'Go,' said Lois, smoothing Faith's hair, and kissing the white, cold cheek, 'or he will wonder why no-one comes to see him, and perhaps think he is not welcome.' Faith went without another word into the keeping-room, and shut the door of communication. Nattee and Lois were left together. Lois felt as happy as if some piece of good fortune had befallen herself. For the time, her growing dread of Manasseh's wild, ominous persistence in his suit, her aunt's coldness, her own loneliness, were all forgotten, and she could almost have danced with joy. Nattee laughed aloud, and talked and chuckled to herself: 'Old Indian woman great mystery. Old Indian woman sent hither and thither; go where she is told, where she hears with her ears. But old Indian woman' – and here she drew herself up, and the expression of her face quite changed – 'know how to call, and then white man must come; and old Indian have spoken never a word, and white man have hear nothing with his ears.' So, the old crone muttered.

All this time, things were going on very differently in the keeping-room to what Lois imagined. Faith sat stiller even than usual; her

eyes downcast, her words few. A quick observer might have noticed a
certain tremulousness about her hands, and an occasional twitching
throughout all her frame. But Pastor Nolan was not a keen observer
upon this occasion; he was absorbed with his own little wonders and
perplexities. His wonder was that of a carnal man – who that pretty
stranger might be, who had seemed, on his first coming, so glad to
see him, but had vanished instantly, apparently not to reappear. And,
indeed, I am not sure if his perplexity was not that of a carnal man
rather than that of a godly minister, for this was his dilemma. It was
the custom of Salem (as we have already seen) for the minister, on
entering a household for the visit which, among other people and in
other times, would have been termed a 'morning call', to put up a
prayer for the eternal welfare of the family under whose roof-tree
he was. Now this prayer was expected to be adapted to the individual character, joys, sorrows, wants, and failings of every member
present; and here was he, a young pastor, alone with a young woman,
and he thought – vain thoughts, perhaps, but still very natural –
that the implied guesses at her character, involved in the minute
supplications above described, would be very awkward in a tête-à-
tête prayer; so, whether it was his wonder or his perplexity, I do not
know, but he did not contribute much to the conversation for some
time, and at last, by a sudden burst of courage and impromptu hit, he
cut the Gordian knot by making the usual proposal for prayer, and
adding to it a request that the household might be summoned. In
came Lois, quiet and decorous; in came Nattee, all one impassive,
stiff piece of wood – no look of intelligence or trace of giggling
near her countenance. Solemnly recalling each wandering thought,
Pastor Nolan knelt in the midst of these three to pray. He was a good
and truly religious man, whose name here is the only thing disguised,
and played his part bravely in the awful trial to which he was afterwards subjected; and if at the time, before he went through his fiery
persecutions, the human fancies which beset all young hearts came
across his, we at this day know that these fancies are no sin. But now
he prays in earnest, prays so heartily for himself, with such a sense of
his own spiritual need and spiritual failings, that each one of his
hearers feels as if a prayer and a supplication had gone up for each of
them. Even Nattee muttered the few words she knew of the Lord's
Prayer; gibberish though the disjointed nouns and verbs might be,
the poor creature said them because she was stirred to unwonted
reverence. As for Lois, she rose up comforted and strengthened, as
no special prayers of Pastor Tappau had ever made her feel. But

Faith was sobbing, sobbing aloud, almost hysterically, and made no effort to rise, but lay on her outstretched arms spread out upon the settle. Lois and Pastor Nolan looked at each other for an instant. Then Lois said: 'Sir, you must go. My cousin has not been strong for some time, and doubtless she needs more quiet than she has had today.'

Pastor Nolan bowed, and left the house; but in a moment he returned. Half opening the door, but without entering, he said: 'I come back to ask, if perchance I may call this evening to inquire how young Mistress Hickson finds herself?'

But Faith did not hear this; she was sobbing louder than ever.

'Why did you send him away, Lois? I should have been better directly, and it is so long since I have seen him.'

She had her face hidden as she uttered these words, and Lois could not hear them distinctly. She bent her head down by her cousin's on the settle, meaning to ask her to repeat what she had said. But in the irritation of the moment, and prompted possibly by some incipient jealousy, Faith pushed Lois away so violently that the latter was hurt against the hard, sharp corner of the wooden settle. Tears came into her eyes; not so much because her cheek was bruised, as because of the surprised pain she felt at this repulse from the cousin towards whom she was feeling so warmly and kindly. Just for the moment, Lois was as angry as any child could have been; but some of the words of Pastor Nolan's prayer yet rang in her ears, and she thought it would be a shame if she did not let them sink into her heart. She dared not, however, stoop again to caress Faith, but stood quietly by her, sorrowfully waiting, until a step at the outer door caused Faith to rise quickly, and rush into the kitchen, leaving Lois to bear the brunt of the newcomer. It was Manasseh, returned from hunting. He had been two days away, in company with other young men belonging to Salem. It was almost the only occupation which could draw him out of his secluded habits. He stopped suddenly at the door on seeing Lois, and alone, for she had avoided him of late in every possible way.

'Where is my mother?'

'At a prayer meeting at Pastor Tappau's. She has taken Prudence. Faith has left the room this minute. I will call her.' And Lois was going towards the kitchen, when he placed himself between her and the door.

'Lois,' said he, 'the time is going by, and I cannot wait much longer. The visions come thick upon me, and my sight grows clearer and clearer. Only this last night, camping out in the woods, I saw in my soul, between sleeping and waking, the spirit come and offer thee two lots, and the colour of the one was white, like a bride's, and the other was black and red, which is, being interpreted, a violent death. And when thou didst choose the latter the spirit said unto me, "Come!" and I came, and did as I was bidden. I put it on thee with mine own hands, as it is preordained, if thou wilt not hearken unto the voice and be my wife. And when the black and red dress fell to the ground, thou wert even as a corpse three days old. Now, be advised, Lois, in time. Lois, my cousin, I have seen it in a vision, and my soul cleaveth unto thee – I would fain spare thee.'

He was really in earnest – in passionate earnest; whatever his visions, as he called them, might be, he believed in them, and this belief gave something of unselfishness to his love for Lois. This she felt at this moment, if she had never done so before, and it seemed like a contrast to the repulse she had just met with from his sister. He had drawn near her, and now he took hold of her hand, repeating in his wild, pathetic, dreamy way: 'And the voice said unto me, "Marry Lois!" ' And Lois was more inclined to soothe and reason with him than she had ever been before, since the first time of his speaking to her on the subject – when Grace Hickson and Prudence entered the room from the passage. They had returned from the prayer meeting by the back way, which had prevented the sound of their approach from being heard.

But Manasseh did not stir or look round; he kept his eyes fixed on Lois, as if to note the effect of his words. Grace came hastily forwards, and lifting up her strong right arm, smote their joined hands in twain, in spite of the fervour of Manasseh's grasp.

'What means this?' said she, addressing herself more to Lois than to her son, anger flashing out of her deep-set eyes.

Lois waited for Manasseh to speak. He seemed, but a few minutes before, to be more gentle and less threatening than he had been of late on this subject, and she did not wish to irritate him. But he did not speak, and her aunt stood angrily waiting for an answer.

'At any rate,' thought Lois, 'it will put an end to the thought in his mind when my aunt speaks out about it.'

'My cousin seeks me in marriage,' said Lois.

'Thee!' and Grace struck out in the direction of her niece with a gesture of supreme contempt. But now Manasseh spoke forth.

'Yea! it is preordained. The voice has said it, and the spirit has brought her to me as my bride.'

'Spirit! An evil spirit then. A good spirit would have chosen out for thee a godly maiden of thine own people, and not a prelatist and a stranger like this girl. A pretty return, Mistress Lois, for all our kindness.'

'Indeed, Aunt Hickson, I have done all I could – Cousin Manasseh knows it – to show him I can be none of his. I have told him,' said she, blushing, but determined to say the whole out at once, 'that I am all but troth-plight to a young man of our own village at home; and, even putting all that on one side, I wish not for marriage at present.'

'Wish rather for conversion and regeneration. Marriage is an un-seemly word in the mouth of a maiden. As for Manasseh, I will take reason with him in private; and, meanwhile, if thou hast spoken truly, throw not thyself in his path, as I have noticed thou hast done but too often of late.'

Lois's heart burnt within her at this unjust accusation, for she knew how much she had dreaded and avoided her cousin, and she almost looked to him to give evidence that her aunt's last words were not true. But, instead, he recurred to his one fixed idea, and said: 'Mother, listen! If I wed not Lois, both she and I die within the year. I care not for life; before this, as you know, I have sought for death' (Grace shuddered, and was for a moment subdued by some recoll-ection of past horror); 'but if Lois were my wife I should live, and she would be spared from what is the other lot. That whole vision grows clearer to me day by day. Yet, when I try to know whether I am one of the elect, all is dark. The mystery of Free-Will and Fore-Knowledge is a mystery of Satan's devising, not of God's.'

'Alas, my son! Satan is abroad among the brethren even now; but let the old vexed topics rest. Sooner than fret thyself again, thou shalt have Lois to be thy wife, though my heart was set far differ-ently for thee.'

'No, Manasseh,' said Lois. 'I love you well as a cousin, but wife of yours I can never be. Aunt Hickson, it is not well to delude him so. I say, if ever I marry man, I am troth-plight to one in England.'

'Tush, child! I am your guardian in my dead husband's place. Thou thinkest thyself so great a prize that I would clutch at thee whether or no, I doubt not. I value thee not, save as a medicine for Manasseh, if his mind get disturbed again, as I have noted signs of late.'

This, then, was the secret explanation of much that had alarmed her in her cousin's manner: and if Lois had been a physician of modern times, she might have traced somewhat of the same temper-ament in his sisters as well – in Prudence's lack of natural feeling and impish delight in mischief, in Faith's vehemence of unrequited love. But as yet Lois did not know, any more than Faith, that the attachment of the latter to Mr Nolan was not merely unreturned, but even unperceived, by the young minister.

He came, it is true – came often to the house, sat long with the family, and watched them narrowly, but took no especial notice of Faith. Lois perceived this, and grieved over it; Nattee perceived it, and was indignant at it, long before Faith slowly acknowledged it to herself, and went to Nattee the Indian woman, rather than to Lois her cousin, for sympathy and counsel.

'He cares not for me,' said Faith. 'He cares more for Lois's little finger than for my whole body,' the girl moaned out in the bitter pain of jealousy.

'Hush thee, hush thee, prairie bird! How can he build a nest, when the old bird has got all the moss and the feathers? Wait till the Indian has found means to send the old bird flying far away.' This was the mysterious comfort Nattee gave.

Grace Hickson took some kind of charge over Manasseh that relieved Lois of much of her distress at his strange behaviour. Yet at times he escaped from his mother's watchfulness, and in such opportunities he would always seek Lois, entreating her, as of old, to marry him – sometimes pleading his love for her, oftener speaking wildly of his visions and the voices which he heard foretelling a terrible futurity.

We have now to do with events which were taking place in Salem, beyond the narrow circle of the Hickson family; but as they only concern us in as far as they bore down in their consequences on the future of those who formed part of it, I shall go over the narrative very briefly. The town of Salem had lost by death, within a very short time preceding the commencement of my story, nearly all its venerable men and leading citizens – men of ripe wisdom and sound counsel. The people had hardly yet recovered from the shock of their loss, as one by one the patriarchs of the primitive little community had rapidly followed each other to the grave. They had been beloved as fathers, and looked up to as judges in the land. The first bad effect of their loss was seen in the heated dissension which sprang up between Pastor Tappau and the candidate Nolan. It had been apparently healed over; but Mr Nolan had not been many weeks in Salem, after his second coming, before the strife broke out afresh, and alienated many for life who had till then been bound together by the ties of friendship or relationship. Even in the Hickson family something of this feeling soon sprang up; Grace being a vehement partisan of the elder pastor's more gloomy doctrines, while Faith was a passionate, if a powerless, advocate of Mr Nolan. Manasseh's growing absorption in his own fancies, and imagined gift of prophecy, making him comparatively indifferent to all outward events, did not tend to either the fulfilment of his visions, or the elucidation of the dark mysterious doctrines over which he had pondered too long for the health either of his mind or body; while Prudence delighted in irritating everyone by her advocacy of the views of thinking to which they were most opposed, and retailing every gossiping story to the person most likely to disbelieve, and be indignant at what she told, with an assumed unconsciousness of any such effect to be produced. There was much talk of the congregational difficulties and dissensions being carried up to the general court, and each party naturally hoped that, if such were the course of events, the opposing pastor and that portion of the congregation which adhered to him might be worsted in the struggle.

Such was the state of things in the township when, one day towards the end of the month of February, Grace Hickson returned from the weekly prayer meeting, which it was her custom to attend at Pastor Tappau's house, in a state of extreme excitement. On her entrance into her own house she sat down, rocking her body backwards and forwards, and praying to herself: both Faith and Lois stopped their spinning, in wonder at her agitation, before either of them ventured to address her. At length Faith rose, and spoke: 'Mother, what is it? Hath anything happened of an evil nature?'

The brave, stern, old woman's face was blenched, and her eyes were almost set in horror, as she prayed; the great drops running down her cheeks.

It seemed almost as if she had to make a struggle to recover her sense of the present homely accustomed life, before she could find words to answer.

'Evil nature! Daughters, Satan is abroad – is close to us. I have this very hour seen him afflict two innocent children, as of old he troubled those who were possessed by him in Judea. Hester and Abigail Tappau have been contorted and convulsed by him and his servants into such shapes as I am afeard to think on; and when their father, godly Mr Tappau, began to exhort and to pray, their howlings were like the wild beasts of the field. Satan is of a truth let loose amongst us. The girls kept calling upon him as if he were even then present among us. Abigail screeched out that he stood at my very back in the guise of a black man; and truly, as I turned round at her words, I saw a creature like a shadow vanishing, and turned all of a cold sweat. Who knows where he is now? Faith, lay straws across on the door-sill.'

'But if he be already entered in,' asked Prudence, 'may not that make it difficult for him to depart?'

Her mother, taking no notice of her question, went on rocking herself, and praying, till again she broke out into narration: 'Reverend Mr Tappau says, that only last night he heard a sound as of a heavy body dragged all through the house by some strong power; once it was thrown against his bedroom door, and would, doubtless, have broken it in, if he had not prayed fervently and aloud at that very time; and a shriek went up at his prayer that made his hair stand on end; and this morning all the crockery in the house was found broken and piled up in the middle of the kitchen floor; and Pastor Tappau says, that as soon as he began to ask a blessing on the morning's meal, Abigail and Hester cried out, as if someone was pinching them. Lord, have mercy upon us all! Satan is of a truth let loose.'

'They sound like the old stories I used to hear in Barford,' said Lois, breathless with affright.

Faith seemed less alarmed; but then her dislike to Pastor Tappau was so great, that she could hardly sympathise with any misfortunes that befell him or his family.

Towards evening Mr Nolan came in. In general, so high did party spirit run, Grace Hickson only tolerated his visits, finding herself often engaged at such hours, and being too much abstracted in thought to show him the ready hospitality which was one of her most prominent virtues. But today, both as bringing the latest intelligence of the new horrors sprung up in Salem, and as being one of the Church militant (or what the Puritans considered as equivalent to the Church militant) against Satan, he was welcomed by her in an unusual manner.

He seemed oppressed with the occurrences of the day: at first it appeared to be almost a relief to him to sit still, and cogitate upon them, and his hosts were becoming almost impatient for him to say something more than mere monosyllables, when he began.

'Such a day as this, I pray that I may never see again. It is as if the devils whom our Lord banished into the herd of swine, had been permitted to come again upon the earth. And I would it were only the lost spirits who were tormenting us; but I much fear, that certain of those whom we have esteemed as God's people have sold their souls to Satan, for the sake of a little of his evil power, whereby they may afflict others for a time. Elder Sherringham hath lost this very day a good and valuable horse, wherewith he used to drive his family to meeting, his wife being bedridden.'

'Perchance,' said Lois, 'the horse died of some natural disease.'

'True,' said Pastor Nolan; 'but I was going on to say, that as he entered into his house, full of dolour at the loss of his beast, a mouse ran in before him so sudden that it almost tripped him up, though an instant before there was no such thing to be seen; and he caught at it with his shoe and hit it, and it cried out like a human creature in pain, and straight ran up the chimney, caring nothing for the hot flame and smoke.'

Manasseh listened greedily to all this story, and when it was ended he smote upon his breast, and prayed aloud for deliverance from the power of the Evil One; and he continually went on praying at intervals through the evening, with every mark of abject terror on his face and in his manner – he, the bravest, most daring hunter in all the settlement. Indeed, all the family huddled together in silent fear, scarcely finding any interest in the usual household occupations. Faith and Lois sat with arms entwined, as in days before the former had become jealous of the latter; Prudence asked low, fearful questions of her mother and of the pastor as to the creatures that were abroad, and the ways in which they afflicted others; and when Grace besought the minister to pray for her and her household, he made a long and passionate supplication that none of that little flock might ever so far fall away into hopeless perdition as to be guilty of the sin without forgiveness – the sin of Witchcraft.

Chapter 3

'The sin of witchcraft.' We read about it, we look on it from the outside; but we can hardly realise the terror it induced. Every impulsive or unaccustomed action, every little nervous affection, every ache or pain was noticed, not merely by those around the sufferer, but by the person himself, whoever he might be, that was acting, or being acted upon, in any but the most simple and ordinary manner. He or she (for it was most frequently a woman or girl that was the supposed subject) felt a desire for some unusual kind of food – some unusual motion or rest – her hand twitched, her foot was asleep, or her leg had the cramp; and the dreadful question immediately suggested itself, 'Is anyone possessing an evil power over me, by the help of

Satan?' and perhaps they went on to think, 'It is bad enough to feel that my body can be made to suffer through the power of some unknown evil-wisher to me, but what if Satan gives them still further power, and they can touch my soul, and inspire me with loathful thoughts leading me into crimes which at present I abhor?' and so on, till the very dread of what might happen, and the constant dwelling of the thoughts, even with horror, upon certain possibilities, or what were esteemed such, really brought about the corruption of imagination at least, which at first they had shuddered at. Moreover, there was a sort of uncertainty as to who might be infected – not unlike the overpowering dread of the plague, which made some shrink from their best-beloved with irrepressible fear. The brother or sister, who was the dearest friend of their childhood and youth, might now be bound in some mysterious deadly pact with evil spirits of the most horrible kind – who could tell? And in such a case it became a duty, a sacred duty, to give up the earthly body which had been once so loved, but which was now the habitation of a soul corrupt and horrible in its evil inclinations. Possibly, terror of death might bring on confession and repentance, and purification. Or if it did not, why away with the evil creature, the witch, out of the world, down to the kingdom of the master, whose bidding was done on earth in all manner of corruption and torture of God's creatures! There were others who, to these more simple, if more ignorant, feelings of horror at witches and witchcraft, added the desire, conscious or unconscious, of revenge on those whose conduct had been in any way displeasing to them. Where evidence takes a supernatural character, there is no disproving it. This argument comes up: 'You have only the natural powers; I have supernatural. You admit the existence of the supernatural by the condemnation of this very crime of witchcraft. You hardly know the limits of the natural powers; how then can you define the supernatural? I say that in the dead of night, when my body seemed to all present to be lying in quiet sleep, I was, in the most complete and wakeful consciousness, present in my body at an assembly of witches and wizards with Satan at their head; that I was by them tortured in my body, because my soul would not acknowledge him as its king; and that I witnessed such and such deeds. What the nature of the appearance was that took the semblance of myself, sleeping quietly in my bed, I know not; but admitting, as you do, the possibility of witchcraft, you cannot disprove my evidence.' This evidence might be given truly or falsely, as the person witnessing believed it or not; but everyone must see what immense and terrible power was abroad for revenge. Then, again, the accused themselves ministered to the horrible panic abroad. Some, in dread of death, confessed from cowardice to the imaginary crimes of which they were accused, and of which they were promised a pardon on confession. Some, weak and terrified, came honestly to believe in their own guilt, through the diseases of imagination which were sure to be engendered at such a time as this.

Lois sat spinning with Faith. Both were silent, pondering over the stories that were abroad. Lois spoke first.

'Oh, Faith! this country is worse than ever England was, even in the days of Master Matthew Hopkins, the witch-finder. I grow frightened of everyone, I think. I even get afeard sometimes of Nattee!'

Faith coloured a little. Then she asked, 'Why? What should make you distrust the Indian woman?'

'Oh! I am ashamed of my fear as soon as it arises in my mind. But, you know, her look and colour were strange to me when first I came; and she is not a christened woman; and they tell stories of Indian wizards; and I know not what the mixtures are which she is sometimes stirring over the fire, nor the meaning of the strange chants she sings to herself. And once I met her in the dusk, just close by Pastor Tappau's house, in company with Hota, his servant – it was just before we heard of the sore disturbance in his house – and I have wondered if she had aught to do with it.'

Faith sat very still, as if thinking. At last she said: 'If Nattee has powers beyond what you and I have, she will not use them for evil; at least not evil to those whom she loves.'

'That comforts me but little,' said Lois. 'If she has powers beyond what she ought to have, I dread her, though I have done her no evil; nay, though I could almost say she bore me a kindly feeling. But such powers are only given by the Evil One; and the proof thereof is, that, as you imply, Nattee would use them on those who offend her.'

'And why should she not?' asked Faith, lifting her eyes, and flashing heavy fire out of them at the question.

'Because,' said Lois, not seeing Faith's glance, 'we are told to pray for them that despitefully use us, and to do good to them that persecute us. But poor Nattee is not a christened woman. I would that Mr Nolan would baptize her; it would, maybe, take her out of the power of Satan's temptations.'

'Are you never tempted?' asked Faith, half scornfully; 'and yet I doubt not you were well baptized!'

'True,' said Lois, sadly; 'I often do very wrong, but, perhaps, I might have done worse, if the holy form had not been observed.'

They were again silent for a time.

'Lois,' said Faith, 'I did not mean any offence. But do you never feel as if you would give up all that future life, of which the parsons talk, and which seems so vague and so distant, for a few years of real, vivid blessedness to begin tomorrow – this hour, this minute? Oh! I could think of happiness for which I would willingly give up all those misty chances of heaven – '

'Faith, Faith!' cried Lois, in terror, holding her hand before her cousin's mouth, and looking around in fright. 'Hush! you know not who may be listening; you are putting yourself in his power.'

But Faith pushed her hand away, and said, 'Lois, I believe in him no more than I believe in heaven. Both may exist, but they are so far away that I defy them. Why, all this ado about Mr Tappau's house – promise me never to tell living creature, and I will tell you a secret.'

'No!' said Lois, terrified. 'I dread all secrets. I will hear none. I will do all that I can for you, cousin Faith, in any way; but just at this time, I strive to keep my life and thoughts within the strictest bounds of godly simplicity, and I dread pledging myself to aught that is hidden and secret.'

'As you will, cowardly girl, full of terrors, which, if you had listened to me, might have been lessened, if not entirely done away with.' And Faith would not utter another word, though Lois tried meekly to entice her into conversation on some other subject.

The rumour of witchcraft was like the echo of thunder among the hills. It had broken out in Mr Tappau's house, and his two little daughters were the first supposed to be bewitched; but round about, from every quarter of the town, came in accounts of sufferers by witchcraft. There was hardly a family without one of these supposed victims. Then arose a growl and menaces of vengeance from many a household – menaces deepened, not daunted by the terror and mystery of the suffering that gave rise to them.

At length a day was appointed when, after solemn fasting and prayer, Mr Tappau invited the neighbouring ministers and all godly people to assemble at his house, and unite with him in devoting a day to solemn religious services, and to supplication for the deliverance of his children, and those similarly afflicted, from the power of the Evil One. All Salem poured out towards the house of the minister. There was a look of excitement on all their faces; eagerness and horror were depicted on many, while stern resolution, amounting to determined cruelty, if the occasion arose, was seen on others.

In the midst of the prayer, Hester Tappau, the younger girl, fell into convulsions; fit after fit came on, and her screams mingled with the shrieks and cries of the assembled congregation. In the first pause, when the child was partially recovered, when the people stood around exhausted and breathless, her father, the Pastor Tappau, lifted his right hand, and adjured her, in the name of the Trinity, to say who tormented her. There was a dead silence; not a creature stirred of all those hundreds. Hester turned wearily and uneasily, and moaned out the name of Hota, her father's Indian servant. Hota was present, apparently as much interested as anyone; indeed, she had been busying herself much in bringing remedies to the suffering child. But now she stood aghast, transfixed, while her name was caught up and shouted out in tones of reprobation and hatred by all the crowd around her. Another moment and they would have fallen upon the trembling creature and torn her limb from limb – pale, dusky, shivering Hota, half guilty-looking from her very bewilderment. But Pastor Tappau, that gaunt, grey man, lifting himself to his utmost height, signed to them to go back, to keep still while he addressed them; and then he told them, that instant vengeance was not just, deliberate punishment; that there would be need of conviction, perchance of confession – he hoped for some redress for his suffering children from her revelations, if she were brought to confession. They must leave the culprit in his hands, and in those of his brother ministers, that they might wrestle with Satan before delivering her up to the civil power. He spoke well, for he spoke from the heart of a father seeing his children exposed to dreadful and mysterious suffering, and firmly believing that he now held the clue in his hand which should ultimately release them and their fellow-sufferers. And the congregation moaned themselves into unsatisfied submission, and listened to his long, passionate prayer, which he uplifted even while the hapless Hota stood there, guarded and bound by two men, who glared at her like bloodhounds ready to slip, even while the prayer ended in the words of the merciful Saviour.

Lois sickened and shuddered at the whole scene; and this was no intellectual shuddering at the folly and superstition of the people, but tender moral shuddering at the sight of guilt which she believed in, and at the evidence of men's hatred and abhorrence, which, when shown even to the guilty, troubled and distressed her merciful heart.

She followed her aunt and cousins out into the open air, with down-cast eyes and pale face. Grace Hickson was going home with a feel-ing of triumphant relief at the detection of the guilty one. Faith alone seemed uneasy and disturbed beyond her wont, for Manasseh received the whole transaction as the fulfilment of a prophecy, and Prudence was excited by the novel scene into a state of discordant high spirits.

'I am quite as old as Hester Tappau,' said she; 'her birthday is in September and mine in October.'

'What has that to do with it?' said Faith, sharply.

'Nothing, only she seemed such a little thing for all those grave ministers to be praying for, and so many folk come from a distance – some from Boston they said – all for her sake, as it were. Why, didst thou see, it was godly Mr Henwick that held her head when she wriggled so, and old Madam Holbrook had herself helped upon a chair to see the better. I wonder how long I might wriggle, before great and godly folk would take so much notice of me? But, I sup-pose, that comes of being a pastor's daughter. She'll be so set up there'll be no speaking to her now. Faith! thinkest thou that Hota really had bewitched her? She gave me corn-cakes, the last time I was at Pastor Tappau's, just like any other woman, only, perchance, a trifle more good-natured; and to think of her being a witch after all!'

But Faith seemed in a hurry to reach home, and paid no attention to Prudence's talking. Lois hastened on with Faith, for Manasseh was walking alongside of his mother, and she kept steady to her plan of avoiding him, even though she pressed her company upon Faith, who had seemed of late desirous of avoiding her.

That evening the news spread through Salem, that Hota had con-fessed her sin – had acknowledged that she was a witch. Nattee was the first to hear the intelligence. She broke into the room where the girls were sitting with Grace Hickson, solemnly doing nothing, because of the great prayer-meeting in the morning, and cried out, 'Mercy, mercy, mistress, everybody! Take care of poor Indian Nattee, who never do wrong, but for mistress and the family! Hota one bad wicked witch, she say so herself; oh, me! oh me!' and stooping over Faith, she said something in a low, miserable tone of voice, of which Lois only heard the word 'torture'. But Faith heard all, and turning very pale, half accompanied, half led Nattee back to her kitchen.

Presently, Grace Hickson came in. She had been out to see a neighbour; it will not do to say that so godly a woman had been gossiping; and, indeed, the subject of the conversation she had held was of too serious and momentous a nature for me to employ a light word to designate it. There was all the listening to and repeating of small details and rumours, in which the speakers have no concern, that constitutes gossiping; but in this instance, all trivial facts and speeches might be considered to bear such dreadful significance, and might have so ghastly an ending, that such whispers were occasionally raised to a tragic importance. Every fragment of intelligence that related to Mr Tappau's household was eagerly snatched at; how his dog howled all one long night through, and could not be stilled; how his cow suddenly failed in her milk only two months after she had calved; how his memory had forsaken him one morning, for a minute or two, in repeating the Lord's Prayer, and he had even omitted a clause thereof in his sudden perturbation; and how all these fore-runners of his children's strange illness might now be interpreted and understood – this had formed the staple of the conversation between Grace Hickson and her friends. There had arisen a dispute among them at last, as to how far these subjections to the power of the Evil One were to be considered as a judgment upon Pastor Tappau for some sin on his part; and if so, what? It was not an unpleasant discussion, although there was considerable difference of opinion; for as none of the speakers had had their families so troubled, it was rather a proof that they had none of them committed any sin. In the midst of this talk, one, entering in from the street, brought the news that Hota had confessed all – had owned to signing a certain little red book which Satan had presented to her – had been present at impious sacraments – had ridden through the air to Newbury Falls – and, in fact, had assented to all the questions which the elders and magistrates, carefully reading over the confessions of the witches who had formerly been tried in England, in order that they might not omit a single inquiry, had asked of her. More she had owned to, but things of inferior importance, and partaking more of the nature of earthly tricks than of spiritual power. She had spoken of carefully adjusted strings, by which all the crockery in Pastor Tappau's house could be pulled down or disturbed; but of such intelligible malpractices the gossips of Salem took little heed. One of them said that such an action showed Satan's prompting, but they all preferred to listen to the grander guilt of the blasphemous sacraments and supernatural rides. The narrator ended with saying that Hota was to be hung the next morning, in spite of her confession, even although her life had been promised to her if she acknowledged her sin; for it was well to make an example of the first-discovered witch, and it was also well that she was an Indian, a heathen, whose life would be no great loss to the community. Grace Hickson on this spoke out. It was well that witches should perish off the face of the earth, Indian or English, heathen or, worse, a baptized Christian who had betrayed the Lord, even as Judas did, and had gone over to Satan. For her part, she wished that the first-discovered witch had been a member of a godly English household, that it might be seen of all men that religious folk were willing to cut off the right hand, and pluck out the right eye, if tainted with this devilish sin. She spoke sternly and well. The last comer said, that her words might be brought to the proof, for it had been whispered that Hota had named others, and some from the most religious families of Salem, whom she had seen among the unholy communicants at the sacrament of the Evil One. And Grace replied that she would answer for it, all godly folk would stand the proof, and quench all natural affection rather than that such a sin should grow and spread among them. She herself had a weak bodily dread of witnessing the violent death even of an animal; but she would not let that deter her from standing amidst those who cast the accursed creature out from among them on the morrow morning.

Contrary to her wont, Grace Hickson told her family much of this conversation. It was a sign of her excitement on the subject that she thus spoke, and the excitement spread in different forms through her family. Faith was flushed and restless, wandering between the keeping-room and the kitchen, and questioning her mother part-icularly as to the more extraordinary parts of Hota's confession, as if she wished to satisfy herself that the Indian witch had really done those horrible and mysterious deeds.

Lois shivered and trembled with affright at the narration, and the idea that such things were possible. Occasionally she found herself wandering off into sympathetic thought for the woman who was to die, abhorred of all men, and unpardoned by God, to whom she had been so fearful a traitor, and who was now, at this very time – when Lois sat among her kindred by the warm and cheerful firelight, anticipating many peaceful, perchance happy, morrows – solitary, shivering, panic-stricken, guilty, with none to stand by her and ex-hort her, shut up in darkness between the cold walls of the town prison. But Lois almost shrank from sympathising with so loathsome an accomplice of Satan, and prayed for forgiveness for her charitable thought; and yet, again, she remembered the tender spirit of the Saviour, and allowed herself to fall into pity, till at last her sense of right and wrong became so bewildered that she could only leave all to God's disposal, and just ask that He would take all creatures and all events into His hands.

Prudence was as bright as if she were listening to some merry story – curious as to more than her mother would tell her – seeming to have no particular terror of witches or witchcraft, and yet to be especially desirous to accompany her mother the next morning to the hanging. Lois shrank from the cruel, eager face of the young girl as she begged her mother to allow her to go. Even Grace was disturbed and perplexed by her daughter's pertinacity.

'No!' said she. 'Ask me no more. Thou shalt not go. Such sights are not for the young. I go, and I sicken at the thoughts of it. But I go to show that I, a Christian woman, take God's part against the devil's. Thou shalt not go, I tell thee. I could whip thee for thinking of it.'

'Manasseh says Hota was well whipped by Pastor Tappau ere she was brought to confession,' said Prudence, as if anxious to change the subject of discussion.

Manasseh lifted up his head from the great folio Bible, brought by his father from England, which he was studying. He had not heard what Prudence said, but he looked up at the sound of his name. All present were startled at his wild eyes, his bloodless face. But he was evidently annoyed at the expression of their countenances.

'Why look ye at me in that manner?' asked he. And his manner was anxious and agitated. His mother made haste to speak: 'It was but that Prudence said something that thou hast told her – that Pastor Tappau defiled his hands by whipping the witch Hota. What evil thought has got hold of thee? Talk to us, and crack not thy skull against the learning of man.'

'It is not the learning of man that I study: it is the word of God. I would fain know more of the nature of this sin of witchcraft, and whether it be, indeed, the unpardonable sin against the Holy Ghost. At times I feel a creeping influence coming over me, prompting all evil thoughts and unheard-of deeds, and I question within myself, "Is not this the power of witchcraft?" and I sicken, and loathe all that I do or say, and yet some evil creature hath the mastery over me, and I must needs do and say what I loathe and dread. Why wonder you, mother, that I, of all men, strive to learn the exact nature of witchcraft, and for that end study the word of God? Have you not seen me when I was, as it were, possessed with a devil?'

He spoke calmly, sadly, but as under deep conviction. His mother rose to comfort him.

'My son,' she said, 'no-one ever saw thee do deeds, or heard thee utter words, which anyone could say were prompted by devils. We have seen thee, poor lad, with thy wits gone astray for a time, but all thy thoughts sought rather God's will in forbidden places, than lost the clue to them for one moment in hankering after the powers of darkness. Those days are long past; a future lies before thee. Think not of witches or of being subject to the power of witchcraft. I did evil to speak of it before thee. Let Lois come and sit by thee, and talk to thee.'

Lois went to her cousin, grieved at heart for his depressed state of mind, anxious to soothe and comfort him, and yet recoiling more than ever from the idea of ultimately becoming his wife – an idea to which she saw her aunt reconciling herself unconsciously day by day, as she perceived the English girl's power of soothing and comforting her cousin, even by the very tones of her sweet cooing voice.

He took Lois's hand.

'Let me hold it. It does me good,' said he. 'Ah, Lois, when I am by you I forget all my troubles – will the day never come when you will listen to the voice that speaks to me continually?'

'I never hear it, Cousin Manasseh,' she said, softly; 'but do not think of the voices. Tell me of the land you hope to enclose from the forest – what manner of trees grow on it?'

Thus, by simple questions on practical affairs, she led him back, in her unconscious wisdom, to the subjects on which he had always shown strong practical sense. He talked on these with all due discretion till the hour for family prayer came round, which was early in those days. It was Manasseh's place to conduct it, as head of the family; a post which his mother had always been anxious to assign to him since her husband's death. He prayed extempore; and tonight his supplications wandered off into wild, unconnected fragments of prayer, which all those kneeling around began, each according to her anxiety for the speaker, to think would never end. Minutes elapsed, and grew to quarters of an hour, and his words only became more emphatic and wilder, praying for himself alone, and laying bare the recesses of his heart. At length his mother rose, and took Lois by the hand, for she had faith in Lois's power over her son, as being akin to that which the shepherd David, playing on his harp, had over king Saul sitting on his throne. She drew her towards him, where he knelt facing into the circle, with his eyes upturned, and the tranced agony of his face depicting the struggle of the troubled soul within.

'Here is Lois,' said Grace, almost tenderly; 'she would fain go to her chamber.' (Down the girl's face the tears were streaming.) 'Rise, and finish thy prayer in thy closet.'

But at Lois's approach he sprang to his feet – sprang aside.

'Take her away, mother! Lead me not into temptation. She brings me evil and sinful thoughts. She overshadows me, even in the presence of my God. She is no angel of light, or she would not do this. She troubles me with the sound of a voice bidding me marry her, even when I am at my prayers. Avaunt! Take her away!'

He would have struck at Lois if she had not shrunk back, dismayed and affrighted. His mother, although equally dismayed, was not affrighted. She had seen him thus before; and understood the management of his paroxysm.

'Go, Lois! The sight of thee irritates him, as once that of Faith did. Leave him to me.'

And Lois rushed away to her room, and threw herself on her bed, like a panting, hunted creature. Faith came after her slowly and heavily.

'Lois,' said she, 'wilt thou do me a favour? It is not much to ask. Wilt thou arise before daylight, and bear this letter from me to Pastor Nolan's lodgings? I would have done it myself, but mother has bidden me to come to her, and I may be detained until the time when Hota is to be hung; and the letter tells of matters pertaining to life and death. Seek out Pastor Nolan wherever he may be, and have speech of him after he has read the letter.'

'Cannot Nattee take it?' asked Lois.

'No!' Faith answered, fiercely. 'Why should she?'

But Lois did not reply. A quick suspicion darted through Faith's mind, sudden as lightning. It had never entered there before.

'Speak, Lois. I read thy thoughts. Thou wouldst fain not be the bearer of this letter?'

'I will take it,' said Lois, meekly. 'It concerns life and death, you say?'

'Yes!' said Faith, in quite a different tone of voice. But, after a pause of thought, she added: 'Then, as soon as the house is still, I will write what I have to say, and leave it here, on this chest; and thou wilt promise me to take it before the day is fully up, while there is yet time for action.'

'Yes! I promise,' said Lois. And Faith knew enough of her to feel sure that the deed would be done, however reluctantly.

The letter was written – laid on the chest; and, ere day dawned, Lois was astir, Faith watching her from between her half-closed eyelids – eyelids that had never been fully closed in sleep the livelong night. The instant Lois, cloaked and hooded, left the room, Faith sprang up, and prepared to go to her mother, whom she heard already stirring. Nearly everyone in Salem was awake and up on this awful morning, though few were out of doors, as Lois passed along the streets. Here was the hastily erected gallows, the black shadow of which fell across the street with ghastly significance; now she had to pass the iron-barred gaol, through the unglazed windows of which she heard the fearful cry of a woman, and the sound of many foot-steps. On she sped, sick almost to faintness, to the widow woman's where Mr Nolan lodged. He was already up and abroad, gone, his hostess believed, to the gaol. Thither Lois, repeating the words 'for life and for death!' was forced to go. Retracing her steps, she was thankful to see him come out of those dismal portals, rendered more dismal for being in heavy shadow, just as she approached. What his errand had been she knew not; but he looked grave and sad, as she put Faith's letter into his hands, and stood before him quietly waiting, until he should read it, and deliver the expected answer. But, instead of opening it, he held it in his hand, apparently absorbed in thought. At last he spoke aloud, but more to himself than to her: 'My God! and is she then to die in this fearful delirium? It must be – can be – only delirium, that prompts such wild and horrible confessions. Mistress Barclay, I come from the presence of the Indian woman appointed to die. It seems, she considered herself betrayed last evening by her sentence not being respited, even after she had made confession of sin enough to bring down fire from heaven; and, it seems to me, the passionate, impotent anger of this helpless creature has turned to madness, for she appals me by the additional revelations she has made to the keepers during the night – to me this morning. I could almost fancy that she thinks, by deepening the guilt she confesses, to escape this last dread punishment of all, as if, were a tithe of what she say true, one could suffer such a sinner to live. Yet to send her to death in such a state of mad terror! What is to be done?'

'Yet Scripture says that we are not to suffer witches in the land,' said Lois, slowly.

'True; I would but ask for a respite till the prayers of God's people had gone up for His mercy. Some would pray for her, poor wretch as she is. You would, Mistress Barclay, I am sure?' But he said it in a questioning tone.

'I have been praying for her in the night many a time,' said Lois, in a low voice. 'I pray for her in my heart at this moment; I suppose;

they are bidden to put her out of the land, but I would not have her entirely God-forsaken. But, sir, you have not read my cousin's letter. And she bade me bring back an answer with much urgency.'

Still he delayed. He was thinking of the dreadful confession he came from hearing. If it were true, the beautiful earth was a polluted place, and he almost wished to die, to escape from such pollution, into the white innocence of those who stood in the presence of God.

Suddenly his eyes fell on Lois's pure, grave face, upturned and watching his. Faith in earthly goodness came over his soul in that instant, 'and he blessed her unaware'.

He put his hand on her shoulder, with an action half paternal – although the difference in their ages was not above a dozen years – and, bending a little towards her, whispered, half to himself, 'Mistress Barclay, you have done me good.'

'I!' said Lois, half affrighted – 'I done you good! How?'

'By being what you are. But, perhaps, I should rather thank God, who sent you at the very moment when my soul was so disquieted.'

At this instant, they were aware of Faith standing in front of them, with a countenance of thunder. Her angry look made Lois feel guilty. She had not enough urged the pastor to read his letter, she thought; and it was indignation at this delay in what she had been commissioned to do with the urgency of life or death, that made her cousin lower at her so from beneath her straight black brows. Lois explained how she had not found Mr Nolan at his lodgings, and had had to follow him to the door of the gaol. But Faith replied, with obdurate contempt: 'Spare thy breath, cousin Lois. It is easy seeing on what pleasant matters thou and the Pastor Nolan were talking. I marvel not at thy forgetfulness. My mind is changed. Give me back my letter, sir; it was about a poor matter – an old woman's life. And what is that compared to a young girl's love?'

Lois heard but for an instant; did not understand that her cousin, in her jealous anger, could suspect the existence of such a feeling as love between her and Mr Nolan. No imagination as to its possibility had ever entered her mind; she had respected him, almost revered him – nay, had liked him as the probable husband of Faith. At the thought that her cousin could believe her guilty of such treachery, her grave eyes dilated, and fixed themselves on the flaming countenance of Faith. That serious, unprotesting manner of perfect innocence must have told on her accuser, had it not been that, at the same instant, the latter caught sight of the crimsoned and disturbed countenance of the pastor, who felt the veil rent off the unconscious secret of his heart. Faith snatched her letter out of his hands, and said: 'Let the witch hang! What care I? She has done harm enough with her charms and her sorcery on Pastor Tappau's girls. Let her die, and let all other witches look to themselves; for there be many kinds of witchcraft abroad. Cousin Lois, thou wilt like best to stop with Pastor Nolan, or I would pray thee to come back with me to breakfast.'

Lois was not to be daunted by jealous sarcasm. She held out her hand to Pastor Nolan, determined to take no heed of her cousin's mad words, but to bid him farewell in her accustomed manner. He hesitated before taking it, and when he did, it was with a convulsive squeeze that almost made her start. Faith waited and watched all, with set lips and vengeful eyes. She bade no farewell; she spake no word; but grasping Lois tightly by the back of the arm, she almost drove her before her down the street till they reached their home.

The arrangement for the morning was this: Grace Hickson and her son Manasseh were to be present at the hanging of the first witch executed in Salem, as pious and godly heads of a family. All the other members were strictly forbidden to stir out, until such time as the low-tolling bell announced that all was over in this world for Hota, the Indian witch. When the execution was ended, there was to be a solemn prayer-meeting of all the inhabitants of Salem; ministers had come from a distance to aid by the efficacy of their prayers in these efforts to purge the land of the devil and his servants. There was reason to think that the great old meeting-house would be crowded, and when Faith and Lois reached home, Grace Hickson was giving her directions to Prudence, urging her to be ready for an early start to that place. The stern old woman was troubled in her mind at the anticipation of the sight she was to see, before many minutes were over, and spoke in a more hurried and incoherent manner than was her wont. She was dressed in her Sunday best; but her face was very grey and colourless, and she seemed afraid to cease speaking about household affairs, for fear she should have time to think. Manasseh stood by her, perfectly, rigidly still; he also was in his Sunday clothes. His face, too, was paler than its wont, but it wore a kind of absent, rapt expression, almost like that of a man who sees a vision. As Faith entered, still holding Lois in her fierce grasp, Manasseh started and smiled; but still dreamily. His manner was so peculiar, that even his mother stayed her talking to observe him more closely; he was in that state of excitement which usually ended in what his mother and certain of her friends esteemed a prophetic revelation. He began to speak, at first very low, and then his voice increased in power: 'How beautiful is the land of Beulah, far over the sea, beyond the mountains! Thither the angels carry her, lying back in their arms like one fainting. They shall kiss away the black circle of death, and lay her down at the feet of the Lamb. I hear her pleading there for those on earth who consented to her death. O Lois! pray also for me, pray for me, miserable!'

When he uttered his cousin's name all their eyes turned towards her. It was to her that his vision related! She stood among them, amazed, awe-stricken, but not like one affrighted or dismayed. She was the first to speak: 'Dear friends, do not think of me; his words may or may not be true. I am in God's hands all the same, whether he have the gift of prophecy or not. Besides, hear you not that I end where all would fain end? Think of him, and of his needs. Such times as these always leave him exhausted and weary, when he comes out of them.'

And she busied herself in cares for his refreshment, aiding her aunt's trembling hands to set before him the requisite food, as he now sat tired and bewildered, gathering together with difficulty his scattered senses.

Prudence did all she could to assist and speed their departure. But Faith stood apart, watching in silence with her passionate, angry eyes.

As soon as they had set out on their solemn, fatal errand, Faith left the room. She had not tasted food or touched drink. Indeed, they all felt sick at heart. The moment her sister had gone upstairs, Prudence sprang to the settle on which Lois had thrown down her cloak and hood: 'Lend me your muffles and mantle, Cousin Lois. I never yet saw a woman hanged, and I see not why I should not go. I will stand on the edge of the crowd; no-one will know me, and I will be home long before my mother.'

'No!' said Lois, 'that may not be. My aunt would be sore displeased. I wonder at you, Prudence, seeking to witness such a sight.' And as she spoke she held fast her cloak, which Prudence vehemently struggled for.

Faith returned, brought back possibly by the sound of the struggle. She smiled – a deadly smile.

'Give it up, Prudence. Strive no more with her. She has bought success in this world, and we are but her slaves.'

'Oh, Faith!' said Lois, relinquishing her hold of the cloak, and turning round with passionate reproach in her look and voice, 'what have I done that you should speak so of me; you, that I have loved as I think one loves a sister?'

Prudence did not lose her opportunity, but hastily arrayed herself in the mantle, which was too large for her, and which she had, therefore, considered as well adapted for concealment; but, as she went towards the door, her feet became entangled in the unusual length, and she fell, bruising her arm pretty sharply.

'Take care, another time, how you meddle with a witch's things,' said Faith, as one scarcely believing her own words, but at enmity with all the world in her bitter jealousy of heart. Prudence rubbed her arm and looked stealthily at Lois.

'Witch Lois! Witch Lois!' said she at last, softly, pulling a childish face of spite at her.

'Oh, hush, Prudence! Do not bandy such terrible words. Let me look at thine arm. I am sorry for thy hurt, only glad that it has kept thee from disobeying thy mother.'

'Away, away!' said Prudence, springing from her. 'I am afeard of her in very truth, Faith. Keep between me and the witch, or I will throw a stool at her.'

Faith smiled – it was a bad and wicked smile – but she did not stir to calm the fears she had called up in her young sister. Just at this moment, the bell began to toll. Hota, the Indian witch, was dead. Lois covered her face with her hands. Even Faith went a deadlier pale than she had been, and said, sighing, 'Poor Hota! But death is best.'

Prudence alone seemed unmoved by any thoughts connected with the solemn, monotonous sound. Her only consideration was, that now she might go out into the street and see the sights, and hear the news, and escape from the terror which she felt at the presence of her cousin. She flew upstairs to find her own mantle, ran down again, and past Lois, before the English girl had finished her prayer, and was speedily mingled among the crowd going to the meeting-house. There also Faith and Lois came in due course of time, but separately, not together. Faith so evidently avoided Lois, that she, humbled and grieved, could not force her company upon her cousin, but loitered a little behind – the quiet tears stealing down her face, shed for the many causes that had occurred this morning.

The meeting-house was full to suffocation; and, as it sometimes happens on such occasions, the greatest crowd was close about the doors, from the fact that few saw, on their first entrance, where there might be possible spaces into which they could wedge themselves. Yet they were impatient of any arrivals from the outside, and pushed and hustled Faith, and after her Lois, till the two were forced on to a conspicuous place in the very centre of the building, where there was no chance of a seat, but still space to stand in. Several stood around, the pulpit being in the middle, and already occupied by two ministers in Geneva bands and gowns, while other ministers, similarly attired, stood holding on to it, almost as if they were giving support instead of receiving it. Grace Hickson and her son sat decorously in their own pew, thereby showing that they had arrived early from the execution. You might almost have traced out the number of those who had been at the hanging of the Indian witch, by the expression of their countenances. They were awe-stricken into terrible repose; while the crowd pouring in, still pouring in, of those who had not attended the execution, looked all restless, and excited, and fierce. A buzz went round the meeting, that the stranger minister who stood along with Pastor Tappau in the pulpit was no other than Dr Cotton Mather himself, come all the way from Boston to assist in purging Salem of witches.

And now Pastor Tappau began his prayer, extempore, as was the custom. His words were wild and incoherent, as might be expected from a man who had just been consenting to the bloody death of one who was, but a few days ago, a member of his own family; violent and passionate, as was to be looked for in the father of children, whom he believed to suffer so fearfully from the crime he would denounce before the Lord. He sat down at length from pure exhaustion. Then Dr Cotton Mather stood forward: he did not utter more than a few words of prayer, calm in comparison with what had gone before, and then he went on to address the great crowd before him in a quiet, argumentative way, but arranging what he had to say with something of the same kind of skill which Antony used in his speech to the Romans after Cæsar's murder. Some of Dr Mather's words have been preserved to us, as he afterwards wrote them down in one of his works. Speaking of those 'unbelieving Sadducees' who doubted the existence of such a crime, he said: 'Instead of their apish shouts and jeers at blessed Scripture, and histories which have such undoubted confirmation as that no man that has breeding enough to regard the common laws of human society will offer to doubt of them, it becomes us rather to adore the goodness of God, who from the mouths of babes and sucklings has ordained truth, and by the means of the sore-afflicted children of your godly pastor, has revealed the fact that the devils have with most horrid operations broken in upon your neighbourhood. Let us beseech Him that their power may be restrained, and that they go not so far in their evil machinations as they did but four years ago in the city of Boston, where I was the humble means, under God, of loosing from the power of Satan the four children of that religious and blessed man, Mr Goodwin. These four babes of grace were bewitched by an Irish witch; there is no end to the narration of the torments they had to submit to. At one time they would bark like dogs, at another purr like cats; yea, they would fly like geese, and be carried with an incredible swiftness, having but just their toes now and then upon the ground, sometimes not once in twenty feet, and their arms waved like those of a bird. Yet at other times, by the hellish devices of the woman who had bewitched them, they could not stir without limping, for, by means of an invisible chain, she hampered their limbs, or, sometimes, by means of a noose, almost choked them. One in especial was subjected by this woman of Satan to such heat as of an oven, that I myself have seen the sweat drop from off her, while all around were moderately cold and well at ease. But not to trouble you with more of my stories, I will go on to prove that it was Satan himself that held power over her. For a very remarkable thing it was, that she was not permitted by that evil spirit to read any godly or religious book, speaking the truth as it is in Jesus. She could read Popish books well enough, while both sight and speech seemed to fail her when I gave her the Assembly's Catechism. Again, she was fond of that prelatical Book of Common Prayer, which is but the Roman mass-book in an English and ungodly shape. In the midst of her sufferings, if one put the Prayer-book into her hands it relieved her. Yet mark you, she could never be brought to read the Lord's Prayer, whatever book she met with it in, proving thereby distinctly that she was in league with the devil. I took her into my own house, that I, even as Dr Martin Luther did, might wrestle with the devil and have my fling at him. But when I called my household to prayer, the devils that possessed her caused her to whistle, and sing, and yell in a discordant and hellish fashion.'

At this very instant, a shrill, clear whistle pierced all ears. Dr Mather stopped for a moment: 'Satan is among you!' he cried. 'Look to yourselves!' And he prayed with fervour, as if against a present and threatening enemy; but no-one heeded him. Whence came that ominous, unearthly whistle? Every man watched his neighbour. Again the whistle, out of their very midst! And then a bustle in a corner of the building, three or four people stirring, without any cause immediately perceptible to those at a distance, the movement spread, and, directly after, a passage even in that dense mass of people was cleared for two men, who bore forwards Prudence Hickson, lying rigid as a log of wood, in the convulsive position of one who suffered from an epileptic fit. They laid her down among the ministers who were gathered round the pulpit. Her mother came to her, sending up a wailing cry at the sight of her distorted child. Dr Mather came down from the pulpit and stood over her, exorcising the devil in possession, as one accustomed to such scenes. The crowd pressed forward in mute horror. At length, her rigidity of form and feature gave way, and she was terribly convulsed – torn by the devil, as they called it. By and by the violence of the attack was over, and the spectators began to breathe once more, though still the former horror brooded over them, and they listened as if for the sudden ominous whistle again, and glanced fearfully around, as if Satan were at their backs picking out his next victim.

Meanwhile, Dr Mather, Pastor Tappau, and one or two others were exhorting Prudence to reveal, if she could, the name of the person, the witch, who, by influence over Satan, had subjected the child to such torture as that which they had just witnessed. They bade her speak in the name of the Lord. She whispered a name in the low voice of exhaustion. None of the congregation could hear what it was. But the Pastor Tappau, when he heard it, drew back in dismay, while Dr Mather, knowing not to whom the name belonged, cried out, in a clear, cold voice, 'Know ye one Lois Barclay; for it is she who hath bewitched this poor child?'

The answer was given rather by action than by word, although a low murmur went up from many. But all fell back, as far as falling back in such a crowd was possible, from Lois Barclay, where she stood – and looked on her with surprise and horror. A space of some feet, where no possibility of space had seemed to be not a minute before, left Lois standing alone, with every eye fixed upon her in hatred and dread. She stood like one speechless, tongue-tied, as if in a dream. She a witch! accursed as witches were in the sight of God and man! Her smooth, healthy face became contracted into shrivel and pallor, but she uttered not a word, only looked at Dr Mather with her dilated, terrified eyes.

Someone said, 'She is of the household of Grace Hickson, a God-fearing woman.' Lois did not know if the words were in her favour or not. She did not think about them, even; they told less on her than on any person present. She a witch! and the silver glittering Avon, and the drowning woman she had seen in her childhood at Barford – at home in England – were before her, and her eyes fell before her doom. There was some commotion – some rustling of papers; the magistrates of the town were drawing near the pulpit and consulting with the ministers. Dr Mather spoke again.

'The Indian woman, who was hung this morning, named certain people, whom she deposed to having seen at the horrible meetings for the worship of Satan; but there is no name of Lois Barclay down upon the paper, although we are stricken at the sight of the names of some – '

An interruption – a consultation. Again Dr Mather spoke: 'Bring the accused witch, Lois Barclay, near to this poor suffering child of Christ.'

They rushed forward to force Lois to the place where Prudence lay. But Lois walked forward of herself.

'Prudence,' she said, in such a sweet, touching voice, that, long afterwards, those who heard it that day, spoke of it to their children, 'have I ever said an unkind word to you, much less done you an ill turn? Speak, dear child. You did not know what you said just now, did you?'

But Prudence writhed away from her approach, and screamed out, as if stricken with fresh agony.

'Take her away! Take her away! Witch Lois, witch Lois, who threw me down only this morning, and turned my arm black and blue.' And she bared her arm, as if in confirmation of her words. It was sorely bruised.

'I was not near you, Prudence!' said Lois, sadly. But that was only reckoned fresh evidence of her diabolical power.

Lois's brain began to get bewildered. Witch Lois! she a witch, abhorred of all men! Yet she would try to think, and make one more effort.

'Aunt Hickson,' she said, and Grace came forwards – 'am I a witch, Aunt Hickson?' she asked; for her aunt, stern, harsh, unloving as she might be, was truth itself, and Lois thought – so near to delirium had she come – if her aunt condemned her, it was possible she might indeed be a witch.

Grace Hickson faced her unwillingly.

'It is a stain upon our family for ever,' was the thought in her mind.

'It is for God to judge whether thou art a witch, or not. Not for me.'

'Alas, alas!' moaned Lois; for she had looked at Faith, and learnt that no good word was to be expected from her gloomy face and averted eyes. The meeting-house was full of eager voices, repressed, out of reverence for the place, into tones of earnest murmuring that seemed to fill the air with gathering sounds of anger, and those who had at first fallen back from the place where Lois stood were now pressing forwards and round about her, ready to seize the young friendless girl, and bear her off to prison. Those who might have been, who ought to have been, her friends, were either averse or indifferent to her; though only Prudence made any open outcry upon her. That evil child cried out perpetually that Lois had cast a devilish spell upon her, and bade them keep the witch away from her; and, indeed, Prudence was strangely convulsed when once or twice Lois's perplexed and wistful eyes were turned in her direction. Here and there girls, women uttering strange cries, and apparently suffering from the same kind of convulsive fit as that which had attacked Prudence, were centres of a group of agitated friends, who muttered much and savagely of witchcraft, and the list which had been taken down only the night before from Hota's own lips. They demanded to have it made public, and objected to the slow forms of the law. Others, not so much or so immediately interested in the sufferers, were kneeling around, and praying aloud for themselves and their own safety, until the excitement should be so much quelled as to enable Dr Cotton Mather to be again heard in prayer and exhortation.

And where was Manasseh? What said he? You must remember, that the stir of the outcry, the accusation, the appeals of the accused, all seemed to go on at once amid the buzz and din of the people who had come to worship God, but remained to judge and upbraid their fellow-creature. Till now Lois had only caught a glimpse of Manasseh, who was apparently trying to push forwards, but whom his mother was holding back with word and action, as Lois knew she would hold him back; for it was not for the first time that she was made aware how carefully her aunt had always shrouded his decent reputation among his fellow-citizens from the least suspicion of his seasons of excitement and incipient insanity. On such days, when he himself imagined that he heard prophetic voices, and saw prophetic visions, his mother would do much to prevent any besides his own family from seeing him; and now Lois, by a process swifter than reasoning, felt certain, from her one look at his face, when she saw it, colourless and deformed by intensity of expression, among a number of others all simply ruddy and angry, that he was in such a state that his mother would in vain do her utmost to prevent his making himself conspicuous. Whatever force or argument Grace used, it was of no avail. In another moment he was by Lois's side, stammering with excitement, and giving vague testimony, which would have been of little value in a calm court of justice, and was only oil to the smouldering fire of that audience.

'Away with her to gaol!' 'Seek out the witches!' 'The sin has spread into all households!' 'Satan is in the very midst of us!' 'Strike and spare not!' In vain Dr Cotton Mather raised his voice in loud prayers, in which he assumed the guilt of the accused girl; no-one listened, all were anxious to secure Lois, as if they feared she would vanish from before their very eyes; she, white, trembling, standing quite still in the tight grasp of strange, fierce men, her dilated eyes only wandering a little now and then in search of some pitiful face – some pitiful face that among all those hundreds was not to be found. While some fetched cords to bind her, and others, by low questions, suggested new accusations to the distempered brain of Prudence, Manasseh obtained a hearing once more. Addressing Dr Cotton Mather, he said, evidently anxious to make clear some new argument that had just suggested itself to him: 'Sir, in this matter, be she witch or not, the end has been foreshown to me by the spirit of prophecy. Now, reverend sir, if the event be known to the spirit, it must have been foredoomed in the councils of God. If so, why punish her for doing that in which she had no free will?'

'Young man,' said Dr Mather, bending down from the pulpit and looking very severely upon Manasseh, 'take care! you are trenching on blasphemy.'

'I do not care. I say it again. Either Lois Barclay is a witch, or she is not. If she is, it has been foredoomed for her, for I have seen a vision of her death as a condemned witch for many months past – and the voice has told me there was but one escape for her, Lois – the voice you know – ' In his excitement he began to wander a little, but it was touching to see how conscious he was that by giving way he would lose the thread of the logical argument by which he hoped to prove that Lois ought not to be punished, and with what an effort he wrenched his imagination away from the old ideas, and strove to concentrate all his mind upon the plea that, if Lois was a witch, it had been shown him by prophecy; and if there was prophecy there must be foreknowledge; if foreknowledge, foredoom; if foredoom, no exercise of free will, and, therefore, that Lois was not justly amenable to punishment.

On he went, plunging into heresy, caring not – growing more and more passionate every instant, but directing his passion into keen argument, desperate sarcasm, instead of allowing it to excite his imagination. Even Dr Mather felt himself on the point of being worsted in the very presence of this congregation, who, but a short half-hour ago, looked upon him as all but infallible. Keep a good heart, Cotton Mather! your opponent's eye begins to glare and flicker with a terrible yet uncertain light – his speech grows less coherent, and his arguments are mixed up with wild glimpses at wilder revelations made to himself alone. He has touched on the limits – he has entered the borders of blasphemy, and with an awful cry of horror and reprobation the congregation rise up, as one man, against the blasphemer. Dr Mather smiled a grim smile, and the people were ready to stone Manasseh, who went on, regardless, talking and raving.

'Stay, stay!' said Grace Hickson – all the decent family shame which prompted her to conceal the mysterious misfortune of her only son from public knowledge done away with by the sense of the immediate danger to his life. 'Touch him not. He knows not what he is saying. The fit is upon him. I tell you the truth before God. My son, my only son, is mad.'

They stood aghast at the intelligence. The grave young citizen, who had silently taken his part in life close by them in their daily lives – not mixing much with them, it was true, but looked up to, perhaps, all the more – the student of abstruse books on theology, fit to converse with the most learned ministers that ever came about those parts – was he the same with the man now pouring out wild words to Lois the witch, as if he and she were the only two present! A solution of it all occurred to them. He was another victim. Great was the power of Satan! Through the arts of the devil, that white statue of a girl had mastered the soul of Manasseh Hickson. So the word spread from mouth to mouth. And Grace heard it. It seemed a healing balsam for her shame. With wilful, dishonest blindness, she would not see – not even in her secret heart would she acknowledge, that Manasseh had been strange, and moody, and violent long before the English girl had reached Salem. She even found some specious reason for his attempt at suicide long ago. He was recovering from a fever – and though tolerably well in health, the delirium had not finally left him. But since Lois came, how headstrong he had been at times! how unreasonable! how moody! What a strange delusion was that which he was under, of being bidden by some voice to marry her! How he followed her about, and clung to her, as under some compulsion of affection! And over all reigned the idea that, if he were indeed suffering from being bewitched, he was not mad, and might again assume the honourable position he had held in the congregation and in the town, when the spell by which he was held was destroyed. So Grace yielded to the notion herself, and encouraged it in others, that Lois Barclay had bewitched both Manasseh and Prudence. And the consequence of this belief was, that Lois was to be tried, with little chance in her favour, to see whether she was a witch or no; and if a witch, whether she would confess, implicate others, repent, and live a life of bitter shame, avoided by all men, and cruelly treated by most; or die impenitent, hardened, denying her crime upon the gallows.

And so they dragged Lois away from the congregation of Christians to the gaol, to await her trial. I say 'dragged her', because, although she was docile enough to have followed them whither they would, she was now so faint as to require extraneous force – poor Lois! who should have been carried and tended lovingly in her state of exhaustion, but, instead, was so detested by the multitude, who looked upon her as an accomplice of Satan in all his evil doings, that they cared no more how they treated her than a careless boy minds how he handles the toad that he is going to throw over the wall.

When Lois came to her full senses, she found herself lying on a short hard bed in a dark square room, which she at once knew must be a part of the city gaol. It was about eight feet square, it had stone walls on every side, and a grated opening high above her head, letting in all the light and air that could enter through about a square foot of aperture. It was so lonely, so dark to that poor girl, when she came slowly and painfully out of her long faint. She did so want human help in that struggle which always supervenes after a swoon; when the effort is to clutch at life, and the effort seems too much for the will. She did not at first understand where she was; did not understand how she came to be there, nor did she care to understand. Her physical instinct was to lie still and let the hurrying pulses have time to calm. So she shut her eyes once more. Slowly, slowly the recollection of the scene in the meeting-house shaped itself into a kind of picture before her. She saw within her eyelids, as it were, that sea of loathing faces all turned towards her, as towards something unclean and hateful. And you must remember, you who in the nineteenth century read this account, that witchcraft was a real terrible sin to her, Lois Barclay, two hundred years ago. The look on their faces, stamped on heart and brain, excited in her a sort of strange sympathy. Could it, oh God! – could it be true, that Satan had obtained the terrific power over her and her will, of which she had heard and read? Could she indeed be possessed by a demon and be indeed a witch, and yet till now have been unconscious of it? And her excited imagination recalled, with singular vividness, all she had ever heard on the subject – the horrible midnight sacrament, the very presence and power of Satan. Then remembering every angry thought against her neighbour, against the impertinences of Prudence, against the overbearing authority of her aunt, against the persevering crazy suit of Manasseh, the indignation – only that morning, but such ages off in real time – at Faith's injustice; oh, could such evil thoughts have had devilish power given to them by the father of evil, and, all unconsciously to herself, have gone forth as active curses into the world? And so, on the ideas went careering wildly through the poor girl's brain – the girl thrown inward upon herself. At length, the sting of her imagination forced her to start up impatiently. What was this? A weight of iron on her legs – a weight stated afterwards, by the gaoler of Salem prison, to have been 'not more than eight pounds'. It was well for Lois it was a tangible ill, bringing her back from the wild illimitable desert in which her imagination was wandering. She took hold of the iron, and saw her torn stocking – her bruised ankle, and began to cry pitifully, out of strange compassion with herself. They feared, then, that even in that cell she would find a way to escape. Why, the utter, ridiculous impossibility of the thing convinced her of her own innocence, and ignorance of all supernatural power; and the heavy iron brought her strangely round from the delusions that seemed to be gathering about her.

No! she never could fly out of that deep dungeon; there was no escape, natural or supernatural, for her, unless by man's mercy. And what was man's mercy in such times of panic? Lois knew that it was nothing; instinct more than reason taught her, that panic calls out cowardice, and cowardice cruelty. Yet she cried, cried freely, and for the first time, when she found herself ironed and chained. It seemed so cruel, so much as if her fellow-creatures had really learnt to hate and dread her – her, who had had a few angry thoughts, which God forgive! but whose thoughts had never gone into words, far less into actions. Why, even now she could love all the household at home, if they would but let her; yes, even yet, though she felt that it was the open accusation of Prudence and the withheld justifications of her aunt and Faith that had brought her to her present strait. Would they ever come and see her? Would kinder thoughts of her – who had shared their daily bread for months and months – bring them to see her, and ask her whether it were really she who had brought on the illness of Prudence, the derangement of Manasseh's mind?

No-one came. Bread and water were pushed in by someone, who hastily locked and unlocked the door, and cared not to see if he put them within his prisoner's reach, or perhaps thought that physical fact mattered little to a witch. It was long before Lois could reach them; and she had something of the natural hunger of youth left in her still, which prompted her, lying her length on the floor, to weary herself with efforts to obtain the bread. After she had eaten some of it, the day began to wane, and she thought she would lay her down and try to sleep. But before she did so, the gaoler heard her singing the Evening Hymn.

> Glory to thee, my God, this night,
> For all the blessings of the light.

And a dull thought came into his dull mind, that she was thankful for few blessings, if she could tune up her voice to sing praises after this day of what, if she were a witch, was shameful detection in abominable practices, and if not – well, his mind stopped short at this point in his wondering contemplation. Lois knelt down and said the Lord's Prayer, pausing just a little before one clause, that she might be sure that in her heart of hearts she did forgive. Then she looked at her ankle, and the tears came into her eyes once again, but not so much because she was hurt, as because men must have hated her so bitterly before they could have treated her thus. Then she lay down, and fell asleep.

The next day, she was led before Mr Hathorn and Mr Curwin, justices of Salem, to be accused legally and publicly of witchcraft. Others were with her, under the same charge. And when the prisoners were brought in, they were cried out at by the abhorrent crowd. The two Tappaus, Prudence, and one or two other girls of the same age were there, in the character of victims of the spells of the accused. The prisoners were placed about seven or eight feet from the justices and the accusers between the justices and them; the former were then ordered to stand right before the justices. All this Lois did at their bidding, with something of the wondering docility of a child, but not with any hope of softening the hard, stony look of detestation that was on all the countenances around her, save those that were distorted by more passionate anger. Then an officer was bidden to hold each of her hands, and Justice Hathorn bade her keep her eyes continually fixed on him, for this reason – which, however, was not told to her – lest, if she looked on Prudence, the girl might either fall into a fit, or cry out that she was suddenly and violently hurt. If any heart could have been touched of that cruel multitude, they would have felt some compassion for the sweet young face of the English girl, trying so meekly to do all that she was ordered, her face quite white, yet so full of sad gentleness, her grey eyes, a little dilated by the very solemnity of her position, fixed with the intent look of innocent maidenhood on the stern face of Justice Hathorn. And thus they stood in silence, one breathless minute. Then they were bidden to say the Lord's Prayer. Lois went through it as if alone in her cell; but, as she had done alone in her cell the night before, she made a little pause, before the prayer to be forgiven as she forgave. And at this instant of hesitation – as if they had been on the watch for it – they all cried out upon her for a witch, and when the clamour ended the justices bade Prudence Hickson come forwards. Then Lois turned a little to one side, wishing to see at least one familiar face; but when her eyes fell upon Prudence, the girl stood stock-still, and answered no questions, nor spoke a word, and the justices declared that she was struck dumb by witchcraft. Then some behind took Prudence under the arms, and would have forced her forwards to touch Lois, possibly esteeming that as a cure for her being bewitched. But Prudence had hardly been made to take three steps before she struggled out of their arms, and fell down writhing as in a fit, calling out with shrieks, and entreating Lois to help her, and save her from her torment. Then all the girls began 'to tumble down like swine' (to use the words of an eye-witness) and to cry out upon Lois and her fellow-prisoners. These last were now ordered to stand with their hands stretched out, it being imagined that if the bodies of the witches were arranged in the form of a cross they would lose their evil power. By and by Lois felt her strength going, from the unwonted fatigue of such a position, which she had borne patiently until the pain and weariness had forced both tears and sweat down her face, and she asked in a low, plaintive voice, if she might not rest her head for a few moments against the wooden partition. But Justice Hathorn told her she had strength enough to torment others, and should have strength enough to stand. She sighed a little, and bore on, the clamour against her and the other accused increasing every moment; the only way she could keep herself from utterly losing consciousness was by distracting herself from present pain and danger, and saying to herself verses of the Psalms as she could remember them, expressive of trust in God. At length she was ordered back to gaol, and dimly understood that she and others were sentenced to be hanged for witchcraft. Many people now looked eagerly at Lois, to see if she would weep at this doom. If she had had strength to cry, it might – it was just possible that it might – have been considered a plea in her favour, for witches could not shed tears, but she was too exhausted and dead. All she wanted was to lie down once more on her prison-bed, out of the reach of men's cries of abhorrence, and out of shot of their cruel eyes. So they led her back to prison, speechless and tearless.

But rest gave her back her power of thought and suffering. Was it, indeed, true that she was to die? She, Lois Barclay, only eighteen, so well, so young, so full of love and hope as she had been, till but these little days past! What would they think of it at home – real, dear home at Barford, in England? There they had loved her; there she had gone about, singing and rejoicing all the day long in the pleasant meadows by the Avon side. Oh, why did father and mother die, and leave her their bidding to come here to this cruel New England shore, where no-one had wanted her, no-one had cared for her, and where now they were going to put her to a shameful death as a witch? And there would be no-one to send kindly messages by to those she should never see more. Never more! Young Lucy was living, and joyful – probably thinking of her, and of his declared intention of coming to fetch her home to be his wife this very spring. Possibly he had forgotten her; no-one knew. A week before, she would have been indignant at her own distrust in thinking for a minute that he could forget. Now, she doubted all men's goodness for a time; for those around her were deadly, and cruel, and relentless.

Then she turned round, and beat herself with angry blows (to speak in images), for ever doubting her lover. Oh! if she were but with him! Oh! if she might but be with him! He would not let her die; but would hide her in his bosom from the wrath of this people, and carry her back to the old home at Barford. And he might even now be sailing on the wide blue sea, coming nearer, nearer every moment, and yet be too late after all.

So the thoughts chased each other through her head all that feverish night, till she clung almost deliriously to life, and wildly prayed that she might not die; at least, not just yet, and she so young!

Pastor Tappau and certain elders roused her up from a heavy sleep, late on the morning of the following day. All night long she had trembled and cried, till morning had come peering in through the square grating up above. It soothed her, and she fell asleep, to be awakened, as I have said, by Pastor Tappau.

'Arise!' said he, scrupling to touch her, from his superstitious idea of her evil powers. 'It is noonday.'

'Where am I?' said she, bewildered at this unusual wakening, and the array of severe faces all gazing upon her with reprobation.

'You are in Salem gaol, condemned for a witch.'

'Alas! I had forgotten for an instant,' said she, dropping her head upon her breast.

'She has been out on a devilish ride all night long, doubtless, and is weary and perplexed this morning,' whispered one, in so low a voice that he did not think she could hear; but she lifted up her eyes, and looked at him, with mute reproach.

'We are come' said Pastor Tappau, 'to exhort you to confess your great and manifold sin.'

'My great and manifold sin!' repeated Lois to herself, shaking her head.

'Yea, your sin of witchcraft. If you will confess, there may yet be balm in Gilead.'

One of the elders, struck with pity at the young girl's wan, shrunken look, said, that if she confessed, and repented, and did penance, possibly her life might yet be spared.

A sudden flash of light came into her sunk, dulled eye. Might she yet live? Was it yet in her power?

Why, no-one knew how soon Ralph Lucy might be here, to take her away for ever into the peace of a new home! Life! Oh, then, all hope was not over – perhaps she might still live, and not die. Yet the truth came once more out of her lips, almost without any exercise of her will.

'I am not a witch,' she said.

Then Pastor Tappau blindfolded her, all unresisting, but with languid wonder in her heart as to what was to come next. She heard people enter the dungeon softly, and heard whispering voices; then her hands were lifted up and made to touch someone near, and in an instant she heard a noise of struggling, and the well-known voice of Prudence shrieking out in one of her hysterical fits, and screaming to be taken away and out of that place. It seemed to Lois as if some of her judges must have doubted of her guilt, and demanded yet another test. She sat down heavily on her bed, thinking she must be in a horrible dream, so compassed about with dangers and enemies did she seem. Those in the dungeon – and by the oppression of the air she perceived that they were many – kept on eager talking in low voices. She did not try to make out the sense of the fragments of sentences that reached her dulled brain, till, all at once, a word or two made her understand they were discussing the desirableness of applying the whip or the torture to make her confess, and reveal by what means the spell she had cast upon those whom she had be-witched could be dissolved. A thrill of affright ran through her; and she cried out, beseechingly: 'I beg you, sirs, for God's mercy sake, that you do not use such awful means. I may say anything – nay, I may accuse anyone if I am subjected to such torment as I have heard tell about. For I am but a young girl, and not very brave, or very good, as some are.'

It touched the hearts of one or two to see her standing there; the tears streaming down from below the coarse handkerchief tightly bound over her eyes; the clanking chain fastening the heavy weight to the slight ankle; the two hands held together as if to keep down a convulsive motion.

'Look!' said one of these. 'She is weeping. They say no witch can weep tears.'

But another scoffed at this test, and bade the first remember how those of her own family, the Hicksons even, bore witness against her.

Once more she was bidden to confess. The charges, esteemed by all men (as they said) to have been proven against her, were read over to her, with all the testimony borne against her in proof thereof. They told her that, considering the godly family to which she be-longed, it had been decided by the magistrates and ministers of Salem that he should have her life spared, if she would own her guilt, make reparation, and submit to penance; but that if not, she, and others convicted of witchcraft along with her, were to be hung in Salem market-place on the next Thursday morning (Thursday being market day). And when they had thus spoken, they waited silently for her answer. It was a minute or two before she spoke. She had sat down again upon the bed meanwhile, for indeed she was very weak. She asked, 'May I have this handkerchief unbound from my eyes, for indeed, sirs, it hurts me?'

The occasion for which she was blindfolded being over, the band-age was taken off, and she was allowed to see. She looked pitifully at the stern faces around her, in grim suspense as to what her answer would be. Then she spoke: 'Sirs, I must choose death with a quiet conscience, rather than life to be gained by a lie. I am not a witch. I know not hardly what you mean when you say I am. I have done many, many things very wrong in my life; but I think God will forgive me them for my Saviour's sake.'

'Take not His name on your wicked lips,' said Pastor Tappau, enraged at her resolution of not confessing, and scarcely able to keep himself from striking her. She saw the desire he had, and shrank away in timid fear. Then Justice Hathorn solemnly read the legal condemnation of Lois Barclay to death by hanging, as a convicted witch. She murmured something which nobody heard fully, but which sounded like a prayer for pity and compassion on her tender years and friendless estate. Then they left her to all the horrors of that solitary, loathsome dungeon, and the strange terror of approaching death.

Outside the prison walls, the dread of the witches, and the excitement against witchcraft, grew with fearful rapidity. Numbers of women, and men, too, were accused, no matter what their station of life and their former character had been. On the other side, it is alleged that upwards of fifty persons were grievously vexed by the devil, and those to whom he had imparted of his power for vile and wicked considerations. How much of malice, distinct, unmistakable personal malice, was mixed up with these accusations, no-one can now tell. The dire statistics of this time tell us, that fifty-five escaped death by confessing themselves guilty, one hundred and fifty were in prison, more than two hundred accused, and upwards of twenty suffered death, among whom was the minister I have called Nolan, who was traditionally esteemed to have suffered through hatred of his co-pastor. One old man, scorning the accusation, and refusing to plead at his trial, was, according to the law, pressed to death for his contumacy. Nay, even dogs were accused of witchcraft, suffered the legal penalties, and are recorded among the subjects of capital punishment. One young man found means to effect his mother's escape from confinement, fled with her on horseback, and secreted her in the Blueberry Swamp, not far from Taplay's Brook, in the Great Pasture; he concealed her here in a wigwam which he built for her shelter, provided her with food and clothing, and comforted and sustained her until after the delusion had passed away. The poor creature must, however, have suffered dreadfully, for one of her arms was fractured in the all but desperate effort of getting her out of prison.

But there was no-one to try and save Lois. Grace Hickson would fain have ignored her altogether. Such a taint did witchcraft bring upon a whole family, that generations of blameless life were not at that day esteemed sufficient to wash it out. Besides, you must remember that Grace, along with most people of her time, believed most firmly in the reality of the crime of witchcraft. Poor, forsaken Lois believed in it herself, and it added to her terror, for the gaoler, in an unusually communicative mood, told her that nearly every cell was now full of witches; and it was possible he might have to put one, if more came, in with her. Lois knew that she was no witch herself; but not the less did she believe that the crime was abroad, and largely shared in by evil-minded persons who had chosen to give up their souls to Satan; and she shuddered with terror at what the gaoler said, and would have asked him to spare her this companionship if it were possible. But, somehow, her senses were leaving her, and she could not remember the right words in which to form her request, until he had left the place.

The only person who yearned after Lois – who would have befriended her if he could – was Manasseh: poor, mad Manasseh. But he was so wild and outrageous in his talk, that it was all his mother could do to keep his state concealed from public observation. She had for this purpose given him a sleeping potion; and, while he lay heavy and inert under the influence of the poppy-tea, his mother bound him with cords to the ponderous, antique bed in which he slept. She looked broken-hearted while she did this office, and thus acknowledged the degradation of her first-born – him of whom she had ever been so proud.

Late that evening, Grace Hickson stood in Lois's cell, hooded and cloaked up to her eyes. Lois was sitting quite still, playing idly with a bit of string which one of the magistrates had dropped out of his pocket that morning. Her aunt was standing by her for an instant or two in silence, before Lois seemed aware of her presence. Suddenly she looked up, and uttered a little cry, shrinking away from the dark figure. Then, as if her cry had loosened Grace's tongue, she began: 'Lois Barclay, did I ever do you any harm?'

Grace did not know how often her want of loving-kindness had pierced the tender heart of the stranger under her roof; nor did Lois remember it against her now. Instead, Lois's memory was filled with grateful thoughts of how much that might have been left undone, by a less conscientious person, her aunt had done for her, and she half stretched out her arms as to a friend in that desolate place, while she answered: 'Oh no, no you were very good! very kind!'

But Grace stood immovable.

'I did you no harm, although I never rightly knew why you came to us.'

'I was sent by my mother on her death-bed,' moaned Lois, covering her face. It grew darker every instant. Her aunt stood, still and silent.

'Did any of mine ever wrong you?' she asked, after a time.

'No, no; never, till Prudence said – Oh, aunt, do you think I am a witch?' And now Lois was standing up, holding by Grace's cloak and trying to read her face. Grace drew herself, ever so little, away from the girl, whom she dreaded, and yet sought to propitiate.

'Wiser than I, godlier than I, have said it. But oh, Lois, Lois! he was my first-born. Loose him from the demon, for the sake of Him whose name I dare not name in this terrible building, filled with them who have renounced the hopes of their baptism; loose Manasseh from his awful state, if ever I or mine did you a kindness!'

'You ask me for Christ's sake,' said Lois. 'I can name that holy name – for oh, aunt! indeed, and in holy truth, I am no witch; and yet I am to die – to be hanged! Aunt, do not let them kill me! I am so young, and I never did anyone any harm that I know of.'

'Hush! for very shame! This afternoon I have bound my first-born with strong cords, to keep him from doing himself or us a mischief – he is so frenzied. Lois Barclay, look here!' and Grace knelt down at her niece's feet, and joined her hands as if in prayer – 'I am a proud woman, God forgive me! and I never thought to kneel to any save to Him. And now I kneel at your feet, to pray you to release my children, more especially my son Manasseh, from the spells you have put upon them. Lois, hearken to me, and I will pray to the Almighty for you, if yet there may be mercy.'

'I cannot do it; I never did you or yours any wrong. How can I undo it? How can I?' And she wrung her hands in intensity of conviction of the inutility of aught she could do.

Here Grace got up, slowly, stiffly, and sternly. She stood aloof from the chained girl, in the remote corner of the prison cell near the door, ready to make her escape as soon as she had cursed the witch, who would not, or could not, undo the evil she had wrought. Grace lifted up her right hand, and held it up on high, as she doomed Lois to be accursed for ever, for her deadly sin, and her want of mercy even at this final hour. And, lastly, she summoned her to meet her at the judgment-seat, and answer for this deadly injury done to both souls and bodies of those who had taken her in, and received her when she came to them an orphan and a stranger.

Until this last summons, Lois had stood as one who hears her sentence and can say nothing against it, for she knows all would be in vain. But she raised her head when she heard her aunt speak of the judgment-seat, and at the end of Grace's speech she, too, lifted up her right hand, as if solemnly pledging herself by that action, and replied: 'Aunt! I will meet you there. And there you will know my innocence of this deadly thing. God have mercy on you and yours!'

Her calm voice maddened Grace, and making a gesture as if she plucked up a handful of dust of the floor, and threw it at Lois, she cried: 'Witch! Witch! Ask mercy for thyself – I need not your prayers. Witches' prayers are read backwards. I spit at thee, and defy thee!' And so she went away.

Lois sat moaning that whole night through. 'God comfort me! God strengthen me!' was all she could remember to say. She just felt that want, nothing more – all other fears and wants seemed dead within her. And when the gaoler brought in her breakfast the next morning, he reported her as 'gone silly'; for, indeed, she did not seem to know him, but kept rocking herself to and fro, and whispering softly to herself, smiling a little from time to time.

But God did comfort her, and strengthen her too. Late on that Wednesday afternoon, they thrust another 'witch' into her cell, bidding the two, with opprobrious words, keep company together. The newcomer fell prostrate with the push given her from without; and Lois, not recognising anything but an old ragged woman lying helpless on her face on the ground, lifted her up; and lo! it was Nattee – dirty, filthy indeed, mud-pelted, stone-bruised, beaten, and all astray in her wits with the treatment she had received from the mob outside. Lois held her in her arms, and softly wiped the old brown wrinkled face with her apron, crying over it, as she had hardly yet cried over her own sorrows. For hours she tended the old Indian woman – tended her bodily woes; and as the poor scattered senses of the savage creature came slowly back, Lois gathered her infinite dread of the morrow, when she too, as well as Lois, was to be led out to die, in face of all that infuriated crowd. Lois sought in her own mind for some source of comfort for the old woman, who shook like one in the shaking palsy at the dread of death – and such a death.

When all was quiet through the prison, in the deep dead midnight, the gaoler outside the door heard Lois telling, as if to a young child, the marvellous and sorrowful story of one who died on the cross for us and for our sakes. As long as she spoke, the Indian woman's terror seemed lulled; but the instant she paused, for weariness, Nattee cried out afresh, as if some wild beast were following her close through the dense forests in which she had dwelt in her youth. And then Lois went on, saying all the blessed words she could remember, and comforting the helpless Indian woman with the sense of the presence of a Heavenly Friend. And in comforting her, Lois was comforted; in strengthening her, Lois was strengthened.

The morning came, and the summons to come forth and die came. They who entered the cell found Lois asleep, her face resting on the slumbering old woman, whose head she still held in her lap. She did not seem clearly to recognise where she was, when she awakened; the 'silly' look had returned to her wan face; all she appeared to know was, that somehow or another, through some peril or another, she had to protect the poor Indian woman. She smiled faintly when she saw the bright light of the April day; and put her arm round Nattee, and tried to keep the Indian quiet with hushing, soothing words of broken meaning, and holy fragments of the Psalms. Nattee tightened her hold upon Lois as they drew near the gallows, and the outrageous crowd below began to hoot and yell. Lois redoubled her efforts to calm and encourage Nattee, apparently unconscious that any of the opprobrium, the hootings, the stones, the mud, was directed towards her herself. But when they took Nattee from her arms, and led her out to suffer first, Lois seemed all at once to recover her sense of the present terror. She gazed wildly around, stretched out her arms as if to some person in the distance, who was yet visible to her, and cried out once with a voice that thrilled through all who heard it, 'Mother!' Directly afterwards, the body of Lois the Witch swung in the air, and everyone stood, with hushed breath, with a sudden wonder, like a fear of deadly crime, fallen upon them.

The stillness and the silence were broken by one crazed and mad, who came rushing up the steps of the ladder, and caught Lois's body in his arms, and kissed her lips with wild passion. And then, as if it were true what the people believed, that he was possessed by a demon, he sprang down, and rushed through the crowd, out of the bounds of the city, and into the dark dense forest, and Manasseh Hickson was no more seen of Christian man.

The people of Salem had awakened from their frightful delusion before the autumn, when Captain Holdernesse and Ralph Lucy came to find out Lois, and bring her home to peaceful Barford, in the pleasant country of England. Instead, they led them to the grassy grave where she lay at rest, done to death by mistaken men. Ralph Lucy shook the dust off his feet in quitting Salem, with a heavy, heavy heart; and lived a bachelor all his life long for her sake.

Long years afterwards, Captain Holdernesse sought him out, to tell him some news that he thought might interest the grave miller of the Avonside. Captain Holdernesse told him that in the previous year, it was then 1713, the sentence of excommunication against the witches of Salem was ordered, in godly sacramental meeting of the church, to be erased and blotted out, and that those who met together for this purpose 'humbly requested the merciful God would pardon whatso-ever sin, error, or mistake was in the application of justice, through our merciful High Priest, who knoweth how to have compassion on the ignorant, and those that are out of the way'. He also said that Prudence Hickson – now woman grown – had made a most touching and pungent declaration of sorrow and repentance before the whole church, for the false and mistaken testimony she had given in several instances, among which she particularly mentioned that of her cousin Lois Barclay. To all which Ralph Lucy only answered: 'No repentance of theirs can bring her back to life.'

Then Captain Holdernesse took out a paper, and read the follow-ing humble and solemn declaration of regret on the part of those who signed it, among whom Grace Hickson was one.

We, whose names are undersigned, being, in the year 1692, called to serve as jurors in court of Salem, on trial of many who were by some suspected guilty of doing acts of witchcraft upon the bodies of sundry persons; we confess that we ourselves were not capable to understand, nor able to withstand, the mysterious delusions of the powers of darkness, and prince of the air, but were, for want of knowledge in ourselves, and better information from others, pre-vailed with to take up with such evidence against the accused, as, on further consideration, and better information, we justly fear was insufficient for the touching the lives of any (Deut. xvii. 6), whereby we fear we have been instrumental, with others, though ignorantly and unwittingly, to bring upon ourselves and this people of the Lord the guilt of innocent blood; which sin, the Lord saith in Scripture, he would not pardon (2 Kings, xxiv. 4), that is, we sup-pose, in regard of his temporal judgments. We do, therefore, signify to all in general (and to the surviving sufferers in special) our deep sense of, and sorrow for, our errors, in acting on such evidence to the condemning of any person; and do hereby declare, that we justly fear that we were sadly deluded and mistaken, for which we are much disquieted and distressed in our minds, and do therefore humbly beg forgiveness, first of God for Christ's sake, for this our error; and pray that God would not impute the guilt of it to ourselves nor others; and we also pray that we may be considered candidly and aright by the living sufferers, as being then under the power of a strong and general delusion, utterly unacquainted with, and not experienced in, matters of that nature.

We do heartily ask forgiveness of you all, whom we have justly offended; and do declare, according to our present minds, we would none of us do such things again on such grounds for the whole world; praying you to accept of this in way of satisfaction for our offence, and that you would bless the inheritance of the Lord, that he may be entreated for the land.

Foreman, THOMAS FISK, &c.

To the reading of this paper Ralph Lucy made no reply save this, even more gloomily than before: 'All their repentance will avail nothing to my Lois, nor will it bring back her life.'

Then Captain Holdernesse spoke once more, and said that on the day of the general fast, appointed to be held all through New England, when the meeting-houses were crowded, an old, old man with white hair had stood up in the place in which he was accustomed to worship, and had handed up into the pulpit a written confession, which he had once or twice essayed to read for himself, acknowledging his great and grievous error in the matter of the witches of Salem, and praying for the forgiveness of God and of his people, ending with an entreaty that all then present would join with him in prayer that his past conduct might not bring down the displeasure of the Most High upon his country, his family, or himself. That old man, who was no other than Justice Sewall, remained standing all the time that his confession was read; and at the end he said, 'The good and gracious God be pleased to save New England and me and my family.' And then it came out that, for years past, Judge Sewall had set apart a day for humiliation and prayer, to keep fresh in his mind a sense of repentance and sorrow for the part he had borne in these trials, and that this solemn anniversary he was pledged to keep as long as he lived, to show his feeling of deep humiliation.

Ralph Lucy's voice trembled as he spoke: 'All this will not bring my Lois to life again, or give me back the hope of my youth.'

But – as Captain Holdernesse shook his head (for what word could he say, or how dispute what was so evidently true?) – Ralph added, 'What is the day, know you, that this justice has set apart?'

'The twenty-ninth of April.'

'Then on that day will I, here at Barford in England, join my prayer as long as I live with the repentant judge, that his sin may be blotted out and no more had in remembrance. She would have willed it so.'

The Doom of the Griffiths

Chapter 1

I have always been much interested by the traditions which are scattered up and down North Wales relating to Owen Glendower (Owain Glendwr is the national spelling of the name), and I fully enter into the feeling which makes the Welsh peasant still look upon him as the hero of his country. There was great joy among many of the inhabitants of the principality, when the subject of the Welsh prize poem at Oxford, some fifteen or sixteen years ago, was announced to be 'Owain Glendwr'. It was the most proudly national subject that had been given for years.

Perhaps, some may not be aware that this redoubted chieftain is, even in the present days of enlightenment, as famous among his illiterate countrymen for his magical powers as for his patriotism. He says himself – or Shakespeare says it for him, which is much the same thing –

> At my nativity
> The front of heaven was full of fiery shapes
> Of burning cressets . . .
> I can call spirits from the vasty deep.

And few among the lower orders in the principality would think of asking Hotspur's irreverent question in reply.

Among other traditions preserved relative to this part of the Welsh hero's character, is the old family prophecy which gives title to this tale. When Sir David Gam, 'as black a traitor as if he had been born in Builth', sought to murder Owen at Machynlleth, there was one with him whose name Glendwr little dreamed of having associated with his enemies. Rhys ap Gryfydd, his 'old familiar friend', his relation, his more than brother, had consented unto his blood. Sir David Gam might be forgiven, but one whom he had loved, and who had betrayed him, could never be forgiven. Glendwr was too deeply read in the human heart to kill him. No, he let him live on, the

loathing and scorn of his compatriots, and the victim of bitter remorse. The mark of Cain was upon him.

But before he went forth – while he yet stood a prisoner, cowering
beneath his conscience before Owain Glendwr – that chieftain passed
a doom upon him and his race.

'I doom thee to live, because I know thou wilt pray for death. Thou
shalt live on beyond the natural term of the life of man, the scorn of
all good men. The very children shall point to thee with hissing
tongue, and say, 'There goes one who would have shed a brother's
blood!' For I loved thee more than a brother, O Rhys ap Gryfydd!
Thou shalt live on to see all of thy house, except the weakling in
arms, perish by the sword. Thy race shall be accursed. Each generation shall see their lands melt away like snow; yea their wealth shall
vanish, though they may labour night and day to heap up gold. And
when nine generations have passed from the face of the earth, thy
blood shall no longer flow in the veins of any human being. In those
days the last male of thy race shall avenge me. The son shall slay
the father.'

Such was the traditional account of Owain Glendwr's speech to
his once-trusted friend. And it was declared that the doom had been
fulfilled in all things; that live in as miserly a manner as they would,
the Griffiths never were wealthy and prosperous – indeed that their
worldly stock diminished without any visible cause.

But the lapse of many years had almost deadened the wonder-
inspiring power of the whole curse. It was only brought forth from
the hoards of Memory when some untoward event happened to
the Griffiths family; and in the eighth generation the faith in the
prophecy was nearly destroyed, by the marriage of the Griffiths
of that day, to a Miss Owen, who, unexpectedly, by the death of a
brother, became an heiress – to no considerable amount, to be sure,
but enough to make the prophecy appear reversed. The heiress and
her husband removed from his small patrimonial estate in Merion-
ethshire, to her heritage in Caernarvonshire, and for a time the
prophecy lay dormant.

If you go from Tremadoc to Criccaeth, you pass by the parochial
church of Ynysynhanarn, situated in a boggy valley running from the
mountains, which shoulder up to the Rivals, down to Cardigan Bay.
This tract of land has every appearance of having been redeemed at
no distant period of time from the sea, and has all the desolate
rankness often attendant upon such marshes. But the valley beyond,
similar in character, had yet more of gloom at the time of which

I write. In the higher part there were large plantations of firs, set too closely to attain any size, and remaining stunted in height and scrubby in appearance. Indeed, many of the smaller and more weakly had died, and the bark had fallen down on the brown soil neglected and unnoticed. These trees had a ghastly appearance, with their white trunks, seen by the dim light which struggled through the thick boughs above. Nearer to the sea, the valley assumed a more open, though hardly a more cheerful character; it looked dark and overhung by sea-fog through the greater part of the year, and even a farm-house, which usually imparts something of cheerfulness to a landscape, failed to do so here. This valley formed the greater part of the estate to which Owen Griffiths became entitled by right of his wife. In the higher part of the valley was situated the family mansion, or rather dwelling-house, for 'mansion' is too grand a word to apply to the clumsy, but substantially-built Bodowen. It was square and heavy-looking, with just that much pretension to ornament necessary to distinguish it from the mere farm-house.

In this dwelling Mrs Owen Griffiths bore her husband two sons – Llewellyn, the future Squire, and Robert, who was early destined for the Church. The only difference in their situation, up to the time when Robert was entered at Jesus College, was, that the elder was invariably indulged by all around him, while Robert was thwarted and indulged by turns; that Llewellyn never learned anything from the poor Welsh parson, who was nominally his private tutor; while occasionally Squire Griffiths made a great point of enforcing Robert's diligence, telling him that, as he had his bread to earn, he must pay attention to his learning. There is no knowing how far the very irregular education he had received would have carried Robert through his college examinations; but, luckily for him in this respect, before such a trial of his learning came round, he heard of the death of his elder brother, after a short illness, brought on by a hard drinking-bout. Of course, Robert was summoned home, and it seemed quite as much of course, now that there was no necessity for him to 'earn his bread by his learning', that he should not return to Oxford. So the half-educated, but not unintelligent, young man continued at home, during the short remainder of his parent's lifetime.

His was not an uncommon character. In general he was mild, in-dolent, and easily managed; but once thoroughly roused, his passions were vehement and fearful. He seemed, indeed, almost afraid of himself, and in common hardly dared to give way to justifiable anger –

so much did he dread losing his self-control. Had he been judiciously educated, he would, probably, have distinguished himself in those branches of literature which call for taste and imagination, rather than any exertion of reflection or judgment. As it was, his literary taste showed itself in making collections of Cambrian antiquities of every description, till his stock of Welsh MSS. would have excited the envy of Dr Pugh himself, had he been alive at the time of which I write.

There is one characteristic of Robert Griffiths which I have omitted to note, and which was peculiar among his class. He was no hard drinker; whether it was that his head was easily affected, or that his partially-refined taste led him to dislike intoxication and its attendant circumstances, I cannot say; but at five-and-twenty Robert Griffiths was habitually sober – a thing so rare in Llyn, that he was almost shunned as a churlish, unsociable being, and passed much of his time in solitude.

About this time, he had to appear in some case that was tried at the Caernarvon assizes; and while there, was a guest at the house of his agent, a shrewd, sensible Welsh attorney, with one daughter, who had charms enough to captivate Robert Griffiths. Though he remained only a few days at her father's house, they were sufficient to decide his affections, and short was the period allowed to elapse before he brought home a mistress to Bodowen. The new Mrs Griffiths was a gentle, yielding person, full of love toward her husband, of whom, nevertheless, she stood something in awe, partly arising from the difference in their ages, partly from his devoting much time to studies of which she could understand nothing.

She soon made him the father of a blooming little daughter, called Angharad after her mother. Then there came several uneventful years in the household of Bodowen; and when the old women had one and all declared that the cradle would not rock again, Mrs Griffiths bore the son and heir. His birth was soon followed by his mother's death: she had been ailing and low-spirited during her pregnancy, and she seemed to lack the buoyancy of body and mind requisite to bring her round after her time of trial. Her husband, who loved her all the more from having few other claims on his affections, was deeply grieved by her early death, and his only comforter was the sweet little boy whom she had left behind. That part of the squire's character, which was so tender, and almost feminine, seemed called forth by the helpless situation of the little infant, who stretched out his arms to his father with the same earnest cooing that happier children make use of to their mother alone. Angharad was almost neglected, while the little Owen was king of the house; still, next to his father, none tended him so lovingly as his sister. She was so accustomed to give way to him that it was no longer a hardship. By night and by day Owen was the constant companion of his father, and increasing years seemed only to confirm the custom. It was an unnatural life for the child, seeing no bright little faces peering into his own (for Angharad was, as I said before, five or six years older, and her face, poor motherless girl! was often anything but bright), hearing no din of clear ringing voices, but day after day sharing the otherwise solitary hours of his father, whether in the dim room, surrounded by wizard-like antiquities, or pattering his little feet to keep up with his 'tada' in his mountain rambles or shooting excursions. When the pair came to some little foaming brook, where the stepping-stones were far and wide, the father carried his little boy across with the tenderest care; when the lad was weary, they rested, he cradled in his father's arms, or the Squire would lift him up and carry him to his home again. The boy was indulged (for his father felt flattered by the desire) in his wish of sharing his meals and keeping the same hours. All this indulgence did not render Owen unamiable, but it made him wilful, and not a happy child. He had a thoughtful look, not common to the face of a young boy. He knew no games, no merry sports; his information was of an imaginative and speculative character. His father delighted to interest him in his own studies, without considering how far they were healthy for so young a mind.

Of course Squire Griffiths was not unaware of the prophecy which was to be fulfilled in his generation. He would occasionally refer to it when among his friends, with sceptical levity; but in truth it lay nearer to his heart than he chose to acknowledge. His strong imagination rendered him peculiarly impressible on such subjects; while his judgment, seldom exercised or fortified by severe thought, could not prevent his continually recurring to it. He used to gaze on the half-sad countenance of the child, who sat looking up into his face with his large dark eyes, so fondly yet so inquiringly, till the old legend swelled around his heart, and became too painful for him not to require sympathy. Besides, the overpowering love he bore to the child seemed to demand fuller vent than tender words; it made him like, yet dread, to upbraid its object for the fearful contrast foretold. Still Squire Griffiths told the legend, in a half-jesting manner, to his little son, when they were roaming over the wild heaths in the autumn days, 'the saddest of the year', or while they sat in the oak-wainscoted room, surrounded by mysterious relics that gleamed strangely forth by the flickering fire-light. The legend was wrought into the boy's mind, and he would crave, yet tremble, to hear it told over and over again, while the words were intermingled with caresses and questions as to his love. Occasionally his loving words and actions were cut short by his father's light yet bitter speech – 'Get thee away, my lad; thou knowest not what is to come of all this love.'

When Angharad was seventeen, and Owen eleven or twelve, the rector of the parish in which Bodowen was situated, endeavoured to prevail on Squire Griffiths to send the boy to school. Now, this rector had many congenial tastes with his parishioner, and was his only intimate; and, by repeated arguments, he succeeded in convincing the Squire that the unnatural life Owen was leading was in every way injurious. Unwillingly was the father wrought to part from his son; but he did at length send him to the Grammar School at Bangor, then under the management of an excellent classic. Here Owen showed that he had more talents than the rector had given him credit for, when he affirmed that the lad had been completely stupefied by the life he led at Bodowen. He bade fair to do credit to the school in the peculiar branch of learning for which it was famous. But he was not popular among his schoolfellows. He was wayward, though to a certain degree generous and unselfish; he was reserved but gentle, except when the tremendous bursts of passion (similar in character to those of his father) forced their way.

On his return from school one Christmas-time, when he had been a year or so at Bangor, he was stunned by hearing that the under-valued Angharad was about to be married to a gentleman of South Wales, residing near Aberystwyth. Boys seldom appreciate their sisters; but Owen thought of the many slights with which he had requited the patient Angharad, and he gave way to bitter regrets, which, with a selfish want of control over his words, he kept expressing to his father, until the Squire was thoroughly hurt and chagrined at the repeated exclamations of 'What shall we do when Angharad is gone?' 'How dull we shall be when Angharad is married!' Owen's holidays were prolonged a few weeks, in order that he might be present at the wedding; and when all the festivities were over, and the bride and bridegroom had left Bodowen, the boy and his father really felt how much they missed the quiet, loving Angharad. She had performed so many thoughtful, noiseless little offices, on which their daily comfort depended; and now she was gone, the household seemed to miss the spirit that peacefully kept it in order; the servants roamed about in search of commands and directions, the rooms had no longer the unobtrusive ordering of taste to make them cheerful, the very fires burned dim, and were always sinking down into dull heaps of gray ashes. Altogether Owen did not regret his return to Bangor, and this also the mortified parent perceived. Squire Griffiths was a selfish parent.

Letters in those days were a rare occurrence. Owen usually received one during his half-yearly absences from home, and occasionally his father paid him a visit. This half-year the boy had no visit, nor even a letter, till very near the time of his leaving school, and then he was astounded by the intelligence that his father was married again.

Then came one of his paroxysms of rage; the more disastrous in its effects upon his character because it could find no vent in action. Independently of slight to the memory of the first wife which children are so apt to fancy such an action implies, Owen had hitherto considered himself (and with justice) the first object of his father's life. They had been so much to each other; and now a shapeless, but too real something had come between him and his father there for ever. He felt as if his permission should have been asked, as if he should have been consulted. Certainly he ought to have been told of the intended event. So the Squire felt, and hence his constrained letter which had so much increased the bitterness of Owen's feelings.

With all this anger, when Owen saw his stepmother, he thought he had never seen so beautiful a woman for her age; for she was no longer in the bloom of youth, being a widow when his father married her. Her manners, to the Welsh lad, who had seen little of female grace among the families of the few antiquarians with whom his father visited, were so fascinating that he watched her with a sort of breathless admiration. Her measured grace, her faultless movements, her tones of voice, sweet, till the ear was sated with their sweetness, made Owen less angry at his father's marriage. Yet he felt, more than ever, that the cloud was between him and his father; that the hasty letter he had sent in answer to the announcement of his wedding was not forgotten, although no allusion was ever made to it. He was no longer his father's confidant – hardly ever his father's companion, for the newly-married wife was all in all to the Squire, and his son felt himself almost a cipher, where he had so long been everything. The lady herself had ever the softest consideration for her stepson; almost too obtrusive was the attention paid to his wishes, but still he fancied that the heart had no part in the winning advances. There was a watchful glance of the eye that Owen once or twice caught when she had imagined herself unobserved, and many other nameless little circumstances, that gave him a strong feeling of want of sincerity in his stepmother. Mrs Owen brought with her into the family her little child by her first husband, a boy nearly three years old. He was one of those elfish, observant, mocking children, over whose feelings you seem to have no control: agile and mischievous, his little practical jokes, at first performed in ignorance of the pain he gave, but afterward proceeding to a malicious pleasure in suffering, really seemed to afford some ground to the superstitious notion of some of the common people that he was a fairy changeling.

Years passed on; and as Owen grew older he became more observant. He saw, even in his occasional visits at home (for from school he had passed on to college), that a great change had taken place in the outward manifestations of his father's character; and, by degrees, Owen traced this change to the influence of his stepmother; so slight, so imperceptible to the common observer, yet so resistless in its effects. Squire Griffiths caught up his wife's humbly advanced opinions, and, unawares to himself, adopted them as his own, defying all argument and opposition. It was the same with her wishes; they met their fulfilment, from the extreme and delicate art with which she insinuated them into her husband's mind, as his own. She sacrificed the show of authority for the power. At last, when Owen perceived some oppressive act in his father's conduct toward his dependants, or some unaccountable thwarting of his own wishes, he fancied he saw his stepmother's secret influence thus displayed, however much she might regret the injustice of his father's actions in her conversations with him when they were alone. His father was fast losing his temperate habits, and frequent intoxication soon took its usual effect upon the temper. Yet even here was the spell of his wife upon him. Before her he placed a restraint upon his passion, yet she was perfectly aware of his irritable disposition, and directed it hither and thither with the same apparent ignorance of the tendency of her words.

Meanwhile Owen's situation became peculiarly mortifying to a youth whose early remembrances afforded such a contrast to his present state. As a child, he had been elevated to the consequence of a man before his years gave any mental check to the selfishness which such conduct was likely to engender; he could remember when his will was law to the servants and dependants, and his sympathy necessary to his father: now he was as a cipher in his father's house; and the Squire, estranged in the first instance by a feeling of the injury he had done his son in not sooner acquainting him with his purposed marriage, seemed rather to avoid than to seek him as a companion, and too frequently showed the most utter indifference to the feelings and wishes which a young man of a high and independent spirit might be supposed to indulge.

Perhaps Owen was not fully aware of the force of all these circumstances; for an actor in a family drama is seldom unimpassioned enough to be perfectly observant. But he became moody and soured; brooding over his unloved existence, and craving with a human heart after sympathy.

This feeling took more full possession of his mind when he had left college, and returned home to lead an idle and purposeless life. As the heir, there was no worldly necessity for exertion: his father was too much of a Welsh squire to dream of the moral necessity, and he himself had not sufficient strength of mind to decide at once upon abandoning a place and mode of life which abounded in daily mortifications; yet to this course his judgment was slowly tending, when some circumstances occurred to detain him at Bodowen.

It was not to be expected that harmony would long be preserved, even in appearance, between an unguarded and soured young man, such as Owen, and his wary stepmother, when he had once left college, and come, not as a visitor, but as the heir to his father's house. Some cause of difference occurred, where the woman subdued her hidden anger sufficiently to become convinced that Owen was not entirely the dupe she had believed him to be. Henceforward there was no peace between them. Not in vulgar altercations did this show itself; but in moody reserve on Owen's part, and in undisguised and contemptuous pursuance of her own plans by his stepmother. Bodowen was no longer a place where, if Owen was not loved or attended to, he could at least find peace, and care for himself: he was thwarted at every step, and in every wish, by his father's desire, apparently, while the wife sat by with a smile of triumph on her beautiful lips.

So Owen went forth at the early day dawn, sometimes roaming about on the shore or the upland, shooting or fishing, as the season might be, but oftener 'stretched in indolent repose' on the short, sweet grass, indulging in gloomy and morbid reveries. He would fancy that this mortified state of existence was a dream, a horrible dream, from which he should awake and find himself again the sole object and darling of his father. And then he would start up and strive to shake off the incubus. There was the molten sunset of his childish memory; the gorgeous crimson piles of glory in the west, fading away into the cold calm light of the rising moon, while here and there a cloud floated across the western heaven, like a seraph's wing, in its flaming beauty; the earth was the same as in his childhood's days, full of gentle evening sounds, and the harmonies of twilight – the breeze came sweeping low over the heather and bluebells by his side, and the turf was sending up its evening incense of perfume. But life, and heart, and hope were changed for ever since those bygone days!

Or he would seat himself in a favourite niche of the rocks on Moel Gest, hidden by a stunted growth of the whitty, or mountain-ash, from general observation, with a rich-tinted cushion of stone-crop for his feet, and a straight precipice of rock rising just above. Here would he sit for hours, gazing idly at the bay below with its background of purple hills, and the little fishing-sail on its bosom, showing white in the sunbeam, and gliding on in such harmony with the quiet beauty of the glassy sea; or he would pull out an old school-volume, his companion for years, and in morbid accordance with the dark legend that still lurked in the recesses of his mind – a shape of gloom in those innermost haunts awaiting its time to come forth in distinct outline – would he turn to the old Greek dramas which treat of a family foredoomed by an avenging Fate. The worn page opened of itself at the play of the *Oedipus Tyrannus*, and Owen dwelt with the craving disease upon the prophecy so nearly resembling that which concerned himself. With his consciousness of neglect, there was a sort of self-flattery in the consequence which the legend gave him. He almost wondered how they durst, with slights and insults, thus provoke the Avenger.

The days drifted onward. Often he would vehemently pursue some sylvan sport, till thought and feeling were lost in the violence of bodily exertion. Occasionally his evenings were spent at a small public-house, such as stood by the unfrequented wayside, where the welcome, hearty, though bought, seemed so strongly to contrast with the gloomy negligence of home – unsympathising home.

One evening (Owen might be four or five-and-twenty), wearied with a day's shooting on the Clenneny Moors, he passed by the open door of The Goat at Penmorfa. The light and the cheeriness within tempted him, poor self-exhausted man! as it has done many a one more wretched in worldly circumstances, to step in, and take his evening meal where at least his presence was of some consequence. It was a busy day in that little hostel. A flock of sheep, amounting to some hundreds, had arrived at Penmorfa, on their road to England, and thronged the space before the house. Inside was the shrewd, kind-hearted hostess, bustling to and fro, with merry greetings for every tired drover who was to pass the night in her house, while the sheep were penned in a field close by. Ever and anon, she kept attending to the second crowd of guests, who were celebrating a rural wedding in her house. It was busy work to Martha Thomas, yet her smile never flagged; and when Owen Griffiths had finished his evening meal she was there, ready with a hope that it had done him good, and was to his mind, and a word of intelligence that the wedding-folk were about to dance in the kitchen, and the harper was the famous Edward of Corwen.

Owen, partly from good-natured compliance with his hostess's implied wish, and partly from curiosity, lounged to the passage which led to the kitchen – not the everyday, working, cooking kitchen, which was behind, but a good-sized room, where the mistress sat, when her work was done, and where the country people were commonly entertained at such merry-makings as the present. The lintels of the door formed a frame for the animated picture which Owen saw within, as he leaned against the wall in the dark passage. The red light of the fire, with every now and then a falling piece of turf sending forth a fresh blaze, shone full upon four young men who were dancing a measure something like a Scotch reel, keeping admirable time in their rapid movements to the capital tune the harper was playing. They had their hats on when Owen first took his stand, but as they grew more and more animated they flung them away, and presently their shoes were kicked off with like disregard to the spot where they might happen to alight. Shouts of applause followed any remarkable exertion of agility, in which each seemed to try to excel his companions. At length, wearied and exhausted, they sat down, and the harper gradually changed to one of those wild, inspiring national airs for which he was so famous. The thronged audience sat earnest and breathless, and you might have heard a pin drop, except when some maiden passed hurriedly, with flaring candle and busy look, through to the real kitchen beyond. When he had finished his beautiful theme on 'The March of the Men of Harlech', he changed the measure again to 'Tri chant o'bunnan' ('Three hundred pounds'), and immediately a most unmusical-looking man began chanting 'Pennillion', or a sort of recitative stanzas, which were soon taken up by another, and this amusement lasted so long that Owen grew weary, and was thinking of retreating from his post by the door, when some little bustle was occasioned, on the opposite side of the room, by the entrance of a middle-aged man, and a young

girl, apparently his daughter. The man advanced to the bench occupied by the seniors of the party, who welcomed him with the usual
pretty Welsh greeting, 'Pa sut mae dy galon?' ('How is thy heart?')
and drinking his health passed on to him the cup of excellent cwrw.*
The girl, evidently a village belle, was as warmly greeted by the
young men, while the girls eyed her rather askance with a half-
jealous look, which Owen set down to the score of her extreme
prettiness. Like most Welsh women, she was of middle size as to
height, but beautifully made, with the most perfect yet delicate
roundness in every limb. Her little mob-cap was carefully adjusted to
a face which was excessively pretty, though it never could be called
handsome. It also was round, with the slightest tendency to the oval
shape, richly coloured, though somewhat olive in complexion, with
dimples in cheek and chin, and the most scarlet lips Owen had ever
seen, that were too short to meet over the small pearly teeth. The
nose was the most defective feature; but the eyes were splendid.
They were so long, so lustrous, yet at times so very soft under their
thick fringe of eyelash! The nut-brown hair was carefully braided
beneath the border of delicate lace: it was evident the little village
beauty knew how to make the most of all her attractions, for the gay
colours which were displayed in her neckerchief were in complete
harmony with the complexion.

Owen was much attracted, while yet he was amused, by the evident
coquetry the girl displayed, collecting around her a whole bevy of
young fellows, for each of whom she seemed to have some gay speech,
some attractive look or action. In a few minutes young Griffiths of
Bodowen was at her side, brought thither by a variety of idle motives,
and as her undivided attention was given to the Welsh heir, her
admirers, one by one, dropped off, to seat themselves by some less
fascinating but more attentive fair one. The more Owen conversed
with the girl, the more he was taken; she had more wit and talent than
he had fancied possible; a self-abandon and thoughtfulness, to boot,
that seemed full of charms; and then her voice was so clear and sweet,
and her actions so full of grace, that Owen was fascinated before he
was well aware, and kept looking into her bright, blushing face, till her
uplifted flashing eye fell beneath his earnest gaze.

While it thus happened that they were silent – she from confusion
at the unexpected warmth of his admiration, he from an unconsciousness of anything but the beautiful changes in her flexile countenance –
the man whom Owen took for her father came up and addressed

* Beer.

some observation to his daughter, from whence he glided into some commonplace though respectful remark to Owen, and at length engaging him in some slight, local conversation, he led the way to the account of a spot on the peninsula of Penthryn, where teal abounded, and concluded with begging Owen to allow him to show him the exact place, saying that whenever the young Squire felt so inclined, if he would honour him by a call at his house, he would take him across in his boat. While Owen listened, his attention was not so much absorbed as to be unaware that the little beauty at his side was refusing one or two who endeavoured to draw her from her place by invitations to dance. Flattered by his own construction of her refusals, he again directed all his attention to her, till she was called away by her father, who was leaving the scene of festivity. Before he left he reminded Owen of his promise, and added: 'Perhaps, sir, you do not know me. My name is Ellis Pritchard, and I live at Ty Glas, on this side of Moel Gest; anyone can point it out to you.'

When the father and daughter had left, Owen slowly prepared for his ride home; but encountering the hostess, he could not resist asking a few questions relative to Ellis Pritchard and his pretty daughter. She answered shortly but respectfully, and then said, rather hesitatingly: 'Master Griffiths, you know the triad, "Tri pheth tebyg y naill i'r llall, ysgnbwr heb yd, mail deg heb ddiawd, a merch deg heb ei geirda" ("Three things are alike: a fine barn without corn, a fine cup without drink, a fine woman without her reputation").' She hastily quitted him, and Owen rode slowly to his unhappy home.

Ellis Pritchard, half farmer and half fisherman, was shrewd, and keen, and worldly; yet he was good-natured, and sufficiently generous to have become rather a popular man among his equals. He had been struck with the young Squire's attention to his pretty daughter, and was not insensible to the advantages to be derived from it. Nest would not be the first peasant girl, by any means, who had been transplanted to a Welsh manor-house as its mistress; and, accordingly, her father had shrewdly given the admiring young man some pretext for further opportunities of seeing her.

As for Nest herself, she had somewhat of her father's worldliness, and was fully alive to the superior station of her new admirer, and quite prepared to slight all her old sweethearts on his account. But then she had something more of feeling in her reckoning; she had not been insensible to the earnest yet comparatively refined homage which Owen paid her; she had noticed his expressive and occasionally handsome countenance with admiration, and was flattered by his so immediately singling her out from her companions. As to the hint which Martha Thomas had thrown out, it is enough to say that Nest was very giddy, and that she was motherless. She had high spirits and a great love of admiration, or, to use a softer term, she loved to please; men, women, and children, all, she delighted to gladden with her smile and voice. She coquetted, and flirted, and went to the extreme lengths of Welsh courtship, till the seniors of the village shook their heads, and cautioned their daughters against her acquaintance. If not absolutely guilty, she had too frequently been on the verge of guilt.

Even at the time, Martha Thomas's hint made but little impression on Owen, for his senses were otherwise occupied; but in a few days the recollection thereof had wholly died away, and one warm glorious summer's day, he bent his steps toward Ellis Pritchard's with a beating heart; for, except some very slight flirtations at Oxford, Owen had never been touched; his thoughts, his fancy, had been otherwise engaged.

Ty Glas was built against one of the lower rocks of Moel Gest, which, indeed, formed a side to the low, lengthy house. The materials of the cottage were the shingly stones which had fallen from above, plastered rudely together, with deep recesses for the small oblong windows. Altogether, the exterior was much ruder than Owen had expected; but inside there seemed no lack of comforts. The house was divided into two apartments, one large, roomy, and dark, into which Owen entered immediately; and before the blushing Nest came from the inner chamber (for she had seen the young Squire coming, and hastily gone to make some alteration in her dress), he had had time to look around him, and note the various little particulars of the room. Beneath the window (which commanded a magnificent view) was an oaken dresser, replete with drawers and cupboards, and brightly polished to a rich dark colour. In the farther part of the room Owen could at first distinguish little, entering as he did from the glaring sunlight, but he soon saw that there were two oaken beds, closed up after the manner of the Welsh: in fact, the domitories of Ellis Pritchard and the man who served under him, both on sea and on land. There was the large wheel used for spinning wool, left standing on the middle of the floor, as if in use only a few minutes before; and around the ample chimney hung flitches of bacon, dried kids'-flesh, and fish, that was in process of smoking for winter's store.

Before Nest had shyly dared to enter, her father, who had been mending his nets down below, and seen Owen winding up to the house, came in and gave him a hearty yet respectful welcome; and then Nest, downcast and blushing, full of the consciousness which her father's advice and conversation had not failed to inspire, ventured to join them. To Owen's mind this reserve and shyness gave her new charms.

It was too bright, too hot, too anything to think of going to shoot teal till later in the day, and Owen was delighted to accept a hesitating invitation to share the noonday meal. Some ewe-milk cheese, very hard and dry, oat-cake, slips of the dried kids'-flesh broiled, after having been previously soaked in water for a few minutes, delicious butter and fresh butter-milk, with a liquor called 'diod griafol' (made from the berries of the *sorbus aucuparia*, infused in water and then fermented), composed the frugal repast; but there was something so clean and neat, and withal such a true welcome, that Owen had seldom enjoyed a meal so much. Indeed, at that time of day the Welsh squires differed from the farmers more in the plenty and rough abundance of their manner of living than in the refinement of style of their table.

At the present day, down in Llyn, the Welsh gentry are not a wit behind their Saxon equals in the expensive elegances of life; but then (when there was but one pewter-service in all Northumberland) there was nothing in Ellis Pritchard's mode of living that grated on the young Squire's sense of refinement.

Little was said by that young pair of wooers during the meal; the father had all the conversation to himself, apparently heedless of the ardent looks and inattentive mien of his guest. As Owen became more serious in his feelings, he grew more timid in their expression, and at night, when they returned from their shooting-excursion, the caress he gave Nest was almost as bashfully offered as received.

This was but the first of a series of days devoted to Nest in reality, though at first he thought some little disguise of his object was necessary. The past, the future, was all forgotten in those happy days of love.

And every worldly plan, every womanly wile was put in practice by Ellis Pritchard and his daughter, to render his visits agreeable and alluring. Indeed, the very circumstance of his being welcome was enough to attract the poor young man, to whom the feeling so produced was new and full of charms. He left a home where the certainty of being thwarted made him chary in expressing his wishes; where no tones of love ever fell on his ear, save those addressed to others; where his presence or absence was a matter of utter indifference; and when he entered Ty Glas, all, down to the little cur which, with clamorous barkings, claimed a part of his attention, seemed to rejoice. His account of his day's employment found a willing listener in Ellis; and when he passed on to Nest, busy at her wheel or at her churn, the deepened colour, the conscious eye, and the gradual yielding of herself up to his lover-like caress, had worlds of charms. Ellis Pritchard was a tenant on the Bodowen estate, and therefore had reasons in plenty for wishing to keep the young Squire's visits secret; and Owen, unwilling to disturb the sunny calm of these halcyon days by any storm at home, was ready to use all the artifice which Ellis suggested as to the mode of his calls at Ty Glas. Nor was he unaware of the probable, nay, the hoped-for termination of these repeated days of happiness. He was quite conscious that the father wished for nothing better than the marriage of his daughter to the heir of Bodowen; and when Nest had hidden her face in his neck, which was encircled by her clasping arms, and murmured into his ear her acknowledgment of love, he felt only too desirous of finding someone to love him for ever. Though not highly principled, he would not have tried to obtain Nest on other terms save those of marriage: he did so pine after enduring love, and fancied he should have bound her heart for evermore to his, when they had taken the solemn oaths of matrimony.

There was no great difficulty attending a secret marriage at such a place and at such a time. One gusty autumn day, Ellis ferried them round Penthryn to Llandutrwyn, and there saw his little Nest become future Lady of Bodowen.

How often do we see giddy, coquetting, restless girls become sobered by marriage? A great object in life is decided; one on which their thoughts have been running in all their vagaries, and they seem to verify the beautiful fable of Undine. A new soul beams out in the gentleness and repose of their future lives. An indescribable softness and tenderness takes place of the wearying vanity of their former endeavours to attract admiration. Something of this sort took place in Nest Pritchard. If at first she had been anxious to attract the young Squire of Bodowen, long before her marriage this feeling had merged into a truer love than she had ever felt before; and now that he was her own, her husband, her whole soul was bent toward making him amends, as far as in her lay, for the misery which, with a woman's tact, she saw that he had to endure at his home. Her greetings were abounding in delicately-expressed love; her study of his tastes unwearying, in the arrangement of her dress, her time, her very thoughts.

No wonder that he looked back on his wedding-day with a thankfulness which is seldom the result of unequal marriages. No wonder that his heart beat aloud as formerly when he wound up the little path to Ty Glas, and saw – keen though the winter's wind might be – that Nest was standing out at the door to watch for his dimly-seen approach, while the candle flared in the little window as a beacon to guide him aright.

The angry words and unkind actions of home fell deadened on his heart; he thought of the love that was surely his, and of the new promise of love that a short time would bring forth, and he could almost have smiled at the impotent efforts to disturb his peace.

A few more months, and the young father was greeted by a feeble little cry, when he hastily entered Ty Glas, one morning early, in consequence of a summons conveyed mysteriously to Bodowen; and the pale mother, smiling, and feebly holding up her babe to its father's kiss, seemed to him even more lovely than the bright gay Nest who had won his heart at the little inn of Penmorfa.

But the curse was at work! The fulfilment of the prophecy was nigh at hand!

Chapter 2

It was the autumn after the birth of their boy; it had been a glorious summer, with bright, hot, sunny weather; and now the year was fading away as seasonably into mellow days, with mornings of silver mists and clear frosty nights. The blooming look of the time of flowers was past and gone; but instead there were even richer tints abroad in the sun-coloured leaves, the lichens, the golden blossomed furze; if it was the time of fading, there was a glory in the decay.

Nest, in her loving anxiety to surround her dwelling with every charm for her husband's sake, had turned gardener, and the little corners of the rude court before the house were filled with many a delicate mountain-flower, transplanted more for its beauty than its rarity. The sweetbrier bush may even yet be seen, old and gray, which she and Owen planted a green slipling beneath the window of her little chamber. In those moments Owen forgot all besides the present; all the cares and griefs he had known in the past, and all that might await him of woe and death in the future. The boy, too, was as lovely a child as the fondest parent was ever blessed with; and crowed with delight, and clapped his little hands, as his mother held him in her arms at the cottage-door to watch his father's ascent up the rough path that led to Ty Glas, one bright autumnal morning; and when the three entered the house together, it was difficult to say which was the happiest. Owen carried his boy, and tossed and played with him, while Nest sought out some little article of work, and seated herself on the dresser beneath the window, where now busily plying the needle, and then again looking at her husband, she eagerly told him the little pieces of domestic intelligence, the winning ways of the child, the re-sult of yesterday's fishing, and such of the gossip of Penmorfa as came to the ears of the now retired Nest. She noticed that, when she men-tioned any little circumstance which bore the slightest reference to Bodowen, her husband appeared chafed and uneasy, and at last avoided anything that might in the least remind him of home. In truth, he had been suffering much of late from the irritability of his father, shown in trifles to be sure, but not the less galling on that account.

While they were thus talking, and caressing each other and the child, a shadow darkened the room, and before they could catch a glimpse of the object that had occasioned it, it vanished, and Squire Griffiths lifted the door-latch and stood before them. He stood and looked – first on his son, so different, in his buoyant expression of content and enjoyment, with his noble child in his arms, like a proud and happy father, as he was, from the depressed, moody young man he too often appeared at Bodowen; then on Nest – poor, trembling, sickened Nest! – who dropped her work, but yet durst not stir from her seat, on the dresser, while she looked to her husband as if for protection from his father.

The Squire was silent, as he glared from one to the other, his features white with restrained passion. When he spoke, his words came most distinct in their forced composure. It was to his son he addressed himself: 'That woman! Who is she?'

Owen hesitated one moment, and then replied, in a steady, yet quiet voice: 'Father, that woman is my wife.'

He would have added some apology for the long concealment of his marriage; have appealed to his father's forgiveness; but the foam flew from Squire Owen's lips as he burst forth with invective against Nest: 'You have married her! It is as they told me! Married Nest Pritchard yr buten!* And you stand there as if you had not disgraced yourself for ever and ever with your accursed wiving! And the fair harlot sits there, in her mocking modesty, practising the mimming airs that will become her state as future Lady of Bodowen. But I will

* The whore.

move heaven and earth before that false woman darken the doors of my father's house as mistress!'

All this was said with such rapidity that Owen had no time for the words that thronged to his lips. 'Father!' (he burst forth at length) 'Father, whosoever told you that Nest Pritchard was a harlot told you a lie as false as hell! Ay! a lie as false as hell!' he added, in a voice of thunder, while he advanced a step or two nearer to the Squire. And then, in a lower tone, he said: 'She is as pure as your own wife; nay, God help me! as the dear, precious mother who brought me forth, and then left me – with no refuge in a mother's heart – to struggle on through life alone. I tell you Nest is as pure as that dear, dead mother!'

'Fool – poor fool!'

At this moment the child – the little Owen – who had kept gazing from one angry countenance to the other, and with earnest look, trying to understand what had brought the fierce glare into the face where till now he had read nothing but love, in some way attracted the Squire's attention, and increased his wrath.

'Yes,' he continued, 'poor, weak fool that you are, hugging the child of another as if it were your own offspring!' Owen involuntarily caressed the affrighted child, and half smiled at the implication of his father's words. This the Squire perceived, and raising his voice to a scream of rage, he went on: 'I bid you, if you call yourself my son, to cast away that miserable, shameless woman's offspring; cast it away this instant – this instant!'

In this ungovernable rage, seeing that Owen was far from complying with his command, he snatched the poor infant from the loving arms that held it, and throwing it to his mother, left the house inarticulate with fury.

Nest – who had been pale and still as marble during this terrible dialogue, looking on and listening as if fascinated by the words that smote her heart – opened her arms to receive and cherish her precious babe; but the boy was not destined to reach the white refuge of her breast. The furious action of the Squire had been almost without aim, and the infant fell against the sharp edge of the dresser down on to the stone floor.

Owen sprang up to take the child, but he lay so still, so motionless, that the awe of death came over the father, and he stooped down to gaze more closely. At that moment, the upturned, filmy eyes rolled convulsively – a spasm passed along the body – and the lips, yet warm with kissing, quivered into everlasting rest.

A word from her husband told Nest all. She slid down from her seat, and lay by her little son as corpse-like as he, unheeding all the agonising endearments and passionate adjurations of her husband. And that poor, desolate husband and father! Scarce one little quarter of an hour, and he had been so blessed in his consciousness of love! the bright promise of many years on his infant's face, and the new, fresh soul beaming forth in its awakened intelligence. And there it was; the little clay image, that would never more gladden up at the sight of him, nor stretch forth to meet his embrace; whose inarticulate, yet most eloquent cooings might haunt him in his dreams, but would never more be heard in waking life again! And by the dead babe, almost as utterly insensate, the poor mother had fallen in a merciful faint – the slandered, heart-pierced Nest! Owen struggled against the sickness that came over him, and busied himself in vain attempts at her restoration.

It was now near noonday, and Ellis Pritchard came home, little dreaming of the sight that awaited him; but though stunned, he was able to take more effectual measures for his poor daughter's recovery than Owen had done.

By and by she showed symptoms of returning sense, and was placed in her own little bed in a darkened room, where, without ever waking to complete consciousness, she fell asleep. Then it was that her husband, suffocated by pressure of miserable thought, gently drew his hand from her tightened clasp, and printing one long soft kiss on her white waxen forehead, hastily stole out of the room, and out of the house.

Near the base of Moel Gest – it might be a quarter of a mile from Ty Glas – was a little neglected solitary copse, wild and tangled with the trailing branches of the dog-rose and the tendrils of the white bryony. Toward the middle of this thicket lay a deep crystal pool – a clear mirror for the blue heavens above – and round the margin floated the broad green leaves of the water-lily, and when the regal sun shone down in his noonday glory the flowers arose from their cool depths to welcome and greet him. The copse was musical with many sounds; the warbling of birds rejoicing in its shades, the ceaseless hum of the insects that hovered over the pool, the chime of the distant waterfall, the occasional bleating of the sheep from the mountain-top, were all blended into the delicious harmony of nature.

It had been one of Owen's favourite resorts when he had been a lonely wanderer – a pilgrim in search of love in the years gone by.

And thither he went, as if by instinct, when he left Ty Glas; quelling the uprising agony till he should reach that little solitary spot.

It was the time of day when a change in the aspect of the weather so frequently takes place; and the little pool was no longer the reflection of a blue and sunny sky: it sent back the dark and slaty clouds above, and, every now and then, a rough gust shook the painted autumn leaves from their branches, and all other music was lost in the sound of the wild winds piping down from the moorlands, which lay up and beyond the clefts in the mountainside. Presently the rain came on and beat down in torrents.

But Owen heeded it not. He sat on the dank ground, his face buried in his hands, and his whole strength, physical and mental, employed in quelling the rush of blood, which rose and boiled and gurgled in his brain as if it would madden him.

The phantom of his dead child rose ever before him, and seemed to cry aloud for vengeance. And when the poor young man thought upon the victim whom he required in his wild longing for revenge, he shuddered, for it was his father!

Again and again he tried not to think; but still the circle of thought came round, eddying through his brain. At length he mastered his passions, and they were calm; then he forced himself to arrange some plan for the future.

He had not, in the passionate hurry of the moment, seen that his father had left the cottage before he was aware of the fatal accident that befell the child. Owen thought he had seen all; and once he planned to go to the Squire and tell him of the anguish of heart he had wrought, and awe him, as it were, by the dignity of grief. But then again he durst not – he distrusted his self-control – the old prophecy rose up in its horror – he dreaded his doom.

At last he determined to leave his father for ever; to take Nest to some distant country where she might forget her first-born, and where he himself might gain a livelihood by his own exertions.

But when he tried to descend to the various little arrangements which were involved in the execution of this plan, he remembered that all his money (and in this respect Squire Griffiths was no niggard) was locked up in his escritoire at Bodowen. In vain he tried to do away with this matter-of-fact difficulty; go to Bodowen he must: and his only hope – nay his determination – was to avoid his father.

He rose and took a by-path to Bodowen. The house looked even more gloomy and desolate than usual in the heavy down-pouring rain, yet Owen gazed on it with something of regret – for sorrowful as his days in it had been, he was about to leave it for many many years, if not for ever. He entered by a side door opening into a passage that led to his own room, where he kept his books, his guns, his fishing-tackle, his writing materials, et cetera.

Here he hurriedly began to select the few articles he intended to take; for, besides the dread of interruption, he was feverishly anxious to travel far that very night, if only Nest was capable of performing the journey. As he was thus employed, he tried to conjecture what his father's feelings would be on finding that his once-loved son was gone away for ever. Would he then awaken to regret for the conduct which had driven him from home, and bitterly think on the loving and caressing boy who haunted his footsteps in former days? Or, alas! would he only feel that an obstacle to his daily happiness – to his contentment with his wife, and his strange, doting affection for the child – was taken away? Would they make merry over the heir's departure? Then he thought of Nest – the young childless mother, whose heart had not yet realised her fulness of desolation. Poor Nest! so loving as she was, so devoted to her child – how should he console her? He pictured her away in a strange land, pining for her native mountains, and refusing to be comforted because her child was not.

Even this thought of the homesickness that might possibly beset Nest hardly made him hesitate in his determination; so strongly had the idea taken possession of him that only by putting miles and leagues between him and his father could he avert the doom which seemed blending itself with the very purposes of his life as long as he stayed in proximity with the slayer of his child.

He had now nearly completed his hasty work of preparation, and was full of tender thoughts of his wife, when the door opened, and the elfish Robert peered in, in search of some of his brother's possessions. On seeing Owen he hesitated, but then came boldly forward, and laid his hand on Owen's arm, saying,

'Nesta yr buten! How is Nest yr buten?'

He looked maliciously into Owen's face to mark the effect of his words, but was terrified at the expression he read there. He started off and ran to the door, while Owen tried to check himself, saying continually, 'He is but a child. He does not understand the meaning of what he says. He is but a child!' Still Robert, now in fancied security, kept calling out his insulting words, and Owen's hand was on his gun, grasping it as if to restrain his rising fury.

But when Robert passed on daringly to mocking words relating to the poor dead child, Owen could bear it no longer; and before the boy was well aware, Owen was fiercely holding him in an iron clasp with one hand, while he struck him hard with the other.

In a minute he checked himself. He paused, relaxed his grasp, and, to his horror, he saw Robert sink to the ground; in fact, the lad was half-stunned, half-frightened, and thought it best to assume insensibility.

Owen – miserable Owen – seeing him lie there prostrate, was bitterly repentant, and would have dragged him to the carved settle, and done all he could to restore him to his senses, but at this instant the Squire came in.

Probably, when the household at Bodowen rose that morning, there was but one among them ignorant of the heir's relation to Nest Pritchard and her child; for secret as he tried to make his visits to Ty Glas, they had been too frequent not to be noticed, and Nest's altered conduct – no longer frequenting dances and merry-makings – was a strongly corroborative circumstance. But Mrs Griffiths' influence reigned paramount, if unacknowledged, at Bodowen, and till she sanctioned the disclosure, none would dare to tell the Squire.

Now, however, the time drew near when it suited her to make her husband aware of the connection his son had formed; so, with many tears, and much seeming reluctance, she broke the intelligence to him – taking good care, at the same time, to inform him of the light character Nest had borne. Nor did she confine this evil reputation to her conduct before her marriage, but insinuated that even to this day she was a 'woman of the grove and brake' – for centuries the Welsh term of opprobrium for the loosest female characters.

Squire Griffiths easily tracked Owen to Ty Glas; and without any aim but the gratification of his furious anger, followed him to upbraid as we have seen. But he left the cottage even more enraged against his son than he had entered it, and returned home to hear the evil suggestions of the stepmother. He had heard a slight scuffle in which he caught the tones of Robert's voice, as he passed along the hall, and an instant afterwards he saw the apparently lifeless body of his little favourite dragged along by the culprit Owen – the marks of strong passion yet visible on his face. Not loud, but bitter and deep were the evil words which the father bestowed on the son; and as Owen stood proudly and sullenly silent, disdaining all exculpation of himself in the presence of one who had wrought him so much graver – so fatal an injury – Robert's mother entered the room. At sight of her natural emotion the wrath of the Squire was redoubled, and his wild suspicions that this violence of Owen's to Robert was a premeditated act appeared like the proven truth through the mists of rage. He summoned domestics as if to guard his own and his wife's life from the attempts of his son; and the servants stood wondering around – now gazing at Mrs Griffiths, alternately scolding and sobbing, while she tried to restore the lad from his really bruised and half-unconscious state; now at the fierce and angry Squire; and now at the sad and silent Owen. And he – he was hardly aware of their looks of wonder and terror; his father's words fell on a deadened ear; for before his eyes there rose a pale dead babe, and in that lady's violent sounds of grief he heard the wailing of a more sad, more hopeless mother. For by this time the lad Robert had opened his eyes, and though evidently suffering a good deal from the effects of Owen's blows, was fully conscious of all that was passing around him.

Had Owen been left to his own nature, his heart would have worked itself to doubly love the boy whom he had injured; but he was stubborn from injustice, and hardened by suffering. He refused to vindicate himself; he made no effort to resist the imprisonment the Squire had decreed, until a surgeon's opinion of the real extent of Robert's injuries was made known. It was not until the door was locked and barred, as if upon some wild and furious beast, that the recollection of poor Nest, without his comforting presence, came into his mind. Oh! thought he, how she would be wearying, pining for his tender sympathy; if, indeed, she had recovered the shock of mind sufficiently to be sensible of consolation! What would she think of his absence? Could she imagine he believed his father's words, and had left her, in this her sore trouble and bereavement? The thought maddened him, and he looked around for some mode of escape.

He had been confined in a small unfurnished room on the first floor, wainscoted, and carved all round, with a massy door, calculated to resist the attempts of a dozen strong men, even had he afterward been able to escape from the house unseen, unheard. The window was placed (as is common in old Welsh houses) over the fire-place; with branching chimneys on either hand, forming a sort of projection on the outside. By this outlet his escape was easy, even had he been less determined and desperate than he was. And when he had descended, with a little care, a little winding, he might elude all observation and pursue his original intention of going to Ty Glas.

The storm had abated, and watery sunbeams were gilding the bay, as Owen descended from the window, and, stealing along in the broad afternoon shadows, made his way to the little plateau of green turf in the garden at the top of a steep precipitous rock, down the abrupt face of which he had often dropped, by means of a well-secured rope, into the small sailing-boat (his father's present, alas! in days gone by) which lay moored in the deep sea-water below. He had always kept his boat there, because it was the nearest available spot to the house; but before he could reach the place – unless, indeed, he crossed a broad sun-lighted piece of ground in full view of the windows on that side of the house, and without the shadow of a single sheltering tree or shrub – he had to skirt round a rude semi-circle of underwood, which would have been considered as a shrub-bery had anyone taken pains with it. Step by step he stealthily moved along – hearing voices now, again seeing his father and stepmother in no distant walk, the Squire evidently caressing and consoling his wife, who seemed to be urging some point with great vehemence, again forced to crouch down to avoid being seen by the cook, return-ing from the rude kitchen-garden with a handful of herbs. This was the way the doomed heir of Bodowen left his ancestral house for ever, and hoped to leave behind him his doom. At length he reached the plateau – he breathed more freely. He stooped to dis-cover the hidden coil of rope, kept safe and dry in a hole under a great round flat piece of rock: his head was bent down; he did not see his father approach, nor did he hear his footstep for the rush of blood to his head in the stooping effort of lifting the stone; the Squire had grappled with him before he rose up again, before he fully knew whose hands detained him, now, when his liberty of person and action seemed secure. He made a vigorous struggle to free himself; he wrestled with his father for a moment – he pushed him hard, and drove him on to the great displaced stone, all unsteady in its balance.

Down went the Squire, down into the deep waters below – down after him went Owen, half consciously, half unconsciously, partly compelled by the sudden cessation of any opposing body, partly from a vehement irrepressible impulse to rescue his father. But he had instinctively chosen a safer place in the deep sea-water pool than that into which his push had sent his father. The Squire had hit his head with much violence against the side of the boat, in his fall; it is, indeed, doubtful whether he was not killed before ever he sank into the sea. But Owen knew nothing save that the awful doom seemed even now present. He plunged down, he dived below the water in search of the body which had none of the elasticity of life to buoy it up; he saw his father in those depths, he clutched at him, he brought him up and cast him, a dead weight, into the boat, and exhausted by the effort, he had begun himself to sink again before he instinctively strove to rise and climb into the rocking boat. There lay his father, with a deep dent in the side of his head where the skull had been fractured by his fall; his face blackened by the arrested course of the blood. Owen felt his pulse, his heart – all was still. He called him by his name.

'Father, father!' he cried, 'come back! come back! You never knew how I loved you! how I could love you still – if – oh God!'

And the thought of his little child rose before him. 'Yes, father,' he cried afresh, 'you never knew how he fell – how he died! Oh, if I had but had patience to tell you! If you would but have borne with me and listened! And now it is over! Oh father! father!'

Whether she had heard this wild wailing voice, or whether it was only that she missed her husband and wanted him for some little everyday question, or, as was perhaps more likely, she had discovered Owen's escape, and come to inform her husband of it, I do not know, but on the rock, right above his head, as it seemed, Owen heard his stepmother calling her husband.

He was silent, and softly pushed the boat right under the rock till the sides grated against the stones, and the overhanging branches concealed him and it from all not on a level with the water. Wet as he was, he lay down by his dead father the better to conceal himself; and, somehow, the action recalled those early days of childhood – the first in the Squire's widowhood – when Owen had shared his father's bed, and used to waken him in the morning to hear one of the old Welsh legends. How long he lay thus – body chilled, and brain hard-working through the heavy pressure of a reality as terrible as a nightmare – he never knew; but at length he roused himself up to think of Nest.

Drawing out a great sail, he covered up the body of his father with it where he lay in the bottom of the boat. Then with his numbed hands he took the oars, and pulled out into the more open sea toward Criccaeth. He skirted along the coast till he found a shadowed cleft in the dark rocks; to that point he rowed, and anchored his boat close in land. Then he mounted, staggering, half longing to fall into the dark waters and be at rest – half instinctively finding out the surest foot-rests on that precipitous face of rock, till he was high up, safe landed on the turfy summit. He ran off, as if pursued, toward Penmorfa; he ran with maddened energy. Suddenly he paused, turned, ran again with the same speed, and threw himself prone on the summit, looking down into his boat with straining eyes to see if there

THE DOOM OF THE GRIFFITHS 189

had been any movement of life – any displacement of a fold of sail-cloth. It was all quiet deep down below, but as he gazed the shifting light gave the appearance of a slight movement. Owen ran to a lower part of the rock, stripped, plunged into the water, and swam to the boat. When there, all was still – awfully still! For a minute or two, he dared not lift up the cloth. Then reflecting that the same terror might beset him again – of leaving his father unaided while yet a spark of life lingered – he removed the shrouding cover. The eyes looked into his with a dead stare! He closed the lids and bound up the jaw. Again he looked. This time he raised himself out of the water and kissed the brow.

'It was my doom, father! It would have been better if I had died at my birth!'

Daylight was fading away. Precious daylight! He swam back, dressed, and set off afresh for Penmorfa. When he opened the door of Ty Glas, Ellis Pritchard looked at him reproachfully, from his seat in the darkly-shadowed chimney-corner.

'You're come at last,' said he. 'One of our kind would not have left his wife to mourn by herself over her dead child; nor would one of our kind have let his father kill his own true son. I've a good mind to take her from you for ever.'

'I did not tell him,' cried Nest, looking piteously at her husband; 'he made me tell him part, and guessed the rest.'

She was nursing her babe on her knee as if it was alive. Owen stood before Ellis Pritchard.

'Be silent,' said he, quietly. 'Neither words nor deeds but what are decreed can come to pass. I was set to do my work, this hundred years and more. The time waited for me, and the man waited for me. I have done what was foretold of me for generations!'

Ellis Pritchard knew the old tale of the prophecy, and believed in it in a dull, dead kind of way, but somehow never thought it would come to pass in his time. Now, however, he understood it all in a moment, though he mistook Owen's nature so much as to believe that the deed was intentionally done, out of revenge for the death of his boy; and viewing it in this light, Ellis thought it little more than a just punishment for the cause of all the wild despairing sorrow he had seen his only child suffer during the hours of this long afternoon. But he knew the law would not so regard it. Even the lax Welsh law of those days could not fail to examine into the death of a man of Squire Griffith's standing. So the acute Ellis thought how he could conceal the culprit for a time.

'Come,' said he; 'don't look so scared! It was your doom, not your fault;' and he laid a hand on Owen's shoulder.

'You're wet,' said he, suddenly. 'Where have you been? Nest, your husband is dripping, drookit wet. That's what makes him look so blue and wan.'

Nest softly laid her baby in its cradle; she was half stupefied with crying, and had not understood to what Owen alluded, when he spoke of his doom being fulfilled, if indeed she had heard the words.

Her touch thawed Owen's miserable heart.

'Oh, Nest!' said he, clasping her in his arms; 'do you love me still – can you love me, my own darling?'

'Why not?' asked she, her eyes filling with tears. 'I only love you more than ever, for you were my poor baby's father!'

'But, Nest – Oh, tell her, Ellis! *You* know.'

'No need, no need!' said Ellis. 'She's had enough to think on. Bustle, my girl, and get out my Sunday clothes.'

'I don't understand,' said Nest, putting her hand up to her head. 'What is to tell? and why are you so wet? God help me for a poor crazed thing, for I cannot guess at the meaning of your words and your strange looks! I only know my baby is dead!' and she burst into tears.

'Come, Nest! go and fetch him a change, quick!' and as she meekly obeyed, too languid to strive further to understand, Ellis said rapidly to Owen, in a low, hurried voice: 'Are you meaning that the Squire is dead? Speak low, lest she hear. Well, well, no need to talk about how he died. It was sudden, I see; and we must all of us die; and he'll have to be buried. It's well the night is near. And I should not wonder now if you'd like to travel for a bit; it would do Nest a power of good; and then – there's many a one goes out of his own house and never comes back again; and – I trust he's not lying in his own house – and there's a stir for a bit, and a search, and a wonder – and, by-and-by, the heir just steps in, as quiet as can be. And that's what you'll do, and bring Nest to Bodowen after all. Nay, child, better stockings nor those; find the blue woollens I bought at Llanrwst fair. Only don't lose heart. It's done now and can't be helped. It was the piece of work set you to do from the days of the Tudors, they say. And he deserved it. Look in yon cradle. So tell us where he is, and I'll take heart of grace and see what can be done for him.'

But Owen sat wet and haggard, looking into the peat fire as if for visions of the past, and never heeding a word Ellis said. Nor did he move when Nest brought the armful of dry clothes.

'Come, rouse up, man!' said Ellis, growing impatient. But he neither spoke nor moved.

'What is the matter, father?' asked Nest, bewildered.

Ellis kept on watching Owen for a minute or two, till on his daughter's repetition of the question, he said: 'Ask him yourself, Nest.'

'Oh, husband, what is it?' said she, kneeling down and bringing her face to a level with his.

'Don't you know?' said he, heavily. 'You won't love me when you do know. And yet it was not my doing: it was my doom.'

'What does he mean, father?' asked Nest, looking up; but she caught a gesture from Ellis urging her to go on questioning her husband.

'I will love you, husband, whatever has happened. Only let me know the worst.'

A pause, during which Nest and Ellis hung breathless.

'My father is dead, Nest.'

Nest caught her breath with a sharp gasp.

'God forgive him!' said she, thinking on her babe.

'God forgive *me*!' said Owen.

'You did not – ' Nest stopped.

'Yes, I did. Now you know it. It was my doom. How could I help it? The devil helped me – he placed the stone so that my father fell. I jumped into the water to save him. I did, indeed, Nest. I was nearly drowned myself. But he was dead – dead – killed by the fall!'

'Then he is safe at the bottom of the sea?' said Ellis, with hungry eagerness.

'No, he is not; he lies in my boat,' said Owen, shivering a little, more at the thought of his last glimpse at his father's face than from cold.

'Oh, husband, change your wet clothes!' pleaded Nest, to whom the death of the old man was simply a horror with which she had nothing to do, while her husband's discomfort was a present trouble.

While she helped him to take off the wet garments which he would never have had energy enough to remove of himself, Ellis was busy preparing food, and mixing a great tumbler of spirits and hot water. He stood over the unfortunate young man and compelled him to eat and drink, and made Nest, too, taste some mouthfuls – all the while planning in his own mind how best to conceal what had been done, and who had done it; not altogether without a certain feeling of vulgar triumph in the reflection that Nest, as she stood there, care-lessly dressed, dishevelled in her grief, was in reality the mistress of Bodowen, than which Ellis Pritchard had never seen a grander house, though he believed such might exist.

By dint of a few dexterous questions he found out all he wanted to know from Owen, as he ate and drank. In fact, it was almost a relief to Owen to dilute the horror by talking about it. Before the meal was done, if meal it could be called, Ellis knew all he cared to know.

'Now, Nest, on with your cloak and haps. Pack up what needs to go with you, for both you and your husband must be half way to Liverpool by tomorrow's morn. I'll take you past Rhyl Sands in my fishing-boat, with yours in tow; and, once over the dangerous part, I'll return with my cargo of fish, and learn how much stir there is at Bodowen. Once safe hidden in Liverpool, no-one will know where you are, and you may stay quiet till your time comes for returning.'

'I will never come home again,' said Owen, doggedly. 'The place is accursed!'

'Hoot! be guided by me, man. Why, it was but an accident, after all! And we'll land at the Holy Island, at the Point of Llyn; there is an old cousin of mine, the parson, there – for the Pritchards have known better days, Squire – and we'll bury him there. It was but an accident, man. Hold up your head! You and Nest will come home yet and fill Bodowen with children, and I'll live to see it.'

'Never!' said Owen. 'I am the last male of my race, and the son has murdered his father!'

Nest came in laden and cloaked. Ellis was for hurrying them off. The fire was extinguished, the door was locked.

'Here, Nest, my darling, let me take your bundle while I guide you down the steps.' But her husband bent his head, and spoke never a word. Nest gave her father the bundle (already loaded with such things as he himself had seen fit to take), but clasped another softly and tightly.

'No-one shall help me with this,' said she, in a low voice.

Her father did not understand her; her husband did, and placed his strong helping arm round her waist, and blessed her.

'We will all go together, Nest,' said he. 'But where?' and he looked up at the storm-tossed clouds coming up from windward.

'It is a dirty night,' said Ellis, turning his head round to speak to his companions at last. 'But never fear, we'll weather it!' And he made for the place where his vessel was moored. Then he stopped and thought a moment.

'Stay here!' said he, addressing his companions. 'I may meet folk, and I shall, maybe, have to hear and to speak. You wait here till I come back for you.' So they sat down close together in a corner of the path.

'Let me look at him, Nest!' said Owen.

She took her little dead son out from under her shawl; they looked at his waxen face long and tenderly; kissed it, and covered it up reverently and softly.

'Nest,' said Owen, at last, 'I feel as though my father's spirit had been near us, and as if it had bent over our poor little one. A strange chilly air met me as I stooped over him. I could fancy the spirit of our pure, blameless child guiding my father's safe over the paths of the sky to the gates of heaven, and escaping those accursed dogs of hell that were darting up from the north in pursuit of souls not five minutes since.'

'Don't talk so, Owen,' said Nest, curling up to him in the darkness of the copse. 'Who knows what may be listening?'

The pair were silent, in a kind of nameless terror, till they heard Ellis Pritchard's loud whisper. 'Where are ye? Come along, soft and steady. There were folk about even now, and the Squire is missed, and madam in a fright.'

They went swiftly down to the little harbour, and embarked on board Ellis's boat. The sea heaved and rocked even there; the torn clouds went hurrying overhead in a wild tumultuous manner.

They put out into the bay; still in silence, except when some word of command was spoken by Ellis, who took the management of the vessel. They made for the rocky shore, where Owen's boat had been moored. It was not there. It had broken loose and disappeared.

Owen sat down and covered his face. This last event, so simple and natural in itself, struck on his excited and superstitious mind in an extraordinary manner. He had hoped for a certain reconciliation, so to say, by laying his father and his child both in one grave. But now it appeared to him as if there was to be no forgiveness; as if his father revolted even in death against any such peaceful union. Ellis took a practical view of the case. If the Squire's body was found drifting about in a boat known to belong to his son, it would create terrible suspicion as to the manner of his death. At one time in the evening, Ellis had thought of persuading Owen to let him bury the Squire in a sailor's grave; or, in other words, to sew him up in a spare sail, and weighting it well, sink it for ever. He had not broached the subject, from a certain fear of Owen's passionate repugnance to the plan;

otherwise, if he had consented, they might have returned to Pen-morfa, and passively awaited the course of events, secure of Owen's succession to Bodowen, sooner or later; or if Owen was too much overwhelmed by what had happened, Ellis would have advised him to go away for a short time, and return when the buzz and the talk was over.

Now it was different. It was absolutely necessary that they should leave the country for a time. Through those stormy waters they must plough their way that very night. Ellis had no fear – would have had no fear, at any rate, with Owen as he had been a week, a day ago; but with Owen wild, despairing, helpless, fate-pursued, what could he do?

They sailed into the tossing darkness, and were never more seen of men.

The house of Bodowen has sunk into damp, dark ruins; and a Saxon stranger holds the lands of the Griffiths.

The Ghost in the Garden Room

Prologue

My friend and solicitor rubbed his bald forehead – which is quite Shakespearean – with his hand, after a manner he has when I consult him professionally, and took a very large pinch of snuff. 'My bedroom,' said he, 'has been haunted by the ghost of a judge.'

'Of a judge?' said all the company.

'Of a judge. In his wig and robes as he sits upon the Bench, at Assize-time. As I have lingered in the great white chair at the side of my fire, when we have all retired for the night to our respective rooms, I have seen and heard him. I never shall forget the description he gave me, and I never have forgotten it since I first heard it.'

'Then you have seen and heard him before, Mr Undery?' said my sister.

'Often.'

'Consequently, he is not peculiar to this house?'

'By no means. He returns to me in many intervals of quiet leisure, and his story haunts me.'

We one and all called for the story, that it might haunt us likewise.

'It fell within the range of his judicial experience,' said my friend and solicitor, 'and this was the judge's manner of summing it up.'

Those words did not apply, of course, to the great pinch of snuff that followed them, but to the words that followed the great pinch of snuff. They were these.

* * *

Not many years after the beginning of this century, a worthy couple of the name of Huntroyd occupied a small farm in the North Riding of Yorkshire. They had married late in life, although they were very young when they first began to 'keep company' with each other. Nathan Huntroyd had been farm-servant to Hester Rose's father, and had made up to her at a time when her parents thought she might do better; and so, without much consultation of her feelings, they had dismissed Nathan in somewhat cavalier fashion. He had drifted far away from his former connections, when an uncle of his died, leaving Nathan – by this time upwards of forty years of age – enough money to stock a small farm, and yet have something over, to put in the bank against bad times. One of the consequences of this bequest was, that Nathan was looking out for a wife and house-keeper, in a kind of discreet and leisurely way, when one day he heard that his old love, Hester, was not married and flourishing, as he had always supposed her to be, but a poor maid-of-all-work, in the town of Ripon. For her father had had a succession of mis-fortunes, which had brought him in his old age to the workhouse; her mother was dead; her only brother struggling to bring up a large family; and Hester herself a hard-working, homely-looking (at thirty-seven) servant. Nathan had a kind of growling satisfaction (which only lasted a minute or two, however) in hearing of these turns of fortune's wheel. He did not make many intelligible remarks to his informant, and to no-one else did he say a word. But, a few days afterwards, he presented himself, dressed in his Sunday best, at Mrs Thompson's back-door in Ripon.

Hester stood there, in answer to the good sound knock his good sound oak-stick made: she, with the light full upon her, he in shadow. For a moment there was silence. He was scanning the face and figure of his old love, for twenty years unseen. The comely beauty of youth had faded away entirely; she was, as I have said, homely-looking, plain-featured, but with a clean skin, and pleasant frank eyes. Her figure was no longer round, but tidily draped in a blue and white bed-gown, tied round her waist by her white apron-strings, and her short red linsey petticoat showed her tidy feet and ankles. Her former lover fell into no ecstasies. He simply said to himself, 'She'll do'; and forth-with began upon his business.

'Hester, thou dost not mind me. I am Nathan, as thy father turned off at a minute's notice, for thinking of thee for a wife, twenty year come Michaelmas next. I have not thought much upon matrimony since. But Uncle Ben has died leaving me a small matter in the bank; and I have taken Nab-end Farm, and put in a bit of stock, and shall want a missus to see after it. Wilt like to come? I'll not mislead thee. It's dairy, and it might have been arable. But arable takes more horses nor it suited me to buy, and I'd the offer of a tidy lot of kine. That's all. If thou'll have me, I'll come for thee as soon as the hay is gotten in'.

Hester only said, 'Come in, and sit thee down'.

He came in, and sat down. For a time, she took no more notice of him than of his stick, bustling about to get dinner ready for the family whom she served. He meanwhile watched her brisk sharp movements, and repeated to himself, 'She'll do!' After about twenty minutes of silence thus employed, he got up, saying 'Well, Hester, I'm going. When shall I come back again?'

'Please thysel', and thou'll please me,' said Hester, in a tone that she tried to make light and indifferent; but he saw that her colour came and went, and that she trembled while she moved about. In another moment Hester was soundly kissed; but, when she looked round to scold the middle-aged farmer, he appeared so entirely composed that she hesitated. He said: 'I have pleased mysel', and thee too, I hope. Is it a month's wage, and a month's warning? Today is the eighth. July eighth is our wedding-day. I have no time to spend a-wooing before then, and wedding must na take long. Two days is enough to throw away, at our time o' life.'

It was like a dream; but Hester resolved not to think more about it till her work was done. And when all was cleaned up for the evening, she went and gave her mistress warning, telling her all the history of her life in a very few words. That day month she was married from Mrs Thompson's house.

The issue of the marriage was one boy, Benjamin. A few years after his birth, Hester's brother died at Leeds, leaving ten or twelve children. Hester sorrowed bitterly over this loss; and Nathan showed her much quiet sympathy, although he could not but remember that Jack Rose had added insult to the bitterness of his youth. He helped his wife to make ready to go by the waggon to Leeds. He made light of the household difficulties, which came thronging into her mind after all was fixed for her departure. He filled her purse, that she might have wherewithal to alleviate the immediate wants of her brother's family. And, as she was leaving, he ran after the waggon. 'Stop, stop!' he cried. 'Hetty, if thou wilt – if it wunnot be too much for thee – bring back one of Jack's wenches for company, like. We've enough and to spare; and a lass will make the house winsome, as a man may say.'

The waggon moved on; while Hester had such a silent swelling of gratitude in her heart, as was both thanks to her husband and thanksgiving to God. And that was the way that little Bessy Rose came to be an inmate of the Nab's-end Farm. Virtue met with its own reward in this instance, and in a clear and tangible shape, too; which need not delude people in general into thinking that such is the usual nature of virtue's rewards! Bessy grew up a bright, affectionate, active girl; a daily comfort to her uncle and aunt. She was so much a darling in the household that they even thought her worthy of their only son Benjamin, who was perfection in their eyes. It is not often the case that two plain, homely people have a child of uncommon beauty; but it is so sometimes, and Benjamin Huntroyd was one of these exceptional cases. The hard-working, labour-and-care-marked farmer, and the mother, who could never have been more than tolerably comely in her best days, produced a boy who might have been an earl's son for grace and beauty. Even the hunting squires of the neighbourhood reined up their horses to admire him, as he opened the gates for them. He had no shyness, he was so accustomed from his earliest years to admiration from strangers and adoration from his parents. As for Bessy Rose, he ruled imperiously over her heart from the time she first set eyes on him. And, as she grew older, she grew on in loving, persuading herself that what her uncle and aunt loved so dearly it was her duty to love dearest of all. At every unconscious symptom of the young girl's love for her cousin, his parents smiled and winked: all was going on as they wished; no need to go far a-field for Benjamin's wife. The household could go on as it was now; Nathan and Hester sinking into the rest of years, and relinquishing care and authority to those dear ones, who, in the process of time, might bring other dear ones to share their love.

But Benjamin took it all very coolly. He had been sent to a day-school in the neighbouring town – a grammar-school in the high state of neglect in which the majority of such schools were thirty years ago. Neither his father nor his mother knew much of learning. All they knew (and that directed their choice of a school) was that they could not, by any possibility, part with their darling to a boarding-school; that some schooling he must have, and that Squire Pollard's son went to Highminster Grammar School. Squire Pollard's son, and many another son destined to make his parents' hearts ache, went to this school. If it had not been so utterly a bad place of education, the simple farmer and his wife might have found it out sooner. But not only did the pupils there learn vice, they also learnt deceit. Benjamin was naturally too clever to remain a dunce; or else, if he had chosen so to be, there was nothing in Highminster Grammar School to hinder his being a dunce of the first water. But, to all appearance, he grew clever and gentleman-like. His father and mother were even proud of his airs and graces, when he came home for the holidays; taking them for proofs of his refinement, although the practical effect of such refinement was to make him express his contempt for his parents' homely ways and simple ignorance. By the time he was eighteen, an articled clerk in an attorney's office at Highminster – for he had quite declined becoming a 'mere clod-hopper', that is to say, a hard-working, honest farmer like his father – Bessy Rose was the only person who was dissatisfied with him. The little girl of fourteen instinctively felt there was something wrong about him. Alas! two years more, and the girl of sixteen worshipped his very shadow, and would not see that aught could be wrong with one so soft-spoken, so handsome, so kind as Cousin Benjamin. For Benjamin had discovered that the way to cajole his parents out of money for every indulgence he fancied, was to pretend to forward their innocent scheme, and make love to his pretty cousin, Bessy Rose. He cared just enough for her to make this work of necessity not disagreeable at the time he was performing it. But he found it tiresome to remember her little claims upon him, when she was no longer present. The letters he had promised her during his weekly absence at Highminster, the trifling commissions she had asked him to do for her, were all considered in the light of troubles; and, even when he was with her, he resented the inquiries she made as to his mode of passing his time, or what female acquaintances he had in Highminster

When his apprenticeship was ended, nothing would serve him but that he must go up to London for a year or two. Poor Farmer Huntroyd was beginning to repent of his ambition of making his son Benjamin a gentleman. But it was too late to repine now. Both father and mother felt this; and, however sorrowful they might be, they were silent, neither demurring nor assenting to Benjamin's proposition when first he made it. But Bessy, through her tears, noticed that both her uncle and aunt seemed unusually tired that night, and sat hand-in-hand on the fireside settle, idly gazing into the bright flame, as if they saw in it pictures of what they had once hoped their lives would have been. Bessy rattled about among the supper-things, as she put them away after Benjamin's departure, making more noise than usual – as if noise and bustle was what she needed to keep her from bursting out crying – and, having at one keen glance taken in the position and looks of Nathan and Hester, she avoided looking in that direction again, for fear the sight of their wistful faces should make her own tears overflow.

'Sit thee down, lass – sit thee down! Bring the creepie-stool to the fireside, and let's have a bit of talk over the lad's plans,' said Nathan, at last rousing himself to speak. Bessy came and sat down in front of the fire, and threw her apron over her face, as she rested her head on both hands. Nathan felt as if it was a chance which of the two women burst out crying first. So he thought he would speak, in hopes of keeping off the infection of tears.

'Didst ever hear of this mad plan afore, Bessy?'

'No, never!' Her voice came muffled and changed from under her apron. Hester felt as if the tone, both of question and answer, implied blame; and this she could not bear.

'We should ha' looked to it when we bound him; for of necessity it would ha' come to this. There's examins, and catechises, and I dunno what all for him to be put through in London. It's not his fault.'

'Which on us said it were?' asked Nathan, rather put out. 'Tho', for that matter, a few weeks would carry him over the mire, and make him as good a lawyer as any judge among 'em. Oud Lawson the attorney told me that, in a talk I had wi' him a bit sin. Na, na! it's the lad's own hankering after London that makes him want for to stay there for a year, let alone two.'

Nathan shook his head.

'And if it be his own hankering,' said Bessy, putting down her apron, her face all flame, and her eyes swollen up, 'I dunnot see harm in it. Lads aren't like lasses, to be teed to their own fireside like th' crook yonder. It's fitting for a young man to go abroad and see the world, afore he settles down.'

Hester's hand sought Bessy's; and the two women sat in sympathetic defiance of any blame that should be thrown on the beloved absent. Nathan only said: 'Nay, wench, dunnot wax up so; whatten's done's done; and worse, it's my doing. I mun needs make my bairn a gentleman; and we mun pay for it.'

'Dear Uncle! he wunna spend much, I'll answer for it; and I'll scrimp and save i' the house, to make it good.'

'Wench!' said Nathan solemnly, 'it were not paying in cash I were speaking on: it were paying in heart's care, and heaviness of soul. Lunnon is a place where the devil keeps court as well as King George; and my poor chap has more nor once welly fallen into his clutches here. I dunno what he'll do, when he gets close within sniff of him.'

'Don't let him go, father!' said Hester, for the first time taking this view. Hitherto she had only thought of her own grief at parting with him. 'Father, if you think so, keep him here, safe under your own eye!'

'Nay!' said Nathan, 'he's past time o' life for that. Why, there's not one on us knows where he is at this present time, and he not gone out of our sight an hour. He's too big to be put back i' th' go-cart, mother, or to keep within doors, with the chair turned bottom-upwards.'

'I wish he were a wee bairn lying in my arms again! It were a sore day when I weaned him; and I think life's been gettin' sorer and sorer at every turn he's ta'en towards manhood.'

'Coom, lass; that's noan the way to be talking. Be thankful to Marcy that thou'st getten a man for thy son as stands five foot eleven in's stockings, and ne'er a sick piece about him. We wunnot grudge him his fling, will we, Bess, my wench? He'll be coming back in a year, or, may be, a bit more, and be a' for settling in a quiet town like, wi' a wife that's noan so fur fra' me at this very minute. An' we oud folk, as we get into years, must gi' up farm, and tak a bit on a house near Lawyer Benjamin.'

And so the good Nathan, his own heart heavy enough, tried to soothe his women-kind. But, of the three, his eyes were longest in closing, his apprehensions the deepest founded.

'I misdoubt me I hanna done well by th' lad. I misdoubt me sore,' was the thought that kept him awake till day began to dawn. 'Summat's wrong about him, or folk would na look me wi' such piteous-like een, when they speak on him. I can see th' meaning of it, thof I'm too proud to let on. And Lawson, too, he holds his tongue more nor he should do, when I ax him how my lad's getting on, and whatten sort of a lawyer he'll mak. God be marciful to Hester an' me, if th' lad's gone away! God be marciful! But, may be, it's this lying waking a' the night through, that maks me so fearfu'. Why, when I were his age, I daur be bound I should ha' spent money fast enoof, i' I could ha' come by it. But I had to arn it; that maks a great differ'. Well! It were hard to thwart th' child of our old age, and we waitin' so long for to have 'un!'

Next morning, Nathan rode Moggy, the cart-horse, into High-minster to see Mr Lawson. Anybody who saw him ride out of his own yard would have been struck with the change in him which was visible when he returned: a change greater than a day's unusual exercise should have made in a man of his years. He scarcely held the reins at all. One jerk of Moggy's head would have plucked them out of his hands. His head was bent forward, his eyes looking on some unseen thing, with long, unwinking gaze. But, as he drew near home on his return, he made an effort to recover himself.

'No need fretting them,' he said; 'lads will be lads. But I didna think he had it in him to be so thowtless, young as he is. Well, well! he'll, may be, get more wisdom i' Lunnon. Anyways, it's best to cut him off fra such evil lads as Will Hawker, and such-like. It's they as have led my boy astray. He were a good chap till he knowed them – a good chap till he knowed them.'

But he put all his cares in the background when he came into the house-place, where both Bessy and his wife met him at the door, and both would fain lend a hand to take off his greatcoat.

'Theer, wenches, theer! ye might let a man alone for to get out on's clothes! Why, I might ha' struck thee, lass.' And he went on talking, trying to keep them off for a time from the subject that all had at heart. But there was no putting them off for ever; and, by dint of repeated questioning on his wife's part, more was got out than he had ever meant to tell – enough to grieve both his hearers sorely: and yet the brave old man still kept the worst in his own breast.

The next day, Benjamin came home for a week or two, before making his great start to London. His father kept him at a distance, and was solemn and quiet in his manner to the young man. Bessy, who had shown anger enough at first, and had uttered many a sharp speech, began to relent, and then to feel hurt and displeased that her uncle should persevere so long in his cold, reserved manner – and Benjamin just going to leave them! Her aunt went, tremblingly busy, about the clothes-presses and drawers, as if afraid of letting herself think either of the past or the future; only once or twice, coming behind her son, she suddenly stooped over his sitting figure, and kissed his cheek, and stroked his hair. Bessy remembered afterwards – long years afterwards – how he had tossed his head away with nervous irritability on one of these occasions, and had muttered – her aunt did not hear it, but Bessy did – 'Can't you leave a man alone?'

Towards Bessy herself he was pretty gracious. No other words express his manner: it was not warm, nor tender, nor cousinly, but there was an assumption of underbred politeness towards her as a young, pretty woman; which politeness was neglected in his authoritative or grumbling manner towards his mother, or his sullen silence before his father. He once or twice ventured on a compliment to Bessy on her personal appearance. She stood still, and looked at him with astonishment.

'Have my eyes changed sin' last thou saw'st them,' she asked, ' that thou must be telling me about 'em i' that fashion? I'd rayther by a deal see thee helping thy mother, when she's dropped her knitting-needle and canna see i' th' dusk for to pick it up.'

But Bessy thought of his pretty speech about her eyes, long after he had forgotten making it, and when he would have been puzzled to tell the colour of them. Many a day, after he was gone, did she look earnestly in the little oblong looking-glass, which hung up against the wall of her little sleeping-chamber, but which she used to take down in order to examine the eyes he had praised, murmuring to herself, 'Pretty, soft grey eyes! Pretty, soft grey eyes!' until she would hang up the glass again, with a sudden laugh and a rosy blush.

In the days when he had gone away to the vague distance and vaguer place – the city called London – Bessy tried to forget all that had gone against her feeling of the affection and duty that a son owed to his parents; and she had many things to forget of this kind that would keep surging up into her mind. For instance, she wished that he had not objected to the home-spun, home-made shirts which his mother and she had had such pleasure in getting ready for him. He might not know, it was true – and so her love urged – how carefully and evenly the thread had been spun: how, not content with bleaching the yarn in the sunniest meadow, the linen, on its return from the weaver's, had been spread out afresh on the sweet summer grass, and watered carefully, night after night, when there was no dew to perform the kindly office. He did not know – for no-one but Bessy herself did – how many false or large stitches, made large and false by her aunt's failing eyes (who yet liked to do the choicest part of the stitching all by herself), Bessy had unpicked at night in her own room, and with dainty fingers had re-stitched, sewing eagerly in the dead of night. All this he did not know; or he could never have complained of the coarse texture, the old-fashioned make of these shirts, and urged on his mother to give him part of her little store of egg and butter money, in order to buy newer-fashioned linen in Highminster.

When once that little precious store of his mother's was discovered, it was well for Bessy's peace of mind that she did not know how loosely her aunt counted up the coins, mistaking guineas for shillings, or just the other way, so that the amount was seldom the same in the old black spoutless teapot. Yet this son, this hope, this love, had still a strange power of fascination over the household. The evening before he left, he sat between his parents, a hand in theirs on either side, and Bessy on the old creepie-stool, her head lying on her aunt's knee, and looking up at him from time to time, as if to learn his face off by heart; till his glances, meeting hers, made her drop her eyes, and only sigh.

He stopped up late that night with his father, long after the women had gone to bed. But not to sleep; for I will answer for it the grey-haired mother never slept a wink till the late dawn of the autumn day; and Bessy heard her uncle come upstairs with heavy, deliberate footsteps, and go to the old stocking which served him for bank, and count out the golden guineas; once he stopped, but again he went on afresh, as if resolved to crown his gift with liberality. Another long pause – in which she could but indistinctly hear continued words, it might have been advice, it might be a prayer, for it was in her uncle's voice – and then father and son came up to bed. Bessy's room was but parted from her cousin's by a thin wooden partition; and the last sound she distinctly heard, before her eyes, tired out with crying, closed themselves in sleep, was the guineas clinking down upon each other at regular intervals, as if Benjamin were playing at pitch and toss with his father's present.

After he was gone, Bessy wished he had asked her to walk part of the way with him into Highminster. She was all ready, her things laid out on the bed; but she could not accompany him without invitation.

The little household tried to close over the gap as best they might. They seemed to set themselves to their daily work with unusual vigour; but somehow, when evening came there had been little done. Heavy hearts never make light work, and there was no telling how much care and anxiety each had had to bear in secret in the field, at the wheel, or in the dairy. Formerly, he was looked for every Saturday – looked for, though he might not come; or, if he came, there were things to be spoken about that made his visit anything but a pleasure: still, he might come, and all things might go right; and then what sunshine, what gladness to those humble people! But now he was away, and dreary winter was come on; old folks' sight fails, and the evenings were long and sad, in spite of all Bessy could do or say. And he did not write so often as he might – so each one thought; though each one would have been ready to defend him from either of the others who had expressed such a thought aloud. 'Surely,' said Bessy to herself, when the first primroses peeped out in a sheltered and sunny hedge-bank, and she gathered them as she passed home from afternoon church – surely, there never will be such a dreary, miserable winter again as this has been.' There had been a great change in Nathan and Hester Huntroyd during this last year. The spring before, when Benjamin was yet the subject of more hopes than fears, his father and mother looked what I may call an elderly middle-aged couple: people who had a good deal of hearty work in them yet. Now – it was not his absence alone that caused the change – they looked frail and old, as if each day's natural trouble was a burden more than they could bear. For Nathan had heard sad reports about his only child, and had told them solemnly to his wife – as things too bad to be believed, and yet, 'God help us if he is indeed such a lad as this!' Their eyes were become too dry and hollow for many tears; they sat together, hand in hand; and shivered, and sighed, and did not speak many words, or dare to look at each other: and then Hester had said: 'We mauna tell th' lass. Young folks' hearts break wi' a little, and she'd be apt to fancy it were true.'

Here the old woman's voice broke into a kind of piping cry; but she struggled, and her next words were all right. 'We mauna tell her: he's bound to be fond on her, and, may be, if she thinks well on him, and loves him, it will bring him straight!'

'God grant it!' said Nathan.

'God shall grant it!' said Hester, passionately moaning out her words; and then repeating them, alas! with a vain repetition.

'It's a bad place for lying, is Highminster,' said she at length, as if impatient of the silence. 'I never knowed such a place for getting up stories. But Bessy knows nought on 'em and nother you nor me belie'es 'em, that's one blessing.'

But, if they did not in their hearts believe them, how came they to look so sad and worn, beyond what mere age could make them?

Then came round another year, another winter, yet more miserable than the last. This year, with the primroses, came Benjamin; a bad, hard, flippant young man, with yet enough of specious manners and handsome countenance to make his appearance striking at first to those to whom the aspect of a London fast young man of the lowest order is strange and new. Just at first, as he sauntered in with a swagger and an air of indifference, which was partly assumed, partly real, his old parents felt a simple kind of awe of him, as if he were not their son, but a real gentleman; but they had too much fine instinct in their homely natures not to know, after a very few minutes had passed, that this was not a true prince.

'Whatten ever does he mean,' said Hester to her niece, as soon as they were alone, 'by a' them maks and wear-locks? And he minces his words, as if his tongue were clipped short, or split like a magpie's. Hech! London is as bad as a hot day i' August for spoiling good flesh; for he were a good-looking lad when he went up; and now, look at him, with his skin gone into lines and flourishes, just like the first page on a copybook.'

'I think he looks a good deal better, aunt, for them new-fashioned whiskers!' said Bessy, blushing still at the remembrance of the kiss he had given her on first seeing her – a pledge, she thought, poor girl, that, in spite of his long silence in letter-writing, he still looked upon her as his troth-plight wife. There were things about him which none of them liked, although they never spoke of them; yet there was also something to gratify them in the way in which he remained quiet at Nab-end, instead of seeking variety, as he had formerly done, by constantly stealing off to the neighbouring town. His father had paid all the debts that he knew of, soon after Benjamin had gone up to London; so there were no duns that his parents knew of to alarm him, and keep him at home. And he went out in the morning with the old man, his father, and lounged by his side, as Nathan went round his fields, with busy yet infirm gait; having heart, as he would have expressed it, in all that was going on, because at length his son seemed to take an interest in the farming affairs, and stood patiently by his side, while he compared his own small galloways with the great shorthorns looming over his neighbour's hedge.

'It's a slovenly way, thou seest, that of selling th' milk; folk don't care whether it's good or not, so that they get their pint-measure of stuff that's watered afore it leaves th' beast, instead o' honest cheating by the help o' th' pump. But look at Bessy's butter, what skill it shows! part her own manner o' making, and part good choice o' cattle. It's a pleasure to see her basket, a' packed ready to go to market; and it's noan o' a pleasure for to see the buckets fu' of their blue starch-water as yon beasts give. I'm thinking they crossed th' breed wi' a pump not long sin'. Hech! but our Bessy's a clever canny wench! I sometimes think thou'lt be for gie'ing up th' law, and taking to th' oud trade, when thou wedst wi' her!' This was intended to be a skilful way of ascertaining whether there was any ground for the old farmer's wish and prayer, that Benjamin might give up the law and return to the primitive occupation of his father. Nathan dared to hope it now, since his son had never made much by his profession, owing, as he had said, to his want of a connection; and the farm, and the stock, and the clean wife, too, were ready to his hand; and Nathan could safely rely on himself never, in his most unguarded moments, to reproach his son with the hardly-earned hundreds that had been spent on his education. So the old man listened with painful interest to the answer which his son was evidently struggling to make, coughing a little and blowing his nose before he spoke.

'Well, you see, father, law is a precarious livelihood; a man, as I may express myself, has no chances in the profession unless he is known – known to the judges, and tip-top barristers, and that sort of thing. Now, you see, my mother and you have no acquaintance that you may call exactly in that line. But luckily I have met with a man, a friend, as I may say, who is really a first-rate fellow, knowing everybody, from the Lord Chancellor downwards; and he has offered me a share in his business – a partnership, in short' – he hesitated a little.

'I'm sure that's uncommon kind of the gentleman,' said Nathan. 'I should like for to thank him mysen; for it's not many as would pick up a young chap out o' th' dirt, as it were, and say "Here's hauf my good fortune for you, sir, and your very good health!" Most on 'em when they're gettin' a bit o' luck, run off wi' it to keep it a' to themselves, and gobble it down in a corner. What may be his name? For I should like to know it.'

'You don't quite apprehend me, father. A great deal of what you've said is true to the letter. People don't like to share their good luck, as you say.'

'The more credit to them as does,' broke in Nathan.

'Ay, but, you see, even such a fine fellow as my friend Cavendish does not like to give away half his good practice for nothing. He expects an equivalent.'

'An equivalent,' said Nathan; his voice had dropped down an octave. 'And what may that be? There's always some meaning in grand words, I take it; though I am not book-larned enough to find it out.'

'Why, in this case, the equivalent he demands for taking me into partnership, and afterwards relinquishing the whole business to me, is three hundred pounds down.'

Benjamin looked sideways from under his eyes, to see how his father took the proposition. His father struck his stick deep down in the ground; and, leaning one hand upon it, faced round at him.

'Then thy fine friend may go and be hanged. Three hunder pounds! I'll be darned an' danged too, if I know where to get 'em, if I'd be making a fool o' thee an' mysen too.'

He was out of breath by this time. His son took his father's first words in dogged silence; it was but the burst of surprise he had led himself to expect, and did not daunt him for long.

'I should think, sir' –

'"Sir" – whatten for dost thou "sir" me? Is them your manners? I'm plain Nathan Huntroyd, who never took on to be a gentleman; but I have paid my way up to this time, which I shannot do much longer, if I'm to have a son coming an' asking me for three hundred pound, just meet same as if I were a cow, and had nothing to do but let down my milk to the first person as strokes me.'

'Well, father,' said Benjamin, with an affectation of frankness; 'then there's nothing for me but to do as I have often planned before – go and emigrate.'

'And *what?*' said his father, looking sharply and steadily at him.

'Emigrate. Go to America, or India, or some colony where there would be an opening for a young man of spirit.'

Benjamin had reserved this proposition for his trump card, expecting by means of it to carry all before him. But, to his surprise, his father plucked his stick out of the hole he had made when he so vehemently thrust it into the ground, and walked on four or five steps in advance; there he stood still again, and there was a dead silence for a few minutes.

'It 'ud, may be, be the best thing thou couldst do,' the father began. Benjamin set his teeth hard to keep in curses. It was well for poor Nathan he did not look round then, and see the look his son gave him. 'But it would come hard like upon us, upon Hester and me; for, whether thou'rt a good 'un or not, thou'rt our flesh and blood, our only bairn; and, if thou'rt not all as a man could wish, it's, may be, been the fault on our pride i' the – it 'ud kill the missus, if he went off to Amerikay, and Bess, too, the lass as thinks so much on him!' The speech, originally addressed to his son, had wandered off into a monologue – as keenly listened to by Benjamin, however, as if it had all been spoken to him. After a pause of consideration, his father turned round: 'Yon man – I wunnot call him a friend o' yourn, to think of asking you for such a mint o' money – is not th' only one, I'll be bound, as could give ye a start i' the law? Other folks 'ud, may be, do it for less?'

'Not one of 'em; to give me equal advantages,' said Benjamin, thinking he perceived signs of relenting.

'Well, then, thou may'st tell him that it's nother he nor thee as 'll see th' sight o' three hundred pound o' my money. I'll not deny as I've a bit laid up again' a rainy day; it's not so much as thatten, though; and a part on it is for Bessy, as has been like a daughter to us.'

'But Bessy is to be your real daughter some day, when I've a home to take her to,' said Benjamin; for he played very fast and loose, even in his own mind, with his engagement with Bessy. Present with her, when she was looking her brightest and best, he behaved to her as if they were engaged lovers; absent from her, he looked upon her rather as a good wedge, to be driven into his parents' favour on his behalf. Now, however, he was not exactly untrue in speaking as if he meant to make her his wife; for the thought was in his mind, though he made use of it to work upon his father.

'It will be a dree day for us, then,' said the old man. 'But God 'll have us in His keeping, and 'll, may-happen, be taking more care on us i' heaven by that time than Bess, good lass as she is, has had on us at Nab-end. Her heart is set on thee, too. But, lad, I hanna gotten the three hunder; I keeps my cash i' th' stocking, thous know'st, till it reaches fifty pound, and then I takes it to Ripon Bank. Now the last scratch they'n gi'en me made it just two hunder, and I hanna but on to fifteen pound yet i' the stockin', and I meant one hunder an' the red cow's calf to be for Bess, she's ta'en such pleasure like i' rearing it'.

Benjamin gave a sharp glance at his father, to see if he was telling the truth; and that a suspicion of the old man, his father, had entered into the son's head, tells enough of his own character.

'I canna do it, I canna do it, for sure; although I shall like to think as I had helped on the wedding. There's the black heifer to be sold yet, and she'll fetch a matter of ten pound; but a deal on't will be needed for seed-corn, for the arable did but bad last year, and I thought I would try – I'll tell thee what, lad! I'll make it as though Bess lent thee her hunder, only thou must give her a writ of hand for it; and thou shalt have a' the money i' Ripon Bank, and see if the lawyer wunnot let thee have a share of what he offered thee at three hunder for two. I dunnot mean for to wrong him; but thou must get a fair share for the money. At times, I think thou'rt done by folk; now I wadna have you cheat a bairn of a brass farthing; same time, I wadna have thee so soft as to be cheated.'

To explain this, it should be told that some of the bills, which Benjamin had received money from his father to pay, had been altered so as to cover other and less creditable expenses which the young man had incurred; and the simple old farmer, who had still much faith left in him for his boy, was acute enough to perceive that he had paid above the usual price for the articles he had purchased.

After some hesitation, Benjamin agreed to receive the two hundred, and promised to employ it to the best advantage in setting himself up in business. He had, nevertheless, a strange hankering after the additional fifteen pounds that was left to accumulate in the stocking. It was his, he thought, as heir to his father; and he soon lost some of his usual complaisance for Bessy that evening, as he dwelt on the idea that there was money being laid by for her, and grudged it to her even in imagination. He thought more of this fifteen pounds that he was not to have than of all the hardly-earned and humbly-saved two hundred that he was to come into possession of. Meanwhile, Nathan was in unusual spirits that evening. He was so generous and affectionate at heart, that he had an unconscious satisfaction in having helped two people on the road to happiness by the sacrifice of the greater part of his property. The very fact of having trusted his son so largely seemed to make Benjamin more worthy of trust in his father's estimation. The sole idea he tried to banish was that, if all came to pass as he hoped, both Benjamin and Bessy would be settled far away from Nab-end; but then he had a childlike reliance that 'God would take care of him and his missus, somehow or anodder. It wur o' no use looking too far ahead.'

Bessy had to hear many unintelligible jokes from her uncle that night, for he made no doubt that Benjamin had told her all that had passed, whereas the truth was, his son had said never a word to his cousin on the subject.

When the old couple were in bed, Nathan told his wife of the promise he had made to his son, and the plan in life which the advance of the two hundred was to promote. Poor Hester was a little startled at the sudden change in the destination of the sum, which she had long thought of with secret pride as 'money i' th' bank'. But she was willing enough to part with it, if necessary, for Benjamin. Only, how such a sum could be necessary, was the puzzle. But even the perplexity was jostled out of her mind by the overwhelming idea, not only of 'our Ben' settling in London, but of Bessy going there too as his wife. This great trouble swallowed up all care about money, and Hester shivered and sighed all the night through with distress. In the morning, as Bessy was kneading the bread, her aunt, who had been sitting by the fire in an unusual manner, for one of her active habits, said: 'I reckon we maun go to th' shop for our bread; an' that's a thing I never thought to come to so long as I lived.'

Bessy looked up from her kneading, surprised. 'I'm sure, I'm noan going to eat their nasty stuff. What for do ye want to get baker's bread, aunt? This dough will rise as high as a kite in a south wind.'

'I'm not up to kneading as I could do once; it welly breaks my back; and, when thou'rt off in London, I reckon we maun buy our bread, first time in my life.'

'I'm not a-going to London,' said Bessy, kneading away with fresh resolution, and growing very red, either with the idea or the exertion.

'But our Ben is going partner wi' a great London lawyer; and thou know'st he'll not tarry long but what he'll fetch thee.'

'Now, aunt,' said Bessy, stripping her arms of the dough, but still not looking up, 'if that's all, don't fret yourself. Ben will have twenty minds in his head, afore he settles, eyther in business or in wedlock. I sometimes wonder,' she said, with increasing vehemence, 'why I go on thinking on him; for I dunnot think he thinks on me, when I'm out o' sight. I've a month's mind to try and forget him this time, when he leaves us – that I have!'

'For shame, wench! and he to be planning and purposing, all for thy sake! It wur only yesterday as he wur talking to thy uncle, and mapping it out so clever; only, thou seest, wench, it'll be dree work for us when both thee and him is gone.'

The old woman began to cry the kind of tearless cry of the aged. Bessy hastened to comfort her; and the two talked, and grieved, and hoped, and planned for the days that now were to be, till they ended, the one in being consoled, the other in being secretly happy.

Nathan and his son came back from Highminster that evening, with their business transacted in the roundabout way which was most satisfactory to the old man. If he had thought it necessary to take half as much pains in ascertaining the truth of the plausible details by which his son bore out the story of the offered partner-ship, as he did in trying to get his money conveyed to London in the most secure manner, it would have been well for him. But he knew nothing of all this, and acted in the way which satisfied his anxiety best. He came home tired, but content; not in such high spirits as on the night before, but as easy in his mind as he could be on the eve of his son's departure. Bessy, pleasantly agitated by her aunt's tale of the morning of her cousin's true love for her ('what ardently we wish we long believe') and the plan which was to end in their marriage – end to her, the woman, at least – looked almost pretty in her bright, blushing comeliness, and more than once, as she moved about from kitchen to dairy, Benjamin pulled her to-wards him, and gave her a kiss. To all such proceedings the old couple were wilfully blind; and, as night drew on, everyone became sadder and quieter, thinking of the parting that was to be on the morrow. As the hours slipped away, Bessy too became subdued; and, by and by, her simple cunning was exerted to get Benjamin to sit down next his mother, whose very heart was yearning after him, as Bessy saw. When once her child was placed by her side, and she had got possession of his hand, the old woman kept stroking it, and murmuring long unused words of endearment, such as she had spoken to him while he was yet a little child. But all this was wearisome to him. As long as he might play with, and plague, and caress Bessy, he had not been sleepy; but now he yawned loudly. Bessy could have boxed his ears for not curbing this gaping; at any rate, he need not have done it so openly – so almost ostentatiously. His mother was more pitiful.

'Thou'rt tired, my lad!' said she, putting her hand fondly on his shoulder; but it fell off, as he stood up suddenly, and said: 'Yes, deuced tired! I'm off to bed.' And with a rough, careless kiss all round, even to Bessy, as if he was 'deuced tired' of playing the lover, he was gone; leaving the three to gather up their thoughts slowly, and follow him upstairs.

He seemed almost impatient at them for rising betimes to see him off the next morning, and made no more of a goodbye than some such speech as this: 'Well, good folk, when next I see you, I hope you'll have merrier faces than you have today. Why, you might be going to a funeral; it's enough to scare a man from the place; you look quite ugly to what you did last night, Bess.'

He was gone; and they turned into the house, and settled to the long day's work without many words about their loss. They had no time for unnecessary talking, indeed; for much had been left undone, during his short visit, that ought to have been done, and they had now to work double tides. Hard work was their comfort for many a long day.

For some time Benjamin's letters, if not frequent, were full of exultant accounts of his well-doing. It is true that the details of his prosperity were somewhat vague; but the fact was broadly and unmistakably stated. Then came longer pauses; shorter letters, altered in tone. About a year after he had left them, Nathan received a letter which bewildered and irritated him exceedingly. Something had gone wrong – what, Benjamin did not say – but the letter ended with a request that was almost a demand, for the remainder of his father's savings, whether in the stocking or in the bank. Now, the year had not been prosperous with Nathan; there had been an epidemic among cattle, and he had suffered along with his neighbours; and, moreover, the price of cows, when he had bought some to repair his wasted stock, was higher than he had ever remembered it before. The fifteen pounds in the stocking, which Benjamin left, had diminished to little more than three; and to have that required of him in so peremptory a manner! Before Nathan imparted the contents of this letter to anyone (Bessy and her aunt had gone to market in a neighbour's cart that day), he got pen and ink and paper, and wrote back an ill-spelt, but very explicit and stern negative. Benjamin had had his portion; and if he could not make it do, so much the worse for him; his father had no more to give him. That was the substance of the letter.

The letter was written, directed, and sealed, and given to the country postman, returning to Highminster after his day's distribution and collection of letters, before Hester and Bessy came back from market. It had been a pleasant day of neighbourly meeting and sociable gossip; prices had been high, and they were in good spirits – only agreeably tired, and full of small pieces of news. It was some time before they found out how flatly all their talk fell on the ears of the stay-at-home listener. But, when they saw that his depression was caused by something beyond their powers of accounting for by any little everyday cause, they urged him to tell them what was the matter. His anger had not gone off. It had rather increased by dwelling upon it, and he spoke it out in good, resolute terms; and, long ere he had ended, the two women were as sad, if not as angry, as himself. Indeed, it was many days before either feeling wore away in the minds of those who entertained them. Bessy was the soonest comforted, because she found a vent for her sorrow in action: action that was half as a kind of compensation for many a sharp word that she had spoken, when her cousin had done anything to displease her on his last visit, and half because she believed that he never could have written such a letter to his father, unless his want of money had been very pressing and real; though how he could ever have wanted money so soon, after such a heap of it had been given to him, was more than she could justly say. Bessy got out all her savings of little presents of sixpences and shillings, ever since she had been a child – of all the money she had gained for the eggs of two hens, called her own; she put the whole together, and it was above two pounds – two pounds five and seven-pence, to speak accurately – and, leaving out the penny as a nest-egg for her future savings, she made up the rest in a little parcel, and sent it, with a note, to Benjamin's address in London.

From a well-wisher.

DR BENJAMIN – Unkle has lost 2 cows and a vast of monney. He is a good deal Angored, but more Troubled. So no more at present. Hopeing this will finding you well As it leaves us. Tho' lost to Site, To Memory Dear. Repayment not kneeded.

Your effectonet cousin,

ELIZABETH ROSE

When this packet was once fairly sent off, Bessy began to sing again over her work. She never expected the mere form of acknowledgment; indeed, she had such faith in the carrier (who took parcels to York, whence they were forwarded to London by coach), that she felt sure he would go on purpose to London to deliver anything entrusted to him, if he had not full confidence in the person, persons, coach and horses, to whom he committed it. Therefore she was not anxious that she did not hear of its arrival. 'Giving a thing to a man as one knows,' said she to herself, 'is a vast different to poking a thing through a hole into a box, th' inside of which one has never clapped eyes on; and yet letters get safe, some ways or another.' (The belief in the infallibility of the post was destined to a shock before long.) But she had a secret yearning for Benjamin's thanks, and some of the old words of love that she had been without so long. Nay, she even thought – when, day after day, week after week, passed by without a line – that he might be winding up his affairs in that weary, wasteful London, and coming back to Nab-end to thank her in person.

One day – her aunt was upstairs, inspecting the summer's make of cheeses, her uncle out in the fields – the postman brought a letter into the kitchen to Bessy. A country postman, even now, is not much pressed for time; and in those days there were but few letters to distribute, and they were only sent out from Highminster once a week into the district in which Nab-end was situated; and, on those occasions, the letter-carrier usually paid morning calls on the various people for whom he had letters. So, half-standing by the dresser, half-sitting on it, he began to rummage out his bag. 'It's a queer-like thing I've got for Nathan this time. I am afraid it will bear ill news in it; for there's "Dead Letter Office" stamped on the top of it.'

'Lord save us!' said Bessy, and sat down on the nearest chair, as white as a sheet. In an instant, however, she was up; and, snatching the ominous letter out of the man's hands, she pushed him before her out of the house, and said, 'Be off wi' thee, afore aunt comes down'; and ran past him as hard as she could, till she reached the field where she expected to find her uncle.

'Uncle,' said she, breathless, 'what is it? Oh, uncle, speak! Is he dead?'

Nathan's hands trembled, and his eyes dazzled. 'Take it,' he said, 'and tell me what it is.'

'It's a letter – it's from you to Benjamin, it is – and there's words written on it, "Not known at the address given"; so they've sent it back to the writer – that's you, uncle. Oh, it gave me such a start, with them nasty words written outside!'

Nathan had taken the letter back into his own hands, and was turning it over, while he strove to understand what the quick-witted Bessy had picked up at a glance. But he arrived at a different conclusion.

'He's dead!' said he. 'The lad is dead, and he never knowed how as I were sorry I wrote to 'un so sharp. My lad! my lad!' Nathan sat down on the ground where he stood, and covered his face with his old, withered hands. The letter returned to him was one which he had written, with infinite pains and at various times, to tell his child, in kinder words and at greater length than he had done before, the reasons why he could not send him the money demanded. And now Benjamin was dead; nay, the old man immediately jumped to the conclusion that his child had been starved to death, without money, in a wild, wide, strange place. All he could say at first was: 'My heart, Bess – my heart is broken!' And he put his hand to his side, still keeping his shut eyes covered with the other, as though he never wished to see the light of day again. Bessy was down by his side in an instant, holding him in her arms, chafing and kissing him.

'It's noan so bad, uncle; he's not dead; the letter does not say that, dunnot think it. He's flitted from that lodging, and the lazy tykes dunna know where to find him; and so they just send y' back th' letter, instead of trying fra' house to house, as Mark Benson would. I've always heerd tell on south-country folk for laziness. He's noan dead, uncle; he's just flitted; and he'll let us know afore long where he's gotten to. May be, it's a cheaper place; for that lawyer has cheated him, ye reck'lect, and he'll be trying to live for as little as he can, that's all, uncle. Dunnot take on so; for it doesna say he's dead.'

By this time Bessy was crying with agitation, although she firmly believed in her own view of the case, and had felt the opening of the ill-favoured letter as a great relief. Presently she began to urge, both with word and action, upon her uncle, that he should sit no longer on the damp grass, She pulled him up; for he was very stiff, and, as he said, 'all shaken to dithers'. She made him walk about, repeating over and over again her solution of the case, always in the same words, beginning again and again, 'He's noan dead; it's just been a flitting,' and so on. Nathan shook his head, and tried to be convinced; but it was a steady belief in his own heart for all that. He looked so deathly ill on his return home with Bessy (for she would not let him go on with his day's work), that his wife made sure he had taken cold; and he, weary and indifferent to life, was glad to subside into bed and the rest from exertion which his real bodily illness gave him. Neither Bessy nor he spoke of the letter again, even to each other, for many days; and she found means to stop Mark Benson's tongue and satisfy his kindly curiosity, by giving him the rosy side of her own view of the case.

Nathan got up again, an older man in looks and constitution by ten years for that week of bed. His wife gave him many a scolding on his imprudence for sitting down in the wet field, if ever so tired. But now she, too, was beginning to be uneasy at Benjamin's long-continued silence. She could not write herself; but she urged her husband many a time to send a letter to ask for news of her lad. He said nothing in reply for some time; at length, he told her he would write next Sunday afternoon. Sunday was his general day for writing, and this Sunday he meant to go to church for the first time since his illness. On Saturday he was very persistent, against his wife's wishes (backed by Bessy as hard as she could), in resolving to go into Highminster to market. The change would do him good, he said. But he came home tired, and a little mysterious in his ways. When he went to the shippon the last thing at night, he asked Bessy to go with him, and hold the lantern, while he looked at an ailing cow; and, when they were fairly out of earshot of the house, he pulled a little shop-parcel from his pocket and said: 'Thou'lt put that on ma Sunday hat, wilt 'ou, lass? It'll be a bit on a comfort to me; for I know my lad's dead and gone, though I dunna speak on it, for fear o' grieving th' old woman and ye.'

'I'll put it on, uncle, if – But he's noan dead.' (Bessy was sobbing.)

'I know – I know, lass. I dunnot wish other folk to hold my opinion; but I'd like to wear a bit o' crape out o' respect to my boy. It 'ud have done me good for to have ordered a black coat; but she'd see if I had na' on my wedding-coat, Sundays, for a' she's losing her eyesight, poor old wench! But she'll ne'er take notice o' a bit o' crape. Thou'lt put it on all canny and tidy.'

So Nathan went to church with a strip of crape, as narrow as Bessy durst venture to make it, round his hat. Such is the contradictoriness of human nature that, though he was most anxious his wife should not hear of his conviction that their son was dead, he was half hurt that none of his neighbours noticed his sign of mourning so far as to ask him for whom he wore it.

But after a while, when they never heard a word from or about Benjamin, the household wonder as to what had become of him grew so painful and strong, that Nathan no longer kept the idea to himself. Poor Hester, however, rejected it with her whole will, heart, and soul. She could and would not believe – nothing should make her believe – that her only child Benjamin had died without some sign of love or farewell to her. No arguments could shake her in this. She believed that, if all natural means of communication between her and him had been cut off at the last supreme moment – if death had come upon him in an instant, sudden and unexpected – her intense love would have been supernaturally made conscious of the blank. Nathan at times tried to feel glad that she should still hope to see the lad again; but at other moments he wanted her sympathy in his grief, his self-reproach, his weary wonder as to how and what they had done wrong in the treatment of their son, that he had been such a care and sorrow to his parents. Bessy was convinced, first by her aunt, and then by her uncle – honestly convinced – on both sides of the argument, and so, for the time, able to sympathise with each. But she lost her youth in a very few months; she looked set and middle-aged, long before she ought to have done, and rarely smiled and never sang again.

All sorts of new arrangements were required by the blow which told so miserably upon the energies of all the household at Nab-end. Nathan could no longer go about and direct his two men, taking a good turn of work himself at busy times. Hester lost her interest in the dairy; for which, indeed, her increasing loss of sight unfitted her. Bessy would either do field-work, or attend to the cows and the shippon, or churn, or make cheese; she did all well, no longer merrily, but with something of stern cleverness. But she was not sorry when her uncle, one evening, told her aunt and her that a neighbouring farmer, Job Kirkby, had made him an offer to take so much of his land off his hands as would leave him only pasture enough for two cows, and no arable to attend to; while Farmer Kirkby did not wish to interfere with anything in the house, only would be glad to use some of the outbuildings for his fattening cattle.

'We can do wi' Hawky and Daisy; it'll leave us eight or ten pound o' butter to take to market i' summer time, and keep us fra' thinking too much, which is what I'm dreading on as I get into years.'

'Ay,' said his wife. 'Thou'll not have to go so far a-field, if it's only the Aster-Toft as is on thy hands. And Bess will have to gie up her pride i' cheese, and tak' to making cream-butter. I'd allays a fancy for trying at cream-butter; but th' whey had to be used; else, where I come fra', they'd never ha' looked near whey-butter.'

When Hester was left alone with Bessy, she said, in allusion to this change of plan: 'I'm thankful to the Lord that it is as it is; for I were allays feared Nathan would have to gie up the house and farm alto-gether, and then the lad would na know where to find us when he came back fra' Merikay. He's gone there for to make his fortune, I'll be bound. Keep up thy heart, lass, he'll be home some day; and have sown his wild oats. Eh! but thatten's a pretty story i' the Gospel about the Prodigal, who'd to eat the pigs' vittle at one time, but ended i' clover in his father's house. And I'm sure our Nathan 'll be ready to forgive him, and love him, and make much of him – may be, a deal more nor me, who never gave in to 's death. It'll be liken to a resurrection to our Nathan.'

Farmer Kirkby, then, took by far the greater part of the land belonging to Nab-end Farm; and the work about the rest, and about the two remaining cows, was easily done by three pairs of willing hands, with a little occasional assistance. The Kirkby family were pleasant enough to have to deal with. There was a son, a stiff, grave bachelor, who was very particular and methodical about his work, and rarely spoke to anyone. But Nathan took it into his head that John Kirkby was looking after Bessy, and was a good deal troubled in his mind in consequence; for it was the first time he had to face the effects of his belief in his son's death; and he discovered, to his own surprise, that he had not that implicit faith which would make it easy for him to look upon Bessy as the wife of another man than the one to whom she had been betrothed in her youth. As, however, John Kirkby seemed in no hurry to make his intentions (if indeed he had any) clear to Bessy, it was only now and then that his jealousy on behalf of his lost son seized upon Nathan.

But people, old, and in deep hopeless sorrow, grow irritable at times, however they may repent and struggle against their irritability. There were days when Bessy had to bear a good deal from her uncle; but she loved him so dearly and respected him so much, that, high as her temper was to all other people, she never returned him a rough or impatient word. And she had a reward in the conviction of his deep, true affection for her, and her aunt's entire and most sweet dependence upon her.

One day, however – it was near the end of November – Bessy had had a good deal to bear, that seemed more than usually unreasonable, on the part of her uncle. The truth was, that one of Kirkby's cows was ill, and John Kirkby was a good deal about in the farmyard; Bessy was interested about the animal, and had helped in preparing a mash over their own fire, that had to be given warm to the sick creature. If John had been out of the way, there would have been no-one more anxious about the affair than Nathan: both because he was naturally kind-hearted and neighbourly, and also because he was rather proud of his reputation for knowledge in the diseases of cattle. But because John was about, and Bessy helping a little in what had to be done, Nathan would do nothing, and chose to assume that 'nothing to think on ailed th' beast; but lads and lasses were allays fain to be feared on something.' Now John was upwards of forty, and Bessy nearly eight-and-twenty; so the terms lads and lasses did not exactly apply to their case.

When Bessy brought the milk in from their own cows, towards half-past five o'clock, Nathan bade her make the doors, and not be running out i' the dark and cold about other folks' business; and, though Bessy was a little surprised and a good deal annoyed at his tone, she sat down to her supper without making a remonstrance. It had long been Nathan's custom to look out the last thing at night, to see 'what mak' o' weather it wur'; and when, towards half-past eight, he got his stick and went out – two or three steps from the door, which opened into the house-place where they were sitting – Hester put her hand on her niece's shoulder and said: 'He's gotten a touch o' rheumatics, as twinges him and makes him speak so sharp. I didna like to ask thee afore him, but how's yon poor beast?'

'Very ailing, belike. John Kirkby wur off for th' cow-doctor when I cam in. I reckon they'll have to stop up wi 't a' night.'

Since their sorrows, her uncle had taken to reading a chapter in the Bible aloud, the last thing at night. He could not read fluently, and often hesitated long over a word, which he miscalled at length; but the very fact of opening the book seemed to soothe those old bereaved parents; for it made them feel quiet and safe in the presence of God, and took them out of the cares and troubles of this world into that futurity which, however dim and vague, was to their faithful hearts as a sure and certain rest. This little quiet time – Nathan sitting with his horn spectacles, the tallow candle between him and the Bible throwing a strong light on his reverent, earnest face; Hester sitting on the other side of the fire, her head bowed in attentive listening; now and then shaking it, and moaning a little, but when a promise came, or any good tidings of great joy, saying 'Amen' with fervour; Bessy by her aunt, perhaps her mind a little wandering to some household cares, or it might be on thoughts of those who were absent – this little quiet pause, I say, was grateful and soothing to this household, as a lullaby to a tired child. But this night, Bessy, sitting opposite to the long, low window, only shaded by a few geraniums that grew in the sill, and to the door alongside that window through which her uncle had passed not a quarter of an hour before, saw the wooden latch of the door gently and almost noiselessly lifted up, as if someone were trying it from the outside.

She was startled, and watched again, intently; but it was perfectly still now. She thought it must have been that it had not fallen into its proper place, when her uncle had come in and locked the door. It was just enough to make her uncomfortable, no more; and she almost persuaded herself it must have been fancy. Before going upstairs, however, she went to the window, to look out into the darkness; but all was still. Nothing to be seen; nothing to be heard. So the three went quietly upstairs to bed.

The house was little better than a cottage. The front door opened on a house-place, over which was the old couple's bedroom. To the left, as you entered this pleasant house-place, and at close right angles with the entrance, was a door that led into the small parlour, which was Hester's and Bessy's pride, although not half as comfortable as the house-place, and never on any occasion used as a sitting-room. There were shells and bunches of honesty in the fireplace; the best chest of drawers, and a company set of gaudy-coloured china, and a bright common carpet on the floor; but all failed to give it the aspect of the homely comfort and delicate cleanliness of the house-place. Over this parlour was the bedroom which Benjamin had slept in when a boy, when at home. It was kept, still, in a kind of readiness for him. The bed was yet there, in which none had slept since he had last done, eight or nine years ago; and every now and then a warming-pan was taken quietly and silently up by his old mother, and the bed thoroughly aired. But this she did in her husband's absence, and without saying a word to anyone; nor did Bessy offer to help her, though her eyes often filled with tears, as she saw her aunt still going through the hopeless service. But the room had become a receptacle for all unused things; and there was always a corner of it appropriated to the winter's store of apples. To the left of the house-place, as you stood facing the fire, on the side opposite to the window and outer door, were two other doors; the one on the right led into a kind of back kitchen, and had a lean-to roof, and a door opening on to the farm-yard and back-premises; the left-hand door gave on the stairs, underneath which was a closet, in which various household treasures were kept; and beyond that was the dairy, over which Bessy slept, her little chamber window opening just above the sloping roof of the back-kitchen. There were neither blinds nor shutters to any of the windows, either upstairs or down; the house was built of stone; and there was heavy framework of the same material around the little casement windows, and the long, low window of the house-place was divided by what, in grander dwellings, would be called mullions.

By nine o'clock this night of which I am speaking, all had gone upstairs to bed; it was even later than usual, for the burning of candles was regarded so much in the light of an extravagance, that the household kept early hours even for country-folk. But, somehow, this evening, Bessy could not sleep; although in general she was in deep slumber five minutes after her head touched the pillow. Her thoughts ran on the chances for John Kirkby's cow, and a little fear lest the disorder might be epidemic and spread to their own cattle. Across all these homely cares came a vivid, uncomfortable recollection of the way in which the door-latch went up and down, without any sufficient agency to account for it. She felt more sure now than she had done downstairs, that it was a real movement, and no effect of her imagination. She wished that it had not happened just when her uncle was reading, that she might at once have gone quick to the door, and convinced herself of the cause. As it was, her thoughts ran uneasily on the supernatural; and thence to Benjamin, her dear cousin and playfellow, her early lover. She had long given him up as lost for ever to her, if not actually dead; but this very giving him up for ever involved a free, full forgiveness of all his wrongs to her. She thought tenderly of him, as of one who might have been led astray in his later years, but who existed rather in her recollection as the innocent child, the spirited lad, the handsome, dashing young man. If John Kirkby's quiet attentions had ever betrayed his wishes to Bessy – if indeed he ever had any wishes on the subject – her first feeling would have been to compare his weather-beaten, middle-aged face and figure with the face and figure she remembered well, but never more expected to see in this life. So thinking, she became very restless, and weary of bed, and, after long tossing and turning, ending in a belief that she should never get to sleep at all that night, she went off soundly and suddenly.

As suddenly she was wide awake, sitting up in bed, listening to some noise that must have awakened her, but which was not repeated for some time. Surely it was in her uncle's room – her uncle was up; but, for a minute or two, there was no further sound. Then she heard him open his door, and go downstairs, with hurried, stumbling steps. She now thought that her aunt must be ill, and hastily sprang out of bed, and was putting on her petticoat with hurried, trembling hands, and had just opened her chamber door, when she heard the front door undone, and a scuffle, as of the feet of several people, and many rude, passionate words, spoken hoarsely below the breath. Quick as thought she understood it all – the house was lonely – her uncle had the reputation of being well-to-do – they had pretended to be belated, and had asked their way or something. What a blessing that John Kirkby's cow was sick, for there were several men watching with him! She went back, opened her window, squeezed herself out, slid down the lean-to roof, and ran barefoot and breathless to the shippon: 'John, John, for the love of God, come quick; there's robbers in the house, and uncle and aunt 'll be murdered!' she whispered, in terrified accents, through the closed and barred shippon door. In a moment it was undone, and John and the cow-doctor stood there, ready to act, if they but understood her rightly. Again she repeated her words, with broken, half-unintelligible explanations of what she as yet did not rightly understand.

'Front door is open, say'st thou?' said John, arming himself with a pitchfork, while the cow-doctor took some other implement. 'Then I reckon we'd best make for that way o' getting into th' house, and catch 'em all in a trap.'

'Run! run!' was all Bessy could say, taking hold of John Kirkby's arm, and pulling him along with her. Swiftly did the three run to the house round the corner, and in at the open front-door. The men carried the horn lantern they had been using in the shippon; and, by the sudden oblong light that it threw, Bessy saw the principal object of her anxiety, her uncle, lying stunned and helpless on the kitchen-floor. Her first thought was for him; for she had no idea that her aunt was in any immediate danger, although she heard the noise of feet, and fierce, subdued voices upstairs.

'Make th' door behind us, lass. We'll not let 'em escape!' said brave John Kirkby, dauntless in a good cause, though he knew not how many there might be above. The cow-doctor fastened and locked the door, saying, 'There!' in a defiant tone, as he put the key in his pocket. It was to be a struggle for life or death, or, at any rate, for effectual capture or desperate escape. Bessy kneeled down by her uncle, who did not speak or give any sign of consciousness. Bessy raised his head by drawing a pillow off the settle, and putting it under him; she longed to go for water into the back kitchen, but the sound of a violent struggle, and of heavy blows, and of low, hard curses spoken through closed teeth, and muttered passion, as though breath were too much needed for action to be wasted in speech, kept her still and quiet by her uncle's side in the kitchen, where the darkness might almost be felt, so thick and deep was it. Once – in a pause of her own heart's beating – a sudden terror came over her; she perceived, in that strange way in which the presence of a living creature forces itself on our consciousness in the darkest room, that someone was near her, keeping as still as she. It was not the poor old man's breathing that she heard, nor the radiation of his presence that she felt; someone else was in the kitchen; another robber, perhaps, left to guard the old man, with murderous intent if his consciousness returned. Now Bessy was fully aware that self-preservation would keep her terrible companion quiet, as there was no motive for his betraying himself stronger than the desire of escape; any effort for which he, the unseen witness, must know would be rendered abortive by the fact of the door being locked. Yet, with the knowledge that he was there, close to her still, silent as the grave – with fearful, it might be deadly, unspoken thoughts in his heart – possibly even with keener and stronger sight than hers, as longer accustomed to the darkness, able to discern her figure and posture, and glaring at her like some wild beast – Bessy could not fail to shrink from the vision that her fancy presented! And still the struggle went on upstairs; feet slipping, blows sounding, and the wrench of intentioned aims, the strong gasps for breath, as the wrestlers paused for an instant. In one of these pauses, Bessy felt conscious of a creeping movement close to her, which ceased when the noise of the strife above died away, and was resumed when it again began. She was aware of it by some subtle vibration of the air, rather than by touch or sound. She was sure that he who had been close to her one minute as she knelt, was, the next, passing stealthily towards the inner door which led to the staircase. She thought he was going to join and strengthen his accomplices, and, with a great cry, she sprang after him; but just as she came to the doorway, through which some dim portion of light from the upper chambers came, she saw one man thrown downstairs, with such violence that he fell almost at her very feet, while the dark, creeping figure glided suddenly away to the left, and as suddenly entered the closet beneath the stairs. Bessy had no time to wonder as to his purpose in so doing, whether he had at first designed to aid his accomplices in their desperate fight or not. He was an enemy, a robber, that was all she knew, and she sprang to the door of the closet, and in a trice had locked it on the outside. And then she stood frightened, panting in that dark corner, sick with terror lest the man who lay before her was either John Kirkby or the cow-doctor. If it were either of those friendly two, what would become of the other – of her uncle, her aunt, herself? But, in a very few minutes, this wonder was ended; her two defenders came slowly and heavily down the stairs, dragging with them a man, fierce, sullen, despairing – disabled with terrible blows, which had made his face one bloody, swollen mass. As for that, neither John nor the cow-doctor was much more presentable. One of them bore the lantern in his teeth; for all their strength was taken up by the weight of the fellow they were bearing.

'Take care,' said Bessy, from her corner; 'there's a chap just beneath your feet. I dunno know if he's dead or alive; and uncle lies on the floor just beyond.'

They stood still on the stairs for a moment. Just then the robber they had thrown downstairs stirred and moaned.

'Bessy,' said John, 'run off to th' stable and fetch ropes and gearing for us to bind 'em; and we'll rid the house on 'em, and thou can'st go see after th' oud folks, who need it sadly.'

Bessy was back in a very few minutes. When she came in, there was more light in the house-place, for someone had stirred up the raked fire.

'That felly makes as though his leg were broken,' said John, nodding towards the man still lying on the ground. Bessy felt almost sorry for him as they handled him – not over-gently – and bound him, only half-conscious, as hardly and tightly as they had done his fierce, surly companion. She even felt sorry for his evident agony, as they turned him over and over, that she ran to get him a cup of water to moisten his lips.

'I'm loth to leave yo' with him alone,' said John, 'though I'm thinking his leg is broken for sartin, and he can't stir, even if he comes to hissel, to do yo' any harm. But we'll just take off this chap, and mak sure of him, and then one on us 'll come back to yo', and we can, may be, find a gate or so for yo' to get shut on him o' th' house. This felly's made safe enough, I'll be bound,' said he, looking at the burglar, who stood, bloody and black, with fell hatred on his sullen face. His eye caught Bessy's, as hers fell on him with dread so evident that it made him smile; and the look and the smile prevented the words from being spoken which were on Bessy's lips. She dared not tell, before him, that an able-bodied accomplice still remained in the house; lest, somehow, the door which kept him a prisoner should be broken open and the fight renewed. So she only said to John, as he was leaving the house: 'Thou'll not be long away, for I'm afeared of being left wi' this man.'

'He'll noan do thee harm,' said John.

'No! but I'm feared lest he should die. And there's uncle and aunt. Come back soon, John!'

'Ay, ay!' said he, half-pleased; 'I'll be back, never fear me.'

So Bessy shut the door after them, but did not lock it, for fear of mischances in the house, and went once more to her uncle, whose breathing, by this time, was easier than when she had first returned into the house-place with John and the doctor. By the light of the fire, too, she could now see that he had received a blow on the head, which was probably the occasion of his stupor. Round this wound, which was bleeding pretty freely, Bessy put cloths dipped in cold water; and then, leaving him for a time, she lighted a candle, and was about to go upstairs to her aunt, when, just as she was passing the bound and disabled robber, she heard her name softly, urgently called: 'Bessy, Bessy!'

At first the voice sounded so close that she thought it must be the unconscious wretch at her feet. But, once again, that voice thrilled through her: 'Bessy, Bessy! for God's sake, let me out!'

She went to the stair-closet door, and tried to speak, but could not, her heart beat so terribly. Again, close to her ear: 'Bessy, Bessy! they'll be back directly; let me out, I say! For God's sake, let me out!' And he began to kick violently against the panels.

'Hush! hush!' she said, sick with a terrible dread, yet with a will strongly resisting her conviction. 'Who are you?' But she knew – knew quite well.

'Benjamin.' An oath. 'Let me out, I say, and I'll be off, and out of England by tomorrow night, never to come back, and you'll have all my father's money.'

'D'ye think I care for that?' said Bessy vehemently, feeling with trembling hands for the lock; 'I wish there was noan such a thing as money i' the world, afore yo'd come to this. There, yo're free, and I charge yo' never to let me see your face again. I'd ne'er ha' let yo' loose but for fear o' breaking their hearts, if yo' hanna killed him already.' But, before she had ended her speech, he was gone – off into the black darkness, leaving the door open wide. With a new terror in her mind, Bessy shut it afresh – shut it and bolted it this time. Then she sat down on the first chair, and relieved her soul by giving a great and exceeding bitter cry. But she knew it was no time for giving way; and, lifting herself up with as much effort as if each of her limbs was a heavy weight, she went into the back kitchen, and took a drink of cold water. To her surprise, she heard her uncle's voice saying feebly: 'Carry me up, and lay me by her.'

But Bessy could not carry him; she could only help his faint exertions to walk upstairs; and, by the time he was there, sitting panting on the first chair she could find, John Kirkby and Atkinson returned. John came up now to her aid. Her aunt lay across the bed in a fainting-fit, and her uncle sat in so utterly broken-down a state that Bessy feared immediate death for both. But John cheered her up, and lifted the old man into his bed again; and, while Bessy tried to compose poor Hester's limbs into a position of rest, John went down to hunt about for the little store of gin which was always kept in a corner cupboard against emergencies.

'They've had a sore fright,' said he, shaking his head, as he poured a little gin and hot water into their mouths with a teaspoon, while Bessy chafed their cold feet; 'and it and the cold have been welly too much for 'em, poor old folk!'

He looked tenderly at them, and Bessy blessed him in her heart for that look.

'I maun be off. I sent Atkinson up to th' farm for to bring down Bob, and Jack came wi' him back to th' shippon, for to look after t'other man. He began blackguarding us all round, so Bob and Jack were gagging him wi' bridles when I left.'

'Ne'er give heed to what he says,' cried poor Bessy, a new panic besetting her. 'Folks o' his sort are allays for dragging other folk into their mischief. I'm right glad he were well gagged.'

'Well! but what I were saying were this: Atkinson and me will take t'other chap, who seems quiet enough, to th' shippon, and it'll be one piece o' work for to mind them and the cow; and I'll saddle t' old bay mare and ride for constables and doctor fra' Highminster. I'll bring Dr Preston up to see Nathan and Hester first; and then, I reckon, th' broken-legged chap down below must have his turn for all as he's met wi' his misfortunes in a wrong line o' life.'

'Ay!' said Bessy. 'We maun ha' the doctor sure enough, for look at them how they lie – like two stone statues on a church monument, so sad and solemn!'

'There's a look o' sense come back into their faces though, sin' they supped that gin-and-water. I'd keep on a-bathing his head and giving them a sup on't fra' time to time, if I was you, Bessy.'

Bessy followed him downstairs, and lighted the men out of the house. She dared not light them carrying their burden even, until they passed round the corner of the house; so strong was her fearful conviction that Benjamin was lurking near, seeking again to enter. She rushed back into the kitchen, bolted and barred the door, and pushed the end of the dresser against it, shutting her eyes as she passed the uncurtained window, for fear of catching a glimpse of a white face pressed against the glass, and gazing at her. The poor old couple lay quiet and speechless, although Hester's position had slightly altered: she had turned a little on her side towards her husband, and had laid one shrivelled arm around his neck. But he was just as Bessy had left him, with the wet cloths around his head, his eyes not wanting in a certain intelligence, but solemn, and unconscious to all that was passing around as the eyes of death.

His wife spoke a little from time to time – said a word of thanks, perhaps, or so; but he, never. All the rest of that terrible night, Bessy tended the poor old couple with constant care, her own heart so stunned and bruised in its feelings that she went about her pious duties almost like one in a dream. The November morning was long in coming; nor did she perceive any change, either for the worse or the better, before the doctor came, about eight o'clock. John Kirkby brought him; and was full of the capture of the two burglars.

As far as Bessy could make out, the participation of that unnatural Third was unknown. It was a relief, almost sickening in the revulsion it gave her from her terrible fear, which now she felt had haunted and held possession of her all night long, and had, in fact, paralysed her from thinking. Now she felt and thought with acute and feverish vividness, owing, no doubt, in part, to the sleepless night she had passed. She felt almost sure that her uncle (possibly her aunt, too) had recognised Benjamin; but there was a faint chance that they had not done so, and wild horses should never tear the secret from her, nor should any inadvertent word betray the fact that there had been a third person concerned. As to Nathan, he had never uttered a word. It was her aunt's silence that made Bessy fear lest Hester knew, somehow, that her son was concerned.

The doctor examined them both closely; looked hard at the wound on Nathan's head; asked questions which Hester answered shortly and unwillingly, and Nathan not at all – shutting his eyes, as if even the sight of a stranger was pain to him. Bessy replied, in their stead, to all that she could answer respecting their state, and followed the doctor downstairs with a beating heart. When they came into the house-place, they found John had opened the outer door to let in some fresh air, had brushed the hearth and made up the fire, and put the chairs and table in their right places. He reddened a little, as Bessy's eye fell upon his swollen and battered face, but tried to smile it off in a dry kind of way: 'Yo' see, I'm an ould bachelor, and I just thought as I'd redd up things a bit. How dun yo' find 'em, doctor?'

'Well, the poor old couple have had a terrible shock. I shall send them some soothing medicine to bring down the pulse, and a lotion for the old man's head. It is very well it bled so much; there might have been a good deal of inflammation.' And so he went on, giving directions to Bessy for keeping them quietly in bed through the day. From these directions she gathered that they were not, as she had feared all night long, near to death. The doctor expected them to recover, though they would require care. She almost wished it had been otherwise, and that they, and she too, might have just lain down to their rest in the churchyard – so cruel did life seem to her; so dreadful the recollection of that subdued voice of the hidden robber smiting her with recognition.

All this time, John was getting things ready for breakfast, with something of the handiness of a woman. Bessy half-resented his officiousness in pressing Dr Preston to have a cup of tea, she did so want him to be gone and leave her alone with her thoughts. She did not know that all was done for love of her; that the hard-featured, short-spoken John was thinking all the time how ill and miserable she looked, and trying with tender artifices to make it incumbent upon her sense of hospitality to share Dr Preston's meal.

'I've seen as the cows is milked,' said he, 'yourn and all; and Atkinson's brought ours round fine. Whatten a marcy it were as she were sick this very night! Yon two chaps 'ud ha' made short work on't, if yo' hadna fetched us in; and, as it were, we had a sore tussle. One on 'em 'll bear the marks on't to his dying day, wunnot he, doctor?'

'He'll barely have his leg well enough to stand his trial at York Assizes; they're coming off in a fortnight from now.'

'Ay, and that reminds me, Bessy, yo'll have to go witness before Justice Royds. Constables bade me tell yo' and gie yo' this summons. Dunnot be feared: it will not be a long job, though I'm not saying as it'll be a pleasant one. Yo'll have to answer questions as to how, and all about it; and Jane' (his sister) 'will come and stop wi' th' oud folks; and I'll drive yo' in the shandry.'

No-one knew why Bessy's colour blenched, and her eye clouded. No-one knew how she apprehended lest she should have to say that Benjamin had been of the gang; if indeed, in some way, the law had not followed on his heels quick enough to catch him.

But that trial was spared her; she was warned by John to answer questions, and say no more than was necessary, for fear of making her story less clear; and, as she was known, by character at least, to

Justice Royds and his clerk, they made the examination as little formidable as possible.

When all was over, and John was driving her back again, he expressed his rejoicing that there would be evidence enough to convict the men, without summoning Nathan and Hester to identify them. Bessy was so tired that she hardly understood what an escape it was; how far greater than even her companion understood.

Jane Kirkby stayed with her for a week or more, and was an unspeakable comfort. Otherwise she sometimes thought she should have gone mad, with the face of her uncle always reminding her, in its stony expression of agony, of that fearful night. Her aunt was softer in her sorrow, as became one of her faithful and pious nature; but it was easy to see how her heart bled inwardly. She recovered her strength sooner than her husband; but, as she recovered, the doctor perceived the rapid approach of total blindness. Every day, nay, every hour of the day, that Bessy dared, without fear of exciting their suspicions of her knowledge, she told them, as she had anxiously told them at first, that only two men, and those perfect strangers, had been discovered as being concerned in the burglary. Her uncle would never have asked a question about it, even if she had withheld all information respecting the affair; but she noticed the quick, watching, waiting glance of his eye, whenever she returned from any person or place where she might have been supposed to gain intelligence if Benjamin were suspected or caught: and she hastened to relieve the old man's anxiety, by always telling all that she had heard; thankful that, as the days passed on, the danger she sickened to think of grew less and less.

Day by day, Bessy had ground for thinking that her aunt knew more than she had apprehended at first. There was something so very humble and touching in Hester's blind way of feeling about for her husband – stern, woebegone Nathan – and mutely striving to console him in the deep agony of which Bessy learnt, from this loving, piteous manner, that her aunt was conscious. Her aunt's face looked blankly up into his, tears slowly running down from her sightless eyes; while from time to time, when she thought herself unheard by any save him, she would repeat such texts as she had heard at church in happier days, and which she thought, in her true, simple piety, might tend to console him. Yet, day by day, her aunt grew more and more sad.

Three or four days before assize-time, two summonses to attend the trial at York were sent to the old people. Neither Bessy, nor John, nor Jane, could understand this: for their own notices had come long before, and they had been told that their evidence would be enough to convict.

But, alas! the fact was, that the lawyer employed to defend the prisoners had heard from them that there was a third person engaged, and had heard who that third person was; and it was this advocate's business to diminish, if possible, the guilt of his clients, by proving that they were but tools in the hands of one who had, from his superior knowledge of the premises and the daily customs of the inhabitants, been the originator and planner of the whole affair. To do this, it was necessary to have the evidence of the parents, who, as the prisoners had said, must have recognised the voice of the young man, their son. For no-one knew that Bessy, too, could have borne witness to his having been present; and, as it was supposed that Benjamin had escaped out of England, there was no exact betrayal of him on the part of his accomplices.

Wondering, bewildered, and weary, the old couple reached York, in company with John and Bessy, on the eve of the day of the trial. Nathan was still so self-contained that Bessy could never guess what had been passing in his mind. He was almost passive under his old wife's trembling caresses. He seemed hardly conscious of them, so rigid was his demeanour.

She, Bessy feared at times, was becoming childish; for she had evidently so great and anxious a love for her husband, that her memory seemed going in her endeavours to melt the stoniness of his aspect and manners; she appeared occasionally to have forgotten why he was so changed, in her piteous little attempts to bring him back to his former self .

'They'll, for sure, never torture them, when they see what old folks they are!' cried Bessy, on the morning of the trial, a dim fear looming over her mind. 'They'll never be so cruel, for sure?'

But 'for sure' it was so. The barrister looked up at the judge, almost apologetically, as he saw how hoary-headed and woeful an old man was put into the witness-box, when the defence came on, and Nathan Huntroyd was called on for his evidence.

'It is necessary, on behalf of my clients, my lord, that I should pursue a course which, for all other reasons, I deplore.'

'Go on!' said the judge. 'What is right and legal must be done.' But, an old man himself, he covered his quivering mouth with his hand as Nathan, with grey, unmoved face, and solemn, hollow eyes, placing his two hands on each side of the witness-box, prepared to give his answers to questions, the nature of which he was beginning to foresee, but would not shrink from replying to truthfully; 'the very stones' (as he said to himself, with a kind of dulled sense of the Eternal justice) 'rise up against such a sinner.'

'Your name is Nathan Huntroyd, I believe?'

'It is.'

'You live at Nab-end Farm?'

'I do.'

'Do you remember the night of November the twelfth?'

'Yes.'

'You were awakened that night by some noise, I believe. What was it?'

The old man's eyes fixed themselves upon his questioner with the look of a creature brought to bay. That look the barrister never forgets. It will haunt him till his dying day.

'It was a throwing-up of stones against our window.'

'Did you hear it at first?'

'No.'

'What awakened you, then?'

'She did.'

'And then you both heard the stones. Did you hear anything else?'

A long pause. Then a low, clear 'Yes.'

'What?'

'Our Benjamin asking us for to let him in. She said as it were him, leastways.'

'And you thought it was him, did you not?'

'I told her' (this time in a louder voice) 'for to get to sleep, and not be thinking that every drunken chap as passed by were our Benjamin, for that he were dead and gone.'

'And she?'

'She said as though she'd heerd our Benjamin, afore she were welly awake, axing for to be let in. But I bade her ne'er heed her dreams, but turn on her other side and get to sleep again.'

'And did she?'

A long pause – judge, jury, bar, audience, all held their breath. At length Nathan said: 'No!'

'What did you do then? (My lord, I am compelled to ask these painful questions.)'

'I saw she wadna be quiet: she had allays thought he would come back to us, like the Prodigal i' th' Gospels.' (His voice choked a little; but he tried to make it steady, succeeded, and went on.) 'She said, if I wadna get up, she would; and just then I heerd a voice. I'm not quite mysel', gentlemen – I've been ill and i' bed, an' it makes me trembling-like. Someone said, "Father, mother, I'm here, starving i' the cold – wunnot yo' get up and let me in?" '

'And that voice was – ?'

'It were like our Benjamin's. I see whatten yo're driving at, sir, and I'll tell yo' truth, though it kills me to speak it. I dunnot say it were our Benjamin as spoke, mind yo' – I only say it were like – '

'That's all I want, my good fellow. And on the strength of that entreaty, spoken in your son's voice, you went down and opened the door to these two prisoners at the bar, and to a third man?'

Nathan nodded assent, and even that counsel was too merciful to force him to put more into words.

'Call Hester Huntroyd.'

An old woman, with a face of which the eyes were evidently blind, with a sweet, gentle, careworn face, came into the witness-box, and meekly curtseyed to the presence of those whom she had been taught to respect – a presence she could not see.

There was something in her humble, blind aspect, as she stood waiting to have something done to her – what her poor troubled mind hardly knew – that touched all who saw her, inexpressibly. Again the counsel apologised, but the judge could not reply in words; his face was quivering all over, and the jury looked uneasily at the prisoner's counsel. That gentleman saw that he might go too far, and send their sympathies off on the other side; but one or two questions he must ask. So, hastily recapitulating much that he had learned from Nathan, he said, 'You believed it was your son's voice asking to be let in?'

'Ay! Our Benjamin came home, I'm sure; choose where he is gone.'

She turned her head about, as if listening for the voice of her child, in the hushed silence of the court.

'Yes; he came home that night – and your husband went down to let him in?'

'Well! I believe he did. There was a great noise of folk downstair.'

'And you heard your son Benjamin's voice among the others?'

'Is it to do him harm, sir?' asked she, her face growing more intelligent and intent on the business in hand.

'That is not my object in questioning you. I believe he has left England; so nothing you can say will do him any harm. You heard your son's voice, I say?'

'Yes, sir. For sure I did.'

'And some men came upstairs into your room? What did they say?'

'They axed where Nathan kept his stocking.'

THE GHOST IN THE GARDEN ROOM

'And you – did you tell them?'

'No, sir, for I knew Nathan would not like me to.'

'What did you do then?'

A shade of reluctance came over her face, as if she began to perceive causes and consequences.

'I just screamed on Bessy – that's my niece, sir.'

'And you heard someone shout out from the bottom of the stairs?'

She looked piteously at him, but did not answer. 'Gentlemen of the jury, I wish to call your particular attention to this fact; she acknowledges she heard someone shout – some third person, you observe – shout out to the two above. What did he say? That is the last question I shall trouble you with. What did the third person, left behind, downstairs, say?'

Her face worked – her mouth opened two or three times as if to speak – she stretched out her arms imploringly; but no word came, and she fell back into the arms of those nearest to her. Nathan forced himself forward into the witness-box: 'My Lord Judge, a woman bore ye, as I reckon; it's a cruel shame to serve a mother so. It wur my son, my only child, as called out for us t' open door, and who shouted out for to hold th' oud woman's throat if she did na stop her noise, when hoo'd fain ha' cried for her niece to help. And now yo've truth, and a' th' truth, and I'll leave yo' to th' judgement o' God for th' way yo've getten at it.'

Before night the mother was stricken with paralysis, and lay on her death-bed. But the broken-hearted go Home, to be comforted of God.

The Grey Woman

Portion 1

There is a mill by the Neckar-side, to which many people resort for coffee, according to the fashion which is almost national in Germany. There is nothing particularly attractive in the situation of this mill; it is on the Mannheim (the flat and unromantic) side of Heidelberg. The river turns the mill-wheel with a plenteous gushing sound; the out-buildings and the dwelling-house of the miller form a well-kept dusty quadrangle. Again, further from the river, there is a garden full of willows, and arbours, and flower-beds not well kept, but very profuse in flowers and luxuriant creepers, knotting and looping the arbours together. In each of these arbours is a stationary table of white painted wood, and light moveable chairs of the same colour and material.

I went to drink coffee there with some friends in 184—. The stately old miller came out to greet us, as some of the party were known to him of old. He was of a grand build of a man, and his loud musical voice, with its tone friendly and familiar, his rolling laugh of wel-come, went well with the keen bright eye, the fine cloth of his coat, and the general look of substance about the place. Poultry of all kinds abounded in the mill-yard, where there were ample means of livelihood for them strewed on the ground; but not content with this, the miller took out handfuls of corn from the sacks, and threw liberally to the cocks and hens that ran almost under his feet in their eagerness. And all the time he was doing this, as it were habitually, he was talking to us, and ever and anon calling to his daughter and the serving-maids, to bid them hasten the coffee we had ordered. He followed us to an arbour, and saw us served to his satisfaction with the best of everything we could ask for; and then left us to go round to the different arbours and see that each party was properly attended to; and, as he went, this great, prosperous, happy-looking man whistled softly one of the most plaintive airs I ever heard.

'His family have held this mill ever since the old Palatinate days; or rather, I should say, have possessed the ground ever since then, for two successive mills of theirs have been burnt down by the French. If you want to see Scherer in a passion, just talk to him of the possibility of a French invasion.'

But at this moment, still whistling that mournful air, we saw the miller going down the steps that led from the somewhat raised garden into the mill-yard; and so I seemed to have lost my chance of putting him in a passion.

We had nearly finished our coffee, and our *kuchen*, and our cinnamon cake, when heavy splashes fell on our thick leafy covering; quicker and quicker they came, coming through the tender leaves as if they were tearing them asunder; all the people in the garden were hurrying under shelter, or seeking for their carriages standing outside. Up the steps the miller came hastening, with a crimson umbrella, fit to cover everyone left in the garden, and followed by his daughter, and one or two maidens, each bearing an umbrella.

'Come into the house – come in, I say. It is a summer-storm, and will flood the place for an hour or two, till the river carries it away. Here, here.'

And we followed him back into his own house. We went into the kitchen first. Such an array of bright copper and tin vessels I never saw; and all the wooden things were as thoroughly scoured. The red tile floor was spotless when we went in, but in two minutes it was all over slop and dirt with the tread of many feet; for the kitchen was filled, and still the worthy miller kept bringing in more people under his great crimson umbrella. He even called the dogs in, and made them lie down under the tables.

His daughter said something to him in German, and he shook his head merrily at her. Everybody laughed.

'What did she say?' I asked.

'She told him to bring the ducks in next; but indeed if more people come we shall be suffocated. What with the thundery weather, and the stove, and all these steaming clothes, I really think we must ask leave to pass on. Perhaps we might go in and see Frau Scherer.'

My friend asked the daughter of the house for permission to go into an inner chamber and see her mother. It was granted, and we went into a sort of saloon, overlooking the Neckar; very small, very bright, and very close. The floor was slippery with polish; long narrow pieces of looking-glass against the walls reflected the perpetual motion of the river opposite; a white porcelain stove, with some old-fashioned ornaments of brass about it; a sofa, covered with Utrecht velvet, a table before it, and a piece of worsted-worked carpet under it; a vase of artificial flowers; and, lastly, an alcove with a bed in it, on which lay the paralysed wife of the good miller, knitting busily, formed the furniture. I spoke as if this was all that was to be seen in the room; but, sitting quietly, while my friend kept up a brisk conversation in a language which I but half understood, my eye was caught by a picture in a dark corner of the room, and I got up to examine it more nearly.

It was that of a young girl of extreme beauty; evidently of middle rank. There was a sensitive refinement in her face, as if she almost shrank from the gaze which, of necessity, the painter must have fixed upon her. It was not over-well painted, but I felt that it must have been a good likeness, from this strong impress of peculiar character which I have tried to describe. From the dress, I should guess it to have been painted in the latter half of the last century. And I after-wards heard that I was right.

There was a little pause in the conversation.

'Will you ask Frau Scherer who this is?'

My friend repeated my question, and received a long reply in German. Then she turned round and translated it to me.

'It is the likeness of a great-aunt of her husband's.' (My friend was standing by me, and looking at the picture with sympathetic curiosity.) 'See! here is the name on the open page of this Bible: "Anna Scherer, 1778." Frau Scherer says there is a tradition in the family that this pretty girl, with her complexion of lilies and roses, lost her colour so entirely through fright, that she was known by the name of the Grey Woman. She speaks as if this Anna Scherer lived in some state of life-long terror. But she does not know details; refers me to her husband for them. She thinks he has some papers which were written by the original of that picture for her daughter, who died in this very house not long after our friend there was married. We can ask Herr Scherer for the whole story if you like.'

'Oh yes, pray do!' said I. And, as our host came in at this moment to ask how we were faring, and to tell us that he had sent to Heidel-berg for carriages to convey us home, seeing no chance of the heavy rain abating, my friend, after thanking him, passed on to my request.

'Ah!' said he, his face changing, 'the aunt Anna had a sad history. It was all owing to one of those hellish Frenchmen; and her daughter suffered for it – the cousin Ursula, as we all called her when I was a child. To be sure, the good cousin Ursula was his child as well. The sins of the fathers are visited on their children. The lady would like to know all about it, would she? Well, there are papers – a kind of apology the aunt Anna wrote for putting an end to her daughter's engagement – or rather facts which she revealed, that prevented cousin Ursula from marrying the man she loved; and so she would never have any other good fellow, else I have heard say my father would have been thankful to have made her his wife.' All this time he was rummaging in the drawer of an old-fashioned bureau, and now he turned round, with a bundle of yellow MSS. in his hand, which he gave to my friend, saying, 'Take it home, take it home, and if you care to make out our crabbed German writing, you may keep it as long as you like, and read it at your leisure. Only I must have it back again when you have done with it, that's all.'

And so we became possessed of the manuscript of the following letter, which it was our employment, during many a long evening that ensuing winter, to translate, and in some parts to abbreviate. The letter began with some reference to the pain which she had already inflicted upon her daughter by some unexplained opposition to a project of marriage; but I doubt if, without the clue with which the good miller had furnished us, we could have made out even this much from the passionate, broken sentences that made us fancy that some scene between the mother and daughter – and possibly a third person – had occurred just before the mother had begun to write.

* * *

'Thou dost not love thy child, mother! Thou dost not care if her heart is broken!' Ah, God! and these words of my heart-beloved Ursula ring in my ears as if the sound of them would fill them when I lie a-dying. And her poor tear-stained face comes between me and everything else. Child! hearts do not break; life is very tough as well as very terrible. But I will not decide for thee. I will tell thee all; and thou shalt bear the burden of choice. I may be wrong; I have little wit left, and never had much, I think; but an instinct serves me in place of judgement, and that instinct tells me that thou and thy Henri must never be married. Yet I may be in error. I would fain make my child happy. Lay this paper before the good priest Schriesheim if, after reading it, thou hast doubts which make thee uncertain. Only I will tell thee all now, on condition that no spoken word ever passes between us on the subject. It would kill me to be questioned. I should have to see all present again.

My father held, as thou knowest, the mill on the Neckar, where thy new-found uncle, Scherer, now lives. Thou rememberest the sur-prise with which we were received there last vintage twelvemonth.

How thy uncle disbelieved me when I said that I was his sister Anna, whom he had long believed to be dead, and how I had to lead thee underneath the picture, painted of me long ago, and point out, feature by feature, the likeness between it and thee; and how, as I spoke, I recalled first to my own mind, and then by speech to his, the details of the time when it was painted; the merry words that passed between us then, a happy boy and girl; the position of the articles of furniture in the room; our father's habits; the cherry-tree, now cut down, that shaded the window of my bedroom, through which my brother was wont to squeeze himself, in order to spring on to the topmost bough that would bear his weight; and thence would pass me back his cap laden with fruit to where I sat on the window-sill, too sick with fright for him to care much for eating the cherries.

And at length Fritz gave way, and believed me to be his sister Anna, even as though I were risen from the dead. And thou rememberest how he fetched in his wife, and told her that I was not dead, but was come back to the old home once more, changed as I was. And she would scarce believe him, and scanned me with a cold, distrustful eye, till at length – for I knew her of old as Babette Müller – I said that I was well-to-do, and needed not to seek out friends for what they had to give. And then she asked – not me, but her husband – why I had kept silent so long, leading all – father, brother, everyone that loved me in my own dear home – to esteem me dead. And then thine uncle (thou rememberest?) said he cared not to know more than I cared to tell; that I was his Anna, found again, to be a blessing to him in his old age, as I had been in his boyhood. I thanked him in my heart for his trust; for were the need for telling all less than it seems to me now I could not speak of my past life. But she, who was my sister-in-law still, held back her welcome, and, for want of that, I did not go to live in Heidelberg as I had planned beforehand, in order to be near my brother Fritz, but contented myself with his promise to be a father to my Ursula when I should die and leave this weary world.

That Babette Müller was, as I may say, the cause of all my life's suffering. She was a baker's daughter in Heidelberg – a great beauty, as people said, and, indeed, as I could see for myself I, too – thou sawest my picture – was reckoned a beauty, and I believe I was so. Babette Müller looked upon me as a rival. She liked to be admired, and had no-one much to love her. I had several people to love me – thy grandfather, Fritz, the old servant Kätchen, Karl, the head apprentice at the mill – and I feared admiration and notice, and the being stared at as the 'Schöne Müllerin', whenever I went to make my purchases in Heidelberg.

Those were happy, peaceful days. I had Kätchen to help me in the housework, and whatever we did pleased my brave old father, who was always gentle and indulgent towards us women, though he was stern enough with the apprentices in the mill. Karl, the oldest of these, was his favourite; and I can see now that my father wished him to marry me, and that Karl himself was desirous to do so. But Karl was rough-spoken, and passionate – not with me, but with the others – and I shrank from him in a way which, I fear, gave him pain. And then came thy uncle Fritz's marriage; and Babette was brought to the mill to be its mistress. Not that I cared much for giving up my post, for, in spite of my father's great kindness, I always feared that I did not manage well for so large a family (with the men, and a girl under Kätchen, we sat down eleven each night to supper). But when Babette began to find fault with Kätchen, I was unhappy at the blame that fell on faithful servants; and by-and-by I began to see that Babette was egging on Karl to make more open love to me, and, as she once said, to get done with it, and take me off to a home of my own. My father was growing old, and did not perceive all my daily discomfort. The more Karl advanced, the more I disliked him. He was good in the main, but I had no notion of being married, and could not bear anyone who talked to me about it.

Things were in this way when I had an invitation to go to Carlsruhe to visit a schoolfellow, of whom I had been very fond. Babette was all for my going; I don't think I wanted to leave home, and yet I had been very fond of Sophie Rupprecht. But I was always shy among strangers. Somehow the affair was settled for me, but not until both Fritz and my father had made inquiries as to the character and position of the Rupprechts. They learned that the father had held some kind of inferior position about the Grand-duke's court, and was now dead, leaving a widow, a noble lady, and two daughters, the elder of whom was Sophie, my friend. Madame Rupprecht was not rich, but more than respectable – genteel. When this was ascertained, my father made no opposition to my going; Babette forwarded it by all the means in her power, and even my dear Fritz had his word to say in its favour. Only Kätchen was against it – Kätchen and Karl. The opposition of Karl did more to send me to Carlsruhe than anything. For I could have objected to go; but when he took upon himself to ask what was the good of going a-gadding, visiting strangers of whom no-one knew anything, I yielded to circumstances – to the pulling of Sophie and the pushing of Babette. I was silently vexed, I remember, at Babette's inspection of my clothes; at the way in which she settled that this gown was too old-fashioned, or that too common, to go with me on my visit to a noble lady; and at the way in which she took upon herself to spend the money my father had given me to buy what was requisite for the occasion. And yet I blamed myself, for everyone else thought her so kind for doing all this; and she herself meant kindly, too.

At last I quitted the mill by the Neckar-side. It was a long day's journey, and Fritz went with me to Carlsruhe. The Rupprechts lived on the third floor of a house a little behind one of the principal streets, in a cramped-up court, to which we gained admittance through a doorway in the street. I remember how pinched their rooms looked after the large space we had at the mill, and yet they had an air of grandeur about them which was new to me, and which gave me pleasure, faded as some of it was. Madame Rupprecht was too formal a lady for me; I was never at my ease with her; but Sophie was all that I had recollected her at school: kind, affectionate, and only rather too ready with her expressions of admiration and regard. The little sister kept out of our way; and that was all we needed, in the first enthusiastic renewal of our early friendship. The one great object of Madame Rupprecht's life was to retain her position in society; and as her means were much diminished since her husband's death, there was not much comfort, though there was a great deal of show, in their way of living; just the opposite of what it was at my father's house. I believe that my coming was not too much desired by Madame Rupprecht, as I brought with me another mouth to be fed; but Sophie had spent a year or more in entreating for permission to invite me, and her mother, having once consented, was too well bred not to give me a stately welcome.

The life in Carlsruhe was very different from what it was at home. The hours were later, the coffee was weaker in the morning, the pottage was weaker, the boiled beef less relieved by other diet, the dresses finer, the evening engagements constant. I did not find these visits pleasant. We might not knit, which would have relieved the tedium a little; but we sat in a circle, talking together, only inter-rupted occasionally by a gentleman, who, breaking out of the knot of men who stood near the door, talking eagerly together, stole across the room on tiptoe, his hat under his arm, and, bringing his feet together in the position we called the first at the dancing-school, made a low bow to the lady he was going to address. The first time I saw these manners I could not help smiling; but Madame Rupprecht saw me, and spoke to me next morning rather severely, telling me that, of course, in my country breeding I could have seen nothing of court manners, or French fashions, but that that was no reason for my laughing at them. Of course I tried never to smile again in company. This visit to Carlsruhe took place in '89, just when everyone was full of the events taking place at Paris; and yet at Carlsruhe French fashions were more talked of than French politics. Madame Rupprecht, especially, thought a great deal of all French people. And this again was quite different to us at home. Fritz could hardly bear the name of a Frenchman; and it had nearly been an obstacle to my visit to Sophie that her mother preferred being called Madame to her proper title of Frau.

One night I was sitting next to Sophie, and longing for the time when we might have supper and go home, so as to be able to speak together, a thing forbidden by Madame Rupprecht's rules of etiquette, which strictly prohibited any but the most necessary conversation passing between members of the same family when in society. I was sitting, I say, scarcely keeping back my inclination to yawn, when two gentlemen came in, one of whom was evidently a stranger to the whole party, from the formal manner in which the host led him up, and presented him to the hostess. I thought I had never seen anyone so handsome or so elegant. His hair was powdered, of course, but one could see from his complexion that it was fair in its natural state. His features were as delicate as a girl's, and set off by two little 'mouches', as we called patches in those days, one at the left corner of his mouth, the other prolonging, as it were, the right eye. His dress was blue and silver. I was so lost in admiration of this beautiful young man, that I was as much surprised as if the angel Gabriel had spoken to me, when the lady of the house brought him forward to present him to me. She called him Monsieur de la Tourelle, and he began to speak to me in French; but though I understood him perfectly, I dared not trust myself to reply to him in that language. Then he tried German, speaking it with a kind of soft lisp that I thought charming. But, before the end of the evening, I became a little tired of the affected softness and effeminacy of his manners, and the exaggerated compliments he paid me, which had the effect of making all the company turn round and look at me. Madame Rupprecht was, however, pleased with the precise thing that displeased me. She liked either Sophie or me to create a sensation; of course she would have preferred that it should have been her daughter, but her daughter's friend was next best. As we went away, I heard Madame Rupprecht and Monsieur de la Tourelle reciprocating civil speeches with might and main, from which I found out that the French gentleman was coming to call on us the next day. I do not know whether I was more glad or frightened, for I had been kept upon stilts of good manners all the evening. But still I was flattered when Madame Rupprecht spoke as if she had invited him, because he had shown pleasure in my society, and even more gratified by Sophie's ungrudging delight at the evident interest I had excited in so fine and agreeable a gentleman. Yet, with all this, they had hard work to keep me from running out of the salon the next day, when we heard his voice inquiring at the gate on the stairs for Madame Rupprecht. They had made me put on my Sunday gown, and they themselves were dressed as for a reception.

When he was gone away, Madame Rupprecht congratulated me on the conquest I had made; for, indeed, he had scarcely spoken to anyone else, beyond what mere civility required, and had almost invited himself to come in the evening to bring some new song, which was all the fashion in Paris, he said. Madame Rupprecht had been out all morning, as she told me, to glean information about Monsieur de la Tourelle. He was a *propriétaire*, had a small château on the Vosges mountains; he owned land there, but had a large income from some sources quite independent of this property. Altogether, he was a good match, as she emphatically observed. She never seemed to think that I could refuse him after this account of his wealth, nor do I believe she would have allowed Sophie a choice, even had he been as old and ugly as he was young and handsome. I do not quite know – so many events have come to pass since then, and blurred the clearness of my recollections – if I loved him or not. He was very much devoted to me; he almost frightened me by the excess of his demonstrations of love. And he was very charming to everybody around me, who all spoke of him as the most fascinating of men, and of me as the most fortunate of girls. And yet I never felt quite at my ease with him. I was always relieved when his visits were over, although I missed his presence when he did not come. He prolonged his visit to the friend with whom he was staying at Carlsruhe, on purpose to woo me. He loaded me with presents, which I was unwilling to take, only Madame Rupprecht seemed to consider me an affected prude if I refused them. Many of these presents consisted of articles of valuable old jewellery, evidently belonging to his family; by accepting these I doubled the ties which were formed around me by circumstances even more than by my own consent. In those days we did not write letters to absent friends as frequently as is done now, and I had been unwilling to name him in the few letters that I wrote home. At length, however, I learned from Madame Rupprecht that she had written to my father to announce the splendid conquest I had made, and to request his presence at my betrothal. I started with astonishment. I had not realised that affairs had gone so far as this. But when she asked me, in a stern, offended manner, what I had meant by my conduct if I did not intend to marry Monsieur de la Tourelle – I had received his visits, his presents, all his various advances without showing any unwillingness or repugnance – (and it was all true; I had shown no repugnance, though I did not wish to be married to him – at least, not so soon) – what could I do but hang my head, and silently consent to the rapid enunciation of the only course which now remained for me if I would not be esteemed a heartless coquette all the rest of my days?

There was some difficulty, which I afterwards learnt that my sister-in-law had obviated, about my betrothal taking place from home. My father, and Fritz especially, were for having me return to the mill, and there be betrothed, and from thence be married. But the Rupprechts and Monsieur de la Tourelle were equally urgent on the other side; and Babette was unwilling to have the trouble of the commotion at the mill; and also, I think, a little disliked the idea of the contrast of my grander marriage with her own.

So my father and Fritz came over to the betrothal. They were to stay at an inn in Carlsruhe for a fortnight, at the end of which time the marriage was to take place. Monsieur de la Tourelle told me he had business at home, which would oblige him to be absent during the interval between the two events; and I was very glad of it, for I did not think that he valued my father and my brother as I could have wished him to do. He was very polite to them; put on all the soft, grand manner, which he had rather dropped with me; and complimented us all round, beginning with my father and Madame Rupprecht, and ending with little Alwina. But he a little scoffed at the old-fashioned church ceremonies which my father insisted on; and I fancy Fritz must have taken some of his compliments as satire, for I saw certain signs of manner by which I knew that my future husband, for all his civil words, had irritated and annoyed my brother. But all the money arrangements were liberal in the extreme, and more than satisfied, almost surprised, my father. Even Fritz lifted up his eyebrows and whistled. I alone did not care about anything. I was bewitched – in a dream – a kind of despair. I had got into a net through my own timidity and weakness, and I did not see how to get out of it. I clung to my own home-people that fortnight as I had never done before. Their voices, their ways were all so pleasant and familiar to me, after the constraint in which I had been living. I might speak and do as I liked without being corrected by Madame Rupprecht, or reproved in a delicate, complimentary way by Monsieur de la Tourelle. One day I said to my father that I did not want to be married, that I would rather go back to the dear old mill; but he seemed to feel this speech of mine as a dereliction of duty as great as if I had committed perjury; as if, after the ceremony of betrothal, no-one had any right over me but my future husband. And yet he asked me some solemn questions; but my answers were not such as to do me any good.

'Dost thou know any fault or crime in this man that should prevent God's blessing from resting on thy marriage with him? Dost thou feel aversion or repugnance to him in any way?'

And to all this what could I say? I could only stammer out that I did not think I loved him enough; and my poor old father saw in this reluctance only the fancy of a silly girl who did not know her own mind, but who had now gone too far to recede.

So we were married, in the Court chapel, a privilege which Madame Rupprecht had used no end of efforts to obtain for us, and which she must have thought was to secure us all possible happiness, both at the time and in recollection afterwards.

We were married; and after two days spent in festivity at Carlsruhe, among all our new fashionable friends there, I bade goodbye for ever to my dear old father. I had begged my husband to take me by way of Heidelberg to his old castle in the Vosges; but I found an amount of determination, under that effeminate appearance and manner, for which I was not prepared, and he refused my first request so decidedly that I dared not urge it. 'Henceforth, Anna,' said he, 'you will move in a different sphere of life; and though it is possible that you may have the power of showing favour to your relations from time to time, yet much or familiar intercourse will be undesirable, and is what I cannot allow.' I felt almost afraid, after this formal speech, of asking my father and Fritz to come and see me; but, when the agony of bidding them farewell overcame all my prudence, I did beg them to pay me a visit ere long. But they shook their heads, and spoke of business at home, of different kinds of life, of my being a Frenchwoman now. Only my father broke out at last with a blessing, and said, 'If my child is unhappy – which God forbid – let her remember that her father's house is ever open to her.' I was on the point of crying out, 'Oh! take me back then now, my father! oh, my father!' when I felt, rather than saw, my husband present near me. He looked on with a slightly contemptuous air; and, taking my hand in his, he led me weeping away, saying that short farewells were always the best when they were inevitable.

It took us two days to reach his château in the Vosges, for the roads were bad and the way difficult to ascertain. Nothing could be more devoted than he was all the time of the journey. It seemed as if he were trying in every way to make up for the separation which every hour made me feel the more complete between my present and my former life. I seemed as if I were only now wakening up to a full sense of what marriage was, and I dare say I was not a cheerful companion on the tedious journey. At length, jealousy of my regret for my father and brother got the better of M. de la Tourelle, and he became so much displeased with me that I thought my heart would break with the sense of desolation. So it was in no cheerful frame of mind that we approached Les Rochers, and I thought that perhaps it was because I was so unhappy that the place looked so dreary. On one side, the château looked like a raw new building, hastily run up for some immediate purpose, without any growth of trees or underwood near it, only the remains of the stone used for building, not yet cleared away from the immediate neighbourhood, although weeds and lichens had been suffered to grow near and over the heaps of rubbish; on the other, were the great rocks from which the place took its name, and rising close against them, as if almost a natural formation, was the old castle, whose building dated many centuries back.

It was not large nor grand, but it was strong and picturesque, and I used to wish that we lived in it rather than in the smart, half-furnished apartment in the new edifice, which had been hastily got ready for my reception. Incongruous as the two parts were, they were joined into a whole by means of intricate passages and unexpected doors, the exact positions of which I never fully understood. M. de la Tourelle led me to a suite of rooms set apart for me, and formally installed me in them, as in a domain of which I was sovereign. He apologised for the hasty preparation which was all he had been able to make for me, but promised, before I asked, or even thought of complaining, that they should be made as luxurious as heart could wish before many weeks had elapsed. But when, in the gloom of an autumnal evening, I caught my own face and figure reflected in all the mirrors, which showed only a mysterious background in the dim light of the many candles which failed to illuminate the great proportions of the half-furnished salon,

I clung to M. de la Tourelle, and begged to be taken to the rooms he had occupied before his marriage. He seemed angry with me, although he affected to laugh, and so decidedly put aside the notion of my having any other rooms but these, that I trembled in silence at the fantastic figures and shapes which my imagination called up as peopling the background of those gloomy mirrors. There was my boudoir, a little less dreary – my bedroom, with its grand and tarnished furniture, which I commonly made into my sitting-room, locking up the various doors which led into the boudoir, the salon, the passages – all but one, through which M. de la Tourelle always entered from his own apartments in the older part of the castle. But this preference of mine for occupying my bedroom annoyed M. de la Tourelle, I am sure, though he did not care to express his displeasure. He would always allure me back into the salon, which I disliked more and more from its complete separation from the rest of the building by the long passage into which all the doors of my apartment opened. This passage was closed by heavy doors and *portières*, through which I could not hear a sound from the other parts of the house, and, of course, the servants could not hear any movement or cry of mine unless expressly summoned. To a girl brought up as I had been in a household where every individual lived all day in the sight of every other member of the family, never wanting either cheerful words or the sense of silent companionship, this grand isolation of mine was very formidable; and the more so, because M. de la Tourelle, as landed proprietor, sportsman, and what not, was generally out of doors the greater part of every day, and sometimes for two or three days at a time. I had no pride to keep me from associating with the domestics; it would have been natural to me in many ways to have sought them out for a word of sympathy in those dreary days when I was left so entirely to myself, had they been like our kindly German servants. But I disliked them, one and all; I could not tell why. Some were civil, but there was a familiarity in their civility which repelled me; others were rude, and treated me more as if I were an intruder than their master's chosen wife; and yet of the two sets I liked these last the best.

The principal male servant belonged to this latter class. I was very much afraid of him, he had such an air of suspicious surliness about him in all he did for me; and yet M. de la Tourelle spoke of him as most valuable and faithful. Indeed, it sometimes struck me that Lefebvre ruled his master in some things; and this I could not make out. For, while M. de la Tourelle behaved towards me as if I were some precious toy or idol, to be cherished, and fostered, and petted, and indulged, I soon found out how little I, or, apparently, anyone else, could bend the terrible will of the man who had on first acquaintance appeared to me too effeminate and languid to exert his will in the slightest particular. I had learnt to know his face better now; and to see that some vehement depth of feeling, the cause of which I could not fathom, made his grey eye glitter with pale light, and his lips contract, and his delicate cheek whiten on certain occasions. But all had been so open and above board at home, that I had no experience to help me to unravel any mysteries among those who lived under the same roof. I understood that I had made what Madame Rupprecht and her set would have called a great marriage, because I lived in a château with many servants, bound ostensibly to obey me as a mistress. I understood that M. de la Tourelle was fond enough of me in his way – proud of my beauty, I dare say (for he often enough spoke about it to me) – but he was also jealous, and suspicious, and uninfluenced by my wishes, unless they tallied with his own. I felt at this time as if I could have been fond of him too, if he would have let me; but I was timid from my childhood, and before long my dread of his displeasure (coming down like thunder into the midst of his love, for such slight causes as a hesitation in reply, a wrong word, or a sigh for my father), conquered my humorous inclination to love one who was so hand-some, so accomplished, so indulgent and devoted. But if I could not please him when indeed I loved him, you may imagine how often I did wrong when I was so much afraid of him as to quietly avoid his company for fear of his outbursts of passion. One thing I remember noticing, that the more M. de la Tourelle was displeased with me, the more Lefebvre seemed to chuckle; and when I was restored to favour, sometimes on as sudden an impulse as that which occasioned my disgrace, Lefebvre would look askance at me with his cold, malicious eyes, and once or twice at such times he spoke most disrespectfully to M. de la Tourelle.

I have almost forgotten to say that, in the early days of my life at Les Rochers, M. de la Tourelle, in contemptuous indulgent pity at my weakness in disliking the dreary grandeur of the salon, wrote up to the milliner in Paris from whom my *corbeille de mariage* had come, to desire her to look out for me a maid of middle age, experienced in the toilette, and with so much refinement that she might on occasion serve as companion to me.

Portion 2

A Norman woman, Amante by name, was sent to Les Rochers by the Paris milliner, to become my maid. She was tall and handsome, though upwards of forty, and somewhat gaunt. But, on first seeing her, I liked her; she was neither rude nor familiar in her manners, and had a pleasant look of straightforwardness about her that I had missed in all the inhabitants of the château, and had foolishly set down in my own mind as a national want. Amante was directed by M. de la Tourelle to sit in my boudoir, and to be always within call. He also gave her many instructions as to her duties in matters which, perhaps, strictly belonged to my department of management. But I was young and inexperienced, and thankful to be spared any responsibility.

I dare say it was true what M. de la Tourelle said – before many weeks had elapsed – that, for a great lady, a lady of a castle, I became sadly too familiar with my Norman waiting-maid. But you know that by birth we were not very far apart in rank: Amante was the daughter of a Norman farmer, I of a German miller; and besides that, my life was so lonely! It almost seemed as if I could not please my husband. He had written for someone capable of being my companion at times, and now he was jealous of my free regard for her – angry because I could sometimes laugh at her original tunes and amusing proverbs, while when with him I was too much frightened to smile.

From time to time families from a distance of some leagues drove through the bad roads in their heavy carriages to pay us a visit, and there was an occasional talk of our going to Paris when public affairs should be a little more settled. These little events and plans were the only variations in my life for the first twelve months, if I except the alternations in M. de la Tourelle's temper, his unreasonable anger, and his passionate fondness.

Perhaps one of the reasons that made me take pleasure and comfort in Amante's society was, that whereas I was afraid of everybody (I do not think I was half as much afraid of things as of persons), Amante feared no-one. She would quietly beard Lefebvre, and he respected her all the more for it; she had a knack of putting questions to M. de la Tourelle, which respectfully informed him that she had detected the weak point, but forebore to press him too closely upon it out of deference to his position as her master. And with all her shrewdness to others, she had quite tender ways with me; all the more so at this time because she knew, what I had not yet ventured to

tell M. de la Tourelle, that by-and-by I might become a mother –
that wonderful object of mysterious interest to single women, who
no longer hope to enjoy such blessedness themselves.

It was once more autumn; late in October. But I was reconciled to
my habitation; the walls of the new part of the building no longer
looked bare and desolate; the débris had been so far cleared away by
M. de la Tourelle's desire as to make me a little flower-garden, in
which I tried to cultivate those plants that I remembered as growing
at home. Amante and I had moved the furniture in the rooms, and
adjusted it to our liking; my husband had ordered many an article
from time to time that he thought would give me pleasure, and I was
becoming tame to my apparent imprisonment in a certain part of the
great building, the whole of which I had never yet explored. It was
October, as I say, once more. The days were lovely, though short in
duration, and M. de la Tourelle had occasion, so he said, to go to that
distant estate the superintendence of which so frequently took him
away from home. He took Lefebvre with him, and possibly some
more of the lacqueys; he often did. And my spirits rose a little at the
thought of his absence; and then the new sensation that he was the
father of my unborn babe came over me, and I tried to invest him
with this fresh character. I tried to believe that it was his passionate
love for me that made him so jealous and tyrannical, imposing, as he
did, restrictions on my very intercourse with my dear father, from
whom I was so entirely separated, as far as personal intercourse was
concerned.

I had, it is true, let myself go into a sorrowful review of all the
troubles which lay hidden beneath the seeming luxury of my life. I
knew that no-one cared for me except my husband and Amante; for it
was clear enough to see that I, as his wife, and also as a parvenue, was
not popular among the few neighbours who surrounded us; and as
for the servants, the women were all hard and impudent-looking,
treating me with a semblance of respect that had more of mock-
ery than reality in it; while the men had a lurking kind of fierceness
about them, sometimes displayed even to M. de la Tourelle, who
on his part, it must be confessed, was often severe even to cruelty
in his management of them. My husband loved me, I said to myself,
but I said it almost in the form of a question. His love was shown
fitfully, and more in ways calculated to please himself than to please
me. I felt that for no wish of mine would he deviate one tittle from
any predetermined course of action. I had learnt the inflexibility
of those thin delicate lips; I knew how anger would turn his fair

complexion to deadly white, and bring the cruel light into his pale blue eyes. The love I bore to anyone seemed to be a reason for his hating them, and so I went on pitying myself one long dreary afternoon during that absence of his of which I have spoken, only sometimes remembering to check myself in my murmurings by thinking of the new unseen link between us, and then crying afresh to think how wicked I was. Oh, how well I remember that long October evening! Amante came in from time to time, talking away to cheer me – talking about dress and Paris, and I hardly know what, but from time to time looking at me keenly with her friendly dark eyes, and with serious interest, too, though all her words were about frivolity. At length she heaped the fire with wood, drew the heavy silken curtains close; for I had been anxious hitherto to keep them open, so that I might see the pale moon mounting the skies, as I used to see her – the same moon – rise from behind the Kaiser Stuhl at Heidelberg; but the sight made me cry, so Amante shut it out. She dictated to me as a nurse does to a child.

'Now, madame must have the little kitten to keep her company,' she said, 'while I go and ask Marthon for a cup of coffee.' I remember that speech, and the way it roused me, for I did not like Amante to think I wanted amusing by a kitten. It might be my petulance, but this speech – such as she might have made to a child – annoyed me, and I said that I had reason for my lowness of spirits – meaning that they were not of so imaginary a nature that I could be diverted from them by the gambols of a kitten. So, though I did not choose to tell her all, I told her a part; and as I spoke, I began to suspect that the good creature knew much of what I withheld, and that the little speech about the kitten was more thoughtfully kind than it had seemed at first. I said that it was so long since I had heard from my father; that he was an old man, and so many things might happen – I might never see him again – and I so seldom heard from him or my brother. It was a more complete and total separation than I had ever anticipated when I married, and something of my home and of my life previous to my marriage I told the good Amante; for I had not been brought up as a great lady, and the sympathy of any human being was precious to me.

Amante listened with interest, and in return told me some of the events and sorrows of her own life. Then, remembering her purpose, she set out in search of the coffee, which ought to have been brought to me an hour before; but, in my husband's absence, my wishes were but seldom attended to, and I never dared to give orders.

Presently she returned, bringing the coffee and a great large cake. 'See!' said she, setting it down. 'Look at my plunder. Madame must eat. Those who eat always laugh. And, besides, I have a little news that will please madame.' Then she told me that, lying on a table in the great kitchen, was a bundle of letters, come by the courier from Strasburg that very afternoon: then, fresh from her conversation with me, she had hastily untied the string that bound them, but had only just traced out one that she thought was from Germany, when a servant-man came in, and, with the start he gave her, she dropped the letters, which he picked up, swearing at her for having untied and disarranged them. She told him that she believed there was a letter there for her mistress; but he only swore the more, saying that if there was it was no business of hers, or of his either, for that he had the strictest orders always to take all letters that arrived during his master's absence into the private sitting-room of the latter – a room into which I had never entered, although it opened out of my husband's dressing-room.

I asked Amante if she had not conquered and brought me this letter. No, indeed, she replied, it was almost as much as her life was worth to live among such a set of servants: it was only a month ago that Jacques had stabbed Valentin for some jesting talk. Had I never missed Valentin – that handsome young lad who carried up the wood into my salon? Poor fellow! he lies dead and cold now, and they said in the village he had put an end to himself, but those of the household knew better. Oh! I need not be afraid; Jacques was gone, no-one knew where; but with such people it was not safe to upbraid or insist. Monsieur would be at home the next day, and it would not be long to wait.

But I felt as if I could not exist till the next day, without the letter. It might be to say that my father was ill, dying – he might cry for his daughter from his death-bed! In short, there was no end to the thoughts and fancies that haunted me. It was of no use for Amante to say that, after all, she might be mistaken – that she did not read writing well – that she had but a glimpse of the address; I let my coffee cool, my food all became distasteful, and I wrung my hands with impatience to get at the letter, and have some news of my dear ones at home. All the time, Amante kept her imperturbable good temper, first reasoning, then scolding. At last she said, as if wearied out, that if I would consent to make a good supper, she would see what could be done as to our going to monsieur's room in search of the letter, after the servants were all gone to bed. We agreed to go together when all was still, and look over the letters; there could be no harm in that; and yet, somehow, we were such cowards we dared not do it openly and in the face of the household.

Presently my supper came up – partridges, bread, fruits, and cream. How well I remember that supper! We put the untouched cake away in a sort of buffet, and poured the cold coffee out of the window, in order that the servants might not take offence at the apparent fanci-fulness of sending down for food I could not eat. I was so anxious for all to be in bed, that I told the footman who served that he need not wait to take away the plates and dishes, but might go to bed. Long after I thought the house was quiet, Amante, in her caution, made me wait. It was past eleven before we set out, with cat-like steps and veiled light, along the passages, to go to my husband's room and steal my own letter, if it was indeed there; a fact about which Amante had become very uncertain in the progress of our discussion.

To make you understand my story, I must now try to explain to you the plan of the château. It had been at one time a fortified place of some strength, perched on the summit of a rock, which projected from the side of the mountain. But additions had been made to the old building (which must have borne a strong resemblance to the castles overhanging the Rhine), and these new buildings were placed so as to command a magnificent view, being on the steepest side of the rock, from which the mountain fell away, as it were, leaving the great plain of France in full survey. The ground-plan was some-thing of the shape of three sides of an oblong; my apartments in the modern edifice occupied the narrow end, and had this grand prospect. The front of the castle was old, and ran parallel to the road far below. In this were contained the offices and public rooms of various descriptions, into which I never penetrated. The back wing (considering the new building, in which my apartments were, as the centre) consisted of many rooms, of a dark and gloomy character, as the mountainside shut out much of the sun, and heavy pine woods came down within a few yards of the windows. Yet on this side – on a projecting plateau of the rock – my husband had formed the flower-garden of which I have spoken; for he was a great cultivator of flowers in his leisure moments.

Now my bedroom was the corner room of the new buildings on the part next to the mountains. Hence I could have let myself down into the flower-garden by my hands on the window-sill on one side, without danger of hurting myself; while the windows at right angles with these looked sheer down a descent of a hundred feet at least. Going still farther along this wing, you came to the old building; in fact, these two fragments of the ancient castle had formerly been attached by some such connecting apartments as my husband had rebuilt. These rooms belonged to M. de la Tourelle. His bedroom opened into mine, his dressing-room lay beyond; and that was pretty nearly all I knew, for the servants, as well as he himself, had a knack of turning me back, under some pretence, if ever they found me walking about alone, as I was inclined to do, when first I came, from a sort of curiosity to see the whole of the place of which I found myself mistress. M. de la Tourelle never encouraged me to go out alone, either in a carriage or for a walk, saying always that the roads were unsafe in those disturbed times; indeed, I have sometimes fancied since that the flower-garden, to which the only access from the castle was through his rooms, was designed in order to give me exercise and employment under his own eye.

But to return to that night. I knew, as I have said, that M. de la Tourelle's private room opened out of his dressing-room, and this out of his bedroom, which again opened into mine, the corner-room. But there were other doors into all these rooms, and these doors led into a long gallery, lighted by windows, looking into the inner court. I do not remember our consulting much about it; we went through my room into my husband's apartment through the dressing-room, but the door of communication into his study was locked, so there was nothing for it but to turn back and go by the gallery to the other door. I recollect noticing one or two things in these rooms, then seen by me for the first time. I remember the sweet perfume that hung in the air, the scent bottles of silver that decked his toilet-table, and the whole apparatus for bathing and dressing, more luxurious even than those which he had provided for me. But the room itself was less splendid in its proportions than mine. In truth, the new buildings ended at the entrance to my husband's dressing-room. There were deep window recesses in walls eight or nine feet thick, and even the partitions between the chambers were three feet deep; but over all these doors or windows there fell thick, heavy draperies, so that I should think no-one could have heard in one room what passed in another. We went back into my room, and out into the gallery. We had to shade our candle, from a fear that possessed us, I don't know why, lest some of the servants in the opposite wing might trace our progress towards the part of the castle unused by anyone except my husband. Somehow, I had always the feeling that all the domestics, except Amante, were spies upon me, and that I was trammelled in a web of observation and unspoken limitation extending over all my actions.

There was a light in the upper room; we paused, and Amante would have again retreated, but I was chafing under the delays. What was the harm of my seeking my father's unopened letter to me in my husband's study? I, generally the coward, now blamed Amante for her unusual timidity. But the truth was, she had far more reason for suspicion as to the proceedings of that terrible household than I had ever known of. I urged her on, I pressed on myself; we came to the door, locked, but with the key in it; we turned it, we entered; the letters lay on the table, their white oblongs catching the light in an instant, and revealing themselves to my eager eyes, hungering after the words of love from my peaceful, distant home. But just as I pressed forward to examine the letters, the candle which Amante held, caught in some draught, went out, and we were in darkness. Amante proposed that we should carry the letters back to my salon, collecting them as well as we could in the dark, and returning all but the expected one for me; but I begged her to return to my room, where I kept tinder and flint, and to strike a fresh light; and I remained alone in the room, of which I could only just distinguish the size, and the principal articles of furniture: a large table, with a deep, overhanging cloth, in the middle, escritoires and other heavy articles against the walls; all this I could see as I stood there, my hand on the table close by the letters, my face towards the window, which, both from the darkness of the wood growing high up the mountain-side and the faint light of the declining moon, seemed only like an oblong of paler purpler black than the shadowy room. How much I remembered from my one instantaneous glance before the candle went out, how much I saw as my eyes became accustomed to the darkness, I do not know, but even now, in my dreams, comes up that room of horror, distinct in its profound shadow. Amante could hardly have been gone a minute before I felt an additional gloom before the window, and heard soft movements outside – soft, but resolute, and continued until the end was accomplished, and the window raised.

In mortal terror of people forcing an entrance at such an hour, and in such a manner as to leave no doubt of their purpose, I would have turned to fly when first I heard the noise, only that I feared by any quick motion to catch their attention, as I also ran the danger of doing by opening the door, which was all but closed and to whose handlings I was unaccustomed. Again, quick as lightning, I bethought me of the hiding-place between the locked door to my husband's dressing-room and the *portière* which covered it; but I gave that up, I felt as if

I could not reach it without screaming or fainting. So I sank down softly, and crept under the table, hidden as I hoped, by the great, deep table-cover, with its heavy fringe. I had not recovered my swooning senses fully, and was trying to reassure myself as to my being in a place of comparative safety, for, above all things, I dreaded the betrayal of fainting, and struggled hard for such courage as I might attain by deadening myself to the danger I was in by inflicting intense pain on myself. You have often asked me the reason of that mark on my hand; it was there, in my agony, I bit out a piece of flesh with my relentless teeth, thankful for the pain, which helped to numb my terror. I say, I was but just concealed when I heard the window lifted, and one after another stepped over the sill, and stood by me so close that I could have touched their feet. Then they laughed and whispered; my brain swam so that I could not tell the meaning of their words, but I heard my husband's laughter among the rest – low, hissing, scornful – as he kicked something heavy that they had dragged in over the floor, and which lay near me; so near, that my husband's kick, in touching it, touched me too. I don't know why – I can't tell how – but some feeling, and not curiosity, prompted me to put out my hand, ever so softly, ever so little, and feel in the darkness for what lay spurned beside me. I stole my groping palm upon the clenched and chilly hand of a corpse!

Strange to say, this roused me to instant vividness of thought. Till this moment I had almost forgotten Amante; now I planned with feverish rapidity how I could give her a warning not to return; or rather, I should say, I tried to plan, for all my projects were utterly futile, as I might have seen from the first. I could only hope she would hear the voices of those who were now busy in trying to kindle a light, swearing awful oaths at the mislaid articles which would have enabled them to strike fire. I heard her step outside coming nearer and nearer; I saw from my hiding-place the line of light beneath the door more and more distinctly; close to it her footstep paused; the men inside – at the time I thought they had been only two, but I found out afterwards there were three – paused in their endeavours, and were quite still, as breathless as myself, I suppose. Then she slowly pushed the door open with gentle motion, to save her flickering candle from being again extinguished. For a moment all was still. Then I heard my husband say, as he advanced towards her (he wore riding-boots, the shape of which I knew well, as I could see them in the light): 'Amante, may I ask what brings you here into my private room?'

He stood between her and the dead body of a man, from which ghastly heap I shrank away as it almost touched me, so close were we all together. I could not tell whether she saw it or not; I could give her no warning, nor make any dumb utterance of signs to bid her what to say – if, indeed, I knew myself what would be best for her to say.

Her voice was quite changed when she spoke; quite hoarse, and very low; yet it was steady enough as she said, what was the truth, that she had come to look for a letter which she believed had arrived for me from Germany. Good, brave Amante! Not a word about me. M. de la Tourelle answered with a grim blasphemy and a fearful threat. He would have no-one prying into his premises; madame should have her letters, if there were any, when he chose to give them to her, if, indeed, he thought it well to give them to her at all. As for Amante, this was her first warning, but it was also her last; and, taking the candle out of her hand, he turned her out of the room, his companions discreetly making a screen, so as to throw the corpse into deep shadow. I heard the key turn in the door after her – if I had ever had any thought of escape it was gone now. I only hoped that whatever was to befall me might soon be over, for the tension of nerve was growing more than I could bear. The instant she could be supposed to be out of hearing, two voices began speaking in the most angry terms to my husband, upbraiding him for not having detained her, gagged her – nay, one was for killing her, saying he had seen her eye fall on the face of the dead man, whom he now kicked in his passion. Though the form of their speech was as if they were speaking to equals, yet in their tone there was something of fear. I am sure my husband was their superior, or captain, or somewhat. He replied to them almost as if he were scoffing at them, saying it was such an expenditure of labour having to do with fools; that, ten to one, the woman was only telling the simple truth, and that she was frightened enough by discovering her master in his room to be thankful to escape and return to her mistress, to whom he could easily explain on the morrow how he happened to return in the dead of night. But his companions fell to cursing me, and saying that since M. de la Tourelle had been married he was fit for nothing but to dress himself fine and scent himself with perfume; that, as for me, they could have got him twenty girls prettier, and with far more spirit in them. He quietly answered that I suited him, and that was enough. All this time they were doing something – I could not see what – to the corpse; sometimes they were too busy rifling the dead body, I believe, to talk; again they let it fall with a heavy, resistless thud, and took to quarrelling. They taunted my husband with angry vehemence, enraged at his scoffing and scornful replies, his mocking laughter. Yes, holding up his poor dead victim, the better to strip him of whatever he wore that was valuable, I heard my husband laugh just as he had done when exchanging repartees in the little salon of the Rupprechts at Carlsruhe. I hated and dreaded him from that moment. At length, as if to make an end of the subject, he said, with cool determination in his voice: 'Now, my good friends, what is the use of all this talking, when you know in your hearts that, if I suspected my wife of knowing more than I chose of my affairs, she would not outlive the day? Remember Victorine. Because she merely joked about my affairs in an imprudent manner, and rejected my advice to keep a prudent tongue – to see what she liked, but ask nothing and say nothing – she has gone a long journey – longer than to Paris.'

'But this one is different to her; we knew all that Madame Victorine knew, she was such a chatterbox; but this one may find out a vast deal, and never breathe a word about it, she is so sly. Some fine day we may have the country raised, and the gendarmes down upon us from Strasburg, and all owing to your pretty doll, with her cunning ways of coming over you.'

I think this roused M. de la Tourelle a little from his contemptuous indifference, for he ground an oath through his teeth, and said, 'Feel! this dagger is sharp, Henri. If my wife breathes a word, and I am such a fool as not to have stopped her mouth effectually before she can bring down gendarmes upon us, just let that good steel find its way to my heart. Let her guess but one tittle, let her have but one slight suspicion that I am not a '*grand propriétaire*', much less imagine that I am a chief of *Chauffeurs*, and she follows Victorine on the long journey beyond Paris that very day.'

'She'll outwit you yet; or I never judged women well. Those still silent ones are the devil. She'll be off during some of your absences, having picked out some secret that will break us all on the wheel.'

'Bah!' said his voice; and then in a minute he added, 'Let her go if she will. But, where she goes, I will follow; so don't cry before you're hurt.'

By this time, they had nearly stripped the body; and the conversation turned on what they should do with it. I learnt that the dead man was the Sieur de Poissy, a neighbouring gentleman, whom I had often heard of as hunting with my husband. I had never seen him, but they spoke as if he had come upon them while they were robbing

some Cologne merchant, torturing him after the cruel practice of
the *Chauffeurs*, by roasting the feet of their victims in order to
compel them to reveal any hidden circumstances connected with
their wealth, of which the *Chauffeurs* afterwards made use; and this
Sieur de Poissy coming down upon them, and recognising M. de
la Tourelle, they had killed him, and brought him thither after
nightfall. I heard him whom I called my husband, laugh his little
light laugh as he spoke of the way in which the dead body had been
strapped before one of the riders, in such a way that it appeared to
any passer-by as if, in truth, the murderer were tenderly supporting
some sick person. He repeated some mocking reply of double meaning, which he himself had given to someone who made inquiry. He
enjoyed the play upon words, softly applauding his own wit. And all
the time the poor helpless outstretched arms of the dead lay close to
his dainty boot! Then another stooped (my heart stopped beating),
and picked up a letter lying on the ground – a letter that had dropped
out of M. de Poissy's pocket – a letter from his wife, full of tender
words of endearment and pretty babblings of love. This was read
aloud, with coarse ribald comments on every sentence, each trying
to outdo the previous speaker. When they came to some pretty
words about a sweet Maurice, their little child away with its mother
on some visit, they laughed at M. de la Tourelle, and told him that
he would be hearing such woman's drivelling some day. Up to
that moment, I think, I had only feared him, but his unnatural,
half-ferocious reply made me hate even more than I dreaded him.
But now they grew weary of their savage merriment; the jewels
and watch had been apprised, the money and papers examined; and
apparently there was some necessity for the body being interred
quietly and before daybreak. They had not dared to leave him where
he was slain for fear lest people should come and recognise him, and
raise the hue and cry upon them. For they all along spoke as if it was
their constant endeavour to keep the immediate neighbourhood of
Les Rochers in the most orderly and tranquil condition, so as never
to give cause for visits from the gendarmes. They disputed a little as
to whether they should make their way into the castle larder through
the gallery, and satisfy their hunger before the hasty interment, or
afterwards. I listened with eager feverish interest as soon as this
meaning of their speeches reached my hot and troubled brain, for at
the time the words they uttered seemed only to stamp themselves
with terrible force on my memory, so that I could hardly keep from
repeating them aloud like a dull, miserable, unconscious echo; but

my brain was numb to the sense of what they said, unless I myself were named, and then, I suppose, some instinct of self-preservation stirred within me, and quickened my sense. And how I strained my ears, and nerved my hands and limbs, beginning to twitch with convulsive movements, which I feared might betray me! I gathered every word they spoke, not knowing which proposal to wish for, but feeling that whatever was finally decided upon, my only chance of escape was drawing near. I once feared lest my husband should go to his bedroom before I had had that one chance, in which case he would most likely have perceived my absence. He said that his hands were soiled (I shuddered, for it might be with life-blood), and he would go and cleanse them; but some bitter jest turned his purpose, and he left the room with the other two – left it by the gallery door. Left me alone in the dark with the stiffening corpse!

Now, now was my time, if ever; and yet I could not move. It was not my cramped and stiffened joints that crippled me, it was the sensation of that dead man's close presence. I almost fancied – I almost fancy still – I heard the arm nearest to me move; lift itself up, as if once more imploring, and fall in dead despair. At that fancy – if fancy it were – I screamed aloud in mad terror, and the sound of my own strange voice broke the spell. I drew myself to the side of the table farthest from the corpse, with as much slow caution as if I really could have feared the clutch of that poor dead arm, powerless for evermore. I softly raised myself up, and stood sick and trembling, holding by the table, too dizzy to know what to do next. I nearly fainted, when a low voice spoke – when Amante, from the outside of the door, whispered, 'Madame!' The faithful creature had been on the watch, had heard my scream, and having seen the three ruffians troop along the gallery down the stairs, and across the court to the offices in the other wing of the castle, she had stolen to the door of the room in which I was. The sound of her voice gave me strength; I walked straight towards it, as one benighted on a dreary moor, suddenly perceiving the small steady light which tells of human dwellings, takes heart, and steers straight onward. Where I was, where that voice was, I knew not; but go to it I must, or die. The door once opened – I know not by which of us – I fell upon her neck, grasping her tight, till my hands ached with the tension of their hold. Yet she never uttered a word. Only she took me up in her vigorous arms, and bore me to my room, and laid me on my bed. I do not know more; as soon as I was placed there I lost sense; I came to myself with a horrible dread lest my husband was by me, with a belief that he was in the room, in hiding, waiting to hear my first words, watching for the least sign of the terrible knowledge I possessed to murder me. I dared not breathe quicker, I measured and timed each heavy inspiration; I did not speak, nor move, nor even open my eyes, for long after I was in my full, my miserable senses. I heard someone treading softly about the room, as if with a purpose, not as if for curiosity, or merely to beguile the time; someone passed in and out of the salon; and I still lay quiet, feeling as if death were inevitable, but wishing that the agony of death were past. Again faintness stole over me; but just as I was sinking into the horrible feeling of nothingness, I heard Amante's voice close to me, saying: 'Drink this, madame, and let us be gone. All is ready.'

I let her put her arm under my head and raise me, and pour something down my throat. All the time she kept talking in a quiet, measured voice, unlike her own, so dry and authoritative; she told me that a suit of her clothes lay ready for me, that she herself was as much disguised as the circumstances permitted her to be, that what provisions I had left from my supper were stowed away in her pockets, and so she went on, dwelling on little details of the most commonplace description, but never alluding for an instant to the fearful cause why flight was necessary. I made no inquiry as to how she knew, or what she knew. I never asked her either then or afterwards, I could not bear it – we kept our dreadful secret close. But I suppose she must have been in the dressing-room adjoining, and heard all.

In fact, I dared not speak even to her, as if there were anything beyond the most common event in life in our preparing thus to leave the house of blood by stealth in the dead of night. She gave me directions – short condensed directions, without reasons – just as you do to a child; and like a child I obeyed her. She went often to the door and listened; and often, too, she went to the window, and looked anxiously out. For me, I saw nothing but her, and I dared not let my eyes wander from her for a minute; and I heard nothing in the deep midnight silence but her soft movements, and the heavy beating of my own heart. At last she took my hand, and led me in the dark, through the salon, once more into the terrible gallery, where across the black darkness the windows admitted pale sheeted ghosts of light upon the floor. Clinging to her I went; unquestioning – for she was human sympathy to me after the isolation of my unspeakable terror. On we went, turning to the left instead of to the right, past my suite of sitting-rooms where the gilding was red with blood, into that unknown wing of the castle that fronted the main road lying parallel far below. She guided me along the basement passages to which we had now descended, until we came to a little open door, through which the air blew chill and cold, bringing for the first time a sensation of life to me. The door led into a kind of cellar, through which we groped our way to an opening like a window, but which, instead of being glazed, was only fenced with iron bars, two of which were loose, as Amante evidently knew, for she took them out with the ease of one who had performed the action often before, and then helped me to follow her out into the free, open air.

We stole round the end of the building, and on turning the corner – she first – I felt her hold on me tighten for an instant, and the next step I, too, heard distant voices, and the blows of a spade upon the heavy soil, for the night was very warm and still.

We had not spoken a word; we did not speak now. Touch was safer and as expressive. She turned down towards the high road; I followed. I did not know the path; we stumbled again and again, and I was much bruised; so doubtless was she; but bodily pain did me good. At last, we were on the plainer path of the high road.

I had such faith in her that I did not venture to speak, even when she paused, as wondering to which hand she should turn. But now, for the first time, she spoke: 'Which way did you come when he brought you here first?'

I pointed, I could not speak.

We turned in the opposite direction; still going along the high road. In about an hour, we struck up to the mountainside, scrambling far up before we even dared to rest; far up and away again before day had fully dawned. Then we looked about for some place of rest and concealment: and now we dared to speak in whispers. Amante told me that she had locked the door of communication between his bedroom and mine, and, as in a dream, I was aware that she had also locked and brought away the key of the door between the latter and the salon.

'He will have been too busy this night to think much about you – he will suppose you are asleep – I shall be the first to be missed; but they will only just now be discovering our loss.'

I remember those last words of hers made me pray to go on; I felt as if we were losing precious time in thinking either of rest or concealment; but she hardly replied to me, so busy was she in seeking out some hiding-place. At length, giving it up in despair, we proceeded onwards a little way; the mountainside sloped downwards rapidly, and in the full morning light we saw ourselves in a narrow valley, made by a stream which forced its way along it. About a mile lower down there rose the pale blue smoke of a village, a mill-wheel was lashing up the water close at hand, though out of sight. Keeping under the cover of every sheltering tree or bush, we worked our way down past the mill, down to a one-arched bridge, which doubtless formed part of the road between the village and the mill.

'This will do,' said she; and we crept under the space, and climbing a little way up the rough stonework, we seated ourselves on a projecting ledge, and crouched in the deep damp shadow. Amante sat a little above me, and made me lay my head on her lap. Then she fed me, and took some food herself; and opening out her great dark cloak, she covered up every light-coloured speck about us; and thus we sat, shivering and shuddering, yet feeling a kind of rest through it all, simply from the fact that motion was no longer imperative, and that during the daylight our only chance of safety was to be still. But the damp shadow in which we were sitting was blighting, from the circumstance of the sunlight never penetrating there; and I dreaded lest, before night and the time for exertion again came on, I should feel illness creeping all over me. To add to our discomfort, it had rained the whole day long, and the stream, fed by a thousand little mountain brooklets, began to swell into a torrent, rushing over the stones with a perpetual and dizzying noise.

Every now and then I was wakened from the painful doze into which I continually fell, by a sound of horses' feet over our head: sometimes lumbering heavily as if dragging a burden, sometimes rattling and galloping; and with the sharper cry of men's voices coming cutting through the roar of the waters. At length, day fell. We had to drop into the stream, which came above our knees as we waded to the bank. There we stood, stiff and shivering. Even Amante's courage seemed to fail.

'We must pass this night in shelter, somehow,' said she. For indeed the rain was coming down pitilessly. I said nothing. I thought that surely the end must be death in some shape; and I only hoped that to death might not be added the terror of the cruelty of men. In a minute or so she had resolved on her course of action. We went up the stream to the mill. The familiar sounds, the scent of the wheat, the flour whitening the walls – all reminded me of home, and it seemed to me as if I must struggle out of this nightmare and waken, and find myself once more a happy girl by the Neckar-side. They were long in unbarring the door at which Amante had knocked: at length, an old feeble voice inquired who was there, and what was sought? Amante answered shelter from the storm for two women; but the old woman replied, with suspicious hesitation, that she was sure it was a man who was asking for shelter, and that she could not let us in. But at length she satisfied herself, and unbarred the heavy door, and admitted us. She was not an unkindly woman; but her thoughts all travelled in one circle, and that was, that her master, the miller, had told her on no account to let any man into the place during his absence, and that she did not know if he would not think two women as bad; and yet that as we were not men, no-one could say she had disobeyed him, for it was a shame to let a dog be out such a night as this. Amante, with ready wit, told her to let no-one know that we had taken shelter there that night, and that then her master could not blame her; and while she was thus enjoining secrecy as the wisest course, with a view to far other people than the miller, she was hastily helping me to take off my wet clothes, and spreading them, as well as the brown mantle that had covered us both, before the great stove which warmed the room with the effectual heat that the old woman's failing vitality required. All this time the poor creature was discussing with herself as to whether she had disobeyed orders, in a kind of garrulous way that made me fear much for her capability of retaining anything secret if she was questioned. By-and-by, she wandered away to an unnecessary revelation of her master's whereabouts: gone to help in the search for his landlord, the Sieur de Poissy, who lived at the château just above, and who had not returned from his chase the day before; so the intendant imagined he might have met with some accident, and had summoned the neighbours to beat the forest and the hillside. She told us much besides, giving us to understand that she would fain meet with a place as housekeeper where there were more servants and less to do, as her life here was very lonely and dull, especially since her master's son had gone away – gone to the wars. She then took her supper, which was evidently apportioned out to her with a sparing hand, as, even if the idea had come into her head, she had not enough to offer us any. Fortunately, warmth was all that we required, and that, thanks to Amante's cares, was returning to our chilled bodies. After supper, the old woman grew drowsy; but she seemed uncomfortable at the idea of going to sleep and leaving us still in the house. Indeed, she gave us pretty broad hints as to the propriety of our going once more out into the bleak and stormy night; but we begged to be allowed to stay under shelter of some kind; and, at last, a bright idea came over her, and she bade us mount by a ladder to a kind of loft, which went half over the lofty mill-kitchen in which we were sitting. We obeyed her – what else could we do? – and found ourselves in a spacious floor, without any safe-guard or wall, boarding, or railing, to keep us from falling over into the kitchen in case we went too near the edge. It was, in fact, the store-room or garret for the household. There was bedding piled up, boxes and chests, mill sacks, the winter store of apples and nuts, bundles of old clothes, broken furniture, and many other things. No sooner were we up there, than the old woman dragged the ladder, by which we had ascended, away with a chuckle, as if she was now secure that we could do no mischief, and sat herself down again once more, to doze and await her master's return. We pulled out some bedding, and gladly laid ourselves down in our dried clothes and in some warmth, hoping to have the sleep we so much needed to refresh us and prepare us for the next day. But I could not sleep, and I was aware, from her breathing, that Amante was equally wakeful. We could both see through the crevices between the boards that formed the flooring into the kitchen below, very partially lighted by the common lamp that hung against the wall near the stove on the opposite side to that on which we were.

Portion 3

Far on in the night there were voices outside which reached us in our hiding-place; an angry knocking at the door, and we saw through the chinks the old woman rouse herself up to go and open it for her master, who came in, evidently half drunk. To my sick horror, he was followed by Lefebvre, apparently as sober and wily as ever. They were talking together as they came in, disputing about something; but the miller stopped the conversation to swear at the old woman for having fallen asleep, and, with tipsy anger, and even with blows, drove the poor old creature out of the kitchen to bed. Then he and Lefebvre went on talking – about the Sieur de Poissy's disappearance. It seemed that Lefebvre had been out all day, along with other of my husband's men, ostensibly assisting in the search; in all probability trying to blind the Sieur de Poissy's followers by putting them on a wrong scent, and also, I fancied, from one or two of Lefebvre's sly questions, combining the hidden purpose of discovering us.

Although the miller was tenant and vassal to the Sieur de Poissy, he seemed to me to be much more in league with the people of M. de la Tourelle. He was evidently aware, in part, of the life which Lefebvre and the others led; although, again, I do not suppose he knew or imagined one-half of their crimes; and also, I think, he was seriously interested in discovering the fate of his master, little suspecting Lefebvre of murder or violence. He kept talking himself, and letting out all sorts of thoughts and opinions; watched by the keen eyes of Lefebvre gleaming out below his shaggy eyebrows. It was evidently not the cue of the latter to let out that his master's wife had escaped from that vile and terrible den; but though he never breathed a word relating to us, not the less was I certain he was thirsting for our blood, and lying in wait for us at every turn of events. Presently he got up and took his leave; and the miller bolted him out, and stumbled off to bed. Then we fell asleep, and slept sound and long.

The next morning, when I awoke, I saw Amante, half raised, resting on one hand, and eagerly gazing, with straining eyes, into the kitchen below. I looked too, and both heard and saw the miller and two of his men eagerly and loudly talking about the old woman, who had not appeared as usual to make the fire in the stove, and prepare her master's breakfast, and who now, late on in the morning, had been found dead in her bed; whether from the effect of her master's blows the night before, or from natural causes, who can tell? The miller's conscience upbraided him a little, I should say, for he was eagerly declaring his value for his housekeeper, and repeating how often she had spoken of the happy life she led with him. The men might have their doubts, but they did not wish to offend the miller, and all agreed that the necessary steps should be taken for a speedy funeral. And so they went out, leaving us in our loft, but so much alone, that, for the first time almost, we ventured to speak freely, though still in hushed voice, pausing to listen continually. Amante took a more cheerful view of the whole occurrence than I did. She said that, had the old woman lived, we should have had to depart that morning, and that this quiet departure would have been the best thing we could have had to hope for, as, in all probability, the housekeeper would have told her master of us and of our resting-place, and this fact would, sooner or later, have been brought to the knowledge of those from whom we most desired to keep it concealed; but that now we had time to rest, and a shelter to rest in, during the first hot pursuit, which we knew to a fatal certainty was being carried on. The remnants of our food, and the stored-up fruit, would supply us with provision; the only thing to be feared was, that something might be required from the loft, and the miller or someone else mount up in search of it. But even then, with a little arrangement of boxes and chests, one part might be so kept in shadow that we might yet escape observation. All this comforted me a little; but, I asked, how were we ever to escape? The ladder was taken away, which was our only means of descent. But Amante replied that she could make a sufficient ladder of the rope lying coiled among other things, to drop us down the ten feet or so – with the advantage of its being portable, so that we might carry it away, and thus avoid all betrayal of the fact that anyone had ever been hidden in the loft.

During the two days that intervened before we did escape, Amante made good use of her time. She looked into every box and chest during the man's absence at his mill; and finding in one box an old suit of man's clothes, which had probably belonged to the miller's absent son, she put them on to see if they would fit her; and, when she found that they did, she cut her own hair to the shortness of a man's, made me clip her black eyebrows as close as though they had been shaved, and by cutting up old corks into pieces such as would go into her cheeks, she altered both the shape of her face and her voice to a degree which I should not have believed possible.

All this time I lay like one stunned; my body resting, and renewing its strength, but I myself in an almost idiotic state – else surely I could not have taken the stupid interest which I remember I did in all Amante's energetic preparations for disguise. I absolutely recollect once the feeling of a smile coming over my stiff face as some new exercise of her cleverness proved a success.

But towards the second day, she required me, too, to exert myself; and then all my heavy despair returned. I let her dye my fair hair and complexion with the decaying shells of the stored-up walnuts, I let her blacken my teeth, and even voluntarily broke a front tooth the better to effect my disguise. But through it all I had no hope of evading my terrible husband. The third night the funeral was over, the drinking ended, the guests gone; the miller put to bed by his men, being too drunk to help himself. They stopped a little while in the kitchen, talking and laughing about the new housekeeper likely to come; and they, too, went off, shutting, but not locking the door. Everything favoured us. Amante had tried her ladder on one of the two previous nights, and could, by a dexterous throw from beneath, unfasten it from the hook to which it was fixed, when it had served its office; she made up a bundle of worthless old clothes in order that we might the better preserve our characters of a travelling pedlar and his wife; she stuffed a hump on her back, she thickened my figure, she left her own clothes deep down beneath a heap of others in the chest from which she had taken the man's dress which she wore; and with a few francs in her pocket – the sole money we had either of us had about us when we escaped – we let ourselves down the ladder, unhooked it, and passed into the cold darkness of night again.

We had discussed the route which it would be well for us to take while we lay *perdues* in our loft. Amante had told me then that her reason for inquiring, when we first left Les Rochers, by which way I had first been brought to it, was to avoid the pursuit which she was sure would first be made in the direction of Germany; but that now she thought we might return to that district of country where my German fashion of speaking French would excite least observation. I thought that Amante herself had something peculiar in her accent, which I had heard M. de la Tourelle sneer at as Norman *patois*; but I said not a word beyond agreeing to her proposal that we should bend our steps towards Germany. Once there, we should, I thought, be safe. Alas! I forgot the unruly time that was overspreading all Europe, overturning all law, and all the protection which law gives.

How we wandered – not daring to ask our way – how we lived, how we struggled through many a danger and still more terrors of danger, I shall not tell you now. I will only relate two of our adventures before we reached Frankfort. The first, although fatal to an innocent lady, was yet, I believe, the cause of my safety; the second I shall tell you, that you may understand why I did not return to my former home, as I had hoped to do when we lay in the miller's loft, and I first became capable of groping after an idea of what my future life might be. I cannot tell you how much in these doubtings and wanderings I became attached to Amante. I have sometimes feared since, lest I cared for her only because she was so necessary to my own safety; but, no! it was not so; or not so only, or principally. She said once that she was flying for her own life as well as for mine; but we dared not speak much on our danger, or on the horrors that had gone before. We planned a little what was to be our future course; but even for that we did not look forward long; how could we, when every day we scarcely knew if we should see the sun go down? For Amante knew or conjectured far more than I did of the atrocity of the gang to which M. de la Tourelle belonged; and every now and then, just as we seemed to be sinking into the calm of security, we fell upon traces of a pursuit after us in all directions. Once I remember – we must have been nearly three weeks wearily walking through unfrequented ways, day after day, not daring to make inquiry as to our whereabouts, nor yet to seem purposeless in our wanderings –

we came to a kind of lonely roadside farrier's and blacksmith's. I was so tired, that Amante declared that, come what might, we would stay there all night; and accordingly she entered the house, and boldly announced herself as a travelling tailor, ready to do any odd jobs of work that might be required, for a night's lodging and food for herself and wife. She had adopted this plan once or twice before, and with good success; for her father had been a tailor in Rouen, and as a girl she had often helped him with his work, and knew the tailors' slang and habits, down to the particular whistle and cry which in France tells so much to those of a trade. At this blacksmith's, as at most other solitary houses far away from a town, there was not only a store of men's clothes laid by as wanting mending when the housewife could afford time, but there was a natural craving after news from a distance, such news as a wandering tailor is bound to furnish. The early November afternoon was closing into evening, as we sat down, she cross-legged on the great table in the blacksmith's kitchen, drawn close to the window, I close behind her, sewing at another part of the same garment, and from time to time well scolded by my seeming husband. All at once she turned round to speak to me. It was only one word, 'Courage!' I had seen nothing; I sat out of the light; but I turned sick for an instant, and then I braced myself up into a strange strength of endurance to go through I knew not what.

The blacksmith's forge was in a shed beside the house, and fronting the road. I heard the hammers stop plying their continual rhythmical beat. She had seen why they ceased. A rider had come up to the forge and dismounted, leading his horse in to be re-shod. The broad red light of the forge-fire had revealed the face of the rider to Amante, and she apprehended the consequence that really ensued.

The rider, after some words with the blacksmith, was ushered in by him into the house-place where we sat.

'Here, good wife, a cup of wine and some galette for this gentleman.'

'Anything, anything, madame, that I can eat and drink in my hand while my horse is being shod. I am in haste, and must get on to Forbach tonight.'

The blacksmith's wife lighted her lamp; Amante had asked her for it five minutes before. How thankful we were that she had not more speedily complied with our request! As it was, we sat in dusk shadow, pretending to stitch away, but scarcely able to see. The lamp was placed on the stove, near which my husband, for it was he, stood and armed himself. By-and-by he turned round, and looked all over the room, taking us in with about the same degree of interest as the inanimate furniture. Amante, cross-legged, fronting him, stooped over her work, whistling softly all the while. He turned again to the stove, impatiently rubbing his hands. He had finished his wine and galette, and wanted to be off.

'I am in haste, my good woman. Ask thy husband to get on more quickly. I will pay him double if he makes haste.'

The woman went out to do his bidding; and he once more turned round to face us. Amante went on to the second part of the tune. He took it up, whistled a second for an instant or so, and then the blacksmith's wife re-entering, he moved towards her, as if to receive her answer the more speedily.

'One moment, monsieur – only one moment. There was a nail out of the off-foreshoe which my husband is replacing; it would delay monsieur again if that shoe also came off.'

'Madame is right,' said he, 'but my haste is urgent. If madame knew my reasons, she would pardon my impatience. Once a happy husband, now a deserted and betrayed man, I pursue a wife on whom I lavished all my love, but who has abused my confidence, and fled from my house, doubtless to some paramour, carrying off with her all the jewels and money on which she could lay her hands. It is possible madame may have heard or seen something of her; she was accompanied in her flight by a base, profligate woman from Paris, whom I, unhappy man, had myself engaged for my wife's waiting-maid, little dreaming what corruption I was bringing into my house!'

'Is it possible?' said the good woman, throwing up her hands.

Amante went on whistling a little lower, out of respect to the conversation.

'However, I am tracing the wicked fugitives; I am on their track' (and the handsome, effeminate face looked as ferocious as any demon's). 'They will not escape me; but every minute is a minute of misery to me, till I meet my wife. Madame has sympathy, has she not?'

He drew his face into a hard, unnatural smile, and then both went out to the forge, as if once more to hasten the blacksmith over his work.

Amante stopped her whistling for one instant.

'Go on as you are, without change of an eyelid even; in a few minutes he will be gone, and it will be over!'

It was a necessary caution, for I was on the point of giving way, and throwing myself weakly upon her neck. We went on; she whistling and stitching, I making semblance to sew. And it was well we did so; for almost directly he came back for his whip, which he had laid down and forgotten; and again I felt one of those sharp, quick-scanning glances, sent all round the room, and taking in all.

Then we heard him ride away; and then, it had been long too dark to see well, I dropped my work, and gave way to my trembling and shuddering. The blacksmith's wife returned. She was a good creature. Amante told her I was cold and weary, and she insisted on my stopping my work, and going to sit near the stove; hastening, at the same time, her preparations for supper, which, in honour of us, and of monsieur's liberal payment, was to be a little less frugal than ordinary. It was well for me that she made me taste a little of the cider-soup she was preparing, or I could not have held up, in spite of Amante's warning look, and the remembrance of her frequent exhortations to act resolutely up to the characters we had assumed, whatever befell. To cover my agitation, Amante stopped her whistling, and began to talk; and, by the time the blacksmith came in, she and the good woman of the house were in full flow. He began at once upon the handsome gentleman, who had paid him so well; all his sympathy was with him, and both he and his wife only wished he might overtake his wicked wife, and punish her as she deserved. And then the conversation took a turn not uncommon to those whose lives are quiet and monotonous; everyone seemed to vie with each other in telling about some horror; and the savage and mysterious band of robbers called the *Chauffeurs*, who infested all the roads leading to the Rhine, with Schinderhannes at their head, furnished many a tale which made the very marrow of my bones run cold, and quenched even Amante's power of talking. Her eyes grew large and wild, her cheeks blanched, and for once she sought by her looks help from me. The new call upon me roused me. I rose and said, with their permission my husband and I would seek our bed, for that we had travelled far and were early risers. I added that we would get up betimes, and finish our piece of work. The blacksmith said we should be early birds if we rose before him; and the good wife seconded my proposal with kindly bustle. One other such story as those they had been relating, and I do believe Amante would have fainted.

As it was, a night's rest set her up; we arose and finished our work betimes, and shared the plentiful breakfast of the family. Then we had to set forth again; only knowing that to Forbach we must not go, yet believing, as was indeed the case, that Forbach lay between us and that Germany to which we were directing our course. Two days more we wandered on, making a round, I suspect, and returning upon the road to Forbach, a league or two nearer to that town than the blacksmith's house. But as we never made inquiries I hardly knew where we were, when we came one night to a small town, with a good large rambling inn in the very centre of the principal street. We had begun to feel as if there were more safety in towns than in the loneliness of the country. As we had parted with a ring of mine not many days before to a travelling jeweller, who was too glad to purchase it far below its real value to make many inquiries as to how it came into the possession of a poor working tailor, such as Amante seemed to be, we resolved to stay at this inn all night, and gather such particulars and information as we could by which to direct our onward course.

We took our supper in the darkest corner of the *salle-à-manger*, having previously bargained for a small bedroom across the court, and over the stables. We needed food sorely; but we hurried on our meal from dread of anyone entering that public room who might recognise us. Just in the middle of our meal, the public diligence drove lumbering up under the *porte-cochère*, and disgorged its passengers. Most of them turned into the room where we sat, cowering and fearful, for the door was opposite to the porter's lodge, and both opened on to the wide-covered entrance from the street. Among the passengers came in a young, fair-haired lady, attended by an elderly French maid. The poor young creature tossed her head, and shrank away from the common room, full of evil smells and promiscuous company, and demanded, in German French, to be taken to some private apartment. We heard that she and her maid had come in the *coupé,* and, probably from pride, poor young lady! she had avoided all association with her fellow-passengers, thereby exciting their dislike and ridicule. All these little pieces of hearsay had a significance to us afterwards, though, at the time, the only remark made that bore upon the future was Amante's whisper to me that the young lady's hair was exactly the colour of mine, which she had cut off and burnt in the stove in the miller's kitchen in one of her descents from our hiding-place in the loft.

As soon as we could, we struck round in the shadow, leaving the boisterous and merry fellow-passengers to their supper. We crossed the court, borrowed a lantern from the ostler, and scrambled up the rude step to our chamber above the stable. There was no door into it; the entrance was the hole into which the ladder fitted. The window looked into the court. We were tired and soon fell asleep. I was wakened by a noise in the stable below. One instant of listening, and I wakened Amante, placing my hand on her mouth, to prevent any exclamation in her half-roused state. We heard my husband speaking about his horse to the ostler. It was his voice. I am sure of it. Amante said so too. We durst not move to rise and satisfy ourselves. For five minutes or so he went on giving directions. Then he left the stable, and, softly stealing to our window, we saw him cross the court and re-enter the inn. We consulted as to what we should do. We feared to excite remark or suspicion by descending and leaving our chamber, or else immediate escape was our strongest idea. Then the ostler left the stable, locking the door on the outside.

'We must try and drop through the window – if, indeed, it is well to go at all,' said Amante.

With reflection came wisdom. We should excite suspicion by leaving without paying our bill. We were on foot, and might easily be pursued. So we sat on our bed's edge, talking and shivering, while from across the court the laughter rang merrily, and the company slowly dispersed one by one, their lights flitting past the windows as they went upstairs and settled each one to his rest.

We crept into our bed, holding each other tight, and listening to every sound, as if we thought we were tracked, and might meet our death at any moment. In the dead of night, just at the profound still-ness preceding the turn into another day, we heard a soft, cautious step crossing the yard. The key into the stable was turned – someone came into the stable – we felt rather than heard him there. A horse started a little, and made a restless movement with his feet, then whinnied recognition. He who had entered made two or three low sounds to the animal, and then led him into the court. Amante sprang to the window with the noiseless activity of a cat. She looked out, but dared not speak a word. We heard the great door into the street open – a pause for mounting, and the horse's footsteps were lost in distance.

Then Amante came back to me. 'It was he! He is gone!' said she, and once more we lay down, trembling and shaking.

This time we fell sound asleep. We slept long and late. We were wakened by many hurrying feet, and many confused voices; all the world seemed awake and astir. We rose and dressed ourselves, and coming down we looked around among the crowd collected in the courtyard, in order to assure ourselves *he* was not there before we left the shelter of the stable.

The instant we were seen, two or three people rushed to us.

'Have you heard? – Do you know? – That poor young lady – oh, come and see!' and so we were hurried, almost in spite of ourselves, across the court, and up the great open stairs of the main building of the inn, into a bed-chamber, where lay the beautiful young German lady, so full of graceful pride the night before, now white and still in death. By her stood the French maid, crying and gesticulating.

'Oh, madame! if you had but suffered me to stay with you! Oh! the baron, what will he say?' and so she went on. Her state had but just been discovered; it had been supposed that she was fatigued, and was sleeping late, until a few minutes before. The surgeon of the town had been sent for, and the landlord of the inn was trying vainly to enforce order until he came, and, from time to time, drinking little cups of brandy, and offering them to the guests, who were all assembled there, pretty much as the servants were doing in the courtyard.

At last the surgeon came. All fell back, and hung on the words that were to fall from his lips.

'See!' said the landlord. 'This lady came last night by the diligence with her maid. Doubtless, a great lady, for she must have a private sitting-room – '

'She was Madame the Baroness de Roeder,' said the French maid.

' – And was difficult to please in the matter of supper, and a sleeping-room. She went to bed well, though fatigued. Her maid left her – '

'I begged to be allowed to sleep in her room, as we were in a strange inn, of the character of which we knew nothing; but she would not let me, my mistress was such a great lady.'

' – And slept with my servants,' continued the landlord. 'This morning we thought madame was still slumbering; but when eight, nine, ten, and near eleven o'clock came, I bade her maid use my pass-key, and enter her room – '

'The door was not locked, only closed. And here she was found – dead is she not, monsieur? – with her face down on her pillow, and her beautiful hair all scattered wild; she never would let me tie it up, saying it made her head ache. Such hair!' said the waiting-maid, lifting up a long golden tress, and letting it fall again.

I remembered Amante's words the night before, and crept close up to her.

Meanwhile, the doctor was examining the body underneath the bedclothes, which the landlord, until now, had not allowed to be disarranged. The surgeon drew out his hand, all bathed and stained with blood, and held up a short, sharp knife, with a piece of paper fastened round it.

'Here has been foul play,' he said. 'The deceased lady has been murdered. This dagger was aimed straight at her heart.' Then putting on his spectacles, he read the writing on the bloody paper, dimmed and horribly obscured as it was.

NUMÉRO UN
Ainsi les Chauffeurs se vengent

'Let us go!' said I to Amante. 'Oh, let us leave this horrible place!'

'Wait a little,' said she. 'Only a few minutes more. It will be better.'

Immediately the voices of all proclaimed their suspicions of the cavalier who had arrived last the night before. He had, they said, made so many inquiries about the young lady, whose supercilious conduct all in the *salle-à-manger* had been discussing on his entrance. They were talking about her as we left the room; he must have come in directly afterwards, and not until he had learnt all about her, had he spoken of the business which necessitated his departure at dawn of day, and made his arrangements with both landlord and ostler for the possession of the keys of the stable and *porte-cochère*. In short, there was no doubt as to the murderer, even before the arrival of the legal functionary who had been sent for by the surgeon; but the word on the paper chilled everyone with terror. *Les Chauffeurs*, who were they? No-one knew, some of the gang might even then be in the room overhearing, and noting down fresh objects for vengeance. In Germany, I had heard little of this terrible gang, and I had paid no greater heed to the stories related once or twice about them in Carlsruhe than one does to tales about ogres. But here in their very haunts, I learnt the full amount of the terror they inspired. No-one would be legally responsible for any evidence criminating the murderer. The public prosecutor shrank from the duties of his office. What do I say? Neither Amante nor I, knowing far more of the actual guilt of the man who had killed that poor sleeping young lady, durst breathe a word. We appeared to be wholly ignorant of everything: we, who might have told so much. But how could we? We were broken down with terrific anxiety and fatigue, with the knowledge that we, above all, were doomed victims; and that the blood, heavily dripping from the bedclothes on to the floor, was dripping thus out of the poor dead body, because, when living, she had been mistaken for me.

At length Amante went up to the landlord, and asked permission to leave his inn, doing all openly and humbly, so as to excite neither ill-will nor suspicion. Indeed, suspicion was otherwise directed, and he willingly gave us leave to depart. A few days afterwards we were across the Rhine, in Germany, making our way towards Frankfort, but still keeping our disguises, and Amante still working at her trade.

On the way, we met a young man, a wandering journeyman from Heidelberg. I knew him, although I did not choose that he should know me. I asked him, as carelessly as I could, how the old miller was now? He told me he was dead. This realisation of the worst apprehensions caused by his long silence shocked me inexpressibly. It seemed as though every prop gave way from under me. I had been talking to Amante only that very day of the safety and comfort of the home that awaited her in my father's house; of the gratitude which the old man would feel towards her; and how there, in that peaceful dwelling, far away from the terrible land of France, she should find ease and security for all the rest of her life. All this I thought I had to promise, and even yet more had I looked for, for myself. I looked to the unburdening of my heart and conscience by telling all I knew to my best and wisest friend. I looked to his love as a sure guidance as well as a comforting stay, and, behold, he was gone away from me for ever!

I had left the room hastily on hearing of this sad news from the Heidelberger. Presently, Amante followed.

'Poor madame,' said she, consoling me to the best of her ability. And then she told me by degrees what more she had learned respecting my home, about which she knew almost as much as I did, from my frequent talks on the subject both at Les Rochers and on the dreary, doleful road we had come along. She had continued the conversation after I left, by asking about my brother and his wife. Of course, they lived on at the mill, but the man said (with what truth I know not, but I believed it firmly at the time) that Babette had completely got the upper hand of my brother, who only saw through her eyes and heard with her ears. That there had been much Heidelberg gossip of late days about her sudden intimacy with a grand French gentleman who had appeared at the mill – a relation, by marriage – married, in fact, to the miller's sister, who, by all accounts, had behaved abominably and ungratefully. But that was no reason for Babette's extreme and sudden intimacy with him, going about everywhere with the French gentleman; and since he left (as the Heidelberger said he knew for a fact) corresponding with him constantly. Yet her husband saw no harm in it all, seemingly; though, to be sure, he was so out of spirits, what with his father's death and the news of his sister's infamy, that he hardly knew how to hold up his head.

'Now,' said Amante, 'all this proves that M. de la Tourelle has suspected that you would go back to the nest in which you were reared, and that he has been there, and found that you have not yet returned; but probably he still imagines that you will do so, and has accordingly engaged your sister-in-law as a kind of informant. Madame has said that her sister-in-law bore her no extreme good-will; and the defamatory story he has got the start of us in spreading, will not tend to increase the favour in which your sister-in-law holds you. No doubt the assassin was retracing his steps when we met him near Forbach, and having heard of the poor German lady, with her French maid, and her pretty blonde complexion, he followed her. If madame will still be guided by me – and, my child, I beg of you still to trust me,' said Amante, breaking out of her respectful form-ality into the way of talking more natural to those who had shared and escaped from common dangers – more natural, too, where the speaker was conscious of a power of protection which the other did not possess – 'we will go on to Frankfort, and lose ourselves, for a time, at least, in the numbers of people who throng a great town; and you have told me that Frankfort is a great town. We will still be husband and wife; we will take a small lodging, and you shall house-keep and live in-doors. I, as the rougher and the more alert, will continue my father's trade, and seek work at the tailors' shops.'

I could think of no better plan, so we followed this out. In a back street at Frankfort we found two furnished rooms to let on a sixth storey. The one we entered had no light from day; a dingy lamp swung perpetually from the ceiling, and from that, or from the open door leading into the bedroom beyond, came our only light. The bedroom was more cheerful, but very small. Such as it was, it almost exceeded our possible means. The money from the sale of my ring was almost exhausted, and Amante was a stranger in the place, speaking only French, moreover, and the good Germans were hating the French people right heartily. However, we succeeded better than our hopes, and even laid by a little against the time of my confinement. I never stirred abroad, and saw no-one, and Amante's want of knowledge of German kept her in a state of comparative isolation.

At length my child was born – my poor worse than fatherless child. It was a girl, as I had prayed for. I had feared lest a boy might have something of the tiger nature of its father, but a girl seemed all my own. And yet not all my own, for the faithful Amante's delight and glory in the babe almost exceeded mine; in outward show it certainly did.

We had not been able to afford any attendance beyond what a neighbouring *sage-femme* could give, and she came frequently, bringing in with her a little store of gossip, and wonderful tales culled out of her own experience, every time. One day she began to tell me about a great lady in whose service her daughter had lived as scullion, or some such thing. Such a beautiful lady! with such a handsome husband. But grief comes to the palace as well as to the garret, and why or wherefore no-one knew, but somehow the Baron de Roeder must have incurred the vengeance of the terrible *Chauffeurs*; for not many months ago, as madame was going to see her relations in Alsace, she was stabbed dead as she lay in bed at some hotel on the road. Had I not seen it in the *Gazette*? Had I not heard? Why, she had been told that as far off as Lyons there were placards offering a heavy reward on the part of the Baron de Roeder for information respecting the murderer of his wife. But no-one could help him, for all who could bear evidence were in such terror of the *Chauffeurs*; there were hundreds of them she had been told, rich and poor, great gentlemen and peasants, all leagued together by most frightful oaths to hunt to the death anyone who bore witness against them; so that even they who survived the tortures to which the *Chauffeurs* subjected many of the people whom they plundered, dared not to recognise them again, would not dare, even did they see them at the bar of a court of justice; for, if one were condemned, were there not hundreds sworn to avenge his death?

I told all this to Amante, and we began to fear that if M. de la Tourelle, or Lefebvre, or any of the gang at Les Rochers, had seen these placards, they would know that the poor lady stabbed by the former was the Baroness de Roeder, and that they would set forth again in search of me.

This fresh apprehension told on my health and impeded my recovery. We had so little money we could not call in a physician, at least, not one in established practice. But Amante found out a young doctor for whom, indeed, she had sometimes worked; and offering to pay him in kind, she brought him to see me, her sick wife. He was very gentle and thoughtful, though, like ourselves, very poor. But he gave much time and consideration to the case, saying once to Amante that he saw my constitution had experienced some severe shock from which it was probable that my nerves would never entirely recover. By-and-by

I shall name this doctor, and then you will know, better than I can describe, his character.

I grew strong in time – stronger, at least. I was able to work a little at home, and to sun myself and my baby at the garret-window in the roof. It was all the air I dared to take. I constantly wore the disguise I had first set out with; as constantly had I renewed the disfiguring dye which changed my hair and complexion. But the perpetual state of terror in which I had been during the whole months succeeding my escape from Les Rochers made me loathe the idea of ever again walking in the open daylight, exposed to the sight and recognition of every passer-by. In vain Amante reasoned – in vain the doctor urged. Docile in every other thing, in this I was obstinate. I would not stir out. One day Amante returned from her work, full of news – some of it good, some such as to cause us apprehension. The good news was this; the master for whom she worked as journeyman was going to send her with some others to a great house at the other side of Frankfort, where there were to be private theatricals, and where many new dresses and much alteration of old ones would be required. The tailors employed were all to stay at this house until the day of representation was over, as it was at some distance from the town, and no-one could tell when their work would be ended. But the pay was to be proportionately good.

The other thing she had to say was this: she had that day met the travelling jeweller to whom she and I had sold my ring. It was rather a peculiar one, given to me by my husband; we had felt at the time that it might be the means of tracing us, but we were penniless and starving, and what else could we do? She had seen that this French-man had recognised her at the same instant that she did him, and she thought at the same time that there was a gleam of more than common intelligence on his face as he did so. This idea had been confirmed by his following her for some way on the other side of the street; but she had evaded him with her better knowledge of the town, and the increasing darkness of the night. Still it was well that she was going to such a distance from our dwelling on the next day; and she had brought me in a stock of provisions, begging me to keep within doors, with a strange kind of fearful oblivion of the fact that I had never set foot beyond the threshold of the house since I had first entered it – scarce ever ventured down the stairs. But, although my poor, my dear, very faithful Amante was like one possessed that last night, she spoke continually of the dead, which is a bad sign for the living. She kissed you – yes! it was you, my daughter, my darling, whom I bore beneath my bosom away from the fearful castle of your father – I call him so for the first time, I must call him so once again before I have done – Amante kissed you, sweet baby, blessed little comforter, as if she never could leave off. And then she went away, alive.

Two days, three days passed away. That third evening I was sitting within my bolted doors – you asleep on your pillow by my side – when a step came up the stair, and I knew it must be for me; for ours were the topmost rooms. Someone knocked; I held my very breath. But someone spoke, and I knew it was the good Doctor Voss. Then I crept to the door, and answered.

'Are you alone?' asked I.

'Yes,' said he, in a still lower voice. 'Let me in.' I let him in, and he was as alert as I in bolting and barring the door. Then he came and whispered to me his doleful tale. He had come from the hospital in the opposite quarter of the town, the hospital which he visited; he should have been with me sooner, but he had feared lest he should be watched. He had come from Amante's death-bed. Her fears of the jeweller were too well founded. She had left the house where she was employed that morning, to transact some errand connected with her work in the town; she must have been followed, and dogged on her way back through solitary wood-paths, for some of the wood-rangers belonging to the great house had found her lying there, stabbed to death, but not dead; with the poniard again plunged through the fatal writing, once more; but this time with the word 'un' underlined, so as to show that the assassin was aware of his previous mistake.

Numéro Un. Ainsi les Chauffeurs se vengent.

They had carried her to the house, and given her restoratives till she had recovered the feeble use of her speech. But, oh, faithful, dear friend and sister! even then she remembered me, and refused to tell (what no-one else among her fellow workmen knew), where she lived or with whom. Life was ebbing away fast, and they had no resource but to carry her to the nearest hospital, where, of course, the fact of her sex was made known. Fortunately both for her and for me, the doctor in attendance was the very Doctor Voss whom we already knew. To him, while awaiting her confessor, she told enough to enable him to understand the position in which I was left; before the priest had heard half her tale Amante was dead.

Doctor Voss told me he had made all sorts of *détours*, and waited thus, late at night, for fear of being watched and followed. But I do not think he was. At any rate, as I afterwards learnt from him, the Baron Roeder, on hearing of the similitude of this murder with that of his wife in every particular, made such a search after the assassins, that, although they were not discovered, they were compelled to take to flight for the time.

I can hardly tell you now by what arguments Dr Voss, at first merely my benefactor, sparing me a portion of his small modicum, at length persuaded me to become his wife. His wife he called it, I called it; for we went through the religious ceremony too much slighted at the time, and as we were both Lutherans, and M. de la Tourelle had pretended to be of the reformed religion, a divorce from the latter would have been easily procurable by German law both ecclesiastical and legal, could we have summoned so fearful a man into any court.

The good doctor took me and my child by stealth to his modest dwelling; and there I lived in the same deep refinement, never seeing the full light of day, although when the dye had once passed away from my face my husband did not wish me to renew it. There was no need; my yellow hair was grey, my complexion was ashen-coloured, no creature could have recognised the fresh-coloured, bright-haired young woman of eighteen months before. The few people whom I saw knew me only as Madame Voss; a widow much older than himself, whom Dr Voss had secretly married. They called me the Grey Woman.

He made me give you his surname. Till now you have known no other father – while he lived you needed no father's love. Once only, only once more, did the old terror come upon me. For some reason which I forget, I broke through my usual custom, and went to the window of my room for some purpose, either to shut or to open it. Looking out into the street for an instant, I was fascinated by the sight of M. de la Tourelle, gay, young, elegant as ever, walking along on the opposite side of the street. The noise I had made with the window caused him to look up; he saw me, an old grey woman, and he did not recognise me! Yet it was not three years since we had parted, and his eyes were keen and dreadful like those of the lynx.

I told M. Voss, on his return home, and he tried to cheer me, but the shock of seeing M. de la Tourelle had been too terrible for me. I was ill for long months afterwards.

Once again I saw him. Dead. He and Lefebvre were at last caught; hunted down by the Baron de Roeder in some of their crimes. Dr Voss had heard of their arrest; their condemnation, their death; but he never said a word to me, until one day he bade me show him that I loved him by my obedience and my trust. He took me on a long carriage journey, where to I know not, for we never spoke of that day again; I was led through a prison, into a closed courtyard, where, decently draped in the last robes of death, concealing the marks of decapitation, lay M. de la Tourelle, and two or three others, whom I had known at Les Rochers.

After that conviction Dr Voss tried to persuade me to return to a more natural mode of life, and to go out more. But although I sometimes complied with his wish, yet the old terror was ever strong upon me, and he, seeing what an effort it was, gave up urging me at last.

You know all the rest. How we both mourned bitterly the loss of that dear husband and father – for such I will call him ever – and as such you must consider him, my child, after this one revelation is over.

Why has it been made, you ask. For this reason, my child. The lover, whom you have only known as M. Lebrun, a French artist, told me but yesterday his real name, dropped because the blood-thirsty republicans might consider it as too aristocratic. It is Maurice de Poissy.

Curious, if True

[Extract from a letter from Richard Whittingham, Esq.]

You were formerly so much amused at my pride in my descent from that sister of Calvin's, who married a Whittingham, Dean of Durham, that I doubt if you will be able to enter into the regard for my distinguished relation that has led me to France, in order to examine registers and archives, which, I thought, might enable me to discover collateral descendants of the great reformer, with whom I might call cousins. I shall not tell you of my troubles and adventures in this research; you are not worthy to hear of them; but something so curious befell me one evening last August, that if I had not been perfectly certain I was wide awake, I might have taken it for a dream.

For the purpose I have named, it was necessary that I should make Tours my headquarters for a time. I had traced descendants of the Calvin family out of Normandy into the centre of France; but I found it was necessary to have a kind of permission from the bishop of the diocese before I could see certain family papers, which had fallen into the possession of the Church; and, as I had several English friends at Tours, I awaited the answer to my request to Monseigneur de — , at that town. I was ready to accept any invitation; but I received very few; and was sometimes a little at a loss what to do with my evenings. The *table d'hôte* was at five o'clock; I did not wish to go to the expense of a private sitting-room, disliked the dinnery atmosphere of the *salle à manger*, could not play either at pool or billiards, and the aspect of my fellow guests was unprepossessing enough to make me unwilling to enter into any *tête-à-tête* gamblings with them. So I usually rose from table early, and tried to make the most of the remaining light of the August evenings in walking briskly off to explore the surrounding country; the middle of the day was too hot for this purpose, and better employed in lounging on a bench in the Boulevards, lazily listening to the distant band, and noticing with equal laziness the faces and figures of the women who passed by.

One Thursday evening, the 18th of August it was, I think, I had gone further than usual in my walk, and I found that it was later than I had imagined when I paused to turn back. I fancied I could make a round; I had enough notion of the direction in which I was, to see that by turning up a narrow straight lane to my left I should shorten my way back to Tours. And so I believe I should have done, could I have found an outlet at the right place, but field-paths are almost unknown in that part of France, and my lane, stiff and straight as any street, and marked into terribly vanishing perspective by the regular row of poplars on each side, seemed interminable. Of course night came on, and I was in darkness. In England I might have had a chance of seeing a light in some cottage only a field or two off, and asking my way from the inhabitants; but here I could see no such welcome sight; indeed, I believe French peasants go to bed with the summer daylight, so if there were any habitations in the neighbourhood I never saw them. At last – I believe I must have walked two hours in the darkness – I saw the dusky outline of a wood on one side of the weariful lane, and, impatiently careless of all forest laws and penalties for trespassers, I made my way to it, thinking that if the worst came to the worst, I could find some covert – some shelter where I could lie down and rest, until the morning light gave me a chance of finding my way back to Tours. But the plantation, on the outskirts of what appeared to me a dense wood, was of young trees, too closely planted to be more than slender stems growing up to a good height, with scanty foliage on their summits. On I went towards the thicker forest, and once there I slackened my pace, and began to look about me for a good lair. I was as dainty as Lochiel's grandchild, who made his grandsire indignant at the luxury of his pillow of snow: this brake was too full of brambles, that felt damp with dew; there was no hurry, since I had given up all hope of passing the night between four walls; and I went leisurely groping about, and trusting that there were no wolves to be poked up out of their summer drowsiness by my stick, when all at once I saw a château before me, not a quarter of a mile off, at the end of what seemed to be an ancient avenue (now overgrown and irregular), which I happened to be crossing, when I looked to my right, and saw the welcome sight. Large, stately, and dark was its outline against the dusky night-sky; there were pepper-boxes and *tourelles* and what-not fantastically going up into the dim starlight. And more to the purpose still, though I could not see the details of the building that I was now facing, it was plain enough that there were lights in many windows, as if some great entertainment was going on.

'They are hospitable people, at any rate,' thought I. 'Perhaps they will give me a bed. I don't suppose French *propriétaires* have traps and horses quite as plentiful as English gentlemen; but they are evidently having a large party, and some of their guests may be from Tours, and will give me a cast back to the Lion d'Or. I am not proud, and I am dog-tired. I am not above hanging on behind, if need be.'

So, putting a little briskness and spirit into my walk, I went up to the door, which was standing open, most hospitably, and showing a large lighted hall, all hung round with spoils of the chase, armour, &c., the details of which I had not time to notice, for the instant I stood on the threshold a huge porter appeared, in a strange, old-fashioned dress, a kind of livery which well befitted the general appearance of the house. He asked me, in French (so curiously pronounced that I thought I had hit upon a new kind of patois), my name, and whence I came. I thought he would not be much the wiser, still it was but civil to give it before I made my request for assistance; so, in reply, I said. 'My name is Whittingham – Richard Whittingham, an English gentleman, staying at — .' To my infinite surprise, a light of pleased intelligence came over the giant's face; he made me a low bow, and said (still in the same curious dialect) that I was welcome, that I was long expected.

'Long expected!' What could the fellow mean? Had I stumbled on a nest of relations by John Calvin's side, who had heard of my genealogical inquiries, and were gratified and interested by them? But I was too much pleased to be under shelter for the night to think it necessary to account for my agreeable reception before I enjoyed it. Just as he was opening the great heavy *battants* of the door that led from the hall to the interior, he turned round and said: 'Apparently Monsieur le Géanquilleur is not come with you.'

'No! I am all alone; I have lost my way,' – and I was going on with my explanation, when he, as if quite indifferent to it, led the way up a great stone staircase, as wide as many rooms, and having on each landing-place massive iron wickets, in a heavy framework; these the porter unlocked with the solemn slowness of age. Indeed, a strange, mysterious awe of the centuries that had passed away since this château was built, came over me as I waited for the turning of the ponderous keys in the ancient locks. I could almost have fancied that I heard a mighty rushing murmur (like the ceaseless sound of a distant sea, ebbing and flowing for ever and for ever), coming forth from the great vacant galleries that opened out on each side of the broad staircase, and were to be dimly perceived in the darkness above us. It was as if the voices of generations of men yet echoed and eddied in the silent air. It was strange, too, that my friend the porter going before me, ponderously infirm, with his feeble old hands striving in vain to keep the tall flambeau he held steadily before him – strange, I say, that he was the only domestic I saw in the vast halls and passages, or met with on the grand staircase. At length we stood before the gilded doors that led into the saloon where the family – or it might be the company, so great was the buzz of voices – was assembled. I would have remonstrated when I found he was going to introduce me, dusty and travel-smeared, in a morning costume that was not even my best, into this grand salon, with nobody knew how many ladies and gentlemen assembled; but the obstinate old man was evidently bent upon taking me straight to his master, and paid no heed to my words.

The doors flew open, and I was ushered into a saloon curiously full of pale light, which did not culminate on any spot, nor proceed from any centre, nor flicker with any motion of the air, but filled every nook and corner, making all things deliciously distinct; different from our light of gas or candle, as is the difference between a clear southern atmosphere and that of our misty England.

At the first moment, my arrival excited no attention, the apartment was so full of people, all intent on their own conversation. But my friend the porter went up to a handsome lady of middle age, richly attired in that antique manner which fashion has brought round again of late years, and, waiting first in an attitude of deep respect till her attention fell upon him, told her my name and something about me, as far as I could guess from the gestures of the one and the sudden glance of the eye of the other.

She immediately came towards me with the most friendly actions of greeting, even before she had advanced near enough to speak. Then – and was it not strange? – her words and accent were that of the commonest peasant of the country. Yet she herself looked high-bred, and would have been dignified had she been a shade less restless, had her countenance worn a little less lively and inquisitive expression. I had been poking a good deal about the old parts of Tours, and had had to understand the dialect of the people who dwelt in the Marché au Vendredi and similar places, or I really should not have understood my handsome hostess, as she offered to present me to her husband, a henpecked, gentlemanly man, who was more quaintly attired than she in the very extreme of that style of dress. I thought to myself that in France, as in England, it is the provincials who carry fashion to such an excess as to become ridiculous.

However, he spoke (still in the patois) of his pleasure in making my acquaintance, and led me to a strange uneasy easy-chair, much of a piece with the rest of the furniture, which might have taken its place without any anachronism by the side of that in the Hôtel Cluny. Then again began the clatter of French voices, which my arrival had for an instant interrupted, and I had leisure to look about me. Opposite to me sat a very sweet-looking lady, who must have been a great beauty in her youth, I should think, and would be charming in old age, from the sweetness of her countenance. She was, however, extremely fat, and on seeing her feet laid up before her on a cushion, I at once perceived that they were so swollen as to render her incapable of walking, which probably brought on her excessive *embonpoint*. Her hands were plump and small, but rather coarse-grained in texture, not quite so clean as they might have been, and altogether not so aristocratic-looking as the charming face. Her dress was of superb black velvet, ermine-trimmed, with diamonds thrown all abroad over it.

Not far from her stood the least little man I had ever seen; of such admirable proportions no-one could call him a dwarf, because with that word we usually associate something of deformity; but yet with an elfin look of shrewd, hard, worldly wisdom in his face that marred the impression which his delicate regular little features would otherwise have conveyed. Indeed, I do not think he was quite of equal rank with the rest of the company, for his dress was inappropriate to the occasion (and he apparently was an invited, while I was an involuntary guest); and one or two of his gestures and actions were more like the tricks of an uneducated rustic than anything else. To explain what I mean: his boots had evidently seen much service, and had been re-topped, re-heeled, re-soled to the extent of cobbler's powers. Why should he have come in them if they were not his best – his only pair? And what can be more ungenteel than poverty? Then again he had an uneasy trick of putting his hand up to his throat, as if he expected to find some-thing the matter with it; and he had the awkward habit – which I do not think he could have copied from Dr Johnson, because most probably he had never heard of him – of trying always to retrace his steps on the exact boards on which he had trodden to arrive at any particular part of the room. Besides, to settle the question, I once heard him addressed as Monsieur Poucet, without any aristo-cratic 'de' for a prefix; and nearly everyone else in the room was a marquis, at any rate.

I say, 'nearly everyone', for some strange people had the entrée; unless, indeed, they were, like me, benighted. One of the guests I should have taken for a servant, but for the extraordinary influ-ence he seemed to have over the man I took for his master, and who never did anything without, apparently, being urged thereto by this follower. The master, magnificently dressed, but ill at ease in his clothes as if they had been made for someone else, was a weak-looking, handsome man, continually sauntering about, and I almost guessed an object of suspicion to some of the gentlemen present, which, perhaps, drove him on the companionship of his follower, who was dressed something in the style of an ambassador's chasseur; yet it was not a chasseur's dress after all; it was something more thoroughly old-world; boots half-way up his ridiculously small legs, which clattered as he walked along, as if they were too large for his little feet; and a great quantity of grey fur, as trimming to coat, court mantle, boots, cap – everything. You know the way in which certain countenances remind you perpetually of some animal, be it bird or beast! Well, this chasseur (as I will call him for want of a better name) was exceedingly like the great Tom-cat that you have seen so often in my chambers, and laughed at almost as often for his uncanny gravity of demeanour. Grey whiskers has my Tom – grey whiskers had the chasseur: grey hair overshadows the upper lip of my Tom – grey mustachios hid that of the chasseur. The pupils of Tom's eyes dilate and contract as I had thought cats' pupils only could do, until I saw those of the chasseur. To be sure, canny as Tom is, the chasseur had the advantage in the more intelligent expression. He seemed to have obtained most complete sway over his master or patron, whose looks he watched, and whose steps he followed, with a kind of distrustful interest that puzzled me greatly.

There were several other groups in the more distant part of the saloon, all of the stately old school, all grand and noble, I conjectured from their bearing. They seemed perfectly well acquainted with each other, as if they were in the habit of meeting. But I was interrupted in my observations by the tiny little gentleman on the opposite side of the room coming across to take a place beside me. It is no difficult matter to a Frenchman to slide into conversation, and so gracefully did my pigmy friend keep up the character of the nation, that we were almost confidential before ten minutes had elapsed.

Now I was quite aware that the welcome which all had extended to me, from the porter up to the vivacious lady and meek lord of the castle, was intended for some other person. But it required either a degree of moral courage, of which I cannot boast, or the self-reliance and conversational powers of a bolder and cleverer man than I, to undeceive people who had fallen into so fortunate a mistake for me. Yet the little man by my side insinuated himself so much into my confidence, that I had half a mind to tell him of my exact situation, and to turn him into a friend and an ally.

'Madame is perceptibly growing older,' said he, in the midst of my perplexity, glancing at our hostess.

'Madame is still a very fine woman,' replied I.

'Now, is it not strange,' continued he, lowering his voice, 'how women almost invariably praise the absent, or departed, as if they were angels of light while as for the present, or the living' – here he shrugged up his little shoulders, and made an expressive pause. 'Would you believe it! Madame is always praising her late husband to monsieur's face; till, in fact, we guests are quite perplexed how to look: for, you know, the late M. de Retz's character was quite notorious – everybody has heard of him.' All the world of Touraine, thought I, but I made an assenting noise.

At this instant, monsieur our host came up to me, and with a civil look of tender interest (such as some people put on when they inquire after your mother, about whom they do not care one straw), asked if I had heard lately how my cat was? 'How my cat was!' What could the man mean? My cat! Could he mean the tailless Tom, born in the Isle of Man, and now supposed to be keeping guard against the incursions of rats and mice into my chambers in London? Tom is, as you know, on pretty good terms with some of my friends, using their legs for rubbing-posts without scruple, and highly esteemed by them for his gravity of demeanour, and wise manner of winking his eyes. But could his fame have reached across the Channel? However, an answer must be returned to the inquiry, as monsieur's face was bent down to mine with a look of polite anxiety; so I, in my turn, assumed an expression of gratitude, and assured him that, to the best of my belief, my cat was in remarkably good health.

'And the climate agrees with her?'

'Perfectly,' said I, in a maze of wonder at this deep solicitude in a tailless cat who had lost one foot and half an ear in some cruel trap. My host smiled a sweet smile, and, addressing a few words to my little neighbour, passed on.

'How wearisome those aristocrats are!' quoth my neighbour, with a slight sneer. 'Monsieur's conversation rarely extends to more than two sentences to anyone. By that time his faculties are exhausted, and he needs the refreshment of silence. You and I, monsieur, are, at any rate, indebted to our own wits for our rise in the world!'

Here again I was bewildered! As you know, I am rather proud of my descent from families which, if not noble themselves, are allied to nobility – and as to my 'rise in the world' – if I had risen, it would have been rather for balloon-like qualities than for mother-wit, to being unencumbered with heavy ballast either in my head or my pockets. However, it was my cue to agree: so I smiled again.

'For my part,' said he, 'if a man does not stick at trifles, if he knows how to judiciously add to, or withhold facts, and is not sentimental in his parade of humanity, he is sure to do well; sure to affix a *de* or *von* to his name, and end his days in comfort. There is an example of what I am saying' – and he glanced furtively at the weak-looking master of the sharp, intelligent servant, whom I have called the chasseur.

'Monsieur le Marquis would never have been anything but a miller's son, if it had not been for the talents of his servant. Of course you know his antecedents?'

I was going to make some remarks on the changes in the order of the peerage since the days of Louis XVI – going, in fact, to be very sensible and historical – when there was a slight commotion among the people at the other end of the room. Lacqueys in quaint liveries must have come in from behind the tapestry, I suppose (for I never saw them enter, though I sat right opposite to the doors), and were handing about the slight beverages and slighter viands which are considered sufficient refreshments, but which looked rather meagre to my hungry appetite. These footmen were standing solemnly opposite to a lady – beautiful, splendid as the dawn, but – sound asleep in a magnificent settee. A gentleman who showed so much irritation at her ill-timed slumbers, that I think he must have been her husband, was trying to awaken her with actions not far removed from shakings. All in vain; she was quite unconscious of his annoyance, or the smiles of the company, or the automatic solemnity of the waiting footman, or the perplexed anxiety of monsieur and madame.

My little friend sat down with a sneer, as if his curiosity was quenched in contempt.

'Moralists would make an infinity of wise remarks on that scene,' said he. 'In the first place, note the ridiculous position into which their superstitious reverence for rank and title puts all these people. Because monsieur is a reigning prince over some minute principality, the exact situation of which no-one has as yet discovered, no-one must venture to take their glass of *eau sucré* till Madame la Princesse awakens; and, judging from past experience, those poor lacqueys may have to stand for a century before that happens. Next – always speaking as a moralist, you will observe – note how difficult it is to break off bad habits acquired in youth!'

Just then the prince succeeded, by what means I did not see, in awaking the beautiful sleeper. But at first she did not remember where she was, and looking up at her husband with loving eyes, she smiled and said: 'Is it you, my prince?'

But he was too conscious of the suppressed amusement of the spectators and his own consequent annoyance, to be reciprocally tender, and turned away with some little French expression, best rendered into English by 'Pooh, pooh, my dear!'

After I had had a glass of delicious wine of some unknown quality, my courage was in rather better plight than before, and I told my cynical little neighbour – whom I must say I was beginning to dislike – that I had lost my way in the wood, and had arrived at the château quite by mistake.

He seemed mightily amused at my story; said that the same thing had happened to himself more than once; and told me that I had better luck than he had on one of these occasions, when, from his account, he must have been in considerable danger of his life. He ended his story by making me admire his boots, which he said he still wore, patched though they were, and all their excellent quality lost by patching, because they were of such a first-rate make for long pedestrian excursions. 'Though, indeed,' he wound up by saying, 'the new fashion of railroads would seem to supersede the necessity for this description of boots.'

When I consulted him as to whether I ought to make myself known to my host and hostess as a benighted traveller, instead of the guest whom they had taken me for, he exclaimed, 'By no means! I hate such squeamish morality.' And he seemed much offended by my innocent question, as if it seemed by implication to condemn some-thing in himself. He was offended and silent; and just at this moment I caught the sweet, attractive eyes of the lady opposite – that lady whom I named at first as being no longer in the bloom of youth, but as being somewhat infirm about the feet, which were supported on a raised cushion before her. Her looks seemed to say, 'Come here, and let us have some conversation together;' and, with a bow of silent excuse to my little companion, I went across to the lame old lady. She acknowledged my coming with the prettiest gesture of thanks possible; and, half apologetically, said, 'It is a little dull to be unable to move about on such evenings as this; but it is a just punishment to me for my early vanities. My poor feet, that were by nature so small, are now taking their revenge for my cruelty in forcing them into such little slippers . . . Besides, monsieur,' with a pleasant smile, 'I thought it was possible you might be weary of the malicious sayings of your little neighbour. He has not borne the best character in his youth, and such men are sure to be cynical in their old age.'

'Who is he?' asked I, with English abruptness.

'His name is Poucet, and his father was, I believe, a woodcutter, or charcoal burner, or something of the sort. They do tell sad stories of connivance at murder, ingratitude, and obtaining money on false pretences – but you will think me as bad as he if I go on with my slanders. Rather let us admire the lovely lady coming up towards us, with the roses in her hand – I never see her without roses, they are so closely connected with her past history, as you are doubtless aware. Ah, beauty!' said my companion to the lady drawing near to us, 'it is like you to come to me, now that I can no longer go to you.' Then turning to me, and gracefully drawing me into the conversation, she said, 'You must know that, although we never met until we were both married, we have been almost like sisters ever since. There have been so many points of resemblance in our circumstances, and I think I may say in our characters. We had each two elder sisters – mine were but half-sisters, though – who were not so kind to us as they might have been.'

'But have been sorry for it since,' put in the other lady.

'Since we have married princes,' continued the same lady, with an arch smile that had nothing of unkindness in it, 'for we both have married far above our original stations in life; we are both un-punctual in our habits, and, in consequence of this failing of ours, we have both had to suffer mortification and pain.'

'And both are charming,' said a whisper close behind me. 'My lord the marquis, say it – say, "And both are charming."'

'And both are charming,' was spoken aloud by another voice. I turned, and saw the wily cat-like chasseur, prompting his master to make civil speeches.

The ladies bowed with that kind of haughty acknowledgement which shows that compliments from such a source are distasteful.

But our trio of conversation was broken up, and I was sorry for it. The marquis looked as if he had been stirred up to make that one speech, and hoped that he would not be expected to say more; while behind him stood the chasseur, half impertinent and half servile in his ways and attitudes. The ladies, who were real ladies, seemed to be sorry for the awkwardness of the marquis, and addressed some trifling quest- ions to him, adapting themselves to the subjects on which he could have no trouble in answering. The chasseur, meanwhile, was talking to himself in a growling tone of voice. I had fallen a little into the background at this interruption in a conversation which promised to be so pleasant, and I could not help hearing his words.

'Really, De Carabas grows more stupid every day. I have a great mind to throw off his boots, and leave him to his fate. I was intended for a court, and to a court I will go, and make my own fortune as I have made his. The emperor will appreciate my talents.'

And such are the habits of the French, or such his forgetfulness of good manners in his anger, that he spat right and left on the parqueted floor.

Just then a very ugly, very pleasant-looking man, came towards the two ladies to whom I had lately been speaking, leading up to them a delicate, fair woman, dressed all in the softest white, as if she were *vouée au blanc*. I do not think there was a bit of colour about her. I thought I heard her making, as she came along, a little noise of pleasure, not exactly like the singing of a tea-kettle, nor yet like the cooing of a dove, but reminding me of each sound.

'Madame de Mioumiou was anxious to see you,' said he, add- ressing the lady with the roses, 'so I have brought her across to give you a pleasure!' What an honest, good face! but oh! how ugly! And yet I liked his ugliness better than most persons' beauty. There was a look of pathetic acknowledgement of his ugliness, and a deprec- ation of your too hasty judgement in his countenance that was positively winning. The soft, white lady kept glancing at my neigh- bour the chasseur, as if they had had some former acquaintance, which puzzled me very much, as they were of such different rank. However, their nerves were evidently strung to the same tune, for at a sound behind the tapestry, which was more like the scuttering of rats and mice than anything else, both Madame de Mioumiou and the chasseur started with the most eager look of anxiety on their countenances, and by their restless movements – madame's panting, and the fiery dilation of his eyes – one might see that commonplace sounds affected them both in a manner very different to the rest of the company. The ugly husband of the lovely lady with the roses now addressed himself to me.

'We are much disappointed,' he said, 'in finding that monsieur is not accompanied by his countryman – le grand Jean d'Angleterre; I cannot pronounce his name rightly' – and he looked at me to help him out.

'Le grand Jean d'Angleterre!' now who was le grand Jean d'Angleterre? John Bull? John Russell? John Bright?

'Jean – Jean' – continued the gentleman, seeing my embarrassment. 'Ah, these terrible English names – "Jean de Géanquilleur!"' '

I was as wise as ever. And yet the name struck me as familiar, but slightly disguised. I repeated it to myself. It was mighty like John the Giant-killer, only his friends always call that worthy 'Jack'. I said the name aloud.

'Ah, that is it!' said he. 'But why has he not accompanied you to our little reunion tonight?'

I had been rather puzzled once or twice before, but this serious question added considerably to my perplexity. Jack the Giant-killer had once, it is true, been rather an intimate friend of mine, as far as (printer's) ink and paper can keep up a friendship, but I had not heard his name mentioned for years; and for aught I knew he lay enchanted with King Arthur's knights, who lie entranced until the blast of the trumpets of four mighty kings shall call them to help at England's need. But the question had been asked in serious earnest by that gentleman, whom I more wished to think well of me than I did any other person in the room. So I answered respectfully that it was long since I had heard anything of my countryman; but that I was sure it would have given him as much pleasure as it was doing myself to have been present at such an agreeable gathering of friends. He bowed, and then the lame lady took up the word.

'Tonight is the night when, of all the year, this great old forest surrounding the castle is said to be haunted by the phantom of a little peasant girl who once lived hereabouts; the tradition is that she was devoured by a wolf. In former days I have seen her on this night out of yonder window at the end of the gallery. Will you, *ma belle*, take monsieur to see the view outside by the moonlight (you may possibly see the phantom-child); and leave me to a little *tête-à-tête* with your husband?'

With a gentle movement the lady with the roses complied with the other's request, and we went to a great window, looking down on the forest, in which I had lost my way. The tops of the far-spreading and leafy trees lay motionless beneath us in the pale, wan light, which shows objects almost as distinct in form, though not in colour, as by day. We looked down on the countless avenues, which seemed to converge from all quarters to the great old castle; and suddenly across one, quite near to us, there passed the figure of a little girl, with the *capuchon* on, that takes the place of a peasant girl's bonnet in France. She had a basket on one arm, and by her, on the side to which her head was turned, there went a wolf. I could almost have said it was licking her hand, as if in penitent love, if either penitence or love had ever been a quality of wolves – but though not of living, perhaps it may be of phantom wolves.

'There, we have seen her!' exclaimed my beautiful companion. 'Though so long dead, her simple story of household goodness and trustful simplicity still lingers in the hearts of all who have ever heard of her; and the country-people about here say that seeing that phantom-child on this anniversary brings good luck for the year. Let us hope that we shall share in the traditionary good fortune. Ah! here is Madame de Retz – she retains the name of her first husband, you know, as he was of higher rank than the present.' We were joined by our hostess.

'If monsieur is fond of the beauties of nature and art,' said she, perceiving that I had been looking at the view from the great window, 'he will perhaps take pleasure in seeing the picture.' Here she sighed, with a little affectation of grief. 'You know the picture I allude to,' addressing my companion, who bowed assent, and smiled a little maliciously, as I followed the lead of madame.

I went after her to the other end of the saloon, noting by the way with what keen curiosity she caught up what was passing either in word or action on each side of her. When we stood opposite to the end wall, I perceived a full-length picture of a handsome, peculiar-looking man, with – in spite of his good looks – a very fierce and scowling expression. My hostess clasped her hands together as her arms hung down in front, and sighed once more. Then, half in soliloquy, she said: 'He was the love of my youth; his stern yet manly character first touched this heart of mine. When – when shall I cease to deplore his loss!'

Not being acquainted with her enough to answer this question (if, indeed, it were not sufficiently answered by the fact of her second marriage), I felt awkward; and, by way of saying something, I remarked: 'The countenance strikes me as resembling something I have seen before – in an engraving from an historical picture, I think; only, it is there the principal figure in a group: he is holding a lady by her hair, and threatening her with his scimitar, while two cavaliers are rushing up the stairs, apparently only just in time to save her life.'

'Alas, alas!' said she, 'you too accurately describe a miserable passage in my life, which has often been represented in a false light. The best of husbands' – here she sobbed, and became slightly inarticulate with her grief – 'will sometimes be displeased. I was young and curious, he was justly angry with my disobedience – my brothers were too hasty – the consequence is, I became a widow!'

After due respect for her tears, I ventured to suggest some commonplace consolation. She turned round sharply: 'No, monsieur: my only comfort is that I have never forgiven the brothers who interfered so cruelly, in such an uncalled-for manner, between my dear husband and myself. To quote my friend Monsieur Sganarelle – *"Ce sont petites choses qui sont de temps en temps nécessaires dans l'amitié; et cinq ou six coups d'épée entre gens qui s'aiment ne font que ragaillardir l'affection."* You observe the colouring is not quite what it should be?'

'In this light the beard is of rather a peculiar tint,' said I.

'Yes: the painter did not do it justice. It was most lovely, and gave him such a distinguished air, quite different from the common herd. Stay, I will show you the exact colour, if you will come near this flambeau!' And going near the light, she took off a bracelet of hair, with a magnificent clasp of pearls. It was peculiar, certainly. I did not know what to say. 'His precious lovely beard!' said she. 'And the pearls go so well with the delicate blue!'

Her husband, who had come up to us, and waited till her eye fell upon him before venturing to speak, now said, 'It is strange Monsieur Ogre is not yet arrived!'

'Not at all strange,' said she, tartly. 'He was always very stupid, and constantly falls into mistakes, in which he comes worse off; and it is very well he does, for he is a credulous and cowardly fellow. Not at all strange! If you will' – turning to her husband, so that I hardly heard her words, until I caught – 'then everybody would have their rights, and we should have no more trouble. Is it not, monsieur?' addressing me.

'If I were in England, I should imagine madame was speaking of the reform bill, or the millennium – but I am in ignorance.'

And just as I spoke, the great folding-doors were thrown open wide, and everyone started to their feet to greet a little old lady, leaning on a thin black wand – and –

'Madame la Féemarraine,' was announced by a chorus of sweet shrill voices.

And in a moment I was lying in the grass close by a hollow oak-tree, with the slanting glory of the dawning day shining full in my face, and thousands of little birds and delicate insects piping and warbling out their welcome to the ruddy splendour.

Disappearances

I am not in the habit of seeing the *Household Words* regularly; but a friend, who lately sent me some of the back numbers, recommended me to read 'all the papers relating to the Detective and Protective Police', which I accordingly did – not as the generality of readers have done, as they appeared week by week, or with pauses between, but consecutively, as a popular history of the Metropolitan Police; and, as I suppose it may also be considered, a history of the police force in every large town in England. When I had ended these papers, I did not feel disposed to read any others at that time, but preferred falling into a train of reverie and recollection.

First of all I remembered, with a smile, the unexpected manner in which a relation of mine was discovered by an acquaintance, who had mislaid or forgotten Mr B.'s address. Now my dear cousin, Mr B., charming as he is in many points, has the little peculiarity of liking to change his lodgings once every three months on an average, which occasions some bewilderment to his country friends, who have no sooner learnt the 19 Belle Vue Road, Hampstead, than they have to take pains to forget that address, and to remember the 27 ½ Upper Brown Street, Camberwell; and so on, till I would rather learn a page of *Walker's Pronouncing Dictionary*, than try to remember the variety of directions which I have had to put on my letters to Mr B. during the last three years. Last summer it pleased him to remove to a beautiful village not ten miles out of London, where there is a railway station. Thither his friend sought him. (I do not now speak of the following scent there had been through three or four different lodgings, where Mr B. had been residing, before his country friend ascertained that he was now lodging at R— .) He spent the morning in making inquiries as to Mr B.'s whereabouts in the village; but many gentlemen were lodging there for the summer, and neither butcher nor baker could inform him where Mr B. was staying; his letters were unknown at the post-office, which was accounted for by the circumstance of their always being directed to his office in town.

At last the country friend sauntered back to the railway-office, and while he waited for the train he made inquiry, as a last resource, of the book-keeper at the station. 'No, sir, I cannot tell you where Mr B. lodges – so many gentlemen go by the trains; but I have no doubt but that the person standing by that pillar can inform you.' The individual to whom he directed the inquirer's attention had the appearance of a tradesman – respectable enough, yet with no pretensions to 'gentility', and had, apparently, no more urgent employment than lazily watching the passengers who came dropping in to the station. However, when he was spoken to, he answered civilly and promptly. 'Mr B.? tall gentleman, with light hair? Yes, sir, I know Mr B. He lodges at No. 8 Morton Villas – has done these three weeks or more; but you'll not find him there, sir, now. He went to town by the eleven o'clock train, and does not usually return until the half-past four train.'

The country friend had no time to lose in returning to the village, to ascertain the truth of this statement. He thanked his informant, and said he would call on Mr B. at his office in town; but before he left R— station, he asked the bookkeeper who the person was to whom he had referred him for information as to his friend's place of residence. 'One of the Detective Police, sir,' was the answer. I need hardly say that Mr B., not without a little surprise, confirmed the accuracy of the policeman's report in every particular.

When I heard this anecdote of my cousin and his friend, I thought that there could be no more romances written on the same kind of plot as Caleb Williams; the principal interest of which, to the superficial reader, consists in the alternation of hope and fear, that the hero may, or may not, escape his pursuer. It is long since I have read the story, and I forget the name of the offended and injured gentleman whose privacy Caleb has invaded; but I know that his pursuit of Caleb – his detection of the various hiding-places of the latter – his following up of slight clues – all, in fact, depended upon his own energy, sagacity, and perseverance. The interest was caused by the struggle of man against man; and the uncertainty as to which would ultimately be successful in his object: the unrelenting pursuer, or the ingenious Caleb, who seeks by every device to conceal himself. Now, in 1851, the offended master would set the Detective Police to work; there would be no doubt as to their success; the only question would be as to the time that would elapse before the hiding-place could be detected, and that could not be a question long. It is no longer a struggle between man and man, but between a vast organised machinery, and a weak, solitary individual; we have no hopes, no fears –

only certainty. But if the materials of pursuit and evasion, as long as the chase is confined to England, are taken away from the store-house of the romancer, at any rate we can no more be haunted by the idea of the possibility of mysterious disappearances; and anyone who has associated much with those who were alive at the end of the last century, can testify that there was some reason for such fears.

When I was a child, I was sometimes permitted to accompany a relation to drink tea with a very clever old lady, of one hundred and twenty – or so I thought then; I now think she, perhaps, was only about seventy. She was lively, and intelligent, and had seen and known much that was worth narrating. She was a cousin of the Sneyds, the family whence Mr Edgeworth took two of his wives; had known Major André; had mixed in the Old Whig Society that the beautiful Duchess of Devonshire and Mrs Crewe of 'Buff and Blue' fame gathered round them; and her father had been one of the early patrons of the lovely Miss Linley. I name these facts to show that she was too intelligent and cultivated by association, as well as by natural powers, to lend an over-easy credence to the marvellous; and yet I have heard her relate stories of disappearances which haunted my imagination longer than any tale of wonder. One of her stories was this.

Her father's estate lay in Shropshire, and his park-gates opened right on to a scattered village of which he was landlord. The houses formed a straggling irregular street – here a garden, next a gable-end of a farm, there a row of cottages, and so on. Now, at the end house or cottage lived a very respectable man and his wife. They were well known in the village, and were esteemed for the patient attention which they paid to the husband's father, a paralytic old man. In win-ter, his chair was near the fire; in summer, they carried him out into the open space in front of the house to bask in the sunshine, and to receive what placid amusement he could from watching the little pass-ings to and fro of the villagers. He could not move from his bed to his chair without help. One hot and sultry June day, all the village turned out to the hayfields. Only the very old and the very young remained.

The old father of whom I have spoken was carried out to bask in the sunshine that afternoon as usual, and his son and daughter-in-law went to the haymaking. But when they came home in the early evening, their paralysed father had disappeared – was gone! and from that day forwards, nothing more was ever heard of him. The old lady, who told this story, said, with the quietness that always marked the simplicity of her narration, that every inquiry which her father could make was made, and that it could never be accounted for. No-one had observed any stranger in the village; no small house-hold robbery, to which the old man might have been supposed an obstacle, had been committed in his son's dwelling that afternoon. The son and daughter-in-law (noted, too, for their attention to the helpless father) had been afield among all the neighbours the whole of the time. In short, it never was accounted for; and left a painful impression on many minds.

I will answer for it, the Detective Police would have ascertained every fact relating to it in a week.

This story, from its mystery, was painful, but had no consequences to make it tragical. The next which I shall tell (and although trad-itionary, these anecdotes of disappearances which I relate in this paper are correctly repeated, and were believed by my informants to be strictly true) had consequences, and melancholy ones, too. The scene of it is in a little country-town, surrounded by the estates of several gentlemen of large property. About a hundred years ago there lived in this small town an attorney, with his mother and sister. He was agent for one of the squires near, and received rents for him on stated days, which, of course, were well known. He went at these times to a small public-house, perhaps five miles from — , where the tenants met him, paid their rents, and were entertained at dinner afterwards. One night he did not return from this festivity. He never returned. The gentleman whose agent he was, employed the Dog-berrys of the time to find him, and the missing cash; the mother, whose support and comfort he was, sought him with all the persev-erance of faithful love. But he never returned; and by-and-by the rumour spread that he must have gone abroad with the money; his mother heard the whispers all around her, and could not disprove it; and so her heart broke, and she died. Years after, I think as many as fifty, the well-to-do butcher and grazier of — died; but, before his death, he confessed that he had waylaid Mr — on the heath, close to the town, almost within call of his own house, intending only to rob him, but, meeting with more resistance than he anticipated, had been provoked to stab him; and had buried him that very night deep under the loose sand of the heath. There his skeleton was found; but too late for his poor mother to know that his fame was cleared. His sister, too, was dead, unmarried, for no-one liked the possibilities which might arise from being connected with the family. None cared if he were guilty or innocent now.

If our Detective Police had only been in existence!

This last is hardly a story of unaccounted-for disappearance. It is only unaccounted for in one generation. But disappearances never to be accounted for on any supposition are not uncommon among the traditions of the last century. I have heard (and I think I have read it in one of the earlier numbers of *Chambers's Journal*) of a marriage which took place in Lincolnshire about the year 1750. It was not then *de rigueur* that the happy couple should set out on a wedding journey; but instead, they and their friends had a merry jovial dinner at the house of either bride or groom; and in this instance the whole party adjourned to the bridegroom's residence, and dispersed, some to ramble in the garden, some to rest in the house until the dinner-hour. The bridegroom, it is to be supposed, was with his bride, when he was suddenly summoned away by a domestic, who said that a stranger wished to speak to him; and henceforward he was never seen more. The same tradition hangs about an old deserted Welsh hall standing in a wood near Festiniog; there, too, the bridegroom was sent for to give audience to a stranger on his wedding-day, and disappeared from the face of the earth from that time; but there, they tell in addition, that the bride lived long – that she passed her three-score years and ten, but that daily, during all those years, while there was light of sun or moon to lighten the earth, she sat watching – watching at one particular window which commanded a view of the approach to the house. Her whole faculties, her whole mental powers, became absorbed in that weary watching; long before she died, she was childish, and only conscious of one wish – to sit in that long high window, and watch the road along which he might come. She was as faithful as Evangeline, if pensive and inglorious.

That these two similar stories of disappearance on a wedding-day 'obtained', as the French say, shows us that anything which adds to our facility of communication, and organisation of means, adds to our security of life. Only let a bridegroom try to disappear from an untamed Katherine of a bride, and he will soon be brought home, like a recreant coward, overtaken by the electric telegraph, and clutched back to his fate by a detective policeman.

Two more stories of disappearance and I have done. I will give you the last in date first, because it is the most melancholy; and we will wind up cheerfully (after a fashion). Some time between 1820 and 1830, there lived in North Shields a respectable old woman, and her son, who was trying to struggle into sufficient knowledge of medicine to go out as ship-surgeon in a Baltic vessel, and perhaps in this manner to earn money enough to spend a session in Edin-burgh. He was furthered in all his plans by the late benevolent Dr G. of that town. I believe the usual premium was not required in his case; the young man did many useful errands and offices which a finer young gentleman would have considered beneath him; and he resided with his mother in one of the alleys (or 'chares') which lead down from the main street of North Shields to the river. Dr G. had been with a patient all night, and left her very early on a winter's morning to return home to bed; but first he stepped down to his apprentice's home, and bade him get up, and follow him to his own house, where some medicine was to be mixed, and then taken to the lady. Accordingly, the poor lad came, prepared the dose, and set off with it some time between five and six on a winter's morning. He was never seen again. Dr G. waited, thinking he was at his mother's house; she waited, considering that he had gone to his day's work. And meanwhile, as people remembered afterwards, the small vessel bound to Edinburgh sailed out of port. The mother expected him back her whole life long; but some years afterwards occurred the discoveries of the Hare and Burke horrors, and people seemed to gain a dark glimpse at his fate; but I never heard that it was fully ascertained, or indeed more than surmised. I ought to add that all who knew him spoke emphatically as to his steadiness of purpose and conduct, so as to render it improbable in the highest degree that he had run off to sea, or suddenly changed his plan of life in any way.

[A correspondent has favoured us with the sequel of the disappear-ance of the pupil of Dr G., who vanished from North Shields, in charge of certain potions he was entrusted with, very early one morning, to convey to a patient: 'Dr G.'s son married my sister, and the young man who disappeared was a pupil in the house. When he went out with the medicine, he was hardly dressed, having merely thrown on some clothes; and he went in slippers – which incidents induced the belief that he was made away with. After some months his family put on mourning; and the G.s (*very* timid people) were so sure that he was murdered, that they wrote verses to his memory, and became sadly worn by terror. But, after a long time (I fancy, but am not sure, about a year and a half), came a letter from the young man, who was doing well in America. His explanation was, that a vessel was lying at the wharf about to sail in the morning, and the youth, who had long meditated evasion, thought it a good opportunity, and stepped on board, after leaving the medicine at the proper door. I spent some weeks at Dr G.'s after the occurrence; and very doleful we used to be about it. But the next time I went they were, naturally, very angry with the inconsiderate young man.]

My last story is one of a disappearance which was accounted for after many years. There is a considerable street in Manchester leading from the centre of the town to some of the suburbs. This street is called at one part Garratt, and afterwards – where it emerges into gentility and, comparatively, country – Brook Street. It derives its former name from an old black-and-white hall of the time of Richard the Third, or thereabouts, to judge from the style of building; they have closed in what is left of the old hall now; but a few years since this old house was visible from the main road; it stood low on some vacant ground, and appeared to be half in ruins. I believe it was occupied by several poor families, who rented tenements in the tumbledown dwelling. But formerly it was Gerrard Hall (what a difference between Gerrard and Garratt!) and was surrounded by a park with a clear brook running through it, with pleasant fish-ponds (the name of these was preserved, until very lately, on a street near), orchards, dovecots, and similar appurtenances to the manor-houses of former days. I am almost sure that the family to whom it belonged were Mosleys, probably a branch of the tree of the Lord of the Manor of Manchester. Any topographical work of the last century relating to their district would give the name of the last proprietor of the old stock, and it is to him that my story refers.

Many years ago there lived in Manchester two old maiden ladies of high respectability. All their lives had been spent in the town, and they were fond of relating the changes which had taken place within their recollection, which extended back to seventy or eighty years from the present time. They knew much of its traditionary history from their father, as well; who, with his father before him, had been respectable attorneys in Manchester during the greater part of the last century; they were, also, agents for several of the county families, who, driven from their old possessions by the enlargement of the town, found some compensation in the increased value of any land which they might choose to sell. Consequently the Messrs. S., father and son, were conveyancers in good repute, and acquainted with several secret pieces of family history, one of which related to Garratt Hall.

The owner of this estate, some time in the first half of the last century, married young; he and his wife had several children, and lived together in a quiet state of happiness for many years. At last, business of some kind took the husband up to London; a week's journey in those days. He wrote and announced his arrival; I do not think he ever wrote again. He seemed to be swallowed up in the abyss of the metropolis, for no friend (and the lady had many powerful friends) could ever ascertain for her what had become of him; the prevalent idea was that he had been attacked by some of the street-robbers who prowled about in those days, that he had resisted, and had been murdered. His wife gradually gave up all hopes of seeing him again, and devoted herself to the care of her children; and so they went on, tranquilly enough, until the heir came of age, when certain deeds were necessary before he could legally take possession of the property. These deeds Mr S. (the family lawyer) stated had been given up by him into the missing gentleman's keeping just before the last mysterious journey to London, with which I think they were in some way concerned. It was possible that they were still in existence; someone in London might have them in possession, and be either conscious or unconscious of their importance. At any rate, Mr S.'s advice to his client was that he should put an advertisement in the London papers, worded so skilfully that anyone who might hold the important documents should understand to what it referred, and no-one else. This was accordingly done; and, although repeated at intervals for some time, it met with no success. But at last a mysterious answer was sent: to the effect that the deeds were in existence, and should be given up; but only on certain conditions, and to the heir himself. The young man, in consequence, went up to London, and adjourned, according to directions, to an old house in Barbican, where he was told by a man, apparently awaiting him, that he must submit to be blindfolded, and must follow his guidance. He was taken through several long passages before he left the house; at the termination of one of these he was put into a sedan-chair, and carried about for an hour or more; he always reported that there were many turnings, and that he imagined he was set down finally not very far from his starting-point.

When his eyes were unbandaged, he was in a decent sitting-room, with tokens of family occupation lying about. A middle-aged gentleman entered, and told him that, until a certain time had elapsed (which should be indicated to him in a particular way, but of which the length was not then named), he must swear to secrecy as to the means by which he obtained possession of the deeds. This oath was taken; and then the gentleman, not without some emotion, acknowledged himself to be the missing father of the heir. It seems that he had fallen in love with a damsel, a friend of the person with whom he lodged. To this young woman he had represented himself as unmarried; she listened willingly to his wooing, and her father, who was a shopkeeper in the City, was not averse to the match, as the Lancashire squire had a goodly presence, and many similar qualities, which the shopkeeper thought might be acceptable to his customers. The bargain was struck; the descendant of a knightly race married the only daughter of the City shopkeeper, and became the junior partner in the business. He told his son that he had never repented the step he had taken; that his lowly-born wife was sweet, docile, and affectionate; that his family by her was large; and that he and they were thriving and happy. He inquired after his first (or rather, I should say, his true) wife with friendly affection; approved of what she had done with regard to his estate, and the education of his children; but said that he considered he was dead to her as she was to him. When he really died he promised that a particular message, the nature of which he specified, should be sent to his son at Garratt; until then they would not hear more of each other, for it was of no use attempting to trace him under his incognito, even if the oath did not render such an attempt forbidden. I dare say the youth had no great desire to trace out the father, who had been one in name only. He returned to Lancashire; took possession of the property at Manchester; and many years elapsed before he received the myst-erious intimation of his father's real death. After that, he named the particulars connected with the recovery of the title-deeds to Mr S., and one or two intimate friends. When the family became extinct, or removed from Garratt, it became no longer any very closely-kept secret, and I was told the tale of the disappearance by Miss S., the aged daughter of the family agent.

Once more, let me say, I am thankful I live in the days of the Detective Police; if I am murdered, or commit bigamy, at any rate my friends will have the comfort of knowing all about it.